Arrows
OF
Revolution

FINAL BOOK OF KINGMAKERS

HONOR RACONTEUR

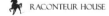 RACONTEUR HOUSE

Published by Raconteur House
Murfreesboro, TN

ARROWS OF REVOLUTION
Final Book of Kingmakers

A Raconteur House book/ published by arrangement with the author

For information address: www.raconteurhouse.com

THE ARTIFACTOR SERIES

The Child Prince
The Dreamer's Curse
The Scofflaw Magician
The Canard Case

DEEPWOODS SAGA

Deepwoods
Blackstone
Fallen Ward

Origins

KINGMAKERS

Arrows of Change
Arrows of Promise
Arrows of Revolution

GÆLDERCRÆFT FORCES

Call to Quarters

*Upcoming

Today the real test of power is not the capacity to make war but capacity to prevent it.

— Anne O'Hare McCormick

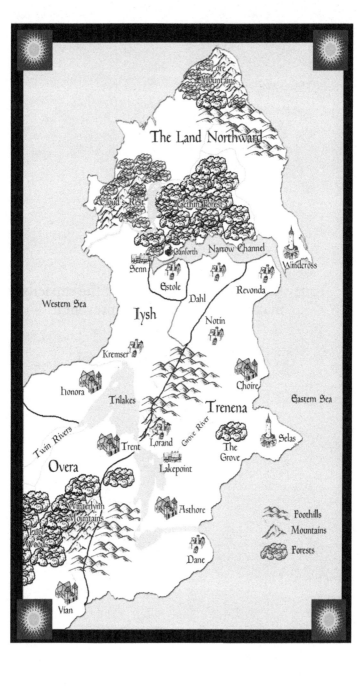

CHAPTER ONE

"Which numbskull of an idiot called this meeting?" Edvard demanded. Or it would've been a demand if he hadn't ended the question in a pained groan. He sat hunched forward, head cradled in both hands with the air of a man that was certain if he let go, the supported appendage would fall right off.

He wasn't alone. In fact, most of the room suffered from some sort of hangover, and more than one bottle had been passed around, each of them offering the others some medication to help ease them through the morning. The Winter Ball last night had been high in fun and gaiety even though there wasn't the overabundance of food to be had, but the spirits might have flown a little too freely.

Riana had never had access to alcohol of any sort growing up. It wasn't the sort of thing her father had encouraged, either. When living in a completely hostile environment, it'd been necessary to keep their wits about them at all times. Broden had never developed the habit of drinking. Riana had never even been able to step into the pub in Cloud's Rest without a riot starting, and being in a room full of drunk men had been extremely dangerous for her to begin with. Last night was the first time she'd been offered a glass.

And she hadn't much cared for it.

It was sour and burned her throat. After that first sip, Riana decided that alcohol must be an acquired taste, and she had no desire to acquire it.

Broden hadn't drunk anything either, so only the two archers were perfectly clearheaded this morning.

Edvard tilted his head enough to glare at Broden. "It was you, wasn't it?"

"It was no'," Broden denied pleasantly.

"You and Riana are the only ones sober," Edvard argued. "And why is that, anyway?"

"I like to remember when I have fun," her father drawled.

Edvard snorted a laugh, which set his head to aching, and he groaned again. "If it wasn't the two of you, then who was it?"

"Me." Hendrix stepped into the room at a brisk stride, a rolled up map under his arm and a stack of what seemed to be reports under the other. He sat both down on the table with a thump loud enough to make people flinch. Looking about the table, he didn't seem to have any pity for their plight. "I hope this is the last time people indulge like this until the war is actually won."

"Right now I'm swearing I'll never drink again," Ash bemoaned against the table top. His forehead had been in contact with the cool surface ever since obeying the summons to the king's study.

"Belike they do no' have enough wine to repeat the experience, lad," Broden assured the frowning prince in good humor. "Do no' fret about it much. Now, what be the meeting about?"

Hendrix spared another dark frown at the table as a whole. Riana had to admit the sight wasn't one to imbue confidence. Edvard, Ashlynn, Ash and Tierone were all very much the worse off for their partying the night before. Tierone refused to even look up or speak, and with the way he sat in his chair, eyes closed, Riana couldn't swear he wasn't already back asleep. Even Troi, sitting next to her, looked a little pale and drawn, and he wasn't the sort to lose complete control of himself.

Master Gerrard had been completely unavailable as he had over a dozen of his students to deal with, all of whom had somehow gotten into the alcohol last night and were paying for it this morning. Kirsty was standing in for him during the meeting and while she did not look hung over, she did seem a little under the weather. But then, since she had been one of the diehards that literally danced until dawn, it was no wonder why she was exhausted.

Seeming to realize the situation wouldn't improve itself until much later in the day, Hendrix cleared his throat and forged on regardless. "I want to hear the battle plan and use the winter months to start making preparations."

Tierone exhaled a sharp breath that sounded suspiciously like a snore and pried one eye open. "We have a plan?"

"Not one we can agree on," Edvard denied, rubbing at his temples as if his headache was escalating, which it likely was. "Go back to sleep."

Tierone amiably let his eye fall closed and he sank a little further into his chair.

A tic started jumping near Hendrix's eye. "You don't have a plan? You formed a country without a plan on how to deal with Iysh?!"

"First of all," Edvard started hotly, only to wince and subside into a volume that wouldn't split his head open, "I did not plan to rebel against Iysh. Your stupid father forced my hand on that one. Second of all, people assumed that I was forming a country, and they flooded in before I could convince them otherwise. I was forced into making a country, it was not my intention. Third of all..." he trailed off, staring blearily at the ceiling. "Do I have a third point to make?"

"We don't have an army?" Ash offered.

His brother gave him a thankful nod, carefully executed and with much support. "I'll take that one, that's a good third point. Hendrix, we've been going around in circles on this ever since day one. Iysh outnumbers us a hundred to one, at least, we'd be overwhelmed if they sent a true army against us instead of several battalions. I have no doubt that's what your brother will spend the winter doing—preparing that army. Aside from strengthening my defenses and doing what I can to weaken their troops, I frankly don't know what to do."

Hendrix gave him the most pensive study in return that Riana had ever seen a human being execute. The prince seemed to be cataloguing every flaw, every virtue, weighing and shifting all that Edvard was. Even the hungover king seemed to realize that the scrutiny was leading up to something as he dared to lift his head, even dropping a hand, so that he could return Hendrix's stare frankly.

What might have been a smile teased up the corners of Hendrix's mouth. In a quiet tone, Hendrix stated, "You are a capable ruler, Edvard Knolton. If all kings were like you, I doubt we'd have much conflict in the world. But it doesn't seem like you have much of a head for strategy."

"I don't," Edvard responded, not a single feather ruffled at this frank appraisal. "I have good people under me that advise me on such matters. Now, Hendrix, I have a feeling that you wanted to see if your plan matched mine. Now that you know I don't have one, why don't you share yours?"

"You're not much of a strategist," Hendrix repeated, and this time the smile was obvious, "but you do read people well. You are correct, I wanted to see what your idea was first, and adjust mine to fit accordingly. You asked, when I first came, how I could help? I think the answer just became clear. I will be your strategist."

Edvard spread his hand, a noncommittal gesture that inclined the person to believe he was amiable to the idea but not sold on it yet. "Tell me your plan."

"You're right, we can't win a full-frontal assault from Iysh. They'd overpower our defenses eventually and it would be a complete bloodbath when they did." Hendrix leaned forward to roll out the map.

Riana half-stood from her chair to help catch the far edge and pull the fabric straight, which Hendrix thanked her for with a nod.

"Maddox is as straightforward as a bull," Hendrix informed the table at large. "He's a military man at heart, a glory-seeker, and it won't occur to him to do anything but charge at our front gates with as strong of a force as he can muster in the next two months. The problem will be his younger twin, Savir. The true strategist in my family is Savir. He's a genius at maneuvering things to go his way. I assure you, if he had been in charge of the first two assaults against you, we would not be having this conversation today."

"Why wasn't he?" Kirsty asked, baffled. "If he's that good."

"My father strangely doesn't trust his opinion. But then, Father has always seemed to hang all hopes on Maddox for some reason. Savir gets very little chance to put in his opinion with Father, which has cost Iysh in the long run, as Maddox isn't a very capable ruler. However, the one and only person that Maddox will always listen to is Savir. And that is where our problem truly comes in. If Savir gives Maddox a battle plan, a strategy on how to get around our defenses, then this battle might well become a retreat altogether." Hendrix tapped the bottom part of Dahl's territory with three fingers. "Ash, Ashlynn, talk to me about wards. Can we maintain a shield around both Estole's and Dahl's borders?"

"Not for long," the twins denied in unison. Ashlynn gestured for Ash to go ahead, which he did. "I'm actually the one in charge of defenses, so I'll answer this. We can for perhaps the space of an afternoon, yes, but it will exhaust the wizards to do it. Part of the challenge is the angles we'll have to go around. A straight square, line, or ball is by far easier to erect and maintain because it's a perfect shape. The more angles you add to that, the more complex the spell gets, and the harder to hold."

Hendrix drew a line straight across Estole's border and then carried through the lower third of Dahl's territory. "A straight line like this, can you hold it?"

"Well, yes, but..." Ash trailed off with an uncertain look at Tierone, who was sitting next to him.

Tierone proved that he was not actually sleeping when he opened his mouth and said, "Mostly farmland in that area. Not many houses or people. If I need to, I can evacuate the area in a couple days and while it would be a loss, it won't be one that impacts us too severely now that we have supplies coming from both Ganforth and Cloud's Rest."

Ashlynn leaned around her brother to demand, "Are you actually napping or not?"

"Light hurts my eyes," Tierone explained, not even trying to look. "If you're asking, Hendrix, if I'm willing to sacrifice a third of my farmland in order to protect my people as a whole, then the answer is yes."

Ash seemed a little unhappy with this answer but even he saw the necessity of it. "Then yes, a straight line like that would be much easier to hold.

We could probably do it for about three days, but again, that would exhaust us and it would tie up every wizard. We wouldn't be available to fight."

Hendrix let out a thoughtful humming noise. "Not the answer I hoped for, but the answer I did expect. We'll talk more about this later. For now, let's focus on the larger scheme of things. What we need to do is delay the army, divert them, and buy me time. Our endgame is this: if we can bankrupt Iysh, then we give the people and the Court the final push it needs to realize that my father and oldest brother are terrible rulers. Once I have them thinking that, I can convince them to put me on the throne instead, overturn my father and his edicts."

"What about Prince Savir?" Kirsty objected. "Is he not a contender for the throne?"

"He abdicated his right to it shortly after the new inheritance law was put into place," Hendrix informed her. "I think Savir did it on purpose so that no one would pay attention to him. So it's literally between me and Maddox now."

"Ye be that confident that ye will win?" Riana marveled. He seemed so matter of fact about it that she almost bought that statement at face value.

"I've spent five years in the country," he said with a smile that didn't quite reach his eyes, "and I've heard every horror story that you can think of about what my family's done to its own citizens. They always thank me, for being so different from them, and it's made me believe that all my people are waiting for is a different choice. It's clear to me that this country is teetering on the edge of a revolution—the reaction to Estole alone illustrates how ready people are to abandon Iysh. If I stood up, asked them if they would support me as king, I have no doubt that I would get a 'yes.'"

"You would," Troi seconded bluntly. "My spies tell me the same thing."

"But can you just assume that and move forward?" Edvard wondered aloud, tone indicating he wasn't expecting an answer immediately, it was more a rhetorical question.

Hendrix shook his head. "I wouldn't dare gamble on that. Almost everyone out here knows me, but I want to visit them again, ask for their support."

"You'd get it," Troi assured him. He was braced against the table with both forearms, as if sitting up straight was beyond him, but those grey eyes of his were calm and clear. "Every report I have says that the people prefer you over either of your brothers."

"That's not much of a compliment," Hendrix sighed, but his expression said he was thankful for Troi's observation, "considering what my brothers are like. But I think this is our only chance. We must find a way to get me on the throne, to divert the army long enough to do so; otherwise Estole and Dahl won't have a prayer."

Edvard sat up hopefully. "Does that mean we can finally use my idea?"

Everyone at the table growled at him.

Hendrix held up a hand and asked the excited king, "What idea?"

"I want to rob the treasury," Edvard explained, happy that someone was listening to him after months of being ignored on this topic.

Hendrix stared thoughtfully at the ceiling for a moment, lips pursed and then nodded once, sharply. "I like it."

Several people voiced protests, words overlapping each other so that they couldn't be distinguished, but their tones enough to carry the message through. Hendrix held up a hand to forestall this. "Wait, I don't mean an actual robbery, where someone sneaks in and does the deed. The treasury is well guarded and has a vast quantity of money in it. It would be a behemoth task."

Edvard actually started pouting. "But you just said—"

"I meant slowly," Hendrix explained, "Well, not that slowly, but in increments. There's several tactics I can think of that will manage it. Troi, as I'm not a master at espionage, tell me: how many men does it take to track down one spy?"

"The general rule of thumb is, for every man that you have in the field, you must have seven that support him," Troi responded. "This is true of military and espionage both. If it's a particularly good spy, then it might take more than that."

"Manpower," Hendrix explained to the table generally, "is the costliest expense of any war. People require lodging, food, clothing, pay, and travel expenditures. The more men that we can force Iysh to employ into the field, the more it empties their coffers, and they don't have a lot of money to spare right now as it is. Overa's giving them trouble along the border, which is diverting some of the army and the budget toward the south end. We, of course, are demanding the bulk of the army and if I know Maddox, he'll want his army equipped well to make this a quick, decisive victory. Troi, your job is to make them deploy as many spies as possible to track down yours, make them think they have a very large infestation in the country to root out."

Troi looked sold on this idea, indeed downright gleeful of it, but he turned to his king for permission.

Edvard still seemed a little put out that he would not be allowed a grand raid into the Iysh treasury but nodded and gave a wave of the fingers. "You have permission to employ a few more. Keep within your budget restraints as much as possible."

"Understood, sire. No worries, Prince Hendrix, I can do what you're asking with ease. It will take a good month to set in place, however."

"I didn't expect anything different. The other thing that I want to do is to start some very costly rumors through you. Say, we've hired a mercenary group from Overa and expect them to be here to supplement our own troops."

The Master of Spies outright grinned at him. "A fine notion, Your Highness. Also, might I suggest that we make use of our bandit connections?"

Hendrix blinked, taken aback. "We have bandit connections?"

"Indeed we do. Or at least we have rumored bandits in that area that we can use to our advantage by playing bandits ourselves."

Leaning over the map, Hendrix traced the distance between Kremser and Estole's border, worrying his bottom lip between his teeth. "If we could somehow force the army up toward Senn, so that they have to re-supply there via the river...we could possibly have a guerilla force hit them there and wrest their supplies from them. It would cost Maddox dearly."

Even Riana could see it. An army of that size could not possibly take enough provisions for a journey and then a battle. Even she and Ash, just two people, had to stop and buy food along their way, and they'd packed as much as they could before leaving Estole. Kremser wasn't as far south as Honora, granted, but it was still a good three week journey for a body of men numbering in the thousands. Mayhap a bit longer than that. "Belike they be supplied by wagon on the march up, though?" she ventured.

"That's probably the case," Hendrix admitted, still staring hard at the map. "It depends on how many troops Maddox will bring and how much of his supplies he will choose to bring with him. Not to mention how he chooses to divide his troops. If he has enough to come at us by land and sea, then we're going to be battling on both fronts. Troi, I need an answer to that question."

"Trust me, Your Highness, we all want an answer to that question. When I have it, you'll be one of the first to know."

Hendrix gave him a shrug and grimace, acknowledging that was a stupid order to have given, but glad that Troi had taken it in the spirit in which it had been meant. "I can't make definite plans on some things until I know. But while we're waiting, I'd like to get what we can started."

Broden, ever sensible, cleared his throat and gave the young prince a meaningful look. "Ye might get better answers, lad, if ye fed people first. Breakfast can do wonders for a man's brain, ye see."

Hendrix blinked, as if food hadn't even occurred to him, then twisted about to stare at the clock on the mantelpiece. "It is time for breakfast, isn't it? Alright, let's adjourn for now. Meet back here in an hour."

Everyone gave Broden grateful looks, all except for Riana, who knew very well that her father's suggestion had not been given for anyone else's benefit aside from his own. Broden Ravenscroft needed a very good reason to skip a meal and war was not a sufficient one to his mind.

CHAPTER TWO

Breakfast (and copious amounts of medicine mixed with potions) did the trick. The hungover kings and their councilors retired back to the study much more alert and clearheaded than they had been before. Broden watched them settle into their seats with a secret smile. Food always made a man better prepared to take on a task, even if it was brain work instead of muscle.

Broden sat next to Ashlynn as a matter of course and waited for the show to begin. He had no doubt there would be one. With three men in the room that were used to dictating how things would be, a storm was inevitable. The only thing that had prevented it before was that two of them had been hungover.

Hendrix did have the sense to not take the seat at the head of the table but was instead on Edvard's right. Tierone chose the seat to the left. Broden wondered if either man questioned where he was sitting, or why he had chosen to position himself so. Historically speaking, the king's sword always sat to his right, and his shield to his left.

Catching Kirsty's eye by accident, Broden

realized he was not the only one to see this positioning or catch its significance. Kirsty, at least, had picked up on it as well.

Clearing his throat, Edvard drew everyone's attention to him. "As I'm not sure how aware we were an hour ago, let me repeat what Hendrix's overall plan is, so that I know we're all on the same page. In order to avoid an open conflict that we can't win, we'll instead divert the army coming at us toward the north, using every tactic we can devise, and stall for time. In that time, Hendrix will go through the country and the Court, solidifying his position with the people, and promote himself as a better candidate as the next king. To cement this, we will employ several tactics to undermine both king and heir apparent in every way possible, so that it would seem the only logical choice would be Hendrix. We want to drive Iysh to the point that it feels like it will collapse under its current rulers. Once Hendrix is on the throne, he will recall the army and we'll formalize a treaty between us."

"Very concisely put," Hendrix approved.

Yes, so it had been. Broden felt surprised as he was not entirely sure Edvard had been completely awake an hour ago. Hendrix's general outline of his plan had also been sidelined several times, making it difficult to follow. So Edvard could think even with a pounding skull and a sick stomach, eh? Good trait for the man to have.

"The trick to this," Hendrix continued to the table at large, "is to come up with tactics that will cost Iysh dearly but will not carry a very high price tag for us. Rumors and half-truths through our spies will be the first and best weapon because of that."

"Iyshian officials have a habit of believing rumor for truth anyway," Troi observed with a dark, twisted glee. "I've seen a few of them that actually wrote reports based on rumor, just to please their superior officers who believed it."

"Wait," Ash demanded incredulously. "They would actually report on a rumor like it's fact? They wouldn't try to verify it or disprove it first?"

"Making their superior officers happy is their first priority," Troi explained, still gleeful. "As long as it sounds even remotely plausible, they'll roll with it. They'll also discount anything that goes against their preconceptions."

Hendrix rubbed at his forehead with both hands, looking beyond pained. "Master Troi, tell me that you have a list of these idiots?"

"Of course I do, Your Highness, they're very dear to my espionage heart."

"I'm sure," the prince drawled darkly. "I'll remove them as soon as I gain the throne."

From Troi's expression, one would think that someone had just informed him that his favorite toys would be taken away. It did make Broden wonder—just what lies had the man been feeding his enemy? And how preposterous were they?

"I also have a list of their favorite lies, if that helps," Troi offered.

"It will," Edvard assured him, adopting his 'thinking pose' of staring up at the ceiling. Broden often thought he did that because the ceiling would not demand immediate answers from him. "But for the purposes of this meeting, I don't think we should go into detail on each aspect of this plan. We'll be here for the next three days. Let's sketch this out in broad lines first, refine it from there."

"But we all need to know what the other is doing so things don't conflict," Hendrix protested.

"Only generally, man," Tierone rumbled and with a very casual circle of the hand that indicated the table as a whole. "You have experts sitting all around you. Trust them to do their job. We only need to confer with each other enough so that one's efforts don't foul up someone else's."

From the expression on Hendrix's face, he did not agree with this at all. "Plans do not stay intact once you encounter the enemy. There should be at least two people who understand everything that's going on, what everyone is supposed to do, so that when alterations need to be made, we have a dedicated decision maker in place."

Broden had to admit the boy talked sense. "Two because if one can no' be reached, mayhap the other can?"

"Exactly," Hendrix agreed, stabbing his finger in Broden's direction.

"You have the two decision makers right here," Edvard said impatiently, gesturing between himself and Tierone. "We don't need to tie up everyone in this room for days at a time hashing out details. We can't afford to, for one thing, they need to be doing their jobs."

"And how are we supposed to know if a plan will work without their input?" Hendrix demanded.

"Actually, Edvard, he might have a point

in keeping people here until we do have a plan, and an alternative," Tierone suggested with a thoughtful look at the table in general. "We get the most interesting ideas from our archers, I know, and sometimes unexpected inspiration comes from people outside of our field."

"You'll also be repeating yourself over and over if you dismiss people too early," Hendrix argued. "You might as well say it all now, even if this meeting does take days."

Broden imagined sitting here listening to people bicker back and forth. For days. Perhaps a full week. He couldn't quite stifle a groan.

Fortunately, Edvard was not having this. "Hendrix, listen to me; we can ill afford to keep people here longer than two hours at a time. They all have vital jobs to do and basically everyone in this room is indispensable. We need them back out there as quickly as we can manage it. Repeating myself is just one of the prices to pay for that. Now, can we focus?"

Ashlynn leaned into Broden's side and murmured, "I predict an argument in five seconds."

"—like my father," Hendrix was saying hotly, "you're terrible at taking any kind of counsel!"

Edvard's temper flared and he slammed his hands against the table, sending his chair catapulting back as he leapt to his feet. "I'm nothing like that two-faced glory hoarder!"

As the men started yelling back and forth, Ashlynn let out a not so subtle sigh of vexation. Broden eyed her sideways. It was never a good sign when she did that. Things tended to either get cursed or broken in short order. "Lass, there be many a good book in here that be hard to replace."

"Dousing them in water is out," she agreed but that look had not left her eye. "However, there are other methods." Raising both hands, she pointed the index finger of her left hand at Hendrix, and the first two fingers of her right hand at Edvard and Tierone. She spoke a word, fingers making a jabbing motion, and a short spark burst forth, hitting all three men simultaneously.

They reacted as if they had been shocked—strongly—yelping and jumping back. Hendrix looked about frantically, confused by the source, but Edvard and Tierone knew exactly where it had come from. Glaring, they protested in unison, "Ashlynn!"

"Do I need to resort to tactics I used when we were ten?" she asked them, finger tapping against the table in a very matronly gesture. "Are you rulers or children?"

"She actually zaps people?" Hendrix demanded incredulously of Edvard and Tierone.

"All the time," Edvard responded sourly, rubbing at his chest and glaring at his sister.

"You're marrying into the family and will be considered her brother-in-law, so we should warn you now," Tierone added, "she's ruthless when it comes to arguments. Won't tolerate them. You'll either get zapped or doused in water if you start one."

"This time we were saved from dousing because of our location, no doubt," Edvard observed as he glanced around the study. "Thank you for not hitting my books."

"And the rest of us," Ash muttered aloud.

"Since the three of you can't decide on this amiably," Ashlynn informed them with that you-will-obey-me tone of voice, "we'll decide for you. We will discuss and plan as a group up until the point where one of us feels he has nothing to contribute and it isn't necessary for him to know the details. When that happens, that person may leave and go back to their job. If you wish to plan things in detail with that person further, then you can catch him later for a private meeting."

Two kings and a prince were not about to cross a woman with a short temper and magic literally in her fingertips. They docilely agreed and regained their seats.

"Now, I'm not a strategist," Ashlynn stated as she regained her seat, "so someone needs to explain this to me. Why are we trying to send the army north?"

"They're going to come this direction anyway," Hendrix explained with a wary eye on her hands. "We can't divert them any other direction without causing trouble with one of our neighboring countries. But the main reason why I want to send them even further north is that I'm hoping we can use the winter storms to trap them up there for a while, buy us more time without tying up manpower or magical resources."

"It be a fine thought, lad," Broden rumbled thoughtfully, "as the snows up there can be fiercesome. But surely yer brothers no' be stupid enough to send soldiers up there during winter."

"It's been a mild winter down here," Kirsty

stated slowly. "Would they think that it's the same up in Cloud's Rest? Or at least above Senn?"

"The trick," Hendrix told them patiently, "is to make them think that's the case. That the winter was mild all around. This is where a campaign of misinformation becomes vital. I need Maddox to believe three things—one, that our main defenses are only on the Estole/Dahl/Iysh border. That we have little to no defenses along the channel."

"You're painting a target on the north side," Tierone realized, sitting up straighter, interest cemented. "Deliberately drawing them around Senn and through Cloud's Rest to get to us."

"Exactly." A wolfish smile appeared on Hendrix's face. "We'll reinforce this idea by making our barrier at least look impenetrable. Make it beyond difficult to attack us from the south side, so they'll try the north out of frustration, if nothing else."

"Especially if their spies report the northern winter was mild, the roads are passable, and they'll have an easier fight if they come through the channel?" Troi's smile matched Hendrix's.

"Master Troi, will it be difficult to convince Iysh of this?"

"Perish the thought, Your Highness. It will be child's play. I have exactly the right spies in mind to leak the information through." Troi's expression reminded Broden of a merchant that knew of a wicked bargain he could make.

Broden realized in that moment that part of the reason why Troi was so good at his job was because he honestly loved doing it. "Lad, no' to put a spike in yer wheel, but Ash said earlier that he can no' keep the barrier up around Estole and Dahl for more than a few days. Be that enough time?"

"Likely not," Hendrix admitted. "Ash, Ashlynn, what are your thoughts?"

The twins turned and gave each other a speaking look that could have filled volumes. After several seconds of this they said in perfect unison, "Moving wall."

Edvard was the only one that said, "Ah!" in recognition.

"We used this once, briefly, in the last battle," Ashlynn told the group. "We were low on magical power, had to think of a way to conserve what we had while defending the city still, and so we set the barrier to be moving. To be attached to a person more than a specific place. It moved up and down according to where the enemy forces were. It's nigh impenetrable, but of course it has a few weak points. It's literally tied to the pillars and it can be burrowed under or around, and if a pillar falls, the whole barrier goes with it."

"Still, the pros outweigh the cons. If we couple this with the right glamour spells," Ash picked up smoothly, "then we can convince the enemy that this isn't a moving barrier, but our actual barrier. It will look nearly impossible to break through."

Hendrix leaned forward, wheels spinning visibly in his eyes. "And how long could you hold that?"

"Weeks, easily," Ash assured him. "Especially if we're doing it in a straight line as we discussed earlier, so that we cut down on the amount of territory we're guarding."

"Weeks," Edvard stated with an evil smile, "would be sufficient time to convince the Iyshian army that attacking us from the south will be too difficult. I like it. Ash, will you need Gerrard's help with this?"

"Absolutely. When I said we can hold this for weeks, I meant with the academy's help. No way just Ashlynn and I can do it."

"I'll let you discuss this with him and get it in place, then. Actually, where would we put it?"

Again, the twins spoke in unison: "Right outside our main wall."

"Not further out than that?" Hendrix protested. "Don't we want more room between us and the enemy?"

"Prince Hendrix," Kirsty explained patiently, "we're over-simplifying how this thing would work, so I understand why you would question this, but in truth this barrier is hideously complex. On a magical level, it's like creating a very complex mathematical equation, giving it instructions, and then turning it loose. Would you create something that's quasi-experimental and then turn it loose without keeping an eye on it?"

"Ah..." Hendrix seemed to think better than to blithely agree. "But it's been done before."

"On a much smaller scale and for a relatively short period of time," Ash reminded him. "This will be a more permanent fixture and much larger than anyone's tried before. Worse, it will take several magicians operating it to make sure that it keeps functioning as we intend it to. We literally need it within throwing distance of us, otherwise we'll be camping out in the snow to get this thing built and maintained."

"And if the enemy somehow finds a weakness and starts exploiting it, we're in trouble if it's too far out, because we won't know something's wrong until it's already happened. And we'll be badly out of position to react to it," Ashlynn added bluntly. "Trust me, it's better to keep it near our wall; at least that way we can keep an eye on it."

"It'll mean sacrificing some of Estole's farmland as well as Dahl's if we do that," Hendrix responded slowly, sneaking a peak at Edvard. He seemed to think an explosion of temper was imminent.

Edvard surprised him by giving a grim smile. "When I told Ash where to build the wall, I was prepared for this possibility. I have to focus on saving lives, not land. My wizards, how long will this take?"

The twins shared a speaking look with Kirsty and she answered: "Putting all of the spells and groundwork in place for an area that large will likely take about a month." Kirsty thought this over and tipped her hand back and forth. "Maybe less; it depends how much help we have setting it up."

"How long does it take to feed the enemy false information?" Hendrix asked Troi.

"You have to be careful on that," Troi warned and he was not speaking to just Hendrix. "You have to time it carefully. Early enough to give them time to respond to the news, but not early enough for them to really validate it. If I feed them a false report now, it will take two weeks maximum to reach the right ears. From there, it will take another week for them to verify it."

"So we want to feed them the false intel no more than a week before they start moving," Hendrix said aloud, more to himself than to anyone else.

"That sounds about right." Tierone leaned forward on the table, bracing himself with his forearms. "Troi, you're keeping tabs on the army's development, I assume?"

"You assume correctly, Your Majesty."

Tierone blinked, then smiled. "It still feels odd hearing myself addressed so. Alright. Then can we say we'll leave this up to Troi's discretion? Let him judge the right moment to start his campaign of misinformation, as Hendrix put it, and notify us when he's done so."

Hendrix looked ready to object to this, but Edvard cut him off before he could do so. "Hendrix, you've only been here a few days, so you likely don't realize what bedlam this place can be. Troi sometimes spends two hours looking for me. We need to give our people the authority to move at their discretion. As long as they continue to update us so we know everyone's progress, we'll be fine."

The prince still did not look sold, but a wary look at Ashlynn made him clamp his mouth shut. Instead, he changed the subject. "I'd like to start my campaign with Senn. Aside from it being nearby, I had a great deal of support the last time I was there, and I believe it will take very little to bring them over to our side."

"I believe you will have minimal trouble

there, Your Highness," Troi seconded this with an encouraging nod. "I hear nothing but praise for you from that quarter. Also, if you can do so, then I can use them to our advantage. They will likely help us convince the army that the winter is mild."

"It will be more convincing if the news comes from another source," Ashlynn agreed. "I think—"

There was a harried knock at the door before a guard burst in. "Sherriff, Broden, we need you."

Ashlynn gave him a weary look. "On a scale of one to ten, how bad?"

"Fifteen?" he offered, still wide around the eyes.

"Duty calls," Broden noted, standing easily and pulling on his quiver as he moved. After being in Estole this long, reports like this from panicked guardsmen no longer worried him. They'd deal with it, whatever it was.

"Update me at dinner," Ashlynn ordered her brothers—and likely Hendrix—even as she strode out the door.

"We'll meet again after dinner!" Edvard commanded as they left. As the door swung shut behind them, Broden heard Edvard say, "See? I told you we can't have a meeting for more than two hours before someone's called away."

Snorting, Broden stretched his legs out to keep up with Ashlynn. They likely had only managed those two hours because most of the city was hungover still from the night before. He privately wished Hendrix luck pulling off another meeting that long again.

CHAPTER THREE

Troi cleared his throat and for some reason had a wary eye on Ash as he spoke. "Sire, if we're speaking of the spy work that needs to be done, there is something I'd like to address."

Edvard gave him an encouraging wave of the hand.

"I've been debating this for some time," Troi hedged, still with that weather eye on Ash. Such behavior was unusual for him and it made Riana wonder just what he was going to say next that he expected Ash to react to. "I have a particular spy that is within the main Court at Iysh. He is, in fact, a dandy in the Court but privy to an amazing amount of information and is somewhat known as a double agent."

"Somewhat?" Hendrix repeated, brows screwing up in confusion. "Clarify that, Master Troi."

"He's not officially a spy for Iysh, or on their payroll as such, but he gives them information as he comes across it, which he's rewarded handsomely for. His information, of course, is always provided by us and we're careful on what we give him. He's one of my best double agents. My most reliable information comes from him and he is, in turn, excellent at feeding false intel to them. Zigzag is his codename."

"Zigzag." The nuance in Ash's tone made it clear he didn't think that was a very good spy name.

Troi gave him a brief, rare smile. "Because I never know which way the man will go. He's completely loyal but terribly unpredictable in some ways."

Ah, so the name was more of a description than anything? Riana found it amusing that a spy's name wasn't a name at all. Shouldn't it be something bland and innocuous so that no one would question it? Or was the temptation for some creativity too much to resist?

"Zigzag has reported something that I think can be vitally useful if done right. My counter-part in Iysh relies heavily on his subordinates for information. The man holds his position because of his family connections and not on his ability. His name is Dunlap."

Tierone held up a hand. "Wait, I know the family. Which Dunlap?"

"Greer Dunlap."

It wasn't quite an eye roll on Tierone's part, but close. "Ah. Things are becoming clearer. Edvard, ever meet the man?"

"No, I don't think I have. What's he like, that you two are sneering so?"

"On the surface he's everything a master spy and information gatherer should be." Troi's hands rose a little in illustration as he painted the picture. "He's tall, has hawkish features that give him a striking look, with blue eyes and dark chestnut hair that's in fashion right now. He has the best of everything—horses, carriages, house, clothes—and he married very well. It was family connections that got him in the department and his smooth-talking abilities that let him rise through the ranks. He actively hunts down people and talks to them, at pubs, at cafes, at dark street corners in the dead of night, and he's responsible for almost half the information that Iysh shifts through every week. There's not a spy in Iysh that doesn't report to him on a semi-regular basis."

"But...?" Edvard encouraged, anticipation rising.

"But in truth, the man's an imbecile. He's terrible at shifting truth from lies, believes anything that matches his preconceptions of events, and has a weakness for a certain type of informant."

Riana felt like Troi had finally gotten back around to his main point. "What type?"

"The female type." Troi was back to staring at Ash out of the corner of his eye. He looked ready to duck under the table, too. "Zigzag reported this to me right before our winter storm passed through. He reports to Dunlap on a regular basis himself and he has his own means of seeing how much Dunlap buys and how much he discounts. About half of what Zigzag tells him actually makes it into a report to his superior and is acted upon. However, Zigzag tried feeding the same information through one of his, ah, female companions, and Dunlap swallowed it hook, line, and sinker."

"Interesting." Hendrix had that look of extreme calculation on his face again. "Same exact information?"

"Almost verbatim, or so Zigzag says. He tested this two other times, using different women, and some of the older information from the week before. Same result. Dunlap doesn't question a single word if it's coming from a woman."

"I believe this." Kirsty actually rolled her eyes. "I've met the man myself on too many occasions to count. Dunlap's got the worst blind spot when it comes to women. He's been trained since toddlerhood to believe that they can do no wrong. It's a miracle, really, that his wife is perfectly faithful to him, as he'd be the perfect husband to cheat on. He'd never suspect a thing."

Hendrix liked this idea a great deal. Riana could tell because all of a sudden the prince had a hard time keeping his seat. He nearly vibrated. "Then, if we use a female spy to report the mild winter, and whatever else we need to, our chances of success...?"

"Double," Troi stated firmly. "At least double. Which is why Zigzag's observation is so invaluable. The problem that I have is this: who do I use? I didn't have many female spies in the Iyshian Court to begin with, and what few I did have, I've had to pull some of them because of various problems. I don't endanger my people unless I can help it. Three of them were on the verge of being compromised so I had to move them out. It doesn't leave me with much manpower in the Court."

"So you need to send in a new face." Edvard's eyes darted between Riana, Ash, and Troi, and the expression on his face was that of realization.

Although what he realized was beyond Riana. Unless...no, surely not.

Ash cottoned on at that moment and he left his chair so fast it went crashing back. Dark anger streaked across his face, eyes narrowed to slits as he stared at Troi. "No."

Troi stood as well, almost pleading. "Ash, I need her."

"No; curse you, no!"

"I need a woman I can trust, someone that knows every aspect of our plans and its variations, someone that has the ability to make judgment calls on the spot when the situation demands it. She needs to be stunningly beautiful so that it's not questioned why she's on Zigzag's arm, and so she has an easier entrance to Dunlap's company. I'm sorry to say that in this case, looks are just as important as brains. It'll be safest if she is also a capable fighter, just in case things go pear-shaped, so that she can fight her way out. On top of all this, it has to be a face that no one in Iysh will recognize. Riana is literally the only woman that fits this description."

Riana stared at Troi with the oddest mix of emotions swirling in her chest. Her? A spy? It was beyond flattering that Troi thought of her as stunning, too, but what was truly flattering was that he thought she had the talent and brains necessary to be a spy in the first place.

Ash moved so that he was nose to nose with the shorter man. "You are not sending my partner into the heart of Iysh without me. No, Troi."

Troi desperately looked like he wanted to argue but didn't quite dare with an angry wizard sparking off magic in front of him. The whole room, in fact, didn't quite dare to take Ash on in this kind of mood. Ashlynn was one thing with her outbursts, but Ash? Mild-mannered Ash that never lost his temper? He was a different kettle of fish entirely.

Riana stared at the spymaster for a long moment. After nearly a year of being here, she recognized desperation when she saw it. Troi would never have asked this if he had another viable option. The truth was he pulled off miracles on a regular basis for them, but this was a war he was ill-equipped to fight. Iysh had more manpower, more resources, and more money to use in this game of espionage. Estole and Dahl combined couldn't begin to compare. The only advantage they had was the man standing in front of them, the man that knew how to play this game and play it well.

Troi's instincts and intelligence had not led Estole astray even once in the past. Riana didn't think he was letting the situation overwhelm him now. If he was asking for her, then he needed her, and he knew that she could do the job. She could not let Ash's fears cripple their efforts.

Taking in a breath, she braced for the argument that was coming.

"Troi," she said quietly, and that single utterance sounded like a death knell in a graveyard.

The Master of Spies dared to look away from

an angry wizard. "Yes, Miss Riana."

"When do ye need me to go?"

There was an exhalation of relief and surprise from different people, but Ash reacted the strongest. He grabbed her wrist and hauled her out of the study, onto the balcony, and slammed the glass doors closed behind them. Whirling to her, she saw and felt every emotion boiling inside her wizard. He was angry, bewildered, determined but overall very, very afraid.

"What," Ash ground out between clenched teeth, "do you think you're doing? Don't you realize how much danger you'll be in?"

Early on in their partnership, Riana had learned that when Ash was upset like this, she needed to deal with emotions first. Arguing with words had no effect with Ash. So she didn't answer that question but instead stepped forward, hugging him around the waist.

His hands closed around her shoulders even as he said, "Don't do that. I hate it when you do that, you always make me look like an idiot for losing my temper."

Even though he said all of that, he didn't let go of her either. Riana hid a smile against his shoulder. "I feel yer fear, Ash."

"Of course you do, that's because there's very good reason to be afraid, and you're not going."

"I feel yer fear but I canna let it govern me actions." She lifted her head enough to meet his eyes, those clear blue eyes that were so stormy now. "If we do no' take risks, we lose it all. We do no' have enough means to fight as it is."

He wanted to argue with her. Oh, he wanted

to do that, she could feel the words boiling and roiling inside of him, itching to burst free. But he could sense her now as strongly as she did him and all he felt from Riana was resolve. Well, resolve mixed with anticipation. And that, more than anything, made him falter. "You're actually looking forward to it."

"Always found it a bit romantic, the darin'-do of spywork," she admitted, trying to tamp down her inner child. "And the bit of spywork I did for Troi afore be quite fun."

Growling a few choice words under his breath, Ash gave her a gentle shake. "When you look at me like that, and feel that way about it, you take the wind completely out of my sails. You know that, right? Don't you have any sense of danger?"

"Why?" she asked him innocently. "If I go, ye be going with me."

That really made him swear and he yanked the doors open, stomping into the room ahead of her. To the room at large he announced, "My good sense and judgment has been overturned."

That made Edvard and Tierone both laugh. Ash shook a finger at them. "Don't add fuel to the fire. I'm mad enough about this as it is, but she wants to do it, and there's too many reasons why she should. Troi, I'm going in with her."

"I would never think of separating you," Troi soothed. It might have been placating on his part but there was something in his tone that suggested he was going to use Ash to the full extent possible. "In fact, I think we can use your bond to our advantage. But we'll discuss the details of this later. Riana, you asked when I need you to go? The answer is, not immediately. It'll take us some time to set this up, as I need to create a new identity for the pair of you. I'll let you know when we start to get close and you need to prepare to go."

Riana nodded agreement, her face straight, even though she was elated by the whole prospect.

"We will need to work on your speech first, make you sound more like an Iyshian lady," Troi added, "which we can start on today."

"You do need to give us a timeline," Ash warned the spymaster. "I have a wall to help build at the very least before I can go."

"The wall might not take precedence," Troi hedged with a sideways glance at the two kings and prince. "I must have a spy in place if we are to pull all of this off."

"Ash, sit," Edvard urged. "Tell us what needs to happen before we can get the wall up. We'll plan accordingly from there."

Troi had stressed to Riana that they would have little time here in Estole before she needed to leave for the palace. After all, there was a delicate sense of timing in all of this. Estole was famous for having a certain pattern in its winter—it always snowed right before or after the All Winter's Festival and then there was a blazing cold period for several weeks, dry and without a snowflake in sight, before true winter hit.

And they had to have an Iyshian army here

before true winter hit. That meant, at most, they had a month and a half to work in. That wasn't much time at all. In fact, considering all that needed to happen, Riana wasn't sure how they'd manage to get it all done without sacrificing things. Like meals. And sleep.

With the logistics whirling in her head, she left the meeting and went straight for the one person she knew would have the time to teach her—Bria. Her friend had caught a bad cold and was currently in bed, suffering through the worst of it. Riana popped her head into Bria's room.

"You awake?"

Bria looked up from the book in her hands. She was curled up in the bed with at least three blankets wrapped around her, red nosed and sniffly, hair in a very messy knot at the top of her head. "I am. Visiting?"

"No' exactly," Riana denied and made herself at home in the chair next to the bed. She didn't dare get any closer than this and even it might be too close. "I need help."

"Certainly, with what?" Bria set the book aside, seemingly happy for some other diversion.

"Well…" Riana rubbed her palms together, not quite sure how to broach this. "Troi asked me to be a spy."

Bria's lips parted, first in surprise, then with indignation. "Why do you get to be a spy and I don't?"

And this was why the two of them were friends. Riana grinned and drawled, "Yer face be known, dear heart."

Pouting, Bria huffed and crossed her arms

over her chest. "Not my fault I'm related to two dukes. Now kings."

"Or betrothed to a prince," Riana couldn't resist adding.

Huffing a tendril of hair off her face, Bria dismissed this and dropped the pout. "You really get to be a spy? Where?"

"Iysh's palace."

Bria let out a soundless whistle. "Wow. How'd you get that past Ash?"

"He be going with me."

"Ah, this makes more sense now. I didn't think he'd let you go into that place without him. Well, what do you need from me? Etiquette lessons?"

"Eh, there be that. And speech lessons, to make me sound like a proper lady."

Nodding—neither of these came as a surprise—Bria agreed. "Yes, I'll help as I can, but I don't know formal etiquette. At least, not palace etiquette. It's on a whole different level. I'll teach you what I know, but you must tell me, why did Troi draft you into this?"

"Can ye teach while I explain?" Riana tried not to fidget in her chair but she literally felt time pressing against her. "There be precious little time for this."

"Certainly, we can. Let's start with your pronouns, shall we?"

CHAPTER FOUR

"The next person stupid enough to jump in there, I'm letting them freeze to death," Ashlynn announced.

Broden was fairly sure she was half-joking, but he also recognized that she was half-serious. Then again, spending the afternoon fishing people out of a freezing cold river would make anyone irate. "Belike the guards we posted will deter the rest."

"I hope for their sakes that is the case." Ashlynn raised her face to the sky and frowned at the sun that almost touched the far horizon. "Why, why would anyone sane jump into that water? It has ice chunks floating in it!"

That it did, likely coming down the river from Cloud's Rest. The channel consisted of half mountain water runoff, after all, and the mountains got much colder than Estole had ever experienced. "A few of them said that it be a tradition where they be from."

"I heard them. A tradition from southern Iysh. Warm, sunny, southern Iysh that barely sees snowflakes." Ashlynn's tone dripped sarcasm.

"Stripping to the waist and diving into water almost cold enough to freeze over is something that only the crazy would do."

It was, and Broden had no excuses for them, because if not for Ashlynn, the men that had jumped in for a lark would have likely lost limbs. As it was, if not for her quick reactions and magic, they would have been dead from hypothermia. It was blistering cold out here even without jumping into icy water. Even Broden, used to mountain climate, found it a mite nippy.

Ashlynn stared at the afternoon sun with a dark frown. "Likely they're no longer in the meeting. Curse it, I needed to talk to Ash. I have no idea how to tackle that moving barrier, not if it's to span Dahl as well."

"Belike ye will need to call a meeting of yer own," Broden suggested. "That sort of talk be best with yer fellow wizards anyway. Or wait for the evening meeting after dinner."

"True enough. But it'll be difficult getting them all at the same place at the same time. Likely we'll have to call each other to manage. Perhaps if I call them now, I can organize a meeting for tomorrow?" This was clearly a rhetorical question as she was already drawing her necklace out from underneath her coat. Lifting it to her mouth, she said clearly, "Lorcan."

Dahl's wizard? Well, trying to coordinate with the most remote person first made sense to Broden. And he was glad that her attention had diverted elsewhere, otherwise she might go back to scalp the idiots that had her running around in this cold weather.

It took a moment, but Lorcan's harried voice came through clearly, "Ashlynn, make this short. I have a collection of idiots over here with a death wish."

"Let me guess. They're stripping to the waist and jumping into the channel."

There was an almost audible double-take. "Did you suddenly develop clairvoyance?"

"No, I just have similar idiots over here. This is apparently some sort of tradition from southern Iysh, to shed your bad luck of the old year and invite good luck for the next."

"Someone needs to explain to the lackheads that shucking off bad luck is all well and good but only if it doesn't make you lose life or limb in the process. What have you been doing to them?"

"We posted guards along the channel to stop them. That's worked the past hour."

"I didn't know you had the guards to spare for that."

"I don't. We hired some men that are looking for work to stand guard for the next three days. They're grateful for the extra coin and they have permission to use force as needed."

"That's brilliant."

"Thank Broden, he thought of it."

"Of course he did. He's the sensible one." The other wizard laughed as if he knew that Ashlynn would be glaring at him if he were within sight, and indeed she was. "I'll do the same here." Lorcan dropped the caller long enough to shout an order to someone standing nearby before his voice became clear and distinct again. "Now, what did you call about?"

"Have you been updated about our meeting this morning?"

"Somewhat. Tierone called earlier saying that I'd need to pair up with you to deal with the barrier along the southern border. Ashlynn, frankly, I don't have the time to travel over there every time for a meeting."

"You won't need to," she assured him. "Calling is fine. If you have the rough outline for this, that's good."

"I do and I've been thinking of different ways we can tackle the design. Either way, you realize that I can't hold up Dahl's end all by my lonesome?"

"Of course. Didn't expect differently. We'll send a few people over there to help you."

"Good. In that case, can I request someone? I found Kirsty Kilpatrick, ah, easy to work with. Our personalities seem, um, very compatible. Yes."

Broden's eyebrows rose slowly into his hairline. What was this interesting undertone to Lorcan's words? He met Ashlynn's eyes and it was apparent from her face that she had caught it as well. "As to that, lad, I do no' think it be a problem, assuming Kirsty do no' have tasks of her own to do."

"Of course, this is only if she's available," Lorcan hastily added. "And of course I'd be willing to take any of the higher ranked students."

"Of course," Ashlynn parroted, a calculated gleam entering her eye. "I'll confer with people here and get back to you. As for a meeting, can you call in around lunchtime tomorrow?"

"Certainly, certainly." There was an aggravated growl. "I need to go. Another idiot just tried to jump in."

"Go," Ashlynn encouraged. "Call me tomorrow." Dropping the necklace, she caught Broden's eye again. "The man's crushing on Kirsty."

"Aye, no doubt of it." Broden chuckled, finding the situation sweet and amusing all at once. "Well, Kirsty be a charming, pretty lass. It be no wonder why the man be attracted."

"I feel this terrible urge to play matchmaker." Ashlynn nearly skipped ahead, smile mischievous.

"Belike ye should ask the lass if she likes him in kind," Broden warned. "Afore ye go shipping her over there."

"Oh, I will, don't you worry. Otherwise the situation would be extremely awkward, which I wouldn't want to do to either of them." This time she did skip, twice, already reaching for the caller again. "I'm calling Kirsty next."

Broden sighed and shook his head. There was no stopping the lass now.

They walked through the streets with Ashlynn calling every trained wizard setting up a meeting for the next day, Broden lost in his own thoughts. As she started in on the problem of the wall, Broden focused on the counterpart to it: the evacuation. Bringing people out of the southern edge of Dahl was sure to be tricky. They had precious little space in Estole, after all, for their own people. Dahl's southern edge, as Broden knew from experience, was mostly farmland. The population was not as high in that region, granted, but it would still be a significant amount of people to find temporary homes for.

Estole proper was out. There was just no place left here. Ganforth was the only option. Broden was not sure if it was a good option, however. He had no notion what sort of defenses they were planning for Ganforth, as the meeting he had been in this morning had not mentioned it more than passing. They were trying to focus on the southern border first, as that was where the army would initially come in from. Could they afford to put people in Ganforth? Did they have enough manpower to protect a large body of people across the channel?

Ashlynn made a sound of aggravation. "I can't reach Kirsty."

Match-making plans temporarily thwarted, eh? Broden carefully bit back a smile. "Belike ye can talk to the lass later."

"If I can even manage a later." Ashlynn went all of two steps before stating, "We'll have to move the evacuated people to Ganforth in easy stages. We don't have enough boats to do it all at once and it will make it obvious what we're doing to the spies in the region if we tried."

Broden eyes nearly went cross-eyed. "Lass, riddle me this: what be it about a woman's brain that lets her think of two things at once?"

She just laughed and did not even try to answer. "I think we'll need to give an alert to Master first. He's going to be in charge of building more houses as a temporary shelter for these people as he's the only one with the spare manpower."

Both thought, 'Even if he does not have the time,' though neither of them said as much, as there was no need to. "How many do we need?"

"That is an excellent question I don't have an answer to. Tierone can tell us, though. The other question is, what do we do with the houses once the people return to their lands?"

"Sell them?" Broden thought that was the only thing that made sense. "Use them for government offices?"

Ashlynn gave a judicial nod and a hum as she thought about it. "I suppose either is a good option. And having branch offices across the way would be helpful, I would think. It gives people immediate access to help instead of having to schedule a trip across the channel."

At the rate Ganforth was growing, branch offices would need to be a reality sooner rather than later. Estole's government offices could barely keep up as it was. Broden shifted his mind to other matters. "Lass, evacuation aside, this moving barrier of yers. Be it difficult?"

"Yes, extremely," she sighed, and for a moment looked ten years older. "I like it better than any other option, though. It'll be easier on us and our defenders in the long run. The setup is what's going to be so horrendously difficult. When Ash and I did this, we had something more or less in place, a safety-net we'd built in case one of us fell in battle, or we ran out of magic power. We were already prepared to use it, which was just as well, as we were forced to in that last battle. But the preparations we'd made can't be used again. For one thing, they've been dismantled to make room for building. For another, what few parts are still up, they're in entirely the wrong place."

Broden had seen her erect enough barriers to be able to follow this explanation without too much trouble. Barriers required markings so that the magic knew the territory and limits it was bound to. Even if this was a mobile, moving wall, it would still need a magical guideline of some sort. "Sounds like a lot of groundwork."

"Understatement," she groaned. "And every person that helps maintain it must have an intimate understanding of exactly where each marker is. They have to know exactly where to go, how far the wall can extend, and so on. For this much territory, it will take at least two people to maintain it for a twelve-hour period. Three would be better, as it lowers the chance of someone magically exhausting themselves."

After having seen what Ash went through, Broden personally would prefer to not have another wizard drop on his watch. That had been a thoroughly alarming experience. He tried to divvy the work up in his mind and frowned when he realized he was not sure if that was the right method. "They work in sync?"

"Hmm? Well, sort of. They work together, certainly, communicating, but each would have their set territory before they'd pass their section off to the next wizard. It would be a magical version of catch, in a way, as each person would hand off part of the barrier to another as the need arose. When I said it would take three people, I don't mean they would be working constantly for twelve hours, but that they would keep the minimum barrier up and then activate the higher end of the spell as necessary. They'd be on watch for a full day at a time."

Ah, now this made more sense. "So one in Dahl, one in Estole, one in the middle?"

"More or less. Although it doesn't solve the question of what to do about Ganforth. I have a feeling we might need to create a separate, hard barrier for them, as even a student can maintain it."

True, it was trained wizards they were lacking, not necessarily magical power. If they could divert some of the responsibilities to the students, that would help the wizards tremendously. "Gerrard think of this yet?"

"It was something he said in passing to me earlier. I think we all know more or less how this will have to work out. Logic will dictate it more than anything." A frown gathered across Ashlynn's forehead, dragging the corners of her mouth down. "The real question is, can we get all of this in place before the first real snows hit?"

CHAPTER FIVE

Ash had regressed back into a child, one that was putting something unpleasant off for as long as he could by lingering over breakfast. His biscuit had made at least three circuits around his plate, so he was obviously full, but wasn't about to admit it.

Riana regarded her wizard partner with open amusement although Ash was so sunk in on himself that he barely noticed. Patting his back sympathetically, she said, "It can't be that bad, Ash."

"We'll have seven trained wizards discussing how to build two separate barriers. Six wizards that are not necessarily used to all working together, who are opinionated, stubborn, and have wildly different approaches on spellwork." Ash lifted his head enough to give her a pitiful look. "This will be a disaster. They'll be arguing with each other all day."

He was likely right, knowing that bunch, but Riana was also confident that by the end of the day, they'd also have a concrete plan to work from. However much they disagreed with one another, they were excellent at pulling through and solving issues.

The biscuit made another circuit. Just the two of them remained at breakfast, everyone else having already finished and left. Riana was of the mindset that he could put things off a little longer if he wished, but not much longer. They both had many things left to do and only about a month to do them in.

The door swung open and Edvard popped his head inside. "Ah, good, you're here. Riana, Troi needs to see you."

Riana was halfway out of her chair before even asking, "What for?"

"He said he needs to start in on your cover identity today. I'm to take you to him as he of course needs my approval as well before he can move ahead."

Starting her new career as a spy sounded much more fun than poking at a moping Ash. Riana cheerfully abandoned her partner to follow Edvard.

The Estolian King took one look at his moping brother and said firmly, "Stop delaying and go."

Ash glared back at him but finally left the biscuit alone.

Biting the inside of her cheek to keep from laughing, Riana followed Edvard through the castle and out the back door. Trying to practice her new linguistic skills, she carefully phrased, "He does not like to argue, our Ash."

Glancing over at her, Edvard approved, "Your accent is much better. Who taught you?"

"Bria."

"Ah, good choice. She's likely the only one available right now anyway. We'll need to start etiquette lessons as well. Remind me tonight. Dinner will be a good place to start."

"I will," she promised.

"Don't worry if you still have a hint of an accent," Edvard continued as he opened a side door through the wall that let out onto the city streets. "Troi mentioned he'd base your identity out of Senn, and if he sticks with that idea, then they'll expect at least a slight accent."

Good to know. Riana hadn't been sure if she could learn the Iyshian accent perfectly in such a short amount of time. But Troi seemed to realize her restrictions and was trying to compensate for them.

They went directly for the Currency Office, a place that Riana had passed many times but never set foot in. She had no idea why they were here, but followed Edvard obediently through the door. It was a wide open space, no dividing walls, with desks arranged in clusters throughout the room. Men and women walked around with large amounts of paper or money in hand. Not one of them reacted to the newcomers aside from, "Welcome, Sire."

Edvard waved a greeting in return but didn't walk all the way inside. Instead, he turned immediately to the left, taking a staircase that was so hidden that Riana hadn't even noticed it. The stairs were a little narrow and led directly into a dimly lit basement that had a hallway stretching either direction, with exactly six doors on each wing.

Bemused, Riana stared first this way, then that. Surely Troi didn't work down here? "Does Troi not have an office near yours?"

"He does," Edvard answered forthrightly, striding down the hall. "He says that too many eyes are on that place, so he only shows up enough to push paper around and make reports to me. The real work happens down here."

Edvard stopped at the third door and pushed the door handle. Abruptly, he stopped with only one foot through the entry. Riana popped up on her toes in order to look over his shoulder and immediately saw why he had stopped. There was precious little room to maneuver. The room wasn't large to begin with, rectangular in shape, and was crammed with multiple desks that sat next to each other in rows. On the far end of the room there was a single table, absolutely buried in all manner of files and papers, with a large map of the world dominating the end wall. There were pins in the maps, string attaching them, all of different hues. Riana assumed they were color-coded to mean something but couldn't decipher it in a glance.

In what little space was between the rows of desks were shelves of different heights and widths, obviously scrounged from all over, that were equally crammed with books, letters, and other rolled up parchments. The light came from multiple lamps and two braziers that gave the room a smoky feeling, as there were only four narrow windows, none of which were open to ventilate the room. It smelled of paper, smoke, and sweat in a somewhat offensive manner, but none of the people in the room seemed to even notice their poor working conditions.

Riana did a quick head count and unless she was mistaken, there were twenty people crammed in here. Wasn't there any other space they could use? So they didn't have elbows in each other's ribs?

Over the cacophony of multiple voices all speaking at once, Edvard called out, "TROI!"

The Master of Spies couldn't have possibly heard him, but still somehow took notice that he had visitors, even though he was bent over a file on the opposite side of the room. He waved a hand of acknowledgement before getting up from the desk and weaving his way forward. It was not a quick trip, as he was constantly stopped every other step by people needing verification or asking a question.

Riana watched as the Master of Spies took a glance at some piece of paper and immediately responded: "Re-do that."

"But it's perfect!" the man protested. "A steamy love-letter to spice up his life."

"It's too perfect, you bloody fool; if she were really writing that thing in a hurry there would be spelling mistakes, blotches of ink, that sort of thing. And don't do that cliché of making one of the girls leave a lip print on it." Troi moved on to the next, pointing at something on the page and commenting, "You can't have him there, I have another spy coming out of there in a week, there's too much overlap."

"Then where should he be, sir?" the young woman asked, rising from her chair.

"Anywhere that the blue or green lines don't intersect." Troi moved on, grabbed the last person trying to catch his attention, and hauled him by the collar towards the door. "The woman you need to ask is standing right behind the king. Riana, what size are you?"

"Size in what?" she asked, not sure how or why this information was needed, but positive they needed to know.

"Dress and shoes, ma'am," the tow-headed man responded with a duck of the head, smile brief but charming.

"Twenty-six dress," Riana informed him, moving more into the room as Edvard slid sideways to give her space, "nineteen wide shoe."

This information was immediately jotted down before the man gave her another duck of the head, this one of thanks, and then he scurried back to his desk.

"We're preparing a wardrobe for you to go along with your new persona," Troi explained to her. "The clothes have to be exactly right and we'll need to pre-order them now so that you're in fashion by the time you arrive."

"Ah, I see." And so she did. Riana would be in High Court after all. "Will this be difficult to arrange?"

"Not at all, not with your partner. He buys clothes—both women's and men's—on a regular basis so he'll know what to do. We have the right contacts to get what you need anyway even if he weren't taking charge of this," Troi said with satisfaction.

To Riana, Edvard explained, "We actually

employ spies and double agents all of the time in every corner of the world. A country has to in order to keep abreast of things. We have at this moment eighty-six spies—"

"Ninety-two," Troi corrected.

Edvard gave him an exasperated look. "I told you I didn't have the budget for more spies."

"It's quite alright, Sire," Troi assured him. "Half of them are fictional."

Riana blinked at him. "Fictional?"

Leaning forward an inch, Troi gave her a wink and grin. "Fictional spies are actually the best kind, in a sense. You don't have to pay them, worry about them double crossing you, or being caught and interrogated. They give the enemy all sorts of wrong information and lead them on a merry chase, which wastes the enemy's resources. Even if they are eventually found out to be a lie, I still win, as they will have to go through considerable time and expense to figure out it is a lie."

"The beauty of it is," Edvard picked up the explanation with the same sort of evil glee as Troi, "that it makes it look like we have a much more broad and comprehensive network of spies in Iysh than we actually do."

Troi nodded agreement. "Of course, the downside is I have over forty personalities to keep straight. None of my fictional spies can once be out of character, otherwise the whole charade falls apart. So I have to keep the details straight, even as I'm sending false information through them, or having them 'move about' with my actual spies. It does get a little confusing at times."

Riana tried to imagine keeping almost a

hundred people straight in her mind, with all of their personalities and tasks, and a headache threatened to form at just the thought.

"That doesn't include our enemy's spies," Troi continued, reading her face with ease. "And they have more spies than I do."

The headache arrived and Riana rubbed a hand to her temple. "Of course. Them too."

"Although they've become almost friends at this point, so it's hard to remember they're enemies."

Edvard gave him a flat look. "Friends? How so?"

"But, Sire," Troi joked with a serious face, "they are so considerate and give me such wonderful information on a consistent basis, how else should I think of them except as friends?"

Several of the staff nearby laughed at this joke, bobbing their heads in agreement, although their hands never stopped moving as they worked. Riana, after a double-take (she had never seen Troi relaxed enough to joke before) grinned at him. "Truly?"

"Not all spies are good spies," Troi informed her. "The more terrible ones give me far more information than they should. I've actually turned a few of them into double agents without their realizing. Spies on another's payroll are the best kind."

Riana almost felt sorry for those particular spies. She pitied anyone that caught Troi's professional attention.

"Let's head next door, there's room to talk there," Troi suggested.

Grateful for this suggestion—hearing Troi had been difficult in that cluttered room—she stepped backwards into the hallway to give the men room to come out. Troi truly did mean right next door, as he led them into a room that was smaller in size, with only a table, chairs, and one bookcase crammed with bound reports. There was a map here, too, not as cluttered with pins and string, but obviously well used.

Taking a seat at random, Riana sat on the edge of her chair in anticipation.

"I've decided to base you out of Senn," Troi informed her, taking the chair at the head of the table. "Senn is very friendly toward us, so they'll go along with your false identity, and it will explain any gaps in your etiquette or education. Senn is considered to be 'backwater' after all."

That made sense to her and Riana nodded.

"You'll actually start in Senn, as we need to lay down a trail for you, in case anyone decides to investigate. You'll stay there for a day or two, exploring the place and getting to know it, before you travel on to the palace. Your partner, Zigzag, will meet you in Senn and take you in. I was going to have the two of you pretend to be lovers—"

Edvard coughed around a laugh. "Are you serious? Ash would hit the roof."

"Which is why I wanted to do it," Troi admitted with a perfectly straight face, setting the other two to laughing, "but in reality it wouldn't work out well. Riana would be snubbed if she was just a nobleman's lover, and wouldn't have the access to the right people, wasting our efforts. So instead you're Zigzag's third cousin, someone he's been tasked to introduce to Court."

Troi's logic was irrefutable, of course, but Riana had a wistful moment where she wished it wasn't so. Just because it was fun tweaking Ash's nose. "Can we pretend otherwise at first?"

Edvard burst out laughing. "I won't tell him if you don't! But please only tell him when I'm in the room, I do not want to miss his reaction."

"I won't," she promised him with a wink. "So I'm a minor noblewoman of Senn?"

"You are," Troi answered, smile approving. "And your accent is coming along nicely. Keep practicing that. I haven't come up with a good name for you yet, as it must be something that would be recorded in Senn as a noblewoman's family, but we should have that wrinkle solved by the end of the week. Now, let's discuss the finer details, shall we?"

CHAPTER SIX

"Broden!"

It was a rare thing indeed for Tierone to be calling out to him. Broden stopped dead and then did a quick side-step off the street to avoid being run over. The Dahlian King caught up in three long strides with a look of abject relief on his face. "Glad I caught you. You weren't at the morning meeting."

"Minor emergency," Broden explained. "Someone left a candle burning in a place they should no' have, and it did a mite of damage."

"Ah. I suppose, considering the cramped conditions, that it's a miracle that doesn't happen more often." Tierone looked about the very crowded tent-city of newcomers that were camped just inside the main wall and grimaced. "And beyond grateful that our sheriff is a wizard that can snuff fire out quickly. Ye gods but that would have been disastrous if it had gotten out of control."

It would have been. They still had people straggling in, and others moving up from the southern edge of Estole in preparation for what was coming. Between Estole's Old Wall and the New Wall (as people coined them) there was a veritable forest of tents and lean-tos. As it was they had lost one tent completely and even now Kirsty was helping to build a place so the family would not be imposing on relatives for more than a few days.

"Ye need me, lad?"

Tierone needed a second to switch mental tracks. "Yes, I certainly did. First, where's Ashlynn?"

"Ah, that? She be working on the wall with Ash and the others any spare second she has. Lass has me playing sheriff while she works her magic."

"Of course," Tierone responded with perfect understanding, "I should have realized that. Let's walk toward the wall, then, as I'll need to speak to her about this as well."

Broden led the way, keeping pace with the man beside him. He was slightly surprised that Tierone was still here, as the man had been making noises last night about needing to return to Dahl; so whatever had happened in the morning meeting must have been serious to delay him.

"Troi reported this morning that there's been an unusual amount of shipping traffic coming out of Kremser, all with indications that they're heading north."

Blinking at him, Broden objected, "North? North where, lad?"

"Not sure. That's what caught my attention. I finally managed to get a shipping manifest for one and it only had Windcross listed as a stopping point," Tierone answered meaningfully.

That did not spell good news to his mind. It was an extremely long trip through the Western Sea, up around the Land Northward, and south again. If a ship was going that direction, they would certainly be heading to more than one destination. Windcross alone was not worth the journey. It smacked of ulterior motives. "What be the cargo?"

"Confidential information."

"This really do no' bode well," Broden growled.

Tierone grimaced. "You're telling me. We threw around several ideas this morning but we're really not sure. Troi can't get anyone close enough to verify what's on there. Are they supplies for the army? Troops? Something totally different that we don't have the right information to predict?"

"Would no' an army need to bring supplies with them on the march? Surely trying to get supplies from the ocean be too much of a jaunt to be feasible," Broden objected, absently dodging a wagon that had random things protruding out the side.

"I would think so." Tierone gave a shrug. "It could be that they're up to something else entirely. We're just so war-oriented right now we can't think of what. But this is where Troi had a flash of genius, and hence why I hunted you down. Broden, didn't you mention before that you have contacts with the pirates?"

"Aye, lad, that I do," Broden agreed slowly, not quite sure where Tierone was going with this.

"How good are your contacts?" Tierone

65

pressed. "Can you get them to raid those ships for us, report what's on them?"

The light dawned. "Lad, they be more than willing to do that. Information for information is a game I've played more times than I can tell. If they know afore when ships be coming up, they can lay in a pretty ambush and be set for the winter storms."

Tierone nodded, satisfied. "Then I need you to go up and broker a deal with the pirates. Even if there's nothing on those ships for us to worry about, it'll help put Iysh in tighter financial straits, so it's a win-win situation for us no matter what the outcome is."

All of that was true enough. Broden just saw one problem with the idea. "Lad, I be willing enough to go, as it be land I know well, but ye do realize that Ashlynn will never agree to me going off into pirate land by me lonesome."

"She can't leave now," Tierone disagreed confidently. "She's working on a wall, and she's sheriff here; she doesn't have the freedom to travel to the other end of the continent with you."

Broden eyed him sideways. For all that the man claimed the lass as a sister, he did not seem to know her very well in some ways. "Tell ye what, lad. If ye can convince her to stay, I will take someone else with me."

"Of course," Tierone assured him hastily, "I never intended you to go in by yourself. I'll talk to her and convince her to stay."

It was better for him to go along, Broden could see that. "Let's find the lass and speak to her, then."

Tierone seemed glad to have backup along for this conversation and readily agreed. The two men fell into step with each other, dodging other pedestrians, making a beeline for the outer barrier through the city. "I do wonder if they're going to be on schedule, since Ash and Riana intend to leave within the next two weeks."

Grunting, Broden agreed, "Aye, the wall will no' be done by the time they leave, but no one wants to delay her going and it lead to trouble."

"I agreed with Troi's timing and reasoning, I just wasn't sure how it was going to affect building the barrier. Ash is our best builder but I'm not sure if the same applies as this is mostly magical construction? With very little physical."

Aside from the posts there to anchor the barrier with, there was nothing physical at all about it. The barrier was made to shuffle back and forth, only presenting a strong front when a physical force impacted against it. "It has no' seemed to slow them down much, lad. I think we should be fine—"

From some distance ahead several voices screamed out in pain and terror all at once. Broden's heart skipped several beats, adrenaline shooting up his spine, as those sounds meant serious trouble. He did not even pause to swear, just broke out into a dead run, following his ears and running in the direction that people were retreating from. Tierone thundered alongside him, pushing hard to keep up. He was a strong man, not a runner, and it showed in the way his lungs strained.

The physical wall around Estole blocked

Broden's view and he could not see what was happening until he breached the main gate. One of the guards recognized them and shouted out, "MAGICAL ASSASSINS!"

This time, Broden did feel like swearing. They had not had an assassin in several weeks—mostly due to the poor traveling conditions the weather brought on, belike—and Broden had naively assumed that they had weathered the worst of it where that was concerned. Why he had, who knew?

Tierone stopped dead, which was wise, as he had no means to fight a magical battle. He was one of those that couldn't tolerate much magic at all without getting the hives from it. "I'll summon help from the academy."

"Go!" Broden encouraged, already slinging his bow off his shoulder and arrows out of his quiver. His eyes darted about, trying to gain a sense of what was happening and where his partner was.

Broden picked out four wizard assassins, all of them dodging or deflecting magical attacks shot at them. They were deadly in their craft and good, curse it. Facing them was Kirsty, Ashlynn, Gerrard and two wizard students, although their backs were to him so he was not quite sure which two. They looked to be middling teens, and having them in this battle made his blood run cold. They were far too young to be facing hardened assassins.

Broden's first duty, always, was Ashlynn. But he could not bear the thought of leaving the kids on their own. Gerrard was doing his level best to get to them, but he had an assassin out for his blood, and that was not happening any time soon.

This was proving to be a perfectly terrible day.

Making a split-second decision, Broden broke for the teenagers, firing as he ran, distracting the wizards. They stumbled, dodged, one even dropped flat on his face to avoid arrows in his chest. It bought Broden the time he needed to reach the students. As he sprinted across that open space, his skin crawled at the excessive exposure, but there was no other option. The land in front of Estole was nothing more than flatland and a few very gently rising hills. There was no cover to be had and hesitating was a sure way of getting killed.

When he was almost upon them, Broden stopped paying strict attention to the wizards and bought a second to see which students they were. His heart sank when he realized that it was Violet and Jayla. They were good students but they hadn't had nearly enough time in battle simulations or training to prepare them for this.

Grabbing them by the shoulders, he spun them about and together, so that their shoulders overlapped. "Shield, both of ye!" he commanded roughly. "Do no' think of attacking, leave that to me. Shield as yer lives depend on it!"

They had already been shielding some, but also dropping it a little to fire off attack spells. After several lessons with him, they obeyed his voice in pure instinct, throwing up the strongest shields that they could muster.

For the first time, Broden truly experienced being in a shield that was not a construct of either Ashlynn's or Ash's and he finally understood why being a partner for a wizard was such a personal thing. He felt like the air around him was statically charged, uncomfortably so, and moving an inch in any direction would send a jolt through him. His first instinct was to escape it but of course he could not. Gritting his teeth, he sought to ignore it, and instead focused on the fight.

Their wizard attackers were up again, and sensing a weakness, one of them focused on the students. He harried them hard, throwing attacks out quickly. Broden knew that the instant he sent out an attack, he would be vulnerable to weaponry, but that was a very fine window to shoot in. It would be a matter of a split second, perhaps less.

"Listen, both of ye," he said calmly, voice barely loud enough to be heard in this chaotic dog fight, "I'll be shooting between yer heads. Do no' move a muscle."

"Sir, if it's you firing, you won't hit us by accident," Jayla declared stoutly. "Fire at will."

"Ye've got mettle, lad," Broden praised and grinned. He knew he liked this kid for a reason. Nocking an arrow, he paused, watching the wizard closely. Several attacks hit and splattered on the shield, different colors, different elements used. Sometimes the shield let off fiery sparks as an attack hit and dissipated harmlessly, the heat of it briefly felt. Broden started to see the rhythm: one, two, three, pause for a moment, then again, one, two, three.

He needed a breath in between attacks.

Broden ducked his head a little, trying to confuse the enemy wizard into thinking he was not paying attention or was focusing elsewhere. He did not need sight to know what the other man was doing. He could hear and feel the attacks in the air as they were unleashed. One, two—

—as the third attack spell was still leaving the man's lips, Broden lifted up and snapped the bow into position, drawing and firing all in one smooth motion. His arrow found its mark with unerring accuracy and lodged itself firmly in the man's heart. He toppled backwards without even a sound.

Whirling in the same moment, Broden sighted the wizard battling Gerrard so ferociously. The man was in profile to him, focused on Gerrard— for good reason, the man fought like a wounded tiger—and was not paying any attention to Broden. Fortunate, that. Broden unleashed two arrows in quick succession at him, both aimed for his body, as he was not sure he could get a clean kill shot at this odd angle.

One found itself in the man's armpit and he went down with a scream. Gerrard took prompt advantage of it and finished the man off without any mercy. He was a little wild-eyed and winded, but not shaken. He proved that as he ran for his students, yelling at Broden as he did so. "Ashlynn!"

"Aye!" Broden agreed, for once perfectly in sync with the other man. He left the students to their master and did another mad sprint for Ashlynn. The ache and strain of battle was starting to enter his legs, feeling the effects of literally running like a madman for the past thirty minutes. He ignored it as best he could, focused on his partner more than anything else.

Ashlynn was back to back with Kirsty, one of them defending while the other fired off an attack. It was the best solution possible in a situation like this, with multiple attackers, and Broden applauded their quick thinking. Fortunately for him, Kirsty's magic was not intolerable to him, as she was the one shielding while Ashlynn attacked. He slid in behind the shield, hoping it was just for magical defense and not physical so he would not get rebuffed. When he made it through, he huffed in relief and nocked an arrow. "Lass, I fire the next with ye."

"Sound thinking," she approved. "On my mark, one, two, mark!"

A wizard could guard against a magical attack or a physical one, but not both at the same time. Their opponent deflected Ashlynn's cleanly enough but he could not switch shields fast enough to do anything about Broden's arrow. He took that one in the chest and stumbled back, going down like a marionette with its strings cut.

That left one. With three very upset wizards and an archer out for his blood, the man did not stand much of a chance. He lasted another ten seconds before he too was down. Broden stared at the bloody aftermath, throat aching from thirst, sweat pouring at his temples, heart beating out a crazy staccato in his ears. He looked to Ashlynn and found that she had that demented grin that signaled she had gone into a berserker rush.

Catching his eye, she said cheerfully, "I'm finally warm. It was freezing out here earlier while working on the wall."

"A few wizard assassins gets the blood

pumping," Kirsty agreed, also looking a little wide around the eyes. "Ye gods, you people dealt with these thugs on a regular basis? I have more respect for Edvard's nerves, now. They must be made of steel."

Ashlynn laughed and didn't deny it. "Broden, Jayla? Violet?"

"Fit as fiddles," he assured her. "I do no' believe anyone got hurt more than scrapes and bruises, which be a minor miracle."

"Our shielding is just that good," Kirsty declared proudly. "That," she added more practically, "and they started attacking the wall first before they noticed us working. I think word of us building a barrier has leaked somehow."

"Not necessarily," Gerrard disagreed, coming up to both of them. His students were safely inside the walls now, and he was studying the area with a keen eye. "It's a logical conclusion to build a barrier to repel an army, if you can. As cramped as we are inside of its borders, Estole is small enough to make a barrier feasible. Someone else in the enemy camp is clearly using their head and anticipating what we'll do."

Now that was not a comfortable thought at all. Broden did not like the taste of it, but conceded privately that Gerrard was likely right.

Ashlynn made a face, agreeing but not liking it either. "Well. Broden, good thing you were nearby."

Was this a good time to mention it...? Was any time a good one to mention it, for that matter. Feeling like he knew how this conversation was going to end before he even opened his mouth, he still felt bound to ask the question Tierone wanted him to. "As to that, lass, Tierone wants to send me north for a while and talk to the pirates. To figure out those mystery trade ships coming out of Iysh, ye ken."

"I ken," she agreed, all smiles. "Why do I hear a 'but you need to stay here' in that speech?"

"The barrier be no' finished," he pointed out lamely.

Ashlynn gave him the same smile that a parent would to a child that is deliberately being obtuse. "Broden. If you think that you're going anywhere alone when there's enemy wizards out here? Then you're sorely mistaken."

Well, as to that, he never thought she would agree. "I think ye and Tierone can hash this out."

"Oh, there will be hashing, alright. If he doesn't see sense."

CHAPTER SEVEN

Broden was not trying to argue with her, but could not help but say, "Lass, there be little need to go up with me."

"You're not going to Runamok alone," his partner stated adamantly.

That was obviously the case, as they were already outside of Ganforth and on the main highway to Cloud's Rest. "Hopefully the city still be in one piece when we get back."

"The city will survive. I don't trust those people with you. Especially since we apparently have wizard assassins running around lose again. You're my priority."

"Ah, now lass, that warms the heart right up, it does." Broden could not help but grin at her.

She mock-scowled at him in return and encouraged her horse to a faster walk with a thump of the heels.

Secretly, Broden was glad that Ashlynn had chosen to go with him. He had not looked forward to going into pirate territory by himself. They did not have the manpower to send much more than him, and Broden admitted that he was likely enough for the job. Probably. He was the one with firm contacts in the pirate world anyway, so he was the better choice to go. Broden understood the situation quite well—despite his reluctance in going.

"How long do you think it will take to get there? Three days?"

Three days was their time limit, although Broden had hoped for four. "Likely so."

"I want to speed this along as much as I can." A frown pulled Ashlynn's brows together.

Broden knew they were both thinking that even if the snows did not come in harshly this winter, neither of them wanted to be riding around in snow-covered mountains, magic or not. Besides, because of the extra precautions and guards now up around the wizards as they constructed the barrier, the progress done on it would be slower than anticipated. And it left the city with a skeletal guard instead of a barely-apt one. They truly could not afford to be out here any longer than necessary.

Hendrix believed his brother would strike now, instead of waiting for spring, as a sensible man would do. Maddox was famous for a "quick, decisive victory" and he likely wanted to prove his mettle to his father sooner rather than later. With the "Estole Problem" solved, as the Iyshians no doubt thought of it, Maddox could easily take over the throne and realize all of his ambitions.

It seemed foolhardy in the extreme for Maddox to launch an offensive now, but Hendrix seemed convinced it would likely happen. Granted, that was exactly what they wanted Maddox to do, and

Broden had no intention of correcting an enemy when they were making a mistake. Still, they had barely started the campaign of misinformation to lead Maddox up here. If he really did come now, that meant he had already planned to do so, belike.

Broden shook his head at the sadness and foolishness of it all.

"What are you thinking about?"

"Maddox's madness," Broden answered with a long sigh.

"Ah," Ashlynn intoned with complete understanding. "I don't expect him to really march soon. I mean, there's still some snow on the ground."

That there was, although trace amounts. "If he does, it means he do no' care what the cost be, he just wants victory."

"Even though he's being stupid about it, he might win, if our plans don't work out." Ashlynn tipped her head back to stare absently at the sky, half-obscured by branches. "By the mite of manpower." She tilted her head back to give him a sorry smile. "Ever think you made a bad bet with me, partner?"

Broden did not even need to think on that. He shook his head immediately. "Life be a struggle, lass. At least here, we be fighting for something instead of against everything."

"And your daughter's found a good man to love," Ashlynn added in a knowing tone, expression challenging him to take on the statement.

Oh, he wanted to, did not he just. But he

could also see the handwriting on the wall and had known for a while now that things would end up that way. So he heaved a gusty sigh instead and stared off into the woods.

Delighted by this win, Ashlynn chuckled. "Not denying it, eh?"

"Lass, I knew from the first moment Ash be taken with me daughter. Man kept staring at her so hard it be a wonder he did no' trip over his own feet."

Ashlynn bobbed her head in agreement. "Completely star-struck, that brother of mine. We've currently got bets going on when he's finally going to confess."

That brought up a good point that Broden had been wondering about for some time. "And why has he no'? Lad's been given the time he needs to."

"It's just how Ash rolls," she explained, not a trace of condemnation in the words, just patient amusement. "He has to think about something, from every possible angle, get used to it, and then he'll move. He's not the type to jump into anything. I think he was giving them both time, too, to get used to their partnership first before he tried for anything more." Ashlynn let loose an evil chuckle. "But judging from Riana's reactions, she's getting tired of waiting on him. I give it any day now, before she pushes the matter."

Aye, he had the same thought. Not that he knew what to think of his little girl seducing a man, but at least he knew it was a good man, and one that would treat her right. It was only that reassurance that kept him from sharpening a few arrows and hunting the man down in the dead of night.

"She best move fast," Ashlynn said, more quietly, a hard look in her eyes. "Maddox's army will be on us soon enough. If he decides to move before the snows, we're likely to get word within three weeks or so, right?"

"No later than that, aye. Belike sooner." Hence why they only had four days up at Runamok. Ashlynn had to get back and prepare the magical defenses along with the other wizards. It was also why Riana had to leave in under two weeks, to make sure that she was well gone before someone could spot her leaving Estole and make the obvious connection.

"I've wondered this before..." Ashlynn trailed off, staring hard at him as if trying to see directly to his mind. "You're really not worried about Riana playing spy in the heart of Iysh?"

"If I said I be no' worried at all, it would be a lie," Broden admitted forthrightly. More forthrightly than when his own daughter had asked the same question, as he did not want his fears to prey on her mind. "Of course I be worried as she be going into the very heart of enemy territory. But lass, me daughter has lived in the heart of enemy territory most of her born days. At least this time she has more than one ally at her back."

Ashlynn gave a grudging nod. "I hadn't thought of it that way, but that's a very good point."

"Also, this spy business, it be akin to cat and mouse games, aye?"

"From what I understand of it."

Broden gave a satisfied grunt. "Then Riana be fine. There be no one better at it than her."

"And you're banking on Ash yanking her out if it does get too dangerous."

"And that," Broden agreed equably.

"You do understand that I feel like we're also walking into enemy territory?" There was not a trace of humor in Ashlynn's expression or tone. "That if I feel like you are in danger up here, that I will also yank you out?"

"It warms this old man's heart, it does, to see ye so up in arms."

"I'm serious, Broden."

"I know ye be, lass, I know ye be." Broden felt like pointing out that they could ill afford to both leave Estole right now, that many of their plans hinged upon her magic, but knew it would not have any impact on her. If Broden was walking into a dangerous situation, she would have his back. She was protective of her loved ones that way. It was part of the reason why Broden absolutely adored her. Knowing this, he changed tactics instead. "I do no' think it will come down to it, but be it no' a better notion to just zap them if they go out of line?"

"Well, of course I'll zap them, but men do get revenge when their enemy's back is turned, y'know."

Aye, did not he just. "They be cowards at heart, lass. It be why me family has been able to survive in Cloud's Rest for generations. They did no' like us, aye, that be truth, but they did no' have the guts to chase us out either. Or deal with the bandits themselves, for that matter. With a wizard at me back, even pirates will no' dare to tussle with me."

Ashlynn looked only half sold on this logic. "Well, we'll see."

It was likely the stress of the situation, the uncertainty of the future, and her worry over her siblings going into danger that she could not protect them from that had set Ashlynn on edge. But she could not do much about any of that. Broden had a feeling that all of her frustration would be unleashed on the first fool that dared to cross them.

"Come to think of it, how do you have contacts with them anyway?"

"Bandits used the pirates as a middleman to offload goods," he explained succinctly. "Sometimes the cargo be people. I be the rescuer more often than no'."

Her face lit in understanding. Ashlynn was bright enough to put the picture together herself. "If you have contacts, then you didn't always fight your way in and out?"

"Be suicide to even try. I always found a way to barter instead. Went over better. After a time, they would contact me and offer a ransom first, afore going elsewhere. It be a business relationship of sorts now."

"You know the most interesting people." Ashlynn shook her head, marveling. "I suppose if I stick around you long enough, I'll be able to say the same. Alright, so, what are we going to bargain with this time in order to get in and strike a deal?"

"That, lass, be a very good question."

"I do not understand the appeal of being either a pirate or a bandit," Ashlynn announced, fortunately in a low enough voice that it would not carry past their table.

"As to that, lass, I never could ken either." Broden kept a wary eye on the door, the room as a whole, and the people near them in particular. Waltzing into a pirate town all by your lonesome was a sure way to get shanghaied. But having Ashlynn with him did not make it less dangerous either, just dangerous in a different sense. "There be times, lass, like this one, that I lament ye be such a pretty gyne."

Ashlynn smirked at him. "It's one of those trials in life you have to bear. No worries, if they do converge on us, I'll just throw up a shield and we can walk back out."

True, the odds of anyone here being able to withstand her magic were slim to none. Broden dared to breathe a little easier.

Coming in had been hairy enough, and it was only Broden naming his contact that had let them in this far. But sitting inside a tavern for ten solid minutes was not doing anything but shortening Broden's life. He really wished the captain in question would just get here.

Runamok had not improved in looks since his last visit. It was just as dank, smelling vaguely of mold and refuse, and a little on the dark side.

It was cold enough to shiver a man's very bones, especially with that crisp sea air blowing through the town. Everyone had their shutters closed, which blocked all light, so they were making do with firelight and lamps. It made for a dreary environment to sit in. Broden was semi-used to it, having been here before, but he understood why it was making Ashlynn uneasy.

"You said this captain is one that you've dealt with many times before." Ashlynn's tone had a lilting question to it.

"Aye. He be no' what a man can describe as 'honorable'—the man's a pirate after all—but he sticks to a bargain he makes." Which was not something that could be said of the rest of this lot. "He be a bit hard to pin down, as to which way he will jump."

"A fine compliment coming from you, Ravenscroft."

Broden had half-sensed the presence just outside the door and was not surprised at this abrupt appearance. Ashlynn jumped a little, although she recovered her composure in the next blink of the eye. Turning his head, he regarded the pirate captain blocking the door, the sun streaming weakly behind him. The man had aged a little in the past year, more grey in his temples and beard, slowly overtaking the dark brown. His skin was still dark and swarthy after so much time in the sun, eyes as penetrating and calculating. He had, however, changed into a more winterish concoction of clothing that was mostly fur-lined, making him seem bulky. Broden knew for a fact the man was more whipcord thin and sinewy.

Were the clothes to help make him intimidating or because he had no natural insulation against the cold? Having never seen him in winter, Broden could not say one way or another.

Standing, he offered a hand. "Captain JJ."

"Broden Ravenscroft." JJ clasped arms with him, the grip strong enough to bend steel. "Never thought I'd see you come back in here. Not after you decimated all my business partners."

"Ye mean yer rivals and general thorns in the side," Broden riposted, deadpanned.

JJ held firm for a full second before a slow smile spread over his face. "Eh, they were that too. Well, man, what do you want this time?"

"To give ye information."

"Give me? For free?" JJ did not believe this for a full second. He dropped into a chair and regarded Ashlynn with frank scrutiny. "You be a mite young for his lover."

"Partner," Ashlynn corrected, eyebrow quirked in what could have been either amusement or challenge. "Ashlynn Fallbright, Wizard."

That got the attention of every person in the room. They all stilled for a long second, regarding her with nervous attention, not at all sure why they had a wizard in their midst. JJ hid this better than the rest but the way his eyes were a trifle too wide in his face gave the game away. "Wizard. Partner. Well, now, things seemed to have changed while I was out at sea. Ravenscroft, seems there's a story here."

"Aye, there be quite the tale. I will tell ye the shorter version if we have the time, but for now, I have a bargain to strike with ye."

JJ waved him on. "Let's hear it, then."

"Word has it that Maddox will soon send an army against Estole." Broden had to gauge this carefully, how much to tell and when to tell it. Too much information all at once, and he would not be able to tell JJ's stance on all of this, and how to negotiate.

JJ grunted understanding. "Maddox is a true half-wit to send an army now, with winter fast approaching, but can't say I'm surprised. We all expected it. And?"

"We also received word that Iysh be sending many ships northward."

The captain stilled, his entire focus on Broden now, eyes narrowing. "How many ships?"

Broden was not about to tell him that. For one thing, all they had was a guess. "What we want be for ye to intercept them, attack them, then report to us what be on them. Ye can keep it all as booty, whatever ye can take."

"And if I agree to the terms, you will tell me everything you know?"

"Aye."

This was a deal too good to be true. JJ knew it. His face said as much. "And what's in it for you two?"

"We're Estolian," Ashlynn stated simply.

JJ let out a short laugh and slapped his hand against the table. "Fallbright! That's where I know the name! You're the same wizard that held off the first two armies of Iysh, aren't you?"

"One of them, yes. The other is my brother."

"Ha!" JJ had an excited gleam in his eyes as he leaned forward. "So you want me to do your work for you? Is that it?"

"Ye get all the booty," Broden reminded him. "A clear target where ye know their course and destination."

JJ drummed his fingertips against the top of the table and regarded both of them. "But I'll be doing the fighting for you."

"Ye fight all the time against targets ye have little ken of," Broden drawled, realizing that this protest was just JJ's way of negotiating. "Man up."

The pirate captain was not deterred. "I want more than the information about the ships."

And here they went. Always the same with JJ. Broden resisted the urge to sigh. "Of course ye do. Out with it, man."

"I want the full story." JJ stabbed a finger between the two of them. "I want your full tale. How did Broden Ravenscroft, archer, become the partner to a famous wizard? How did a wizard from a peaceful duchy start a rebellion against Iysh and found a country? I want the full story."

Ashlynn blinked, not at all expecting this, but Broden was not surprised. JJ liked to have a good yarn to spin on a cold night, and he gathered up rumors and stories like a miser would gold. To him, sometimes, a good story was a better coin to offer than actual currency. But Broden could not just agree and give in, that would tilt their balance, and it would hurt the deal.

"Ye want a full story, knowing well it will take hours to tell, and ye not even offering to feed us? After we rode all this way? For shame, JJ."

Sensing he about to get his way, JJ

slammed a fist against the table. "A fine dinner for you both! Plus a little food to carry with you on the way back. Wizard, you help me repair the docks, as they are in bad shape, I'll get the tale, you tell me all you know about these mystery ships, and we'll call it a bargain."

Now that sounded like a fair enough trade to Broden. He regarded Ashlynn, silently asking if she was willing to stick around for that long. She gave the place another slow, thorough look, nose not quite wrinkling in disgust. Then she shrugged and held her hand out to JJ. "A bargain."

JJ immediately clasped it. "A bargain!" he boomed out, his normal volume when he was excited about something. It set any innocent bystanders' ears to ringing. "Bring me food and ale!" he demanded of the serving women. "Now, first off, let's hear this story—"

"First off," Ashlynn cut in, with some exasperation, "you should show me the docks, shouldn't you? Before the light fails us?"

Considering this, JJ spread out a palm. "Docks, then. Ravenscroft, you can tell me the story as we go."

Not going to wait that long, eh? Broden bit back a grin. "Aye, that I will do."

CHAPTER EIGHT

Broden watched his partner sitting at a table full of men and women, swapping stories and laughing, and wondered just what had happened. Ashlynn had been dead set against this place when they first arrived, and now, not six hours later, she was as comfortable here as if she had been born and raised in the place. Having never really traveled with her—apart from Cloud's Rest, and that had been a disastrous trip in some ways—Broden had not ever really seen her outside of her comfort zone. It turned out she was amazingly adaptable. If he had not known better, he would almost mistake her for a pirate, she was so included in the group.

The light had failed before Ashlynn had finished repairing the docks, and so they were forced to stay the night. JJ was taking advantage of this and getting every possible story out of them, which Ashlynn was happy to oblige. They had even been given rooms in a decent enough place, and while it looked a little worn, it also seemed to be bug-free. Broden had slept in worse. Ashlynn seemed glad to not be camping out in the woods for a fourth night in a row.

Well, they were likely safe for the night, leastways. Normally Broden would not ever dream of staying overnight in this place, but he could see healthy fear in every person's eyes. They in no way wanted to get on a wizard's bad side, and on top of that, they were not about to meddle with JJ when he had a bargain in place. This might be the only time that Broden could walk around freely in the village.

Lass seemed to be having a good time. Broden sat slightly sideways in his chair, watching her with a bemused smile on his face. Now, what would her brothers think of this? Her sitting amongst pirates and eating dinner as if there be no issue.

She was in full swing, telling the stories of some of the crazier law-breaking events they had had in the very beginning. "I swear those idiots were purposefully getting on my last nerve. Like that—" she cut herself off abruptly and lifted the caller toward her mouth. "What? I can't hear you, speak louder."

This time the voice was audible enough for Broden to hear it, although barely. "I said, Maddox's army is already on the move!"

Broden barely registered Edvard's voice before the realization sank in what the man had just said. He shoved his way past two people, leaning over Ashlynn's shoulder to be able to speak. "He WHAT?!"

"Troi's not sure how he managed this, but he got his army on the move days ago. We just got a pigeon informing us."

By pigeon? Broden was aware that Troi employed carrier pigeons as they were the fastest way to receive news and also one of the more reliable methods. That meant the news was at least four hours old, as it took that long for one of the birds to fly that distance.

"What's his estimated time of arrival?" Ashlynn demanded, half-standing in her chair, nearly vibrating with the urgency and desire to leave.

"Here's the aggravating part. The army is at the crossroads already."

Broden started swearing creatively. The major crossroad division lay thirty miles out from Kremser.

"He apparently has no intention of going towards Senn. Instead he's heading straight for us. At best, we have thirteen days before they arrive at the border."

Thirteen days might not be enough time to get the bulk of their plans in place. Broden felt like swearing some more but did not dare interrupt Edvard.

"We've already done what we set out to do," Ashlynn assured her brother, a light of determination in her eyes. "We'll get home as quickly as possible."

"Go, go. The ships didn't leave all at once, they're staggered out, and reports of winter storms likely means they won't be traveling as fast as usual."

A glance at JJ's face confirmed all of this. The captain was nodding along as if this was information he either already knew or had guessed at. "I need to know more than that," Broden protested. "How many ships?"

"About six, we think. There's still no declared destination on the ships' manifests except a stop at Windcross. Hopefully the pirates can figure out where they are now. If we hear anything else, I'll update you as I can. I need to go, good luck, keep me updated!" The connection broke abruptly.

The whole tap room remained silent. Most people did not even seem to breathe for a moment. Then they all started talking, their words overlapping each other. Broden sat there, rubbing at his forehead, logistics and timetables running amok in his head.

JJ came and thumped a boot into a chair, leaning on it so that he was eye-level with Broden and Ashlynn, more or less. "Ravenscroft. Wizard. How about a second bargain?"

Broden slowly looked up at the man. He trusted JJ about as far as he could throw him, but the man seemed to hold bargains sacred, so odds were this might not be a bad deal. "Let's hear it."

"Aside from the docks, there is one more thing we'd like fixed. Only one good well in town, and it's far out. We've been searching for another site to dig a well in, but haven't had any luck. Wizard, if you would find us another site? In return, I'll take you by ship to Gethin and drop you off right and proper."

Ashlynn stared right back at him, her face expressionless, but Broden knew she was thinking hard. "How long does it take to get to Gethin by ship?"

"Six hours, more or less." JJ had a smirk on

his face like he knew he'd get his way shortly.

Six hours? From Gethin to Ganforth was an hour at most on horseback. They'd be back in Estole by tomorrow afternoon. Even with the delay of finding a new well site, it would beat riding hard through mountains for three days.

Standing, Ashlynn offered a hand. "A bargain."

JJ accepted the handshake with a broad grin that revealed a missing tooth. "A bargain! How long will this take?"

"Depends on how many fresh water sources you have near here. I might stumble across one in an hour, it might take me until lunch. Who knows? But I can find you one, that I'm sure of." Ashlynn looked out the door thoughtfully as if she were tempted to look right now.

Broden heaved a sigh. Looks like he would be stomping around in the cold for a few hours. In poor lighting. "If ye stay in the village proper, ye can look tonight."

Ashlynn gave him a slow smile. "You can read my mind, now?"

"No, lass, ye just be predictable." Shaking his head, he glanced about. "JJ, a few volunteers with lanterns will no' be amiss."

JJ grinned and then threw his head back before booming out, "Ahoy, you seadogs! Some lanterns, a shovel, and let's go hunting for buried water!"

A few people laughed and stood, heading different directions. JJ seemed to think they were his volunteers, as he gave Ashlynn a courtly bow and extended his hand gallantly. "Lead me away,

Wizard."

Laughing, Ashlynn took the proffered arm and strolled out of the taproom. Broden trailed along behind and was suddenly grateful that Edvard, Tierone, and Ash were not able to witness this. They would go up like a smoke stack.

Ashlynn likely would not sleep well tonight, too worried about home, but at least with their efforts here they would be able to get home that much sooner.

Broden had been on a ship exactly four times in his life, but this was the first time he had ever been on a pirate ship. As it was the only safe to be, he stood near the prow of the ship and stayed out of everyone's way. Most of the river leading to Gethin was deep and wide but there were spots, like the one they were in now, that narrowed and made it a little tricky for a full-sized ship to navigate through. Fortunately, JJ had been doing exactly that for nigh on thirty years and could likely do it in his sleep.

Ashlynn perched on a barrel next to him, staring straight ahead. The lass had been unusually quiet most of the morning. Broden did not even try to start a conversation with her, knowing full well what she was doing. She was planning out what needed to be done, who should do it, and what to do when things went wrong. For all that she teased her brother about being overly cautious and planning things to death, she was equally worse. Just did it in a different way, that was all.

It was just as well that Ashlynn had gone looking for the well last night as it had taken five hours for her to find fresh water in a place that could actually be tapped into. Three places had been so inconveniently placed that there was no way to build a well there. It meant only getting a handful of hours to sleep, as they both demanded an early start this morning, but no one complained. Perhaps even the pirates realized that Iysh winning this war would not profit them in any way.

The irreverent part of his brain wondered: Even if it was only for six hours, did that make him a defacto pirate?

They remained in silence up until they reached Gethin. It was not a proper town by any means, barely more than a set of docks and a dozen houses clustered together. Broden normally did not see Gethin as the road they had made to Cloud's Rest did not actually pass within view of it. He had been here a handful of times as a caravan guard, but had not come this direction in years. The place had not changed a whit. It still looked half-abandoned, as if the life was gone even though people remained.

They dismounted from the ship, bringing their horses down the gangplank. Judging from the huffing and blowing they did, both steeds were very glad to have their hooves back on solid ground again. Ashlynn turned to JJ with an offered hand. "A bargain well met, Captain."

JJ gave her a toothy grin. "Indeed, Wizard, indeed. Next time you get in trouble, invite me, eh?"

For a moment, she shelved her worries long enough to grin at him impishly. "You bet I will. For now, you have ships to sink and loot."

"I do indeed." JJ rubbed his hands together, nigh chortling. "Ravenscroft, you bring this woman to us more often. We'll spin some stories and drink good ale."

If he ever did such a thing, Edvard would scalp him. "I shall do that." Never. He would do that never.

JJ heard the never, as did Ashlynn, and they both grinned at him like co-conspirators.

It was a terrible idea on his part to introduce Ashlynn to the pirates. He now regretted it sorely but there was no un-doing things. Hopefully she would not go visit them without him.

"Good luck to all!" JJ boomed out, waved a hand, and then ascended the gangplank to his ship. "Ya scurvy miscreants, what are you fooling about for? Get her under way! We have money to make!"

There was a general cheer of enthusiasm even as they went about pulling the ship away from the docks.

Broden and Ashlynn equally wasted no time tightening the girth straps and swinging into their saddles, heading for home. They went at a fast trot, the only speed a horse could easily maintain on these roads, and the noise of it kept them from talking. They reached Ganforth in amazingly good time, abandoned the horses at the inn, and took the first boat across the channel. As they gained the docks, several guardsmen let out wordless sounds of relief and called out greetings. Ashlynn waved, acknowledging them, but no one came to report issues, so she headed directly through town.

A little confused that she was not heading for Edvard's study, Broden stretched out his legs to keep up with her. "Lass, where be we heading?"

"The barrier." She did not even glance at him as she moved, moving at a slow lope, the fastest she could go in this dense street traffic. "Before anything else, we have to get that barrier up and running, otherwise all of our other plans will collapse like a house of cards."

Excellent point. Broden did nothing but keep up until she gained Ash's wall, then ascended it to the very top, giving her the best vantage point possible.

Pulling out a pair of magical glasses from her coat pocket, she put them on, enhancing her vision so that she could see far out in all directions. For several minutes, Ashlynn panned the full area, taking it all in. Regarding the wall in progress with satisfaction, she said, "It might have gone faster if we hadn't left, but it's not bad progress."

Considering the considerable length of magical markers in place for their barrier-wall, all of which happened in the four days that Broden had been gone, he was hard-pressed to think of this as not-bad progress. It was exceptional progress no matter how a man looked at it. Most of the Dahl-Estolian border was up, with only a stretch in the middle left to be bridged. Edvard and Tierone had already ordered the evacuation of southern Dahl to start, and even as he watched, there were people randomly streaming in. Some of them came in under their own power, others had members of the guard helping them along, but they came.

Broden dared to ask the question that was known to invite bad luck, cautiously hoping that he would not be drawing in fortune's attention as he uttered the words: "Be we ahead of schedule, then?"

"Not sure of that," Ashlynn denied thoughtfully, turning to watch some of the people pass her. "But I think we're more or less on schedule. Which, all things considered, is a minor miracle."

Actually it was more like a miracle of epic proportions to his mind, considering their lack of manpower and their overwhelming number of tasks to do. Without a firm deadline to meet, mind. It was enough to drive a man to drink.

A family trundled past, loaded up in a cart, the young man leading a team of mules with what looked to be wife, children, elderly parents and perhaps a sibling or two all piled on top. The grandmother was giving young Seth an earful as the guardsman walked alongside. "I ain't seen any sign of an army yet. Why do we have to go? What about my house? My chickens? Someone has to feed everything and keep up with it or the dogs will get into it, I know they will; why I lost more chickens this past year because of those two scurvy dogs that live next door—"

Seth gave them a pained smile, more of a

grimace, and a salute to them both as he passed by. Broden gave him a little wave of the fingers and silently wished him the best. Not everyone had the sense to move or be thankful for the help in moving, he knew, but to be actively ranted at the entire trip up had to strain a man's nerves to the breaking point.

It was just as well that Ashlynn was NOT in charge of the evacuations. She would have already hexed half of them.

As it was, she stared at the family, the grandmother in particular, with a frown on her face. "Evacuation still going on?"

"Apparently so."

She gave a nod, not of agreement but of confirmation that whatever internal decision she had made was a good one. "Now I want to talk to Edvard."

Edvard looked up at them with open relief as they strode into his study. "You made remarkable time! I know you said you would arrive this evening, but how did you do it?"

"The pirates gave us a ride," Ashlynn stated, as if that was the most obvious thing in the world.

Tierone and Edvard gave each other speaking looks and then turned to stare at their sister with open exasperation. "You made friends with them, didn't you?" Tierone half-accused.

Oh, was she known for doing things like this? Excellent. That meant he was not responsible for any part of it.

"Of course I did, they're a good resource. And they're fun to play with, as long as you don't trust them." She gave a double snap of the fingers. "Now, focus. Catch me up to date, what's happening?"

"Strange things, that's what's happening." Edvard waved them forward and into a chair, looking perplexed instead of stressed, which Broden took as a good sign. "I initially assumed that the message we received warning us of the army's deployment was from Zigzag."

"And it no' be from him?" Broden inquired, taking the chair with supreme gratitude. It was the first time he had been able to just sit without having both eyes trained for trouble in four days.

"No, it isn't," Tierone confirmed. Picking up a plate of sliced fruit, he offered it to Broden, who immediately took it. It was the first food he'd seen in almost eleven hours, and breakfast was a distant memory. Ashlynn immediately put her fingers in as well, snagging several slices of pear. "Actually, we have no idea who the message is from."

Broden stopped chewing and asked around a mouth full of fruit, "Wha?"

"My reaction precisely," Edvard acknowledged sourly. "Who would warn someone of an enemy's approach and not take credit for it? Apparently Troi sat on this message for a full two days, trying to verify it, before he finally mentioned it to me. It was another agent of his that gave us the confirmation yesterday, hence my call to you, Ashlynn."

"Curiouser and curiouser." Ashlynn chewed, then reached for more fruit. "Alright, we have a spy vigilante. Has he told us anything else?"

"That's all so far." Shaking his head, Edvard put the matter aside. "We'll have to figure this out later. Right now, we have a more pressing matter. Have you checked on the status of the barrier?"

"I have before coming here. It looks like good progress. Will we finish in time?"

"Ash is whining about you deserting him," Tierone answered with a hint of dryness in his tone.

In other words, likely not.

Ashlynn caught the inflection as well and rolled her eyes. "There's been a hiccup of some sort, I take it."

"Slight emergency involving damage to the docks took some of the wizards away. We'll finish on time, technically, but he wants to stress-test the wall to make sure it will do as intended instead of blindly trusting it to work. Also, we deemed it unwise for Hendrix to gallivant around the country without at least some way to contact us. So someone was diverted to make him several callers and a magical shield or three as protection."

It was a good thought, that. If Hendrix fell, so did their plans for ending this war without it turning into an all-out war. Even if it meant sacrificing some of their magic manpower now, it was likely worth it in the end.

Ashlynn seemed to feel the same way as she gave an approving hum. "Then is Hendrix gone already?"

"Left as soon as he could. He has the lengthier

campaign, after all, with all of the traveling he has to do through Iysh."

There was truth. Poor lad and the lot with him were sure to be saddle-sore in the extreme after all of this.

Broden turned his thoughts back to the wall. He did not know much of magic, but testing something that was basically a prototype before having it protect a country sounded like a fine idea to him. "So the lass be needed to finish the wall?"

"Exactly." Edvard pointed a finger at him. "Which makes you default sheriff until she's free to resume her duties."

His eyes nearly crossed. "Me again?!"

"You're her partner. You get to take up her slack." Edvard's manner brooked no nonsense. "Actually, I think we should just make you a deputy sheriff and be done with it."

Ashlynn laughed in open delight. "I love this idea!"

Giving her a weary look, Broden tried not to groan. Of course she did.

"Consider it officially done. Deputy Sherriff, you should know that we're running short on supplies," Tierone continued as if Broden had no say in the matter. (Which he did not.) "It's not a true emergency at this moment but we're having to ration people."

They had been on and off rations so many times that Broden was not even fazed by this news anymore. "Any solutions?"

Tierone glanced uncertainly at Edvard. "I think we should approach Windcross."

Windcross was much closer, as they sat on the mouth of the channel, and it would literally be a few hours trip up and down for them. Because of their location they were a major trade hub, if not a large one, as they were more or less on a mini peninsula of sorts. Broden saw sense in the suggestion immediately but for some reason Edvard frowned.

"We have no trade agreements with them and there's precious little that we have to offer," Edvard argued. Only, he himself didn't seem completely convinced. "You think you can do something?"

"You might not have much of a relationship, but I do. I want to at least try."

Edvard gave a provisional nod. "It can't hurt. I think that's about all the news I have to share. Ashlynn, Broden, you best get back to it."

"Not until I have a proper meal," Ashlynn riposted, firmly putting her foot down. "We've been run pillar to post, and while the pirates might be a fun lot, they're not very good cooks."

There was truth.

Somewhere around late evening, well after the sun had gone down, Broden dared to think it might be safe for him to get some sleep. He had managed on very little over the past four days and being horizontal sounded like a dream to him. In fact, when he got to the point that he was fantasizing about taking his boots off, he knew he had been on his feet too long. Turning things over to the night watch, he trudged back to his room in the castle.

As he reached the right hallway, he saw light coming out from underneath the doorway from Riana's room. Was she still up, then? As he neared her door, he could hear her speaking, in a proper dialect like a high lady would use. Still practicing, eh? The thought made him smile even as it made him nervous.

Knocking lightly on her door, he heard an, "Enter!" and did so. "Daughter, ye sounded like a proper lady."

Riana made a face at him. "I still make a fashrie of it from time to time." Pausing, she asked uncertainly, "Fashrie isn't a word I should be using, is it?"

"Belike no'," he concurred, sitting on the edge of her bed. Ahh, sitting was a blissful thing. His fatigue steadily creeped up on him, ready to pounce any second, but he wanted to steal a few minutes to speak with Riana. It felt like ages since he had managed a father-daughter talk with her. "Be ye ready to go, then?"

"Not at all," Riana denied, but she laughed as she said it. "Bria's been helping me with my speech, Kirsty meets up with me whenever we can to discuss court etiquette and the like. Still, there's so much to learn, and most of it isn't second-nature to me no matter how I practice. Troi keeps reminding me that being from Senn, my cover-identity shouldn't know everything about court etiquette, so not to worry over it, but..." she trailed off uncertainly.

"Ye will be fine," he assured her and meant

every word. "Whenever we go somewhere new, ye always be the first to adapt to the place. Here, for instance."

Riana paused, sitting on the bed next to him, really thinking about it. "I suppose so. I'll be taught more on the trip to Kremser as well. I suppose I shouldn't be borrowing trouble."

"The worst mistake a man can make," Broden counseled, "be this: to be so afraid of making a mistake that he sets himself up for one."

Putting a hand over her heart, she vowed, "I'll remember."

In a lighter vein, the father teased, "Belike Ash be doing just such in regards to the two of ye."

"Oh, that be why he be dragging his feet, now?" she retorted, reverting back to her own tongue. "I been wondering what be the holdup."

"Well, that and war taking up the man's spare time," Broden added.

"I gave him as much time as me patience has allowed." Riana's eyes narrowed, a dangerous gleam in them. "A woman can only be so patient. I be thinking I should take steps soon."

It was odd, but there were moments like now that Riana strongly reminded him of her mother. That steel determination must be hereditary along with that expression, as Riana could be the spitting image of her mother in that moment. It made Broden smile wistfully. "Ye do that, daughter."

"Oh? Have I yer blessing, then?"

Repeating what he had said to Ashlynn, he drawled, "I knew from the first moment Ash set eyes on ye this would come about eventually. I have two eyes, Riana. Both work quite well."

She threw both arms around his neck and hugged him. Broden hugged her back and smiled into her hair. "Love ye, Riana. Ye stay safe out there and no matter how tempting it be, do no' stomp the little lordlings flat."

Giggling, she responded, "Love ye too, Da."

No promise about the lordlings, eh? Ah well.

CHAPTER NINE

It was strange how perception worked. When Riana had first seen Senn, all those many months ago, it had seemed unbelievably large to her. Cloud's Rest could fit inside Senn's city walls ten times over without strain. She hadn't entered the city properly then, simply skirted around it for Estole, but doing that had told her well enough how big the place was.

Now that she had actually lived in Estole, and seen its amazing growth, Senn didn't look nearly as impressive in comparison. In fact, it couldn't really compare to Estole now, being half the size and without nearly as much activity in it. It was, in a way, impressive in a completely different way. As they rode through the main street, Riana leaned her head a little out of the carriage to take in the street better. "It's so organized and quiet here," she marveled.

Ash, sitting next to her, chuckled. "The first time you saw the place, you were saying how noisy and crowded it looked."

"Compared to Estole, the place is quiet," she shot back, without retreating. The air was crisp and cold against her face and after the hours of stuffy air inside the carriage, it felt very welcome.

"Oh, I grant you that, I just find it funny how your opinion has completely flip-flopped in the matter of months. We'll make a city girl out of you yet, Riana."

That part she doubted as she would always feel more at home in the mountains and the forests, but it was true the city didn't bother her as it had before. Humans were highly adaptable creatures. Given enough time, it all seemed comfortable and familiar to her.

It was a little premature, her leaving Estole now, but they had no other choice in the matter. It was vital that Riana be out of the city before the army arrived. She would simply have to continue her education in the finer manners on the way and pray that she retained it all.

Riana only had a few days in Senn, long enough to meet "her family," get to know them and a little about the city so casual remarks wouldn't catch her off-guard. It didn't leave her much time, which was the other reason why she had her head hanging out of the window. She needed to memorize every facet of this place that she could, while she could, and pray that it all stuck in her head.

The drive was a short one, taking them directly to a snug inn that lay only a short distance from the main gate. Ash took a moment to don his glamour mask, one that made him seem like a man with nondescript looks. They pulled out in front and Ash, proving that he could play the part of a gentleman well when necessary, stepped out first before giving her a hand down. Riana truly appreciated the gesture as she was not used to all of these voluminous skirts. She'd been in them near constantly for the past four days, striving to get accustomed to them, but how was a woman supposed to adapt to eight extra layers overnight? And heeled shoes for that matter? Maneuvering that bulk through a narrow carriage door was no mean feat.

With her feet on solid ground, she looked up at the charmingly decorated inn. Supposedly, Riana was to meet her new spy partner here, a Cyr Woelfel. She felt a little nervous at this meeting, butterflies jumping about, and she kept smoothing a hand over her stomach to try and settle herself.

Ash put his arm around her shoulders for a brief moment, leaning in to murmur against the top of her head, "No need to be nervous. If he steps out of line, I'll hex him for you."

The offer made her smile. "You are a dear, Ash."

"Of course. It's why you like me. Now, chin up and in we go." Extending his arm, he waited until she put her hand in the crook of his elbow, then led them confidently inside.

A scarecrow thin man with a handlebar mustache and deep blue eyes met them near the door and gave a bow. "Welcome to Sparrow Hill. Would you like a room?"

"We're here to meet someone," Ash denied. "Is Lord Woelfel here?"

The professional smile of welcome sharpened into one of recognition. Riana knew, by that expression, that this man had an idea of who they really were and why they were here. It made her wonder—just how much of Senn would be in on this deception? "He is and waiting on you. I will show you the way."

They followed him quietly out through a side door that led into a narrow hallway, continuing down it until they reached an airy room made mostly of windows. It was a sunny place, and with the modest fire going in the back corner, the space was borderline too warm. Seated at a small table near the windows was the only other occupant of the room, supposedly Lord Cyr Woelfel.

Riana studied the man openly. So this was the spy that was to be her partner for the upcoming weeks? He didn't look like a spy at all, but a dandy. His black hair was artlessly combed back in a rakish style, blue eyes sparkled with humor, every line of his clothes perfectly pressed and without an errant piece of lint anywhere on him. He looked, in every respect, like the playboy he was rumored to be.

She was not about to believe her first impression. After everything Troi had told her, she knew better.

"You have visitors, Lord Woelfel," the innkeeper announced with a deferential bow.

"Yes, so I see. My thanks, Venn."

Dismissed, Venn quietly left and closed the door behind him.

Cyr Woelfel crossed to her and gave an elaborate bow even as he smoothly picked up her hand to place the barest hint of a kiss on her knuckles. "My lady. I am perfectly enchanted."

Not missing a beat, she gave him a curtsey, snapping open her fan so as to cover the lower half of her face in a demure gesture. "My lord, I am flattered in return, to be greeted by so handsome a man."

There was a half a second where he was surprised, pleasantly so, then his mouth spread in a rakish grin. Closing in, he held a hand at her waist that didn't quite touch but gave the impression of doing so. "No, my lady, truly I am enchanted by your beauty. And such a lovely voice. Surely the heavens are conspiring against me, to place such a temptress before my eyes."

Deep down, Riana was not really that comfortable with such attentions, and if they had been more sincere, she would have been looking for an exit right about now. However, she recognized that he was testing her by playing this game of flirtation, and she wasn't about to cower, so upped her own smile a notch and closed her fan with a flick of the wrist. "You say so, but consider my feelings, my lord. I find myself quite out of breath on our meeting. Pray, what is your name? I want to know what to call you when you appear in my dreams tonight."

"Cyr Woelfel," he responded, moving closer still so that their faces were barely inches apart. "My lady, I beg of you, your name? I must know it."

She almost slipped, an automatic habit of saying her true name, but caught herself in the nick of time. "Saira Vaulx, ever at your service, Lord Woelfel."

"Lady Saira, your name was perfectly crafted

for you. I cannot imagine one more fitting."

From the behind Riana, Ash cleared his throat, the sound irritated. "The two of you can stop any moment."

Biting back a smile—or trying to, and likely failing at it—Riana took a full step back. Ash radiated jealousy and anger like a bonfire, and while it was fun to tweak his nose, she didn't want the men at odds with each other. The situation was dangerous enough as it was; there was no need to add fuel to the fire.

Ash stood, his movements sharp and agitated, brows taut in a borderline frown, but he still held out a hand. "Ashtian Fallbright. Harmony find you, Woelfel."

The spy took this in stride and grasped the hand in a firm handshake. "Fallbright. You are to be our backup, I take it?"

"I am."

"Forgive me for saying so, but I'm not sure how useful you'll be. I can't take anything magical in with me that doesn't have a frivolous purpose to it. It's a sure sign to my enemies. How are we to signal if we do need a rescue?"

"That is partially why I was chosen to come in," Riana explained, not at all surprised he didn't know the basics. There had been no time to send word to him, not without risking the message being intercepted. "Our bond is such that I can send him a signal."

The playboy façade fell away and Woelfel's eyes sharpened on the two of them. "I have heard reports that a wizard pairing can hear each other, if they are close enough."

"We're not quite there yet," Riana informed him cheerfully before Ash could take umbrage at the 'if' of that statement. With the mood he was in, he would. "But we feel each other's emotions very strongly. Given a bit more practice, we'll progress to that level."

"Ah?" Woelfel now regarded them with an indecipherable expression that masked some emotion Riana couldn't put a finger on. "Such a close partnering is rare. I take it, then, that I can flirt as much as I like? You're close enough that petty emotions won't mix in."

Ash smiled. It was not a nice expression. "Are you trifling with a wizard, Woelfel?"

Proving that he had a warped sense of humor, Woelfel beamed back at him. "Perish the thought. Merely establishing the boundaries."

Ash's lips drew further back. It was not a smile. "I trust they are set?"

"Perfectly, old chap, not to worry." Woelfel's expression was both rueful and highly amused.

Riana tried very hard not to burst out laughing. She had just known that Ash would not react well to this situation, but seeing it play out in front of her eyes was another matter entirely. Woelfel didn't have an ounce of sincerity towards her, but still it had been enough to stir Ash up. What would it be like if a man truly did try to court her?

"Don't even wonder that," Ash warned her, a visible tic at the corner of his eye. "The idiot wouldn't survive."

Riana regarded him with frank amazement. "Did you hear that?"

"I didn't have to, your emotions were painting a clear enough picture. And this situation is not at all amusing, Riana."

Patting him fondly on the cheek, she whispered for his ears alone, "I disagree, partner-mine." Then with a wink, she disengaged and switched tracks entirely. "Lord Woelfel, since we are to play cousins, should I address you by your given name?"

"You certainly should, Saira." He said her cover name pointedly even as he gestured them all into chairs. "I shall of course do the same. The situation stands as such: Troi was able to give me enough warning of your coming, and your identity, that I could start laying down the groundwork. I have been mock-complaining that I had been volunteered by the family to introduce a backwater cousin to Court. Those that know me are amused about this and anxious to meet her. Just in the interest of tweaking my nose, you understand. I shall, of course, play the part of an older, put-upon cousin."

Having never had a cousin, and with limited experience in regards to extended family, Riana wasn't quite sure what that meant, but could play it by ear. She would simply react to whatever he did and play the part along with him. "I understand. Did you give them any hints of my personality?"

"I said that I hadn't seen you since you were three, and had no idea what you'd be like, as I wasn't sure if Troi had crafted your identity down to that detail."

Smart of him. "He didn't. I'm simply to be naïve and a bit of a chatterbox. Those were his only stipulations."

Woelfel gave her a frank appraisal. "You do not strike me as a chatterbox."

"Not at all," she admitted ruefully. "So this will likely take a stretch on my part. But I'll do my best."

"A person pushing themselves out of their comfort zone can only do it for so long before they need a break." Woelfel said this with a knowing tone, as if he had experience with it firsthand. "When you need a rescue, or simply a few minutes, splay your fan in front of your heart. I'll provide it."

Riana was very glad to hear this. She needed such help and having a signal was very welcome. "I shall, thank you."

Turning to Ash, Woelfel frowned, tapping a finger against his knee. "I have no idea where to install you."

"You can't," Ash told him bluntly. "My face is too well-known in Court, for various reasons. I'll wear a minor glamour and be in the outer palace courtyards, or thereabouts, so that I'm close if needed. But there's no way I can enter freely even with a disguise. Magic has its own aura and the magicians of the Court, if they spot me, will see through any disguise in a thrice."

"I see. In that case, I shan't worry about you."

"Don't. I'll see to myself." The words were saved from being curt by Ash's reassuring nod to the two of them. "That said, don't hesitate to call me if something does go awry. I have several methods of getting in and out of the palace that I can use if need be. I'd just rather not use them unless an emergency demands so. Most of my methods can only be reliably used once."

"Understood, old chap, we'll be careful." Woelfel rocked back on his heels, wheels spinning hard. "I'd rather not be found out at this juncture at any rate. Troi would be hard pressed to replace me and I'd find being a normal citizen dreadfully dull."

That did beg the question, "Then what will you do when Estole wins and this is all over?"

"Rather a good question, isn't it?" Woelfel responded, smile suggesting that he wouldn't really mind the 'tedium' of a normal life. "But let's set that aside for now. Fallbright, if you're going to be separate from us, you'll either have to find your own way there or wear a glamour of some sort. It won't do for you to be in the carriage with us."

"Of course. I'll wear a glamour throughout the trip. I brought my horse just in case, however. If something happens, I'll go in ahead of you."

"We'll leave the day after tomorrow," Woelfel continued. "Saira, that doesn't give you much time here, but I've narrowed this place down to the highlights that anyone in the capital would know, so we'll just tour those. I've also prepared a few family stories from the aristocracy here that will be taught to you over dinner this evening. Family anecdotes and such are always the most convincing to a fake identity."

It was an excellent suggestion and Riana fully intended to take it. "I'll meet the whole family over dinner, then?"

"All but the oldest brother, who is actually in

the army. But he's been notified about you and I'll make sure the two of you meet if he hasn't been sent out with Maddox." Woelfel's eyes glanced toward the window and the day passing outside. "For now, let's walk and talk, as we have precious little time."

Riana automatically took the arm he extended her and walked with him out of the room and toward the outside. It was, fortunately, a mild day for winter and the cloak, muff, and hood kept the worst of the chill at bay. She was able to walk down the streets without shivering. With the dusting from the night before, there were patches of ice, all of it covered in a thin layer of snow so she had to watch her step. Still, she tried to study the place as much as she could and memorize it. The buildings were charming, with tiled roofs in different colors, like well to-do cottages.

The 'highlights' that Woelfel mentioned were all regarding different spots that a child would know well—parks and ponds for ice skating, different sweet shops. Then he deviated and went to other places a young woman would spend time in such as a hat shop, a music school, and the like. Riana didn't just speed past these places but stopped into each one, gaining an impression of them, and spoke with the people that worked there. It helped cement it all a little better in her mind.

They spent the entire day in this pursuit before Woelfel steered her back toward the castle. "You make a natural spy," he complimented her, ignoring Ash who tagged along behind them. "You just charm people into talking to you."

While Riana appreciated the compliment she didn't quite understand what he meant by that either. "But I wasn't trying to be charming?"

Woelfel gave her a slight double take, slowing in his tracks so that he could study her more frankly. "Oh dear. I now understand why your partner is worried."

"At least someone does," Ash grumbled to the world in general.

Giving Ash a sympathetic nod, Woelfel prodded them back in motion. "So, then, tell me why you spoke to them as you did, dear cousin."

"People respond best if you look them in the eye and truly give them your full attention," she responded, not at all sure why this was even a question. Wasn't this obvious? "My da—ah, father always said that giving a compliment opens doors. It's the best way to start a conversation with a stranger."

"He is not wrong." Woelfel had that calculating look in his eye again. "If you use this technique at Court, then you'll do swimmingly. They won't know how to defend themselves against sincerity, having never experienced it before."

Ash choked on a laugh.

"Well, cousin dearest, I am considerably relieved to see that you do indeed have at least some of the social skills necessary. I trust that your court etiquette is simply nonexistent, but not to worry, I'll give you a crash course on that and whatever blunder you'll make will be excused by your background. For now, let's go meet your 'family,' shall we?"

CHAPTER TEN

"Shall we begin?" Woelfel asked with a certain dryness to his tone.

Riana struggled to bring her full attention to him. Something about traveling just exhausted her. Even though she sat in a carriage the entire time (and it was a plush, comfortable one), and wasn't doing anything that could be considered strenuous, she always arrived at the inn beyond tired. Was it the constant change of environment? The unfamiliarity of the place where her brain felt the need to analyze and catalogue everything as she moved? Or was it a consequence of basically only living in two places the majority of her life? She'd felt similarly when they'd moved the academy to Estole, but it hadn't been this bad.

The constant lessons every day also contributed, as Riana wasn't used to studying. She'd been doing little else for the past two weeks straight. The drain had apparently become noticeable, as she had Ash looking at her with some concern, and even Woelfel had picked up on it.

With a mental slap, she forced her brain to

stop wandering. "Yes, please do."

There was an undertone from Ash, a query of are you alright? She reached over and grasped his hand, squeezing in reassurance.

"Did you hear me?" he asked hopefully.

"No," she denied patiently.

Ash let out a sigh, half-resigned.

"You two still working on that, eh?" Woelfel asked knowingly. "Granted, it would be handy to have the ability by the time we arrived in Kremser, but it's not absolutely vital, alright? We spies have our ways of sending information to each other without handy magical links."

"I know." Ash might have said the words but his tone implied he absolutely was not giving up anytime soon. Perhaps ever.

Wisely, Woelfel decided to leave it alone. "Then let's continue our lessons. We'll review court etiquette later when we stop for lunch, and put all of those manners to practice. That will help more than me rattling them off, I think. For this morning, why don't we talk about the players in this dramatic play?"

That sounded good to Riana. She felt sure that she could retain people's names better than arbitrary manners that Court demanded. "Certainly. Who do we start with?"

"Let's start at the top and work our way down. Queen Rosalind, Savir, and Maddox you of course know."

"Actually," she corrected, "I haven't heard much at all of Queen Rosalind."

"Ah?" Woelfel had been on some sort of rehearsed spiel but with her interruption he had to reset himself. "Troi didn't explain all of that? No? Shame on him. Then again, it's rather common knowledge I expect he thought you already knew and forgot that you were politically out of touch with the world until recently. Let me start there, then. Queen Rosalind is in fact the second queen for Zelman. The first died when the twins were barely two years old. The actual cause of her death is a state secret but she was found dead at the foot of the stairs with a broken neck, so..." he trailed off suggestively.

Riana's eyes threatened to fall out of her head. "Zelman didn't kill his own wife, did he?"

"She was not well loved by him and was not well behaved, either. It is an interesting question. Regardless, Zelman was quick to re-marry—a little too quick by anyone's standards—and Queen Rosalind became his wife before his mourning year was out. It took her a year to bear him Hendrix, and she hasn't been pregnant once since. Quite honestly, I don't think she wanted to bear him a child at all, not seeing how he treated Savir."

And considering how he did treat the one child she gave him? Riana didn't blame her at all. "But this queen, is she liked?"

"Yes indeed. And she's a good mother to the older two princes as well. She just won't take an active role in trying to quell Zelman's temper, which is what we all wish she would do." Woelfel sighed. "Even when Hendrix was banished at Court she didn't seem capable of stopping her husband in any way. If she were a stronger queen...well, regardless.

"There are two other contenders for the throne aside from Hendrix. And it's an interesting mix, shall we say. First, we have a retired general by the name of Quillin. He's not actually that old—fifty-six this year, I believe—and he's more retired because he took an arrow to the knee in the last campaign than anything else. He's actually a good man, if all the reports about him are to be believed, and he's personally not interested in being king."

Riana blinked. "If he's not interested, why is he a contender?"

"Because there's quite a few people that want him to be king. Quillin has been protesting for at least a year now that he has no desire to be embroiled in politics and people are stoutly pushing him forward anyway. It's mostly the older generation that is supporting him, understandably, as he's someone they know well." Woelfel gave a shrug. "Personally speaking, if we didn't have Hendrix, I'd throw my vote in for him as well. The problem is, he's not directly blood-related to either king or queen, and while he has a great deal of power and influence, I'm not sure if legally he can even ascend the throne without it being considered a revolution."

Ash gave a thoughtful hum. "Knowing this, people are still supporting his candidacy?"

"Many illegal things have been happening in Kremser," Woelfel drawled, mouth drawn up in a crooked sneer. "What's one more?"

"Ah. Point." Ash gave him a small wave of the hand, encouraging him to continue. "Who else is contending?"

"Axley, cousin of the three princes, son of

Zelman's younger brother." Woelfel had a look of absolute disgust on his face as he answered. "He's the last person that anyone should want on the throne. He's worse than Zelman in many ways and has many a perverted hobby on top of it all. Zelman's bad but at least his tastes in pleasure aren't in the gutter."

That did not sound at all pleasant. "This is well known?"

"It's certainly not a secret." Woelfel gave a dark shake of the head. "I really don't understand what people are thinking, supporting him. He's convinced some of the younger generation by promising them an 'exemption' to the Inheritance Law. He can't undo it completely, of course, that brings Hendrix back into the running. So instead he's using it as a bargaining chip. The older generation despises him, the younger ones are hanging on him like he's their only hope, and everyone else is praying for a better option. It's quite the political mess."

"Isn't it always?" Ash responded, looking tired and world-weary for a moment. "It's what drove Edvard and Tierone to split from Iysh to begin with. Are those the only contenders?"

"There's a few others but they have such little support that they're barely footnotes, really. Those are the main two we need to worry about. Riana, you and I will be trying to steal their supporters over to Hendrix as much as possible."

"Understood." Riana knew how to convince Axley's supporters well enough, but how to reach Quillin's? The older generation didn't have as much to lose; it might take some thought on her part to think of a tactic.

"Now, my immediate support. I have a full staff at the townhouse that not only keeps the place running but also serves as informants. Mrs. Pennington is my main pillar of strength as she's the one that keeps up with everything for me—house and spywork. If she ever chooses to retire, the world will sputter to a stop, I'm quite convinced of it."

This was the first time that Woelfel had ever spoken highly of anyone, and the tone he used was that of a son speaking of a mother-figure he adored. It made this polished gentleman seem more human for a moment and Riana warmed to him a little more. "I look forward to meeting her. Who else?"

"Outside of my main house, we have The Gossiping Quartet, as I like to think of them. They are very dear to my espionage heart. Indeed," Woelfel put a dramatic hand over his heart, "I'd be a little lost without them."

"Only a little?" Ash repeated, deadpan.

Still looking off in a dramatic pose, Woelfel reiterated, "Only a little." Dropping the pose, he continued more seriously, "The first of these is Lord Sudenga. Pompous little windbag is the kindest way I can describe him. He's technically the Minister of Music, not that anyone knows what the Minister of Music is supposed to do, as I've certainly never seen him doing anything that resembled work. He spends his entire time gossiping. If I want some bit of news to get about quickly, he's the first person I track down.

"Lady McAdaragh is the second person. She's

roughly," Woelfel gave Riana a thoughtful look, "your age, I think. How old are you, Riana?"

"Twenty-one in a few months," she responded forthrightly.

"Then yes, I do believe the two of you are exactly the same age. Unlike you, however, she has the most naturally empty head of anyone I've ever met. She's one of those types that will actually forget to breathe at times."

Riana's eyes crossed at his description. Surely the man was exaggerating a little. Surely people weren't so stupid they actually forgot how to breathe. "But you like her?"

"I adore her," Woelfel oozed with false affection. "She's the most faithful parakeet that I've ever encountered. She repeats nearly verbatim everything that she hears and never questions any of it. She's actually one of the people I tested Dunlap with, to see if he would believe her over me, that's how easily she's manipulated."

That poor girl. Riana felt sorry for her but wondered if the sympathy would last past their first meeting. Riana had a low tolerance for fools, it was one of her weak points. "So I can literally tell her anything. Noted. Who's the other two?"

"Bexton. Now, he's not a lord but in fact a page. He's roughly, hmm, thirteen? But he runs messages for literally anyone and everyone and because of that, he's like this fly on the wall. He's constantly in places that he technically shouldn't be in, hears things he's not supposed to, and repeats all of it to anyone that will give him the time of day. You know that phrase, loose lips sinks ships?"

Riana and Ash nodded.

"This boy could sink an entire armada. He's one of my favorites to pass 'confidential' notes through, as I'm guaranteed to have a copy of that note to everyone in Kremser before the hour has struck. He's terribly efficient when it comes to gossip. He is not, sadly, always credible, however. I have found holes in his information as he will sometimes mix things up a little."

Which meant he wasn't a very good spy. "But doesn't that make anything he says dangerous?"

"Indeed so, but for our purposes of misdirection, he's invaluable as he'll put a spin on things in the most creative of ways. Now, for our last person: Lady Sircy. She's an interesting one. She's the wife of Lord Sircy, Minister of Finance. If you ask her, she abhors gossip, wouldn't touch it with a ten-foot pole. She's a very uptight and self-righteous woman."

"But...?" Ash encouraged, eyes crinkling up in amusement. "That's not at all the case, I take it."

"Not at all," Woelfel agreed cheerfully. "For a woman that doesn't gossip, it's amazing how many rumors pass through her hands. She has bat ears, I swear she does, as she'll pick up on things that my other three don't. And while she's above the whole thing, if you ask her about some subject or person, she'll tell you every single thing she knows all while informing you that it was just rumor and you shouldn't pay attention to any part of it."

Ah, one of those types. Riana knew them well. She'd encountered women like her before. They were easily enough handled, as long as you played along with the game. "Surely those aren't the only Court gossips?"

"No, there are others, these four are just my favorites. Of course, I'll introduce you to them. Before I forget to mention this, there are two people specifically that you need to watch out for: Hyde and Larcinese. Hyde is the new Captain of the Guard."

"Wait," Ash interrupted, "I met the Captain of the Guard when we came in for that disastrous audience with Zelman. You mean to tell me that Halloway got replaced?"

"Child of a second wife," Woelfel explained with a grimace.

Ash puffed out a breath of disbelief. To Riana, he explained, "There's a few people that are actually worth their salt and keep Iysh from crumbling to the ground. Halloway is—was—one of those people."

"As to Larcinese, he's one of Axley's compatriots and I dare say his strongest supporter. His tastes in pleasure are even more questionable than Axley's and believe me, that's saying something. I do not want you anywhere near him."

Riana blinked. For a moment there, Woelfel looked as protective of her as Ash was. "He's truly that terrible?"

"Worse. I can't describe how bad without going into detail, which I'm loathe to do. For one, its offensive, for another, Ash would have my head if I were to taint your ears in such a way."

Ash gave a confirming nod, expression impenetrable behind a mild smile.

Woelfel nodded back, lips tucked up into a wry quirk. "I thought as much. Suffice it to say, no lady of any breeding would be caught near him. Especially since you are playing the part of a sweet, naïve girl, you should avoid him at all costs. I do mean all costs. Even if it means getting physical, do not make contact with him."

"Point him out to me the first night in Court," Riana requested. "So I can avoid him properly."

"Of course, of course. Other than that, I have other minor people that are either useful or should be avoided, but those are the main ones."

Riana's head swam with names, roles, and information so she was glad that he chose to stop there for the time being.

With a finger, Woelfel lifted the curtain aside on the carriage windows and looked outside for a moment. "We seem to be nearing Vailwood. It's the perfect place to stop for lunch. Let's take a break, shall we, and continue later this afternoon."

Riana hoped her brain could hold out. This trip was wearing out her memory and they still had four days to go until reaching Kremser.

CHAPTER ELEVEN

Riana actually didn't get to see most of Kremser on the ride in. They came in mid-afternoon, during the busiest time of the day. Riana had a clear view of the city as they came in, seen from her carriage window. Kremser was built on a succession of low rolling hills, making it possible to see other sections of the city's roofline. In the far distance, she could see part of the palace rising up and above, noticeable because of the banners flying high on top of the towers. It didn't seem to reside in the exact center of the city, but closer toward this northern gate. Perhaps it originally was in the center, and then the city just grew every which way until it was in this lopsided shape instead.

The place bustled with people of all types, at least a third of them foreigners in the city, which didn't come as much of a surprise. Surely a capital city would attract any and everyone. The streets were flat and paved, the buildings mostly brick or stone, and it all seemed tidy and well kept. Since they were in wartime, she'd expected some sort of martial law to be in place, or at least a heightened sense of security, but there was little evidence of that. Guards were on the gate, certainly, but the crest on the side of the carriage door was enough to grant them immediate entrance into the city.

Having lived in dangerous climes most of her life, this lax attitude made her head hurt.

Perhaps Woelfel sensed her thoughts, as he gave her a rakish grin. "Relaxed security makes a spy's playground, my lady. Do not complain when your enemy is in the midst of making a mistake."

"Wouldn't dream of it, my lord," she drawled back. "Even if I do think it is stupid."

"Well, how do you think Edvard, Ashlynn, and I waltzed in here, then managed to escape again?" Ash queried them both, voice rich with amusement. "By the time an alarm sounded, the guards were too badly out of position to catch us, even though they scrambled to do so."

Seeing it with her own eyes, it now made more sense. "And here I thought it was because of your amazing magical prowess."

Ash, without batting an eye, shrugged. "But of course. That too."

Woelfel clearly realized she was teasing but still had to ask, "How much of it is rumor? That you and your sister were the reason why you won the first two battles with Iysh."

Regarding him steadily, Ash responded simply, "We had thirty-five guardsmen in Estole during the first two battles."

The full implications hit and Woelfel let out a low whistle. He didn't say another word but the impressed look he gave the wizard spoke volumes.

Privately, Riana was glad to see this. Woelfel

had seemed to take Ash more or less for granted, like an extra addition to Riana and little more. Now that they had been traveling for the past eight days, getting to know each other better, that attitude had been altered. She always wanted people to properly appreciate Ash, of course, but it also was a matter of safety. Woelfel needed to know that when the chips were down, their wizard backup was a force to be reckoned with.

They rode through the city streets and straight to Woelfel's townhome. It was here that they had to be semi-tricky, as no word of Ash's presence could be leaked to the outside. At least, not his true identity. He had been posing as Woelfel's servant throughout the trip. As a spy house, Woelfel only had the most trusted of staff inside, so Ash was safe enough once he was in the house. He just had to be extremely careful entering or exiting it. His arrival today would be especially watched as Woelfel had made a show of fetching his "cousin" from Senn. Anyone that was curious enough to keep tabs on his whereabouts would be on the lookout for the lord and his backwater guest.

The plan was for Ash to stay in the carriage after the other two had left, ride into the stable, then don a glamour to copy Woelfel's livery so that he could pose as a servant simply entering the house after fulfilling his duties. As long as no one had any magical detectors, this plan should go flawlessly. It was a fine line that they tread, as they needed word of Riana's arrival to spread, and had planned their arrival for this busy time of the day for that reason.

Riana was swept into the house with a bit of flair, which relieved her, as she was deathly tired of being trapped in the narrow confines of the carriage. A petite woman with a whipcord frame and iron grey hair pulled back in a tight bun stood just inside the door, waiting on them. Something about her reminded Riana of the very capable housekeeper in Estole. Perhaps it was that air of competence? The two women didn't look anything alike.

For the first time in days, Woelfel relaxed a hair and gave someone a heartfelt smile. "Penny."

The woman gave him a brief curtsey and a smile in return, just like a mother welcoming a son home. "Master Cyr. You made good time. Who is your companion?"

"Saira Vaulx," Woelfel introduced with a sweep of the hand. As previously discussed, Riana's name would never be used in Kremser, not even here. "Saira, this is Mrs. Pennington, my very capable majordomo, housekeeper, and keeper of all secrets."

So this was the woman that kept track of all the informants and the intel they gave? Woelfel had bragged about her off and on while they rode, and Riana was very curious to know what kind of woman could multi-task so flawlessly. This hardened grandmother was outside her expectations, but if there was anything she had learned about spies at this point, the nondescript people often excelled in the craft. "A great pleasure, Mrs. Pennington."

"We are pleased to have you, Lady Saira." The woman's blue eyes raked over her from head to toe and she gave a nod. "You'll be wanting a bath after your long journey, I think, and some good food. I'll show you up myself. Master Cyr, our other guest?"

"Will come through the backdoor in a few minutes under glamour. See to him as well, Penny, and put him in a room adjacent to Lady Saira's." Half teasing, half serious, Woelfel confided, "They're bonded partners and Fallbright won't take any true separation kindly."

Riana thought about correcting this. Then she pondered Ash's behavior of late and decided Woelfel might have a point after all.

"Very well." Pennington gestured for Riana to follow her, discreetly giving orders to a maid and footman as she moved, like a general dispatching officers. Riana took the opportunity to study the man's home as she moved. In a way, it was rather like Edvard's castle—not as large, not quite as grand, but it had the same sort of rich furnishing and elegant touches. Marble floors, polished paneling, beautiful landscapes hanging on the walls. The place spoke a little of age, as if it had been here for at least fifty years, but it was all immaculately kept and one couldn't beg a piece of dust to land anywhere.

With all due efficiency, Pennington had her in a drawn bath, soaking away the stiffness of the journey and enjoying the hot water. Riana was loathe to move and did not even dream of doing so until every ounce of heat from the water was gone. Only then did she begrudgingly climb out, towel dry and think to join the men for an early dinner. A maid came in to help her with her hair, which was another odd thing for Riana to get used to, as she normally just tied it off and moved on with life. But now it was all pins and updos that took time and effort to do and undo.

Really, why did women do this to themselves?

When she finally made it downstairs, she found the men were already seated at the table and waiting on her. Neither of them seemed the least impatient, which made her think they expected Riana to take this long, if not longer. Was this normal for society women, then?

She took the seat next to Ash, which he pulled out for her, playing the part of gentleman to perfection. Riana was dead certain he did it in part to draw lines with Woelfel. For some reason, the man challenged Ash on an instinctive level. Not sure why, but Riana was not above taking advantage of it.

Woelfel nodded to a man hovering nearby, although Riana wasn't clear what position the man held, just that he was in staff uniform of grey on grey. Then he turned his attention to the two guests at his table. "I thought to start you off easy, Saira. There's an informal—well, informal for Court—gathering before dinner tomorrow. It happens twice a week, just a chance for people to mingle, gossip, and politick. I can introduce you to some of the key players and expose you to the public."

The sooner she started, the better, in Riana's opinion. "I'm ready to start when you are, cousin."

A glint in his eye, Woelfel purred, "Excellent. Don't glare at me, Fallbright, it wounds me to the quick."

"Do not take advantage of your supposed relationship," Ash warned in a low timbre. "I'll know if you do."

"Perish the thought, old chap." Woelfel beamed at him, oozing sincerity.

Riana didn't buy it for a moment. Was the man incapable of remaining serious for more than three seconds? Or was tweaking Ash's nose just that irresistible? Trying to drag him back on track, she asked, "Will you give me a quick overview of who I will likely meet tomorrow?"

"It varies," Woelfel denied with a thoughtful frown at the ceiling. "But there are a few that routinely show up. I should be able to give you at least half a list."

That was better than nothing at all. Riana nodded in acquiescence.

Dinner was mentally exhausting in a way, as she tried to remember everything told to her, and she felt glad when it ended. The men chose to retire early, as they were all a little exhausted from the long journey they had just completed. Riana withdrew to her very stately bedroom, an opulent affair of greens and dark maple wood, and promptly escaped the dress. It took some wrangling to get it off herself, without any aid from the maid, but she managed it. Climbing into a baggy shirt and some loose leggings, she brushed out her hair while sitting next to the fire. Even this far south, the air had a slight nip to it in the evenings, so the fire was a very welcome thing. Staring at the flames and not-thinking was also a welcome relief after the past three weeks.

A flash of worry, mixed with irritation, came from Ash. Riana paused mid-stroke and turned to stare at their connecting door with considerable exasperation. Was he stressing on that again? She sent a firm feeling of Stop that to him. They weren't at a telepathic level, certainly, but she had caught on to the finer art of emotional messages.

It worked, as Ash openly flinched and a guilty feeling came back to her. He always thought he had somehow closed himself off from her, so that she wouldn't know when he was chewing on something that should be left alone. Why he thought this, Riana had no idea, as she caught him every time.

A little cautiously, there was a knock on their shared door. "Come in," she encouraged dryly. "It's better you talk to me than chewing on it silently."

Tentatively, Ash poked his head around, but upon seeing her next to the fire, relaxed and immediately joined her. Really, what did the man think, that she would invite him in while she was half-dressed?

Sitting cross legged next to her, he gave her a game smile. "I think you're ready for tomorrow."

That was not what he meant at all to say and she knew it. "You wish we could hear each other properly."

Ash collapsed in on himself, running a hand roughshod through his hair. "I swear at times you really can hear me. You have pinpoint accuracy, you really do."

"No, Ash, I cannot hear you." Shaking her head, she tried not to groan. Or laugh. Or some mix of the two. "You're just very predictable."

"I would just feel so much better about all of this if you could communicate to me properly when something is wrong," he said for what was likely the hundredth time. Perhaps the thousandth. "And yes," he interrupted before she could repeat herself, again, "I know that emotions are enough to tell me when you're in danger, and I know I can find you with my eyes closed, but that doesn't give me a lot of warning. If you could tell me when something just feels off, or ask me a question so that you don't say or do the wrong thing, wouldn't that be better? If we just had a bit more time..." he trailed off unhappily.

"Time is the one thing we never seem to have enough of," Riana opined, waxing philosophical for a moment. "If a man could bottle time and sell it, why, he'd be richer than a king. And we'd beggar ourselves buying it."

"Truly." Ash stared blindly into the fireplace, falling pensive and silent.

She stared at his profile and wondered if he knew just what it was that kept them from forming that last bond. Riana knew exactly what it was. Had, in fact, known it for at least a month now. If he would just admit to himself what he felt for her.... But telling him wouldn't do an ounce of good, as it was something he had to realize himself or it lost half its power.

That didn't mean she wouldn't nudge him now and again.

Scooting over, she cuddled into his side, her head on his shoulder. Ash accommodated her with an arm around her waist, laying his head softly on top of hers. "Riddle me this: why does Cyr Woelfel set you so ill at ease?"

"The man's an uncompromising flirt and you're gorgeous, of course he makes me nervous," Ash retorted, although he sounded and felt more amused than upset.

Hmm. That was not the response she'd been aiming for. Riana tried again with a different tactic. "Even though you know I'm not the least bit interested?"

"It doesn't stop him from trying something. And in your position as spy you can't openly respond as you normally would. He knows that. I'm afraid he's going to put you in an awkward and delicate situation just to watch you squirm and make me squawk."

Knowing Woelfel as she did, Riana was entirely inclined to agree with that analysis. But again, that wasn't what she was aiming for. "You realize that when I'm alone with him he's not at all flirty. He only does it in front of you to tweak your nose."

Ash gave her a dirty look. "Which is easily tweaked."

"Just so." She grinned up at him.

Giving a harrumph, Ash turned again to stare at the fire.

Riana pursed her lips and frowned up at him. Still no closer to realization, was he? At this rate, they'd never make any progress to speak of.

Manipulation was not something she cared

for, and Riana felt like it had no business being in relationships, so it wasn't something she would try. Being frank and outright sat better with her. She did recognize that in Kremser, while playing spy, was not the best time or place to force Ash out of this comfort zone he'd fallen into.

Silently, she made a promise to herself. If Ash didn't come to an awakening by the time they left Kremser, she would make sure it happened. Even if it meant slapping it into him.

CHAPTER TWELVE

So this was the high Court of Iysh. The ceilings were high and vaulted, numerous chandeliers sparkling light onto highly polished granite floors. It certainly looked impressive and it was definitely expensive, but to Riana, it looked cold. Empty. There was not a trace of warmth or home comfort to be found anywhere. People sacrificed, bribed, and manipulated to get into this place? Whatever for?

Riana firmly pinned a smile on her face to hide her distaste and followed Woelfel into the room. Not that he strode into the center of it. Instead, he veered to the right.

"Woelfel!" a jovial voice slurred. Riana turned and found a man not a foot away, slightly swaying as if fighting to stay upright. His blond hair stuck out in a windswept fashion, his skin was flushed, and his clothes, while fashionable, were half-untucked and askew. Despite having called for her companion, he instead stared straight at Riana.

In a blink, Woelfel donned his polished smile,

manner genial. "Halloway. You're in high spirits this evening. May I introduce my cousin, Saira Vaulx?"

"A distinct pleasure, Lady Saira," Halloway gave a hiccup, ducking into a bow that almost ended in a face plant at her feet. Miraculously, he caught his balance at the last possible second and lurched back upright.

Halloway, the ex-captain? Riana wasn't sure how to respond to this obviously drunk lordling. She tried a game smile. "A pleasure, I'm sure, Lord Halloway."

Flinging his arms out wide, Halloway rocked back on his heels, stumbled, and caught himself again. "What do you think of the place?"

When in doubt, compliment? "It's very grand."

That amused him and he laughed boisterously. "Grand, she says! And she's not wrong." For just a moment, he looked sober. "Woelfel, guide her properly."

Woelfel gave him a half-bow, accepting the order.

Satisfied, Halloway went back to being drunk and a little too loud. "Enjoy Court, Lady Saira! For it offers many pleasures."

"I shall try," she promised. Watching him stagger off, she glanced at Woelfel and asked in a bare whisper, "Friend?"

"Yes." He mouthed, Later.

Too complicated to explain in this crowd of eavesdroppers, eh? She'd ask later, then. Still, she had the impression that his drunken behavior was just a charade of Halloway's.

As they moved, she heard multiple conversations about the war, the troops deployed to Estole and the amazing progress they had already made in winning. This last part had Woelfel and Riana hiding smiles. The truth was quite the opposite. The troops likely had just barely arrived! It appeared the war propaganda machine was working zealously well.

Since the topic was already in play, the stage was very well set for a campaign of misinformation. Riana had a slight stumbling block of not knowing more than two souls in the entire room, but Woelfel was with her for that reason. To introduce her and open doors so she could get to work.

"Woelfel!" a voice called.

Riana automatically turned toward it, thinking that this might be her chance to start, but Woelfel caught her by the elbow and stopped her short. "Not him," he denied even as he smiled and gave a wave to the person hailing him. "No one would introduce a woman to that lot with a clear conscious. That's Larcinese."

Riana took good note of that face. So that was the contender, Axley's, favorite lackey, eh? She'd need to avoid that crowd at all times if possible.

"Go get some punch," Woelfel encouraged.

That was their code phrase for when Riana needed to be elsewhere. Nodding in understanding, she moved off. There was a refreshment table over here somewhere. In eight layers and in a more southern clime, Riana felt a little overheated. And this was still winter. Perhaps it was due to the press of bodies in here and the two roaring fires on either side of the room that made it feel this hot?

A buffet table with a variety of delectables and three separate punch bowls were arrayed for the pleasure of anyone in attendance. Riana scooped up a delicate glass of punch, took one sip, and realized it had been made with a significant portion of rum. Erk. She didn't care for alcohol to begin with, but to get tipsy here? Incredibly stupid decision. She was caught, though, as she couldn't just put it back down.

Well, perhaps she could use it as a prop while she made the rounds. Putting on a smile, she went looking for a handy target. There were several people clustered in front of the orchestra so she headed there, rehearsing in her head an opening line or three that might get a conversation started.

One man seemed to be standing more or less on his own, so she started with him. He was a bit round around the gut, dark brown hair thinning on top, with a very styled mustache that curled up on either side. He also had a gold pin on his lapel that was in the shape of a musical note on a staff line. This wouldn't happen to be that useless Minister of Music, would it?

"Forgive me, my lord?"

He turned and gave her a once-over, eyes widening a little. "My dear lady, I do not believe we are acquainted."

And it was rude to just introduce yourself, Riana had been taught that, but spies couldn't depend on propriety all of the time. "We are not, pray forgive me, I am just dying to know what music is playing now. It's quite enchanting. Do you know the name of the song?"

He puffed out his chest, pleased with her praise as if he were the one actually performing. "Indeed I do, young lady. It is called Nightingale's Love Song and was written by Sir Robert Duningham. Sterling composer, that one, no wonder why Zelman knighted him." Giving a wave to the orchestra, he expounded without any encouragement from her. "They are playing it quite admirably this evening. Indeed so. I almost pulled the song from the program as they were abysmal during rehearsals but here they're doing grand."

"Oh, perhaps you are the Minister of Music," she asked with an airheaded delight, "Lord Sudenga?"

The man actually flushed like a giddy schoolboy. "I am. You've heard of me?"

"Indeed, my lord," and nothing charitable either. "Pray forgive my self-introduction. I am Saira Vaulx of Senn."

"My dear Lady Saira, to have someone from even Senn that knows of me," there were tears in the man's eyes, "I feel like all of my hard work is truly appreciated."

She should never, ever, mention that the man was famous because no one could figure out what he actually did. She gave him a brilliant smile instead.

He moved in a half step closer, animated and excited. "You said that you are from Senn? Your arrival must be very recent, as I swear that I have not seen you before."

"You are correct, my lord, I arrived this week.

My cousin, Cyr Woelfel, escorted me in and is acting as my chaperone during my Season here." Seeing a good opportunity to turn the conversation where she wanted it to go, she lowered her voice a hair. "I'm very glad he did. We saw such troubling signs of war while we traveled."

Lord Sudenga pounced on this, mustache quivering. "Pray, do tell, my lady."

Riana went into her rehearsed speech of mercenaries on the road, mild winters in Estole, and all of the other lies Troi wanted her to spread about the Court. Lord Sudenga swallowed every single one, then introduced her to two of his friends and asked her to repeat it all over again, which of course she willingly did.

Eventually the conversation started to wind down. Claiming that she needed to refresh her punch, Riana wandered away from them, feeling like she'd gotten a good start on this crowd. Retreating to the buffet table, she stared down at the glass in her hands and tried to figure out what to do with it. Adding more to the glass was the furthest thing that she wanted. Perhaps she could "forget" it on the balcony.

With that goal in mind, she peeked around a curtain, found an unoccupied balcony, and escaped into the cooler night air.

The balcony, alas, was not as unoccupied as she had first assumed. A lone man hid in the shadows just to the left of the doors, completely out of sight unless one stepped onto the middle of the balcony. Riana realized her mistake when he lifted a glass from the stone banister, making a slight scraping sound. Whirling, she dampened the first three impulses to reach for a stiletto and quickly dipped into a curtsey. "Oh! I do beg your pardon, my lord, I assumed this place to be empty."

"It's quite alright," a pleasant baritone answered. He was still in shadows, giving her the impression of dark hair and a thin figure, but little more detail than that. "I believe you are like me? Wishing for a bit of quiet and fresh air."

She gave him her best smile. "Indeed so, my lord. It is strangely overheated in the room even though it is winter."

"Yes, I find it interesting that you seem to be fine out here even though you have no mantle on."

Sensing she might have an opening to employ a little misinformation, Riana confided easily, "I'm from Senn, my lord. It's much colder up there at this time of year. To me, this feels like early fall."

"Senn, indeed? Is this your first Season in Court, then?"

Riana's ears caught the nuance in that question and knew he was asking if she was a complete novice to Court. "Quite so, my lord. My parents have entrusted me to a cousin in hopes that I might find a good match." Daring two steps closer, she went to lean lightly against the banister. The stone was icy to the touch but she didn't let it bother her much. She'd be roasting again in that room soon enough. "I think they sent me on in part to keep me from the war coming toward Estole. It was perfectly frightful the first two times, and all rumors we heard suggested that Prince Maddox would take no quarter this time."

"Yes, so rumors have said. If you just arrived...? Then you must have passed the army coming in."

Riana felt a little exaltation in sucking him into the topic she wanted to discuss. "I did, my lord. It was awe-inspiring, seeing so many troops marching along. Do you think with that number, that they'll win against Estole?"

"One would certainly think, wouldn't you?"

"I know little of strategy," she demurred with false modesty. "But I do worry about the troops, and Prince Maddox, of course."

"Worry?" He shifted a little, standing slightly more in a sliver of light cast out from the doorway. She could see very angular features and deep-set eyes set in a pale face. "Do you think they'll fall in battle?"

"Men always fall in battle, my lord, but that's not what I meant. The winter season has been uncharacteristically warm so far. Do you think it will stay that way? If it gets cold, as it normally does, all of those poor men will be stranded out in the snow."

He cocked his head, lifting a hand as if to say that anything was possible. "I believe that Prince Maddox brought a larger force than necessary to do a quick, decisive victory in order to avoid such a future. Our prince is not known to be fond of the cold."

"Truly?" She bit on her bottom lip and looked worried, a look she had been taught by Bria and practiced dutifully in the mirror until she had the slightly lost and airheaded expression of a young girl down pat. "Do you think he factored in the mercenaries that were hired too?"

Her conversational partner went very still. "Mercenaries?"

"Didn't you know? We passed them on the way here as well. There were mercenaries heading toward Estole. Their commander shared a table with us one night at the inn and he said they'd been hired on by Estole for the upcoming battle."

The man rocked back on his heels, surprise or some other emotion she couldn't define darting over his face. "Is that so. This is news to me."

"Oh dear. Oh my." Riana put a hand to her heart and did her best to look troubled. "You do think that Prince Maddox knows? Well, he must know by now, as he's surely arrived at Estole at this point."

"One would think." Swirling the liquid in his glass, he took a slow sip before replacing it on the banister. "How many mercenaries?"

Riana pretended to think. As previously planned, she kept her numbers deliberately vague. Rumor mills exaggerated the matter best when it had only sketchy information to build on. "I'm sorry, I didn't do a proper headcount of them. I'm not sure if I saw all of them, for that matter, as they took up three inns. Or was it four? We saw them coming in and out of three inns, at least."

"That's quite the number, then. Inns can hold how many? A hundred or so?"

"Comfortably speaking, I would assume so, my lord."

"True, they could be cramming more than

two people per room. So we can safely assume at least three hundred and on the outside possibly six hundred. Quite the number indeed for Estole to hire. One does wonder where they got the funds to hire people with."

Where indeed, Riana mused ruefully. Never mind three hundred, Estole would be lucky to have the funds to hire three dozen. "I wouldn't know, my lord. Senn has such limited contact with Estole these days. But if you're correct, then Prince Maddox might not have enough troops with him."

"Perhaps. Regardless, it's too late for him now, as he's probably already arrived, as you said." Retrieving his glass, he suggested, "Perhaps you should speak to Greer Dunlap and pass along your information to him? He is our master spy here in Court."

Riana knew perfectly well the reason why, but as a bumpkin from Senn, she should be surprised by this. "My lord, is it safe to noise it about who your spymaster is?"

The lord just laughed. "My dear lady, he is well-known for a reason, have no fear. Spies themselves must of course always be in secret, but a spymaster must be known and accessible. It's not just spies that he communicates with, but informants and even citizens like yourself who have valuable information. If you don't know who our spymaster is, how would you know who to give information to?"

"Oh, I see. Yes, that does make sense."

"He has his own spies, of course, but it never hurts to make sure that the man has the latest information. Having just arrived, you might know something he does not at this point."

"You think so? I'd hate to be presumptuous."

"No, indeed, please speak with him. In fact, let me be your escort to him, as I wish to ascertain that such vital information is given directly to him."

Riana had already made plans to report to this man with Woelfel as her companion, but this might work out better, assuming this man had some sort of importance in the Court. "Pray, might I have your name first? I'm Saira Vaulx."

"Ah, forgive me, we never did properly introduce ourselves. I'm Savir. A pleasure, Lady Saira."

Riana didn't try to mask her surprise. PRINCE Savir, Maddox and Hendrix's brother?! How in the world had she stumbled into him on her first night? She dropped into another, deeper curtsey. "A pleasure, Your Highness."

"You now understand my desire to make sure this information gets directly to our spymaster, do you not?" Prince Savir asked with a quiet smile that was somehow charming. "Please, let me escort you directly to him."

Riana jerked her brain back into motion before it could continue to splutter. "I would be honored, Your Highness." She accepted the arm he extended to her, putting her hand in the crook of his elbow and following his lead out.

Ash was sending her an urgent emotional query, a basic, Is something wrong?

Not wanting him to jump in here with magic blazing, she quickly sent reassuring signals back to him. Granted, she had probably scared ten years off of his life with her emotional spike of disbelief and panic. It had been such a shock that she still reeled with it even as they stepped back into the room. Troi had said that spies needed nerves of steel. She now understood completely what he meant.

Every noble in the room took notice of this newcomer on the prince's arm. Riana kept a pleasantly blank expression firmly fixed on her face and tried to ignore the outright stares. Now that she had proper light to see by, she observed Savir from the corner of her eye. He was tall, like Ash, with a similar build as him, and he strangely didn't look a bit like Hendrix. His hair was blue-black, eyes dark, skin pale, with a hawkish nose. He looked the studious sort, not a fighter like his twin was rumored to be. Could twins be such opposites? Then again, there was Ash and Ashlynn to consider.

Woelfel appeared like magic at her side, smile in place but his wide eyes gave away his surprise. "Your Highness, good evening."

"Good evening, Lord Woelfel." Savir inclined a nod in his direction, acknowledging Woelfel's bow. "I just chanced upon your charming cousin. She told me a little of her journey here, and what she saw on the way. I do believe she has information that is vital to the war effort. You served as her escort here, did you not?"

Woelfel had been at this game too long to be ruffled for more than a split second and he played along beautifully. "I did, Your Highness. Saira, I'm not quite sure what he's referring to...?"

"The mercenaries from Overa," Riana supplied helpfully, giving the man the clues he needed to realize that they were going with the story Troi had fabricated for them. "The ones that stayed in all of those inns around us, remember?"

"Ah yes. We had dinner with the commander," Woelfel explained more directly to Savir. "The inns were completely crowded, so much so that complete strangers were sharing table space with each other. The commander, a man named Draughon, proved to be a good conversationalist however."

"Indeed, he was," Riana confirmed with a reminiscent smile. "But cousin, His Highness said that there's been no word of mercenaries being hired by Estole."

Woelfel frowned at her as if in confusion. "Truly? But they were such a large body of men, surely...."

"That is why I wish for Lady Saira to come and report to our spymaster, Greer Dunlap," Savir encouraged. "Since you are also a witness, Lord Woelfel, please do come with us. I believe I saw Dunlap over here, near the gardens, and I wish to catch him and pass along this news as quickly as I can. If my brother has miscalculated on how many troops he needs, we need to correct it if possible."

"Yes, of course," Woelfel agreed immediately. "Do lead the way, Your Highness."

Savir started again for the opposite side of the room. Riana rehearsed the story in her head, making sure she had all of the details right, and then reminded herself that she was supposed to be a little airheaded so it was alright for her to be uncertain and verify with Woelfel. It would look odd if a strange woman strode in with all sorts of information that was of vital importance even with Woelfel backing her. Better that there be some question and spies sent out to verify her claims.

"Dunlap!" Savir waved a hand above the crowd, caught the man's attention, and pointed him to an open balcony door, the only clear space for more than three people to gather.

Dunlap was exactly as Troi had first described him—the epitome of the handsome spy with exactly the right looks, clothes, and bearing. On the surface he looked imminently confident and capable. It was a pity that appearances were so deceiving. "Your Highness, is ought amiss?"

"Dunlap, I must introduce to you Lady Saira Vaulx, and of course you know her cousin, Lord Woelfel."

"Indeed I do, Your Highness." Dunlap's voice and manners turned smooth as honey as he greeted Riana. "Lord Woelfel. Lady Saira, a very great pleasure."

Riana dipped into a curtsey and smiled back at him. "The pleasure is mine, I assure you, Lord Dunlap."

Savir wasn't about to let them get sidetracked. "Dunlap, Lady Saira arrived in Kremser very recently and she saw something on the way here that I felt you must be informed of. Lady Saira, if you would?"

"On our journey here," Riana launched into her prepared speech, "we stopped along the way at an inn. The town was nearly full to capacity with mercenary soldiers from Overa. The conditions being what they were, no one had any private tables to offer, and we ended up sharing our dinner table with the commander of the mercenaries, a Mr. Draughon. Perfectly charming gentleman, actually."

With a gentle clearing of the throat, Woelfel reminded her, "Saira, that part isn't what's important."

"Oh? Yes, that's true, I'm sorry. The point, Lord Dunlap, is that Mr. Draughon told us he had been hired by Estole to help fend off the Iyshian army."

Dunlap's face lost all color. He physically reeled as if someone had slapped him. "Your Highness, this is the first that I've heard anything about this."

"I felt that must be so, Dunlap, otherwise you would have informed us. Pray, please take these two aside and debrief them as much as possible. I will alert my father about this turn of events and we'll set a carrier pigeon to my brother to inform him. Hopefully we are not too late in our warning."

Dunlap gave him a brief bow and then urged Riana to follow him. "Pray, this way; there's a quiet alcove over here that will give us space to talk in. Lady Saira, how many mercenaries were there?"

Riana made a show of being uncertain. "I am so sorry, Lord Dunlap, but I'm not sure. A great many, to be sure. Cyr, how many do you think there were? We saw them coming in and out of at least three inns, didn't we...?"

It was very difficult, but Riana somehow managed to keep an exultant look off her face while Dunlap bought all of their false intel hook, line, and sinker. Troi had been right—the man was a sucker for women. Riana sat there in the alcove, spinning a yarn, and enjoyed herself immensely.

CHAPTER THIRTEEN

The trick to spreading rumors lay in not presenting a full story to the listener, but instead giving them a setting, a few facts, and then letting their imagination take it from there. Riana had learned this tactic the first few days of being at Court and continued to roll with it. She also took advantage of her gender and went to the Ladies Only social events that Woelfel would not be invited to attend—ladies' tea parties and luncheons and so forth. It made both men extremely nervous for her to go by herself, but, as Riana pointed out, it would be very strange if she turned any invitations down. The whole point of her being here was to make connections and find a husband. Both of those things were done best through the mothers.

The first woman to make a friendly invitation to her was Lady Vailwood, a matronly sort with very pale coloring and a kind smile. She likely invited Riana out of sympathy more than anything else, but Riana took her up on it, as she couldn't afford not to. It was an "informal" luncheon near the palace, in a charming tea shop that catered to the very elite. It boasted delicate water fountains in the corners, flower beds in between the tables, and every piece of furniture was a white wrought iron with cushions. Riana stepped into the place and nearly gagged on femininity.

"Oh, Lady Saira, I'm glad you're here." Lady Vailwood bustled up and took her arm, drawing her into the main dining area that abutted a small, decorative garden. "Have you met either Lady Odom or Lady Sircy?"

Riana managed a smile at both women and a curtsey. "I believe Lady Sircy and I bumped into each other my first night at Court."

Alice Sircy gave her a pleased nod. This was a woman that was at the height of power in Kremser, as her husband was the Minister of Finance. She had a high brow, iron grey hair with streaks of white in it, and fine lines around her eyes and mouth that suggested she did not often smile. She came off as a very cold, rather aloof, woman. Riana was particularly glad to have her here as this was one of Woelfel's favorite gossips. "Indeed we did. You have an excellent memory, Lady Saira."

"Not at all, Lady Sircy," Riana denied honestly. "You make a very strong impression."

Sircy liked this compliment and almost smiled. "Indeed."

"I do not believe that Lady Odom and I have been acquainted?" Riana ventured with an inquiring lift of the brows at the woman in question.

She was a mousy little woman, short and dumpy, hair fuzzy and badly contained into a bun at the top of her head. But her smile was nice, as if she truly was delighted to meet her. "We have not. Rachel Odom, pleased to meet you."

"Likewise, Lady Odom."

"Here, let's all sit," Vailwood encouraged.

Riana breathed a silent sigh of relief that it seemed this was to be the full party for the luncheon. Sometimes these affairs could host fifty or more people, or so Woelfel had told her. She did not think she could handle a crowd of fifty on her own.

They settled around the table, ordered tea and a delicate snack of pastries or sandwiches from a discreet waiter, then set to the real reason why they were here: gossiping.

The first several minutes they discussed a woman that Riana didn't know, and how she might be having an affair with someone else, as Lady Vailwood's sister's friend's cousin had seen them out together. It all seemed a little far-fetched to Riana, but she didn't know either party, and frankly didn't care.

Their teas and food arrived, providing a break, and Riana dove into it to see if she could change the subject. "I'm very glad that I came to Kremser when I did. Considering the dreadful rumors about what is happening around Estole, it seemed I left Senn at just the right time."

Lady Odom gave her a puzzled look as she stirred sugar into her tea. "Whatever do you mean, disturbing rumors? I thought Prince Maddox was winning against Estole."

Riana gave her a blank stare. "Heavens, Lady Odom, while I do not doubt the prince's fighting expertise, it seems a bit early to declare his victory. I passed the army on the way in; there's no way that he could have arrived in Estole before I came into Kremser."

All three women looked at each other, but it was Lady Sircy that seemed the least surprised. Considering her husband's position in the government, it was likely that she had overheard things that were at odds with the war propaganda.

"Yes, I suppose that's true," Lady Odom allowed. "Perhaps we're all optimistic and eager for the situation to be solved."

That seemed to be a mild way of stating the situation. Riana had heard the most ridiculous statements from these people. "He had those mercenaries from Overa to contend with as well, poor man." The ladies nodded—they'd heard that rumor already. Riana tried to add another twist into the tale, as Troi had directed her. "I suppose that's why he's drafting people as he is."

Now all three stopped and stared at her with poised expectation. A new rumor was to be had. "Oh, you hadn't heard?" Riana asked, putting her tea back down before even tasting it. "Heavens, I overheard it myself, I thought it was common knowledge."

"Heard what, my dear?" Lady Vailwood prompted impatiently.

"Why, that the prince is taking people from any area he passes through."

No one seemed to know what to say to that.

"I would think that he would only need the

men if he needed to augment his army," Lady Sircy stated slowly, staring blindly ahead as she weighed the matter.

"Even that doesn't make sense," Lady Odom protested. "Prince Maddox didn't bring extra weapons with him. I heard that straight from you, Lady Sircy, as you said your husband was complaining about how much this war was costing, and how Prince Maddox stretched the budget to the max by so finely outfitting his army. He didn't bring anything extra with him, so what are these newly drafted men supposed to fight with? Hoes?"

An excellent question. Riana applauded it. "But that's what makes this so disturbing. I heard that it wasn't just the men—everyone was taken by him."

"Whatever for?" Lady Vailwood asked, bewildered.

Riana splayed her hands in an open shrug, acting just as bewildered. Silence was often the best thing to employ to encourage their imaginations to run wild.

"How are you hearing about this?" Lady Odom pressed.

"I do get regular correspondence from home," Riana said honestly. "I received a carrier pigeon just the other night telling me sternly to stay in Kremser until the affair at Estole was all over. They do not want me on the roads at all."

"Oh dear," Lady Odom fretted, fanning her face with a flapping hand. "Oh my. I don't like the sound of any of this. I know Prince Maddox has been under a great deal of pressure from the king to solve Estole quickly and bring them back to heel, but do you think the stress of it has made him do something reckless? I can't imagine what he would need the common people for, can you?"

"I can," Lady Sircy stated grimly. "And it is not at all pleasant. Cannon fodder, that's all they would be good for."

A ring of gasps, Riana playing along and doing the same, eyes wide with horror above the hands covering her mouth. "Oh. Oh, do you think that's why my brother said that after the people were taken, no one saw them again?"

"Don't say that," Lady Vailwood practically wailed. "What a dreadful thought. Surely our prince wouldn't do such a heartless thing."

"There's been many a heartless thing done recently in our fair country," Lady Sircy stated flatly. "I'm very afraid this rumor might have too much basis to not have some truth to it. Lady Saira, has your brother witnessed all of this himself?"

"Only part," Riana said, again half-truthfully. "He did see the people taken. He said as of the time he wrote the letter, none of them had returned to their homes."

"I do not like the sound of any of this." Lady Sircy brooded into her tea cup with a glower fierce enough a dragon would envy it. "It's very grim indeed. Lady Saira, I heard that you were the one that gave the report of the mercenaries headed toward Estole?"

"I am, yes, we had dinner with their commander on the way here. Perfectly charming man, although understandably rough around the edges."

"How many mercenaries were with him?" Lady Sircy pressed. "Were they likely to beat our army to Estole?"

Riana built another layer to the tangled web she wove, answering questions just enough to let them take the thought and run it into entirely different directions. By the time the luncheon was over, every single woman was dreadfully afraid that Prince Maddox had turned into a monster on the battlefield. They also lamented that Prince Maddox seemed to be the only viable heir to the throne, and why couldn't one of the other princes step up instead?

The way for Hendrix had been started. Now to continue paving the road.

Riana hovered in a strange mood. She felt tired, extremely so, but not in the mood to go to bed. It was late at night, she had three events lined up for tomorrow, so she really needed to rest. But she felt restless and edgy. The idea of lying in bed did not sound even remotely tempting.

From next door, there came an emotional equivalent from Ash of: You too?

It seemed she was not the only one still awake. Throwing on a robe, she went straight through the connecting door and found him sitting cross-legged in front of the fire, his back braced against a chair. Wordlessly, he extended an arm and encouraged her to come in for a cuddle.

Snuggling for a moment might be exactly

what she needed. Riana tucked herself into his side, head on his shoulder, and let out a weary sigh.

"Homesick?" he asked her softly.

"Aye," she responded, reverting to her native speech. "I miss da, too."

He gave her a slight squeeze in comfort. "I know you do."

He wasn't just saying that. He truly did. Riana tuned more into his feelings and found that he was just as restless as she was, only for different reasons. There was frustration there, emotions rolling because he was caged in this house and unable to actively help. While Riana and Woelfel's jobs were dangerous, Riana felt that Ash actually had the hardest role of all—that of staying in the background as support until he was needed. "Waiting be the hardest."

"The first few days, it wasn't bad," Ash said, staring directly into the flames. "I've been run so hard for the past year that being able to sit and rest was actually nice. I felt nervous for you, but other than that, it's the most peaceful time I've had in ages. My magical level is finally restored to its normal levels. Now I'm all rested up and with nothing to do."

"In yer shoes, I'd feel the same, Ash."

"In my shoes, you would be ready to shoot your way out," he said with a soft snort of laughter. "Speaking of, how does it feel to be fighting without a bow in your hands?"

Pondering that question for a moment, she finally responded, "Odd. It be fun at times, but there be moments I want to shoot these young lordlings. They be so full of it."

"Trust me, I know."

"I canna ken why people want to live here," she continued, letting her eyes fall closed. Being able to talk about this aloud was actually helping her settle her emotions. Not that she was willing to go to bed yet, but still, it felt nice. "They do no' say what they actually mean, they smile when they'd rather curse, and they stab each other in the back without blinking an eye. It be the worst sort of battlefield, where lies and whispers do more damage than an arrow can."

"Now you understand why Edvard hated Court politics here so much."

"Aye, I ken it all too well. And why he do no' tolerate it in Estole."

"He's developed a fondness for plain speech. It's served him well. People will tell him outright when something is wrong, instead of making up pretty lies like they do with Zelman." Turning his head a little, he asked against her skin, "Can you continue?"

She snuggled in a little harder. "Aye. Just let me rest here a little."

"Anytime," he assured her, warm affection flooding through their bond and into her. "Anytime you need it, I'll always be here."

CHAPTER FOURTEEN

It was a perfectly awful day.

The blame lay only partially on the weather. It was not truly cold enough to snow, and so it was an icy drizzle instead, more or less steady ever since the predawn hours. The wind came in fits and bursts, just enough to throw up a man's cover so the rain could penetrate and hit skin. No one wanted to be outside any time at all. But they did not have much chance of hiding indoors.

An army had come knocking at their door.

Actually, the Iyshian army had arrived late, very late, yesterday. As soon as Broden and Ashlynn had gotten word that the army was closing in around Dahl, they traveled over to see for themselves what they would do and to be on hand if the barrier needed reinforcing.

The Iyshian army shot a few arrows along the perimeter of the wall, just to get a feel for how good their shield was, and then stopped so they could make camp. Broden had the feeling that the commander over there wanted to test how long it would take to conquer Estole—if it was a matter of hours, he'd have bulled ahead. But since it was obviously going to take at least a few days, he preferred to make camp first. Truly, it was the sensible approach. No commander worth his salt would think Estole would be an easy win, not after the last two battles.

Broden stood in the shelter of the guardhouse and watched the Iyshian army in the bleak morning light. They appeared to be not in the mood to stand about in this miserable weather and were quite gung-ho about breaking through the wall. Seeing no discernible progress did not seem to discourage them, instead encouraging them to try harder.

He stole a glance at the woman standing next to him. Ashlynn had been uncharacteristically quiet most of this morning. It was never a good sign when the lass was still and thoughtful like this. It meant that like as not, something had gone badly awry.

He was a little scared to ask what.

Ashlynn had one of her magical eyespecs up on her right eye, gaze trained out of the small square window for another minute more before asking, "Broden. While you were playing deputy sheriff, did anyone report to you about the evacuation of Dahl's southern edge?"

"Aye, lass, that they did." Broden had handled so many logistics and numbers over the past dozen days in Ashlynn's shoes that it took him a moment to remember what the last report had been. He frowned when he recalled it. "If I ken right, Seth said there be still people down there, and it be a fashrie trying to fetch them out. That be day afore yesterday. He did no' report to me if he got them all out or no'."

"I'm seeing something I shouldn't." Ashlynn lowered the glass slowly and replaced it in a breast pocket. "I'm seeing prisoners in the far back, although it's too far away for me to make out details. There shouldn't be prisoners in the army at this point."

Broden's ominous feeling from before tripled. "Best we speak with Seth."

"Yes, I definitely want this confirmed." Ashlynn's tone indicated that it had better not be what the situation looked like.

For Seth's sake, Broden sent a prayer heavenward that the lad really had managed to get everyone out. Ashlynn would skin his hide otherwise.

It was not as simple as them leaving and finding Seth, of course. Moving about in the city never was. Even here in Dahl, that was not the case. Broden noted that even though Ashlynn had done nothing but work on the wall for nigh on two weeks, she still stopped at every marker and gave it a thorough once-over, making sure that the army's attacks on the other side were not slowly wearing down the magical construct. Every time that she gave a satisfied nod and moved on, Broden breathed a little easier.

Before this, Broden had only been in Dahl a handful of times. It did not have the same cluttered, nearly claustrophobic feel that Estole did. Until this past week, anyway. With all of the refugees from the southern end now in the city proper, there were tents on top of tents, and even in this drizzling rain there was still many a cookfire sputtering as the women tried to cook. Ashlynn weaved in and out of them, chastising anyone for being too close to the wall but not harshly, as she realized that no one in their right mind got close to the enemy unless there was no other choice. Even the ones that were too close still had more than a stone's throw of space in between. It would hopefully be enough.

A loud, shattering sound, like a boulder splintering, rent through the air. Broden's heart skipped right of his chest and he jumped and spun like a cat, hand automatically reaching for bow and a fistful of arrows. Ashlynn paused with him and drawled, "Settle, partner. It's just the catapults."

"Just, ye say," he spluttered, trying to put his heart back in his chest. "That be a horrendous sound, lass!"

"I know it. But after two battles, you get used to it." She gave him a heartless smile and walked on as if there was not a thing to worry about.

Perhaps for her there was not. For all of their efforts, even the catapults could not seem to make a dent in the wall. Broden kept a weather eye on the other side as he walked and saw three more boulders hit, shatter, and spray over the Iyshian soldiers. In that sense, the catapult was doing more harm than good for the Iyshian side.

They finally tracked Seth down in the impromptu guardhouse/sherriff's office that was, oddly enough, in the center of the tents. The poor lad looked like he had gotten nothing more than a snatch of sleep the night before (like Broden) and was running off of hot tea this morning. He snapped to attention when Ashlynn entered. "Sheriff. Broden. Emergency?"

And what a state they were in, if that was the first question out of the poor boy's mouth. "We hope no', lad. The question stands as such: did ye get everyone out of the area and properly moved up here? Yer last report to me said there still be some left behind."

Seth's wince was answer enough but he dutifully reported, "We were unfortunately not able to get everyone out."

Ashlynn gave Seth a look that would make a lesser man quake in his boots and call pitifully for his mother. "Why are there still people there?"

Seth had worked under the sheriff long enough to not quake or call for his mother, but he did look ready to bolt out the door at the first opportunity. "Um. About that. We tried?"

Deciding he had better intervene before Ashlynn started giving off magical sparks, Broden asked, "What went wrong, lad?"

The young guardsman looked pitifully thankful for Broden's patient query. "Sir, we evacuated everyone willing to go, but we had a surprising number that refused to leave. Mostly elderly folks that don't travel well, or were worried about leaving their houses behind, that kind of thing. Had a few rebellious ones, too, that just escaped us completely. We did our best to reason with them, but it finally got to the point where we'd have to resort to physical violence to get them out. After my last report to you, it came down to a matter of hours before Iysh was on top of us. Captain Bragdon chose to cut our losses and focus on getting everyone we could."

It was the only sensible approach and Broden did not blame the man for it. But the mental picture this conjured up made him wince. Old folks and rebellious souls that did not have the sense to leave when help was offered? And now they were stuck in a prisoner of war camp until someone came along and rescued them.

With a weather eye on Ashlynn, Seth offered tentatively, "Sorry?"

Ashlynn let out a long stream of air, visibly calming as she did so. Or at least, she went from inherent destruction down to smoldering anger. "I don't blame my people, Seth. You did the best you could. I do blame the idiots that I'm going to have to rescue, however. They just made my life more difficult."

"Once we have them back perhaps we can charge a stupidity tax?" Broden offered, completely deadpan.

Instead of laughing, Ashlynn contemplated him thoughtfully. "A stupidity tax."

That did not have the effect he had hoped for. Seeing that she was actually taking him seriously, Broden rapidly backpedaled. "Wait, lass, I be jesting!"

"I know."

That was not an agreement. Broden tried again. "Edvard will no' pass such a thing."

"Oh, he might," Ashlynn stated with a knowing nod. "Think about it. It will take manpower, hazard pay, and additional housing in order to rescue these idiots. All of which costs money and time that we don't have. What do you think he'll do if I give him an expense report of this operation and then propose he tax our rescued prisoners for the mission?"

Broden ran that hypothetical through his head and then groaned. "He'd put a stamp of approval on it and pass it back afore the ink could dry."

Ashlynn gave him a beatific smile. "My thought exactly. Hence why I'll do it. Seth, make sure that everyone tracks every single expense, no matter how trivial, and submit it to me."

Now Seth was smiling. "Absolutely, Sheriff."

There were times when Broden regretted that his mouth often said things before his brain could think it through. This might be one of those times. Although he had to admit that the stubborn people that they were going to rescue should be penalized in some way for not being smart enough to move the first time. He was also of the opinion that being a prisoner of war was penalty enough, though. Now that his suggestion was out, no way would Ashlynn drop it, and the way that Seth had that gleam in his eye said that as soon as the guardsman had left the tent, he was going to spread this idea far and wide.

Sometimes, Broden really should just bite his tongue.

Heaving a resigned sign, the archer asked, "So? How we do go about this bit of chicanery?"

"Slash and grab is out of the question," Ashlynn stated after giving it a moment's thought. "We have too many elderly to transport. Seth, what was the exact number?"

"Seventy-six, Sheriff."

"Far too many," Ashlynn grumbled, borrowing Edvard's habit of staring thoughtfully up at the ceiling. The way her head rested on the back of the chair would give Broden a crick in the neck, but she seemed to find it comfortable enough, as she didn't move. "We'd need wagons to pull them all out of there. And wagons are slow."

Terribly so. A man could walk alongside and keep up easily with a wagon. Mounting everyone on horseback was not an option, however. To begin with, they did not have that many horses to spare. Just coming up with enough wagons was going to be taxing.

"I'm not sure how we're going to pull this off," Ashlynn finally admitted, turning her eyes away from the ceiling, "but I do know that the wagons are a necessity. Seth, rustle me up some wagons. Broden, we need to go speak with Master."

"Gerrard?" Broden did not think this was one of those habitual things, of a student asking the master just because they didn't know the answer off-hand. "Why?"

"Master's got a long and involved history of breaking into places he had no cause to be in," Ashlynn explained with a wicked smile. "He used to regale us with the stories on long, cold winter nights. If anyone can figure out how to sneak into an enemy's camp, break people out, and sneak back again, it will be him. So, let's go talk to the expert."

Gerrard took in Ashlynn's explanation of the problem with a pained expression. They had caught him in the guardhouse, in a makeshift office for the wizards to use while monitoring the barrier. It must be about time for a shift change, as Broden knew that Lorcan and Kirsty were on the barrier now. Gerrard displayed every indication of intending to only grab something before leaving again. Ashlynn's timing in catching her master had been impeccable. Broden had a feeling that she was only this good at it because of years of practice.

No one sat, or tried to get comfortable, as the conditions were not such that it would allow anyone to take it easy. They stayed standing even as Gerrard pondered the question. He did not let them stew for long. "Only one thing to do. Bait and lure."

Proving she was not just his student in magic, Ashlynn caught on quickly. "Create a fake 'weakness' in the border wall, lure the army away from the prisoner of war camp, and then use that opening to rescue them? Will it really be that easy?"

"Certainly, if done well. The trick is to not make the bait too obvious. Make it a flicker, intermittent, so that it makes it look like we're running out of power to keep that thing going. They'll hover around the area that seems weakest, ready to pounce." A reminiscent smile took over

Gerrard's face. "I did this once as a younger man, about your age actually, and it worked beautifully. The Iyshian army is not yet primed for this, however. Only a day in, they're not very frustrated. We need to wait a few days until they are over eager to take advantage of any sign of weakness. But Ashlynn, take heed—this tactic will only work once and it's not going to give you a very wide window to work in. You need to use all speed and have a backup plan in case they catch you before you can get back to safety."

"That much I knew. We have so many elderly though that we'll have to use wagons to transport them all here."

That was not the answer Gerrard wanted to hear. He frowned at her, mouth going into a flat line. "Don't do all wagons, then. Prioritize the wagons for the ones that really need it, get everyone else on horseback, and send them back into Dahl as soon as they can move. Waiting to have everyone mounted will be the death of you. Save who you can, abandon the ones you can't."

Harsh advice, but Broden knew that it was sound. These people had already dug their own grave by refusing to leave when it was safe to do so. They could only afford to sacrifice so much in order to get them back without jeopardizing everyone. Estole and Dahl combined had precious little in terms of a fighting force. They could not allow casualties.

The tight expression on Ashlynn's face said she did not like this answer but understood it. "I'll do what I can to avoid that extreme. But warning taken, Master. Broden, let's go over the deployment of this again, see if we can do a hybrid of horses and wagons. Master, can I count on you to do the bait?"

"I'll handle it," he promised her. "When do you want it done?"

"You said we have to give this a little time. How much time?"

"Two or three days at least."

"Then you might as well start your flickers two nights from now. It'll seem more natural if done over the space of a day with the worst happening on the third night."

Gerrard's brows rose in surprise. "You want to pull together a rescue mission in two days?!"

"No choice," she denied with a grim shake of the head. "I don't have time. There's too many other problems heading my direction that will demand manpower. If I'm going to rescue anyone, it has to be soon or I simply won't have the people to pull this off later."

Broden could not disagree with her there. "We will make it work, man, do no' fret so."

He really wanted to argue this, but Gerrard knew as well as he that Ashlynn did not dramatize anything. If she said it was that dire, it was, and he needed to act accordingly. "I'll go straight to the wall and start strategizing with everyone else, teaching them what needs to be done. It won't happen regularly, I can't promise that, but I'll make it frequent enough to make them shift away from the prisoners."

"That's all I can ask, Master. Thank you." Ashlynn, in a rare affectionate moment, darted in to give him a quick, hard hug. Then she grinned and darted out of the office.

Gerrard looked completely surprised by this hug attack but smiled as she bounced away.

Knowing that the lass was unpredictable in the best of times, Broden did not question the hug, knowing that it was likely a mix of relief and a need for reassurance. Instead he silently followed her out.

By the time that Broden caught up with her at the bottom of the stairs, Ashlynn's mood had switched again to being somber and pensive. She lengthened her stride so that Broden had to stretch his legs just to keep up with her, and even then he was a half-step behind. The lass could move when she was of a mind to.

Not sure if he should ask, but needing to know, Broden forced the question out: "Lass, if they do no' take the bait, then what?"

"Then it goes to the worst case scenario," she said softly, the words barely audible.

Having a sinking feeling what she meant, he said more than asked, "We leave them there."

The dark glance she gave him was answer enough.

CHAPTER FIFTEEN

Gerrard was good to his word and started putting 'flickers' in the wall. It was nothing more than a patchiness, visible to the naked eye, so that it appeared that the power hiccupped for a moment. Never more than three seconds at a time, long enough to notice, but too short of a time for anyone to properly react to it.

The enemy reacted immediately, gravitating to any point that had a flicker. They did not move far, as Gerrard started on the barrier just north of their main encampment. It was also, naturally, the spot that saw the most action as the soldiers pounded away at it. Gerrard might have chosen to start there for that reason, or perhaps he wanted to make sure he caught their attention by keeping it visible for them, but either way, it worked.

In fact, it worked a little too well. The citizens also took note of this new development and an outcry of panic hit the streets. It took Ashlynn and Broden issuing orders to all the guardsmen to quietly assure them that it was all fine, just another tactic to confuse their enemy, for the worst of the clamor to die down. Not that it stopped completely, as it took a while for the word to spread, but the worst of it did. Broden harbored a suspicion that some were convinced it really was a problem and the government officials just would not own up to it, but there was nothing to be done about the paranoid ones. Time would show them the truth. As long as they did not make too much of a fuss, Broden let them stay paranoid.

Seth, bless him, had pulled together twenty wagons and fourteen horses. Each wagon had two men on it, a driver and guardsman, some of them volunteers. They met behind Dahl's physical wall, out of sight, and waited for the cover of darkness. Broden spent his time on the top of the wall, watching the magical one with a keen eye. "Gerrard's playing this well."

Ashlynn, sitting on the ground below him, cocked her head around to ask, "It's working?"

"Oh, aye, no doubt of that. They be moving steadily north without seeming to realize it. Gerrard's throwing in just enough flickers toward the south as to make it seem a natural fault in the middle of the line."

"Master's good at this," she agreed without a trace of doubt in her voice. Then again, she knew from experience that her master had the right feel for the timing necessary. "How many guards are still with the prisoners?"

"A dozen, mayhap? A few be resting inside tents, so I can no' get a proper headcount."

Ashlynn panned her immediate area, checking her own people, and nodded. She did not need to say another word. Broden knew that they did not quite have enough manpower to deal with possibly twenty guards, and it would rest on the two of them to make up for the lack of fighting power. Broden had been up against worse odds. They would make it through fine.

Assuming, of course, that the Iyshian army stayed focused on the wall and not on their backsides.

It was dusk, nearing twilight, that Gerrard proved he might have grown older but the daredevil in him was still as young as ever. Instead of just a patchiness, there was an outright fault straight down the middle, lasting a full five seconds, enough so that one soldier actually managed to get through. The whole army, frustrated and tired of beating themselves against something immovable, roared with renewed energy and threw themselves forward.

Broden hissed out an unbelieving breath. "Cutting it fine, is he no'?"

"And you wonder where I get my recklessness from," Ashlynn responded with a dark chuckle. She sat on the wall with him now, out of sight behind one of the guard turrets, so that she could keep her own eye on the situation. "Look at them move. We have a skeletal guard around the prisoners now."

So they did, a bare dozen. They were a good distance away, as well, barely within sight of their prisoners even on this flat land. If they were going to move, now would be the time to do it.

Their feeling was so unanimous that both of them moved at the same time. Broden mounted his horse and led off, not waiting for the rest to mount up first. They were all so tired of waiting that most were eager to get this over with, instantly climbing aboard.

Broden focused on getting free of the barrier, keeping an eagle eye on the encampment to make sure that no one was looking their direction. They were not—their attention remained riveted toward the "fluctuating" wall. He could not see the barrier well from this angle, nor did he try to, as the shouts of the army painted a clear enough picture.

Gerrard was letting men leak through, but only a few, no more than a handful, and then of course there were Estolian guardsmen waiting on the other side to handily deal with them. The Iyshian army was torn—they wanted to get through, but dodging inside a few at a time was suicidal. They did not want brief breaks in the wall, they wanted it completely down; and since they could not decide what to do, they hovered and cursed instead.

Which was hardly effective behavior, but who could blame them?

Either way it was a fine drama to keep a man entertained by, and the rescue party took full advantage of it by riding recklessly forward at the fastest clip they could manage with the wagons in tow. The distracted attention of the guards was such that the Estolians were nearly on top of them before they realized that they were in trouble. It was more than close enough for Ashlynn to throw up a barrier around them, blocking them from running forward. Their shouts for help could not possibly be heard over the bedlam near the barrier, even though all of them tried.

Broden rode mercilessly forward, using his knees and heels to guide the horse even as his fingers went for his arrows. A quick nock and draw, aiming for anyone he had a good line of sight on.

Ashlynn quickly bust open the manacles on the prisoners' hands and feet, urging them up and into a guard's hands. They acted like a relay system, any guard not fighting grabbing people bodily and shoving them either in the wagon or on a horse, depending on their fitness to ride.

In no way did Broden think they would get out of here scot-free before someone else noticed. In fact, the prisoners' guards were down, and they still had ten people left to move when someone in the back of the army turned around. That signaled their undoing as the cry of alarm went up.

Ashlynn swore, realizing in the same moment as Broden what would happen next, and bellowed, "MOVE THEM NOW!"

Any guardsman still there grabbed the nearest person to them, slinging them like a sack of potatoes over their shoulder, and then ran for a wagon. The wagons were already starting to move, gaining speed, sometimes with a person barely on board. Broden grabbed a person himself, an elderly woman that was protesting something—he did not care what she was saying and did not have the time to stop and listen—before throwing her over his horse's saddle, mounting up, and riding hard for the barrier. She bounced around something terrible, and likely would have bruises to show for it, but he could not take the time to seat her properly.

There was one facet to this rescue that was understood, even though no one would say it aloud. They absolutely could not, under any circumstance, allow Iysh to realize how their barrier worked. Right now the Iyshian soldiers were under the illusion that this was a solid barrier like any other permanent barrier. It would have to be modified or temporarily lowered to allow people through. If they failed to get in under the right timing, then the whole façade fell apart. They would realize that this barrier was of a completely different type, and anyone with magical know-how would realize the weaknesses in a thrice. And that would doom all of Estole and Dahl.

Broden did not count how many people they left behind, if any. His heart could not take knowing that there were people he had had to abandon. He resolutely looked forward and tracked the enemy soldiers' movements from the corner of his eye. They were running for all they were worth, but it did not look like they would quite catch up. Broden was near the back and mounted—the pursuers on foot did not stand much of a chance.

Still, they were closer than he liked, and he focused on getting in as quickly as he could.

Gerrard must have been watching from somewhere nearby, as he opened up another "hole" in the barrier wall for them to escape through with impeccable timing. It was a mite narrow, but passable enough, and Broden spun through and to the left, clearing the space for anyone following after him but giving himself a chance to see what was going on behind them.

Iyshian soldiers, red faced and panting from that mad sprint, were nipping at their heels. They were still ten feet away, at least, when the last Estolian guardsman pounded through. Gerrard snapped the barrier shut with admirable quickness, and when the first Iyshian soldier reached the barrier, he was immediately shocked back as the magic repelled him.

There came a general howl of frustration from their pursuers that made Broden's lips twitch. Aye, a rough night for all involved, but that howling did give him a sense of satisfaction.

"Let me down!" the old woman in front of him begged.

Oh, right, she probably was gasping for breath in that position. Broden swung off, a little gingerly as the saddle moved under his weight, and then lifted her as carefully as he could back to the ground.

She glared up at him, tears in her eyes, as soon as she had her feet back under her. "I do not want to live in Dahl proper."

Broden stared at her. Still stubborn, eh? Well, he did not expect to be thanked by this lot. "You be welcome to waltz right back out and be a prisoner again."

That made her flinch, although her mouth tightened in a mutinous manner. Broden did not care at this point what she thought or what she did. His duty was done as far as he was concerned. Although it made him a little sick, thinking that he had saved this woman instead of someone else, who honestly regretted their choice and wanted to come back into Dahl. Pushing past her, he went to Ashlynn.

He hated to ask, but was duty-bound to know, so he forced the words out regardless. "Lass? How many did we leave behind?"

"Three," she answered in a tired voice. "None of them would look at me or try to help the guards to leave. It would have been a fight to get them, so we left them. I do feel a little bad about it, but... what can you do with such special snowflakes?"

Broden grunted agreement. Three people who did not want to leave and would rather stay prisoners he did not have any sympathy for. His heart eased. "Aye. Well, let's get this lot sorted and go to bed."

"The sorting is not our job." Ashlynn gave him a genuine smile at this. "I have that delegated to someone else. Our job is to return the horses. Then we can go to bed."

"Lass," he marveled, a smile taking over his face, "I knew I liked ye for a reason."

"My amazing delegation ability?"

"Aye, that too." Broden had his mouth open to ask a question when a strange sensation landed on his exposed face. Looking up, he realized that it was a snowflake, one of many. "It be cold enough to snow?"

"Apparently." Ashlynn also turned her face to the sky. "Talk about timing. If we had delayed this operation even one more day, we might have been thwarted. It's already falling harder by the second."

Truly. This might be the first big snow of the winter season. It had been threatening to storm all day but Broden had not realized it was quite cold enough to snow yet. He looked toward the wall, and the Iyshian soldiers camped outside of it. From what he had seen, they were not equipped to camp out in true winter conditions. Those poor sods.

A tiny voice came from Ashlynn's throat. "Ashlynn. Are you done yet?"

Ashlynn lifted the necklace up in front of her nose and glared at it. "Edvard. I am done for the night unless this is an emergency. Emergency defined as your pants being on fire."

"It's more serious than that. Stay on, I'm having trouble getting everyone else on a caller."

Broden and Ashlynn shared a muted, frustrated look. It was never good when Edvard issued these emergency meetings of his. Edvard was not one for meetings to begin with, so if he gathered people, it was because he truly needed them.

They stayed on but delayed just long enough to make sure that everyone was heading in the right directions and things were properly delegated before heading indoors. Ashlynn stopped by the guards' kitchen and gathered them up a snack of biscuits, jam, and hot cider, which Broden certainly appreciated. They had had a very light dinner while waiting for the sunset and he for one was still hungry. If they were going to be up for some hours yet, then they would need the extra energy.

Ashlynn commandeered a guard's bedroom so they had privacy and warmth. It was a narrow space with nothing more than a bed, a chest, and a writing table. Ashlynn took the bed, stretching out and getting her feet up. Broden did not trust himself on a bed—he would fall straight to sleep—so instead took the chair at the desk. Broden managed to cram the last of the biscuit into his mouth just as Ashlynn picked the caller up, demanding, "What now?"

Edvard responded, "Hold on, I'm not quite sure we're all here. Tierone?"

"I'm here, Edvard. Now, tell me that for once you're calling with good news."

"I wish I was. We don't believe Maddox is with his army."

Broden choked on the biscuit still in his mouth. While they'd suspected this...surely not!

"What?!" Ashlynn wailed. Turning, she pounded Broden on the back helpfully even as she demanded, "We've got no sightings of him at all? Troi, are you sure?"

"I've been keeping an eagle eye on the commander's tent ever since their arrival. I've had two spies in place since we got word of the army watching them. We've seen no sign of Maddox except his flags."

True, neither he nor Ashlynn had seen hide nor hair of him either, but they were not always watching the army. Knocking back the rest of his cider cleared the obstruction in his throat enough that Broden was able to croak, "If the man no' be with his army, then where did he get himself off to?"

"Now that is the question, isn't it?" Tierone more grumbled the words than said them. "The only thing we can think of is, did he choose to come up later? Maybe he came up by sea?"

Ashlynn gave Broden a wide-eyed look, and they said in near unison, "The ships?"

One could hear the grimace in Edvard's voice. "I have no idea. I'm just throwing out possibilities. Have either of you received any word from the pirates?"

"No, not one," Ashlynn denied readily. Then she paused and frowned. "Although I'm not sure if they would think to contact us."

"If they succeeded, they would," Broden corrected. "To brag if naught else. Silence means they have nothing to brag about. If he had been on a ship, belike we would have heard something. Troi, have ye heard any word of ships making it to Windcross?"

"I don't have any spies over there to report something to me," Troi denied in frustration. "We have so little manpower, and so many other areas to send them, I was relying on the pirates to tell me if the ships came by."

Which made perfect sense and in his shoes, Broden would likely have done the same.

"They might not be able to, though, if Maddox has seized control over the area," Edvard pointed out. "Broden. You know that area better than anyone. Can you scout around that area and see if Maddox is trying to come up behind us? It's unorthodox for him to not do a frontal assault, but he's obviously not, and I can't think of what else he'd be trying."

All of that was true enough and Broden nodded agreement. "Edvard, I normally be willing to go," he said hesitantly, "but do ye realize it be snowing outside?"

There was a pregnant pause. Had they been so wrapped up in the problem that they had failed to realize what was happening? "Heavens, it is," Edvard said in disbelief. "Well. Scratch that, I can't send you outside in these conditions."

Ashlynn gave the caller a snarky look. "Not that I would have agreed to Broden going by himself."

Did not he know it. "If the snow clears, I can take Tant or Seth with me?" he offered, trying to set her mind at ease. "They be decent enough at skulking, even in a forest. Riana taught them a few tricks."

While this was not the outcome she had wanted, it was apparently a palpable compromise. "Seth, then," she agreed a little reluctantly. "But only if it proves to be necessary. We might get word yet before the snow clears enough for you to go."

True enough. Broden frankly hoped for that, as he was too tired to go gallivanting around the country anyway.

Edvard sounded as if he were well past exhaustion. "Maybe I'm just too tired to think, but I can't understand what Maddox is doing if he's not at my borders. I know we talked of sending him north of Ganforth and playing some tricks on him, but he's completely out of position for half of our plans and he's not making a move to boot. This goes against all of the intelligence that we have on him. We're not even sure where he is. What by Macha's beard is he doing?"

CHAPTER SIXTEEN

Entering the townhouse, she greeted Mrs. Pennington with a smile as she handed off her gloves, hat, and cloak. "Mrs. Pennington, where is everyone?"

"The study, Lady Saira." Pennington had a knowing expression on her face. "It went well, I take it?"

Riana had come from a formal ladies' luncheon and now understood the difference between an informal and a formal version. Informal meant less people, to begin with, but formal also meant that one had a certain agenda as well. Mostly the agenda was introducing eligible young women to eligible young men. Riana had flirted and used these introductions blithely to her own ends. In fact, she had learned that flirting might just be the best way for her to spread rumors about. She was, after all, supposedly here to catch a husband. What better way to meet everyone in Court than through her cover story?

"They bought the story hook, line, and sinker and then threw their own bait into the water. It was marvelous. Best yet, I finally met one of Woelfel's favorite gossips—Lady McAdaraugh. I feel that she'll be marvelously useful in the future."

"She always is," Pennington agreed knowingly. "If you're looking for the men, they're in the study."

"Thank you, Mrs. Pennington." Rubbing her hands together in delight, Riana went for the study, anxious to tell the men of her success.

She'd barely made the hallway when Ash's voice floated toward her from the end of it: "I can feel you gloating from here, dearheart!"

Laughing, she called back, "And for good reason!" With a skip in her step, she rounded the doorway with a flair of skirt and bounced to a stop. "Gentlemen, I return victorious."

"Of course you do," Ash acknowledged, smiling in turn. Only it wasn't a true smile, that slight downturn of the mouth cuing her into his tension. She had been so elated that she hadn't been as in tune with Ash as normal.

Instantly, she went to the table where both of them were sitting. "What's gone wrong?"

"It's truly amazing how well you can feel each other," Woelfel marveled. "He said you were in high spirits even before you returned. And now, even though he's trying to mask it, you can still tell something's off? I'm beginning to put more clout into those stories I heard as a youngster about the legendary wizards and their partners."

Ash gave him an acknowledging, lofty nod. "As you should."

Not about to be sidetracked by this banter as the men intended, she drove a finger into Ash's ribs. "Out with it."

"Ow, ow, owowowowowow, Riana! Quit it. I'll tell you, just don't bore a hole into my ribs." Rubbing at his abused side, Ash tried to scoot back into his chair and put a little space between them. "Truth is, we just received a very disturbing message from Troi. The army arrived, the barrier is holding, so all of that is good news. The bad news is...Maddox isn't there."

"Not there?" she parroted in confusion. "Then where is he?"

"Troi was hoping we'd know," Woelfel sighed glumly. "But I haven't a clue. I know we wanted to draw him north, to trap him up in the mountains, but Troi reports they haven't seen hide nor hair of him."

Riana thought fast, going through every facet of what she knew of their plans. "Da was going to barter with the pirates, get them to help. Did he succeed?"

"He did, but they haven't heard from the pirates either."

She now completely understood why Ash had a headache brewing. She felt one coming on herself. "So not only are we missing a prince, but all of our mystery ships, and the pirates?"

"It's quite the tally." Ash rubbed at his temples. "I don't even know where to start looking, either."

Woelfel pondered the problem with his hands over his belly, head cocked a little to the side. "The first task, I think, is Maddox. If we can figure out where he went, then half of our questions are solved and we can surely guess the other half. To that end, my lovely partner in crime must assist me tonight. There's a soiree of some sort being thrown by Lord and Lady Westhaven. I do believe the guest list has more than one government official attending. If we're lucky, perhaps Lady Saira will bump into Savir again," he drawled with a pointed look at her.

Riana blinked at him, all innocence. Was it her fault that she didn't know what the royal family looked like? Besides, it was dark, the man had been completely obscured in shadows. "It worked in our favor, didn't it?"

"And nearly gave me heart failure, but yes, I suppose it did." Rolling his eyes in a prayer, Woelfel moved on. "At any rate, we best start digging for answers tonight. We need to know where Maddox went. We've kept our eyes strictly on the roads, but perhaps we need to broaden our search a little. I have a few contacts at the shipping companies as well. They only used the royal navy for this mission, but they all use the same docks, perhaps someone saw something."

"It's not a bad thought," Ash agreed. "Do so. I assume my lovely partner has a report to send to Troi?"

"I do," Riana confirmed. "The rumors are taking an interesting turn, shall we say. All of it to our advantage."

"He likes to stay abreast of things like that. Let's write one up for him and send it along by carrier pigeon. Heaven knows the man could use some good news right about now."

Lady McAdaragh was indeed a chatterbox

that couldn't think a single concept for herself but happily repeated everything she heard. Riana had concluded on her first meeting with the girl that she was sweet for the simple reason that she didn't have the brains to be mean.

An uncharitable thought, but true, nonetheless.

For a spy, she was the best possible resource, and Riana hunted her down at every social event. Speaking with Lady McAdaragh was more efficient, for one thing. She spoke with literally anyone and everyone, and because of that, Riana didn't have to do the same thing. Instead, she listened to the girl chatter on, with the occasional re-direction in topics, and weeded through who she needed to speak with. When something caught her attention, she would casually ask who Lady McAdaragh had heard that from, make note of the name, and hunt the person down later.

Zelman had thrown an extravagant New Beginnings Festival at his palace. Everyone came dressed in pale blues, whites, and greys, as if they were limited to the colors of winter. It made a pretty sight, granted, but for some absurd reason they also wore half-masks over the top of their faces and that made it harder to tell who was who. If not for Lady McAdaragh's rather striking midnight hair, Riana would have had the devil of a time finding her in this crowd.

Even the ballroom had undergone a transformation of sorts. Riana hoped that most of it had been done by magic, otherwise the cost would have been hideously expensive. All of the curtains were now white, there was blue and silver ribbons wrapping the columns from floor to ceiling, even the food had white and blue themed decorations to it. How could Zelman afford to throw a party like this when he was fighting a war on one front and having to defend his borders on another?

Oops, her attention had wandered around the room again. That tended to happen when Lady McAdaragh got on the topic of clothes. Which the girl spoke of. A lot. Riana tuned in enough to find a way to divert her attention.

"—Prince Savir look dashing in that stark white? With his dark complexion, it's a truly heady contrast," Lady McAdaragh was gushing, goggling off toward the left somewhere.

Riana didn't do more than pretend to glance in that direction. "I do agree. Actually, speaking of contrast, I find all three princes to be an odd contrast to each other."

Lady McAdaragh blinked at her, not at all following.

"Think about it," Riana encouraged, not for one second believing the girl actually could do such a thing, "Prince Maddox is strong, but not known for being a strategist, Prince Savir is very much the scholarly sort, and then Prince Hendrix is a people-person. That seems to be all he does, is go around, speaking to and supporting people."

"Ohhh," Lady McAdaragh said, mouth forming a perfect O. "I hadn't thought of that. But I suppose that's true, isn't it?"

Good, the idea was planted. Now the misdirect. "I've heard from several people that it's a pity Prince Hendrix can't inherit because of the new Inheritance Law, as he would be a more fitting candidate in some ways for the throne. Of course, I'm not sure if they're right or not, and King Zelman seems to be set on having Prince Maddox inherit."

Head bobbing up and down, Lady McAdaragh agreed, "The king does seem set on that. I've heard other people were contending, but I'm not sure if they stand much of a chance—"

At that point, a voice that Riana did not know spoke up near her ear. "I'm afraid, dear ladies, that you are quite mistaken."

The oiliness behind it sent a shiver straight up her spine. She jumped a little and spun so that this man was no longer at her back.

"Oh, my apologies, I'm sure," he crooned to her, a smile underneath his white half-mask. "I had no intention of startling you."

Riana stared at him hard, frantically trying to place who this was even as she feigned a smile in return. "Not at all. I do not believe we are acquainted."

"Indeed, we are not. Allow me to be so boorish as to introduce myself. My name is Axley—"

All of the blood just drained south.

"—and I am one of those contenders for the Iyshian throne," he finished with a bow and a flourish of the hand. "A pleasure."

"Oh, Lord Axley, I've heard of you," Lady McAdaragh gushed, thankfully covering Riana's frozen horror at being caught near this man. "I'm Lady McAdaragh, charmed."

"No, no, I'm the one charmed," Axley responded smoothly. "Who is your companion?"

"Lady Saira," Lady McAdaragh promptly introduced, not at all catching onto the dangerous tension that was filling the air.

Axley gave her another bow but this time there was a sharp, weighing look in his eyes. "Lady Saira, enchanted."

Riana's smile was so brittle it neared the breaking point. "Lord Axley, it is quite the thing to finally meet the man of report." Where, where, was Woelfel, curse him?! She could not find a good way to excuse herself out of this situation without being rude, and Lady McAdaragh, curse her, would stupidly tell everyone about it without realizing the consequences. Having her name linked to this man in any way would harm the work that Riana had already done. She wanted to use their trouble signal of the fan over the heart, but couldn't, as she didn't have line of sight with him.

"As you ladies were discussing," Axley picked up the original conversational thread, "I wish to correct your assumption that all is set for Maddox to take the throne. Indeed, that is not the case, as he has yet to truly solve the problem with Estole."

"That's true," Lady McAdaragh allowed, blue eyes blinking ingeniously, "but isn't that practically set? He led an army northward after all."

"My dear, Lady McAdaragh, I put no faith in it succeeding. Iysh has led an army twice previously against Estole and it has nothing but graves and defeat to show for it."

All very true but this time the force was much more sizeable and Estole was at its limits trying to protect all of the people inside of its borders. Hence why Riana was in this role, playing spy and trying to find a bloodless solution to the problem. "Yes, well, time will tell in that regard, will it not?" she stated gamely. "If you will excu—"

"No, no, Lady Saira, I do not believe that we should wait for our army's defeat," Axley objected, still in that same polished tone. "Indeed, that is a sad waste of lives, is it not?"

While Riana rather agreed, she knew that he couldn't give two shakes about anyone's life but his own. He was stringing the conversation along until he found a way to win them over to his side. That was all he was doing. She gave a neutral hum and looked away. Somewhere in this crowd, there was surely an excuse for her to get away from this man. Another five minutes and it would be rumored that she was seen to be in an "intimate" conversation with him.

"Ah, Lady Saira, there you are."

Riana jumped all over again when Savir's voice came from behind her. She turned with a smile on her face and a very conflicted heart. While she dearly wanted to escape from Axley, that did not necessarily mean that she was willing to jump from the frying pan and into the fire! "Your Highness."

Everyone in the immediate vicinity gave a bow or curtsey. Savir pinned Axley with a look that promised not nice things—iron maidens and thumb screws would be the beginning of it. "Lady Saira, I must steal you away from this conversation."

Axley regarded him coldly. "Surely whatever

it is can wait, Your Highness. We were deeply engrossed in the talk."

Savir's enigmatic smile stayed in place, as strong as a magical barrier, not revealing what the prince was truly thinking. "If so, I do apologize. My mother has requested to meet her. Lady Saira?" he offered his arm courteously.

Not at all sure what the right thing to do would be, Riana took his arm and let him lead her away. Did he truly mean to introduce her to the queen? Or was that an excuse he knew would work to get her out of a tight spot? Riana tried to feel sorry for leaving Lady McAdaragh trapped with him, but odds were, the girl wouldn't get his political double-talk anyway. She'd be fine. She didn't have an agenda to push like Riana did. "Am I truly going to meet the queen?"

"Indeed you are." Savir's mask fell away and he looked more human as he answered. "Two reports have coincided to make my mother interested in you. We understand that you only recently left Senn?"

"Well, yes," Riana admitted. Relatively.

"We have had reports that my brother Hendrix has also been in Senn recently. Did you cross paths?"

Was it wise of Riana to admit to that? On the other hand, if she said no, and he had actual intelligence saying Hendrix was in Senn, that would look very odd. In this case, the truth might be better. "I did. Prince Hendrix often dines with my family if he is in town."

"Then it is as we thought." Savir offered no more explanation than that as he led her straight through the ballroom and into a corner with a slightly raised dais. King Zelman and Queen Rosalinda often sat there during events like this. Riana's heart clenched at the thought of being anywhere near Zelman. Would she be able to stand it?

As they passed through the last of the crowd, she realized that Zelman was not in his customary chair but mingling. Only Queen Rosalinda was present, comfortably ensconced in a wing backed chair, wearing pure white, her blond hair twisted up elaborately around her face. This was the first time that Riana had seen her this close and she was startled by how alike Hendrix and his mother looked. Savir didn't look a thing like her.

Ah, right, of course. Savir and Maddox were not this woman's sons. She was their step-mother, and only Hendrix was blood related to her, hence why the Inheritance Law was passed. Riana had forgotten that for a moment.

"Mother, this is Lady Saira Vaulx," Savir introduced, releasing Riana and stepping back a half-step. "Lady Saira, Queen Rosalinda of Iysh."

Riana sank into the deepest curtsey that she could manage. "Your Majesty."

"Lift your head, Lady Saira," the Queen invited.

Riana started to only to remember at the last second that this was one of those arbitrary rules of Court. In front of royalty, you had to be invited twice before actually coming out of a bow.

"Please, Lady Saira, raise your head," Queen Rosalinda invited again.

Glad to straighten, Riana did and gave her a

smile. "It is a very great honor, Your Majesty."

"Thank you, Lady Saira. I have had a report that you recently met my son, Hendrix."

"I have." Although why this woman was asking was another question entirely.

For a moment, she looked wistful. "Is he well?"

It hit Riana like a ton of bricks. She was not facing the Queen of Iysh but a mother who dearly missed her son. Knowing how hard this must be on her, to have her own husband banish their son, without any real means to stay in contact with him, Riana felt a pang of pity. "He is, Your Majesty. He had dinner with my family and he is hale and hearty, if a little road weary."

Rosalinda gave her a sad smile. "I am glad to know he is well."

Perhaps this would come back later to bite her, but Riana was trusting her instincts on this. "Did you know that he is engaged?"

The queen's head jerked up. "I have heard rumors, but nothing concrete. You know this for a certainty?"

Oh yes. There was a door open for her here, and a beautiful way to gain some clout very quickly in Court. Riana had to squash an evil chuckle. Gesturing to a plush footstool nearby, she asked, "Perhaps I may sit with you for a spell? I happen to know the story of how he and his fiancé Bria Knolton first met. Have you heard it?"

"Not a whisper." Rosalinda pushed the stool a little closer and quickly gestured her into it. "Do, tell me. Bria Knolton, you say? Surely not related to Edvard Knolton."

"The same, Your Majesty. I believe she is his next to youngest sister. Bria grew up in Senn during her teenage years, you see, I happen to know her rather well." Actually, Bria had spent her teenage years in Honora, but it didn't hurt to bend the truth a little here. Blessing that she wouldn't have to come up with any other lies for the next short while, Riana launched into the story.

Queen Rosalinda listened enthralled and asked a great many details. No one dared to get too close to them, even though they were likely insanely curious what the women were discussing, as Savir stayed planted at the edge of the dais like a guard dog. For all the onlookers knew, they could be discussing clothes or secret information.

Even as she spoke, Riana could hear the buzzing from the other nobles, all of them whispering to each other and wondering what the queen was speaking about to the newcomer. Oh yes. Riana could use this connection quite well.

If Woelfel didn't kill her for this, he might just kiss her.

CHAPTER SEVENTEEN

Six days of being under siege takes a toll on a city. Even when the city was prepared for it.

Because they had no idea where Maddox was, they had to assume that he was coming in some other direction to attack. Whether that was Estole, Dahl, or Ganforth was anyone's guess. The majority believed it would be Ganforth as it remained the only weak chink in Estole's armor, and if he was not at their front door, surely he was heading for the back. That meant that a shield had to be constantly up around Ganforth as well as Estole. It wore on the magicians heavily and Broden sent more than one prayer heavenward that they now had a full school of magicians instead of the three they had possessed before. If this battle had come to them before moving Gerrard here, they would have lost the war before it could have gone more than three days.

The snow arrived in full force over those days and then stayed, as it never got warm enough to melt. Traveling across land became difficult, leaving the only means of reliable travel by sea, as the channel was not iced over enough to prevent ships coming in and out. Fortunate, that, in more than one sense. Ashlynn and Broden had actually returned to Estole via boat as it was the best way to travel. Their duty was done in Dahl, but the same could never be said in Estole.

They'd barely arrived in Estole when they were faced with an old problem—food. They had stored as much as they could, but a good portion of their food came from the southern edge of Dahl and Cloud's Rest. Both of those were lost to them at the moment and there was precious little that could be done about it. Now the only real source that they had for food was the channel, and there was many a man that threw his line in, trying to catch something for dinner.

The price for food in the market was astronomical and it would have become insane if Edvard had not put a cap on it. Ashlynn took it upon herself to go through the market at least twice a day and she kept an eagle eye on the prices. Anyone that tried to jack it up a little got a harsh scolding from her and was forced to sell things at a discount for the rest of the day. After that first day, the merchants had learned their lesson, and they did not try any other shenanigans.

It did not stop Ashlynn from keeping an eye on matters though. She stalked through the marketplace with the caller held up to her mouth, held so that Broden could hear as well. "No, they seem to be behaving after that first day. I'm just making sure they understand that the matter hasn't changed."

"Good, that's probably wise," Edvard responded.

Tierone spoke up, "Do you really not have the time to come here? Meetings over caller are a little awkward."

"We have an army pounding at our gates and you're still asking me that question?" his sister retorted tartly.

"To be precise, they're not pounding anymore."

Truly, after the first few days, the army's morale had more or less plummeted. Broden thought it might have something to do with Gerrard raising their hopes with his flickers in the wall only to dash them by making the wall even more impregnable than before. They had moved further up toward Estole, randomly attacking it, only to fail every time. They were obviously testing for a weakness but had not found one yet. Since yesterday afternoon the army had fallen into this waiting mode where they kept an eye on the wall but did not try to bust through it.

Broden could not really blame them. A man could only try something so many times before the lack of results would get to him. Smarter thing for them to do would be to wait it out. Eventually, either their magic would fail or hunger would force them out. It was the basics of siege warfare.

"It's a technicality and you know it. Now, where do we stand on supplies?"

There was a happy note in Tierone's voice as he answered, "Windcross has agreed to trade as of last night. The message came in too late for me to tell anyone. They've given me a list of things that they wanted, but they agreed to send food immediately. Considering that they are so close I expect an initial shipment this afternoon."

Broden stared at the caller in Ashlynn's hands with complete surprise. "Already? Lad, be that a bit too soon? Surely they be needing a few days to gather things up and actually load it on a ship."

"They've been doing that while we were negotiating," Tierone answered dryly. "Really, they wanted to take advantage of our situation and expand their markets; it was the price we were arguing about. While we were finagling, they were loading four ships with foodstuffs. Two for Estole, two for Dahl."

Broden let out a breath of relief. Two ships' worth of food would be a very welcome sight indeed. They were down to one full meal a day and a snack in the morning to tide the belly over. And a man could only survive on short rations for so long.

"While I'm happy to hear this," and Ashlynn truly did have a smile on her face, "I'm also a little worried. When word of this breaks, do we expect food riots?"

"It's not a thought I had before but you make a good point. People are feeling rather desperate right now." Edvard hummed in a noncommittal noise of contemplation. "Prepare for the worst. Tierone, what time are we expecting the ships?"

"Late afternoon is what they told me."

"Then, Ashlynn, I want you on the docks with guards set up. If anyone asks, tell them we're getting in a shipment of supplies and it will be available at normal market prices by morning."

Broden thought that was a good way to arrange things, but was also aware that a great many people were displaced right now with no source of income. If they did not give some means to those people to earn the food, then they would be inviting trouble.

"Edvard, we have many a refugee that do no' have much money to his name. Can we hire these people to help on the docks in off-loading and delivery? With them, it can be payment in kind."

There was a pregnant pause. "And this is why I bless Ash for bringing you to us, Broden. You always see the angle that I somehow miss. Yes, do exactly that. From your tone, you already have people in mind?"

Broden felt unsure what to do with this unexpected praise, and had to clear his throat before answering. "I do."

"Then you contact them and arrange things. Tierone, how much food did you order?"

"Enough to feed everyone three full meals for about two days."

That was a ridiculous amount of food. Broden did not underestimate the sheer volume of groceries it took to feed this many people. Just how large were these ships?

"Then, Broden, for anyone that works for you, they can carry off two days' worth of food for one person."

Broden wanted to protest, but that actually was about fair, payment-wise. "If I can find other tasks for them to do, the same payment can apply? Most of these men have more than one mouth to feed after all."

"Of course. Be creative," Edvard encouraged, tone upbeat. "I want my people fed, I just can't afford to do it for free. Find things that need doing, something that will take the pressure off of us."

"I can think of something right now," Ashlynn piped up. "I'll hire a dozen housewives and a few children to monitor market prices for me. They'll report to Miss Hadley. That will buy me a few hours a day."

"Do it," Edvard encouraged. "If there's anything you can delegate, by all means, do so. You only needed to give the initial threat and follow through with a punishment—the merchants know you're serious now. As long as you have information coming in to ensure that they aren't playing while your back is turned, it's fine."

He, for one, was happy Ashlynn had thought of this idea. There was no one more sensitive to prices than a housewife who had a household budget to manage. Broden could think of several women that would be good at it, too. Ashlynn likely planned to use the children as runners, sending the information back and forth quickly, so the women were not run ragged trying to do it. It spread the work out and gave more than one family means to bring food in. All in all, a good system.

"Is there anything else?" Ashlynn prompted.

"Not that I know of. Keep me updated on the progress at the docks."

"I will." Ashlynn ended the call and stopped dead on the side of the street, thinking hard. For several seconds she stared blindly ahead before speaking. "A dozen women likely won't be enough for this task. Miss Hadley will need help when the information is given to her, to make sure that all the numbers are staying consistent. I better get two dozen together, some to work at the castle, some to be here in the market."

She was likely right. The only reason that enabled Ashlynn to manage it alone before this was that she just scared the merchants into line, not that she was able to track all of the prices at every shop. "Then we best gather people up quick-like."

"Divide and conquer," Ashlynn stated decisively. "You get the men together, I'll get the women, and we'll meet at the docks in the afternoon."

With a nod, Broden agreed and took himself off. The first place to go would be the Dahl refugee camp, on the outskirts of Estole proper. He did not know many people there, just a handful, but a handful was all he needed to start with. If they wanted to move food quickly off the ships and into merchant hands by morning, then they would need quite a number of people. Broden had done so many things similar to this that he could work out the logistics in his head even as he walked into the camp.

He knew who he needed to speak with first and went past a good two dozen tents before finding the right one. "Ho, Master Larek!"

Larek was a blacksmith, a stropping man that looked like he ate five dozen eggs for breakfast and wrestled bears for the fun of it. His smile, though, made him look a decade younger than his fifty years. They had met in the aftermath of that crazy rescue mission, as Larek had been the one to sort people out and get them settled. Broden looked forward to the day that war was not hovering over their heads like a dark cloud, as he wanted to take Larek fishing. The man struck him as someone that would make a good friend. "Ho, Master Broden! What brings you here?"

Broden gestured him to step in closer and said in a confidential tone, "We have ships bringing in food."

This cemented the other man's attention and he too lowered his voice. "That's very welcome news. How can we get some over here?"

"King Edvard has mandated that the food be available in the morning at normal market prices. So people can buy it, aye, but he's also given permission for me to hire people to move the food to the marketplace. We'll pay in kind, two days' worth of food for anyone that works."

Larek unconsciously licked his lips. He had a wife and three children himself to feed, and that amount of food would be very welcome. "How many can you hire?"

"I have two ships, laden to the gills. I need people to off-load and other people to deliver it to all the shops. I be thinking I need at least thirty men for that. I'd like to hire another two dozen men to act as guards for the docks, to prevent riots." Repeating himself, Broden emphasized, "Every man that works gets two days' worth of food, no matter the task. Who can ye recommend to me?"

"I know most of the people you need," Larek promised. "How soon?"

"Now, man. The ships come in later this afternoon."

Larek swore softly, staring up at the morning sun. "Then we only have about six hours to pull everyone together and organize this."

"Aye, about that," Broden agreed. "Why do ye think I came to ye for help? Let's be about it."

Larek immediately spun on his heel, encouraging as he started off, "Keep up with me, I need you to vouch for things." Spotting someone, he bellowed, "HENRY!"

"What!" Henry yelled back.

"Come here, I have work for you!"

The other man obeyed with alacrity and Broden noticed that at least three other men immediately ducked out of the tent, anxious to see if they could somehow be included in this.

Gathering up people to work, that would not be the issue. Finding enough work to go around, that...that would take some creativity on his part. Broden silently prayed his brain would be up to it.

Broden felt a little more than frayed by the time he made it to the docks. He had fifty-six people all set to work, some as guards, some as dockmen, others as deliverymen. Without Larek, he truly would have been lost, as the man settled arguments before they could even form. Even then, they had to turn some men down, as they just did not have the work to go around. They did not want people working on top of each other—that would be completely counter-productive. Broden had to settle on a rotation system, where the next time he needed workers, he'd take the ones he had to refuse. It was not what he wanted to do, but sometimes common sense just had to win out.

Now he stood with anxiously waiting men deployed in every direction, with Ashlynn standing next to him. She looked as harried as he felt. Giving her a tired grin, he asked, "Did ye get swarmed by people too, lass?"

"Don't ask," she grouched back. "I'm going to have nightmares as it is."

Chuckling, he stared out toward the channel. Time seemed to pass slowly until he finally spotted ships on the horizon. His brow wrinkled in confusion. Granted, his eyes might not be as good as they once were, but even still there seemed to be more shapes than expected. Blinking, he lifted a hand to shield his eyes from the sun and stared harder. "Lass. I be counting four ships."

Ashlynn stopped doing her calculations of how much food to set aside and turned to stare in the same direction. "You're right. There's four. What's that about?"

He did not know. "Call Tierone."

Ashlynn was already doing so. "Tierone. Tierone!"

"Ashlynn I'm in the middle of something, can this wait?"

"No, it can't. We have four ships coming in, not two. Did you negotiate for more and forget to tell us? Did they get mixed up and all four are coming here instead of two going to Dahl's docks?"

There was a clack as Tierone put something heavy down. "No. Our two have already arrived. Four, are you sure?"

"I'm very sure, I'm watching them with my own eyes. Did you try brokering a deal with anyone else?"

"Well, I sent out queries to other places but I didn't get a very good response. Windcross was willing to barter for lumber and ore as we gathered it at Ganforth. No one else wanted to do that; they were more interested in fine goods and money."

Broden had been wondering what Tierone used as a bartering chip. It did make sense—they had plenty of lumber and ore over there; all it would take was some work to get it out. "Lad, whether ye knew of these or no', they be coming in. I need more men to deal with it all."

"Hire what you need," Tierone encouraged. "I'll tell Edvard."

Not having any time to waste, Broden immediately turned and hailed Larek. The man trotted over, pointing to the ships as he did so. "I thought you said two ships."

"Aye, man, that be what the kings be expecting. We have no notion where the other two be coming from, but I know we do no' have the manpower to offload them with. We have permission to hire more men on. Fetch that other lot that wanted work, will ye?"

"I'll be right back with them," he promised, and immediately set off to running.

Broden felt nervous about this turn of events.

He had no way of knowing that these ships were safe to board. Just on the off chance that they had been sent with nefarious intentions, he went and called for a few guardsmen so that they could do a quick inspection of the ships. If that turned out fine, only then would he set men to offload it.

With the guards getting ready behind him, Broden turned back to the men at hand and set about restructuring them, as four ships was an entirely different matter than two. The way he had organized them would not work and he needed to clarify which ships they would focus on first. He just hoped that the timing would work such that they could figure out what cargo was on the other ships and what to do with it before his new recruits arrived.

CHAPTER EIGHTEEN

The ships were not in any way booby trapped or carrying Iyshian soldiers. Broden felt frankly relieved because if they had been, Estole was ill-suited to deal with a sudden invasion by sea.

Troi met them at the docks to investigate by the time all four ships had anchored in. Broden did no more than point people in the right direction and then stay in a central place, on top of a crate, so that he could see what was going on and be available for questions. Ashlynn sat at his feet, ready to take the ships manifests given to her and issue orders of what needed to go where.

The Rose, Maria, Falcon, and Pirate's Bane were all fine merchant ships, as wide as could be and stocked to the gills. Their captains came one by one to speak to them, every one of them looking like the sailors they were, finely outfitted for this winter cold. Broden went down on one knee so that he could be more eye level with them, offering a hand of greeting. "Broden Ravenscroft. May harmony find ye, Captain."

"Jemond Ridiger, Master Broden. Harmony find you." Ridiger was of perfectly normal height, with a touch of iron grey hair at his temples that made him look like a dignified forty. "I'm to report to either King Edvard or his Voice."

Ashlynn popped up from her seat and offered a hand. "I'm Ashlynn Fallbright, Sherriff of Estole and Edvard's Voice."

The captain looked suitably impressed by this and took her hand in a firm grip. "Harmony find you, Sherriff. This is my brother, Captain Julian Ridiger."

Julian looked like his brother except that he had blond hair instead of brown. He gave them a smile and shook hands with both of them. "Pleasure, pleasure. Where do we want to offload?"

"We have people here set to help you offload and they know where to take it all," Ashlynn stated with a confidence that Broden did not entirely share. "Just direct them on the ships and they'll take it from there."

"Fair enough, Sheriff. Our employer indicated that you might have goods to give us in return?"

"We do, Captain, but they're not ready to be shipped out just yet. We were caught a bit off guard by how quickly this shipment came in. If you could give us about five days? We'll have plenty for you to transport back by that point."

"Understood. Even we were surprised by how quickly we were sent out." Quillin gave them both a nod. "Then I'll get back to the Maria."

"I would like to sit and speak with you for a while after this is sorted," Jemond stated with a lilt in his voice to make it more a question.

"Of course, Captain," Broden encouraged. "Come and have dinner with us. Give yer men a bit of liberty tonight to go about the town and stay until the morning tide."

"I'd be pleased to. Thank you." Jemond gave them both a brief, blinding smile, then returned to the ship to oversee the off-loading.

"Good going," Ashlynn praised in a low voice. "The more connections we have with merchants, the better."

"Aye, that be me thought as well."

Troi's attention was trained on the last two captains that headed their direction, obvious by the caps on their head and the merchant crests on their coats. "The real question is, who are these two? I can tell in a glance they're not from Windcross."

No indeed, as the man and woman approaching possessed the swarthy black skin and features of southern Overan.

The woman was the taller of the two, looking stout and hearty, a professional smile on her face. "I'm Crescencia Versch, captain of Pirate's Bane. This is my colleague, Skaff Auman of the Falcon. Who am I speaking with?"

Ashlynn stepped up and offered a greeting. "Ashlynn Fallbright, Sheriff of Estole and Voice for King Edvard. May harmony find you."

"Well, now," Crescencia said with a true smile this time. "A female sheriff. I'm beginning to like Estole already."

Grinning back, Ashlynn introduced, "This is my partner, Broden Ravenscroft and our spymaster, Troi. Captain Versch, Captain Auman, we were not expecting you."

"Oh? Well, true enough, we weren't paid by Estole for this shipment."

Auman nodded in support of this, eyes darting about in curiosity even as he joined the conversation. "True, our employer used a third-party broker to do everything, remained anonymous the whole time. Even we find it strange."

Strange? Broden thought the word "strange" an understatement in the extreme. Who would purchase two ships worth of cargo and then send it to a country anonymously? Only the very wealthy could afford to do so. Why not take credit for it, if you were going to take the risk?

"What are your cargos?" Ashlynn pressed.

They both handed over the ships' manifests readily, but Crescencia gave a verbal answer as well. "Mostly food, as you can see, a few other supplies such as blankets, thick tents, coal and such to tide people through winter. The broker was very specific in that we were to bring goods that would help refugees. Now that I've seen a glimpse of the place coming in, I realize why. You're near overrun with people."

Broden thought that was probably the best description of the situation he had heard in a while. "Aye, that we be."

"And apparently you have people coming in from all over." Crescencia gave him a frank appraisal. "That accent, where is it from?"

"Cloud's Rest."

"Ahhh now that's a place I've never been.

Must be quite the story of how you came to be here, and her partner." Crescencia gave him a wink. "I'll buy you a drink later, so tell me the story when the work is done."

Were all sailors like this? Constantly on the search for a good story? Broden agreed readily, "Aye, we can do that. The other two captains will join us for dinner, if ye'd like to do the same?"

"Oh? I thank you for the invitation, and I certainly will. Skaff, you going to join us?"

"Don't mind if I do." Skaff paused, finger at his chin, and stared hard at Troi. "You're the spymaster for Estole? That right?"

"Yes, Captain, so I am," Troi responded politely.

"In that case, got a message for you." Skaff pulled a sealed envelope from his breast pocket, one that had clearly been riding there for some time, as it looked extremely creased. "Our anonymous employer was very specific that this was to be handed to you, and only to you."

This just got progressively stranger. Broden was very curious as Troi took the envelope and drew out the paper inside. It was a single sheet, the handwriting neat and plain. It was not a letter, as Broden expected, but instead seemed to be a list of names.

Troi read through it in a blink and then started swearing loudly, in the most foul language that Broden had ever heard from a man.

Ashlynn regarded their spymaster with open alarm. "Troi! I've never heard such language from you. What in Lugh's name—"

Waving the paper in front of her nose, Troi

snarled, "THIS lists a quarter of the spies I have in Kremser right now!"

All blood drained south and left Broden feeling light headed. "Man. Do no' say me daughter's name be on it."

"No, fortunately," Troi calmed himself down enough to answer but he was still nearly purple with rage. "But this is bad. It's not even my fake spies, it's my flesh-and-blood ones." Enraged, he ripped the sheet into shreds and then threw it to the ground, stomping on it for good measure. "WHO? Who found my spies?!"

Ashlynn, in her normally delicate and sensitive manner, slapped him in the back of the head. "Throw a fit later, be grateful for the information and go and contact those spies now! You need to get them out before they're caught."

Troi swore, fetched up the scraps, and then sprinted for his office.

Both captains were left staring after him, Auman in appreciation for the sheer creativity of the cursing, Crescencia in narrow eyed speculation. "Now I'm very curious about our employer. Which is more the gift, I wonder? The supplies or the information?"

That was indeed the question. "Captain," Broden said firmly, "there be a great many questions we need to ask of ye."

"That I can see. Let's offload the supplies and go for that dinner, shall we? I'll tell you all I know and some of what I suspect. Maybe with enough heads put together, we can figure this out."

Broden hoped so as well.

Ashlynn gave a noise of agreement and went

back to sitting. "We'll do that. If you don't mind, though, I need to alert my kings of what just happened."

"Of course, of course. Let's all get back to work and speculate later." Crescencia returned to her a ship with a thoughtful look on her face.

Feeling a headache coming on, Broden did the same.

Neither of the captains had much to offer when it came to facts. Most of what they spoke about were guesses and supposition. While all of that was interesting in its own right, they did not have a solid enough basis to build any assumptions on, so it became nothing more than an intellectual exercise.

Their best guess was that a supporter of Estole was, in their own way, rebelling against Iysh. Someone wealthy and with their hands deep in politics, someone that could not show their interests openly without reprisal. After going around and around several times in a row, they let the topic rest.

In the limited amount of time they had before the light failed, they were unable to completely offload all four ships. There just was not enough dock space to unload four merchants' ships at the same time. The food came off first, as no one wanted to give it a chance to spoil, and then the rest of the cargo was slated to be unloaded in the morning.

Ashlynn had the hard job of making sure

the food went to the right places while Broden's responsibility was the rest of the cargo. He stood on his crate again, pointing and giving directions, trying to keep track of the list in his hands to make sure that he was not misguiding people. As he did, he noticed a commotion at the ferry side of the docks. Scanning the three guardsmen involved in the tussle, he found a face he recognized and called out, "Amber! What be this about?"

"We have a pirate!" she yelled back.

A what? Hoping rising in his chest, Broden hopped down, shoved the manifest list into Larek's hands, and went straight for her. Could this be a messenger?

Seeing him approach, Amber shifted to one side to make way, a scowl on her face. "Sir. I know you have contacts with pirates; do you know this whelp?"

"So I do," Broden responded, regarding JJ's ship boy with open delight. "The name be Kyne, I believe?"

"Aye, sir." Kyne rubbed his hands together, looking more than a little cold, and his nose kept trying to run. His clothes were not really thick enough to ward off the snowfall they had seen over the past few days. He must have been traveling for quite some time to get here, so his half-frozen state was understandable. "Captain JJ has his hands full, but he 'xpressly promised ye a message when he be done, so here I be."

"Well, lad, that be a kindness. Let's have it."

As if reciting verbatim, Kyne puffed his chest out a little and stated plainly, "We caught most of them. There were eight ships, we managed to stop five, but three got through. There was a schooner with Maddox's colors on it, and I believe that the prince was on board. The rest had either supplies or soldiers." Dropping the imitation, Kyne added candidly, "The Cap'n dropped me off on land and I followed 'em a ways, just to make sure. Only so far, though, had to double back to Gethin to make it here. Cap'n said ye'd reward me if I spied a bit."

"I certainly will, lad," Broden responded whole-heartedly. He knew better than to press for an immediate answer, although he wanted one. This was the moment when bartering came into place. Kyne had information, he wanted something in return, and he would not say a peep until he got some sort of deal in place. Even if the lad was barely a teenager, he knew the basics of this life. Broden threw out what he thought was a reasonable price. "Supplies for the way back, a fur-lined coat, and matching hat."

Kyne's eyes lit up. He was in skimpy gear, ankles and wrists sticking out from his clothes, and it was clear he was in a growing spree and did not have the funds to get anything better. "Plus boots."

Broden was tempted to get the boy a whole outfit, and would, if he could find anything that would fit. But for now, this would do. He held out a hand and sealed the bargain with a firm handshake. "A bargain it be. Kyne, me lad, be the prince on that schooner?"

"Aye, he be. If he followed the course he set on, he should now be in Gethin Forest and heading this way with nigh on a thousand soldiers. I counted 'em three times to be sure," Kyne added proudly.

"For that, lad, I'll make sure ye get a full outfitting," Broden swore. The information was worth more than that, but they did not have the funds to give him more.

Face lighting up, Kyne demanded, "Ye word on that?"

"Aye, me word on it. Are you sure on his course?"

"Could only follow him so far afore I had to go back to the ship. But aye, he was heading straight as the crow flies towards Ganforth."

That was a good enough answer for Broden. "Then ye've earned yer pay, lad. In fact, come and speak to the spymaster here. Tell him all ye know. As yer doing that, I'll find the best clothes available." Bending down a little, he added confidentially, "Perhaps a bit too long, eh, to last through this growth spurt ye be in?"

"I'd like that fine," Kyne responded thankfully. "Sir," he added almost belatedly.

Grateful enough to remember his manners, eh? Broden bit back a smile. "Amber, escort our young spy direct to Troi. I will finish up here, see to his payment, and report to Edvard." Not exactly in that order. But he had to give her an idea of what places he would be in if she needed to find him later.

"Of course, sir." Amber was a little gentler with the boy as she led him off, now that she knew he was not there just to make mischief.

Broden was not as sure about that. Pirates would make mischief whether they were on a mission or not. He was not too worried about the matter, as between Amber and Troi, they would keep him out of the worst of it.

A thousand soldiers north of them. And Maddox. Broden felt unsure whether to be relieved at the news or overwhelmed by it. He was heartily glad to know the location of the prince and the number of troops heading his direction, but by the same token, what could they do to defend their northern border? More than they were already?

"Larek!" he bellowed out as he moved. "Take over here!"

"Of course," Larek agreed readily, having already taken over Broden's spot on top of the crate. "But where will you go?"

"To report to a king."

CHAPTER NINETEEN

"Lady Saira." Robert Elwood gave a slight bow over her hand, trying his best to look roguish and handsome. He missed by a large margin because of a weak chin and a nervous tic near his left eye but his smile was sincere. "Enchanted to see you."

"Lord Robert," she returned the greeting with a genuine smile of her own. Robert Elwood was one of the sadly disinherited ones, which was a pity, as she rather liked him. He had been kind to her since their first introduction. "The music tonight is quite splendid, is it not?"

"Ah," he turned to take notice of the contralto singing in the front of the garden. "In truth, Lady Saira, I've heard her perform often over the years. But since you are new to Kremser, I suppose this is your first time hearing her?"

"Indeed, yes." Riana had never heard music performed professionally before. She'd never had the opportunity. The first half hour of this musical soiree she had been sitting near the woman's stage, completely spellbound. It had taken Woelfel almost manhandling her to get her back to work. "I find her voice quite stunning."

Robert turned to look at the singer again, as if seeing her through new eyes. "Yes. Yes, I suppose she does possess a remarkable voice. I am very glad that you are here, Lady Saira, to give me a fresh perspective on life."

Riana unfurled her fan with a soft snap and lifted it to her face, obscuring all but her eyes, manner demure. "Lord Robert, you'll make me blush with such statements."

Feeling as if he were gaining some ground with her, he tried to press on the moment. "Indeed, my lady, it is not my intent, but I want to express to you how invigorated I feel whenever in your company."

Mentally, Riana could feel a rumble from Ash, like a thunderstorm that was just cresting the horizon. She wasn't quite sure how, but somehow he had picked up on an emotional cue that told him when she was flirting. It was probably that particular mix of patience, amusement, and manipulation that told him what she was up to. Riana found this jealously perfectly hilarious and didn't even try to squelch it.

"My." She fluttered her fan a little and peeked up at him through her lashes, a move specifically taught to her by Bria. It did its designed effect and Robert looked back at her in a stargazed fashion.

Hmm, that look was remarkably effective. Riana wasn't at all sure why, but men seemed truly weak to it. Perhaps she should try it on Ash tonight when she returned.

Nervously licking his lips, Robert took a half

step forward. "My dear Lady Saira, I—"

"Lady Saira!" Someone knocked into her, upsetting her balance, but fortunately not enough to send them both to the ground. "Oh, I do beg your pardon, clumsy of me."

Riana could smell the wine on him and she tried to hide a grimace. "Not at all, Lord Halloway."

He had a firm grip on her elbow, whether to hold her up or to keep his own balance was anyone's guess. For a moment, just a brief moment, his eyes focused on her with clear lucidity. "Lady Saira, I have been trying to find your cousin. Is Lord Woelfel with you this evening?"

Seriously, what was this man? Woelfel kept forgetting to explain to her who he was but Riana absolutely knew that he had to be an agent of some sort, as both men's behavior didn't make sense otherwise. "Indeed he is, my lord. I saw him next to the stage not a moment ago. Perhaps you can start your search there?"

Lapsing back into his drunk behavior, he gave her a grin and toasted her with a mostly empty wine glass. "My thanks, fair lady!" With that, he staggered off.

Riana waved her fan in front of her face, trying to dissipate the smell of alcohol. The man fairly reeked of it, so much so that she suspected he doused his clothes in it instead of merely drinking it. Stealing a peek at Robert, she found that he was watching Halloway with distinct pity and a dash of annoyance. Annoyance she understood, but pity? "Are you acquainted with Lord Halloway?"

"Yes. Well, no, not really. More like I know of him." Robert wanted to dismiss this with a wave of the fingers.

Riana wasn't about to let him, she sensed an excellent way to turn topics. "Indeed? I have run into him thrice now but I have little idea of his family or connections. Why does the poor man always seem to be drunk, for that matter?"

"Ah, that." Robert heaved a resigned sigh. "He's like my poor brother in that sense. One of the victims to the Inheritance Law."

"Oh, how dreadful! I am so sorry to hear it."

"We all are, in different senses. My brother has found a way to take care of me, as we're close enough that he's not about to leave me high and dry. But some of the lords and ladies aren't as lucky. Halloway is a good example of that." This time, Robert took another step forward but with the intent of sharing gossip. "What I'm about to tell you is well known but considered a semi-taboo subject."

She leaned forward. "I'm all ears. Do tell me."

"I have all of this second hand, mind you, but from a reliable source. Halloway was actually the captain of the City Guard. Quite good at his job, too, although it might be hard to believe it seeing him now. He was a well-known supporter of Prince Hendrix right before Estole rebelled. In fact, it was in part why he lost his position. You see, they blamed him when Edvard Knolton escaped the city after attacking King Zelman."

Several more pieces clicked into place. "Should they have?"

"Well," Robert hedged, "the man was actually outside of the city on the king's command dealing with something else entirely, and wasn't even aware an attack had taken place until he came back the next day. Draw your own conclusions."

In other words, no. But he was a good scapegoat for it.

"The hypocrisy comes later, when the current captain of the Palace Guard replaced him. And if anyone should be blamed for that disaster, I would think it's him."

"Truly," she murmured, staring after Halloway thoughtfully. So, he was disinherited by Zelman, lost his position do to Zelman's poor management skills and bad politics, and now was cut off from any true position or power. If the man wasn't a spy for Estole with that kind of background, Riana would eat both boots. "I do wonder at King Zelman's passing of that law. I realize that he dislikes Prince Hendrix, but there's so many others suffering because of it."

Robert realized they were speaking directly of a taboo subject and lowered his voice to a bare whisper. "I do agree but it's dangerous to say such things."

"Oh, you're right," she agreed with a slightly surprised expression. It was hard to make it seem genuine and not fake. "I just feel so sorry for those lords and ladies that have lost everything. Why, can you imagine—"

"Lady Saira!" a cheerful voice rang out.

Riana just about jumped out of her skin as she spun about.

Smiling down at her was Savir, expression not at all indicating that he had just interrupted a conversation. "Lord Robert, do forgive me, I wish to steal your companion away for a moment. My mother has requested that I bring her along this evening. She quite enjoys Lady Saira's company."

Not at all happy about the interruption, but powerless to do otherwise, Robert put a game smile on. "Of course, who am I to deny Her Majesty? Lady Saira, I hope to be able to speak with you again."

Dratted prince. He was interrupting her work. This was the fourth time this week alone. Riana gave Robert her best smile and watched him melt. "I shall look forward to it, Lord Robert."

Savir extended his arm and she accepted it instead of sticking a dagger into his ribs as she was first inclined to do. After leading her several feet away, he leaned in enough to whisper near her ear, "You must stop smiling at the men like that. You'll give them ideas."

She wanted to give them ideas. That was the whole point of her flirting to begin with. "Your Highness, did you forget that my parents sent me here to find a good match?"

"I have not. But there are more suitable connections that you can make." He steered her around a group of people, an impish twinkle in his eye. "Come. Let me introduce you to a few people on the way."

"I don't know whether to kiss him or kill him," Riana announced, flinging her cape and hat onto the couch as she stomped into the main study.

Ash had been ensconced in a chair, a book

in his hands, but upon their entry he set it aside. Glowering at his partner, he snarked, "I'm inclined to thank him, whoever he is, because he finally stopped you from flirting with every male thing that moved."

"I'm supposed to be flirting, it's the best way to plant ideas," she reminded him, again, for what was probably the hundredth time.

"That's true," Woelfel agreed, sinking wearily into a chair next to the fire. He toed off both shoes and stretched them outward with a sigh of relief. "I do hate garden soirees. They're cold even in this mild weather and there's no good place to sit down."

Riana wasn't as tired as he was, but then, she was used to standing or running for long periods of time as well.

"You only say that as you're the one that taught her that technique," Ash groused. "It's making my skin crawl whenever she does. Riana, who am I to thank for the interruption?"

"Prince Savir," she stated succinctly and flopped into the space next to him on the couch.

Her partner didn't entirely like that answer. "Again? The man seems to be seeking you out at every opportunity."

"I know it." She felt a headache coming on and futilely rubbed at her temples. "I don't understand why. The queen is honestly delighted to hear stories about Hendrix, she makes sense, but Savir?"

"Your connection to both royals is helping you open many doors," Woelfel commented, eyes closed. "Even if it is cumbersome at times.

How close were you to turning Robert over to our side?"

"Another ten minutes and I would have had him." Riana had to struggle to keep a pout off. "On the other hand, Savir was introducing me to people I haven't met before and had no good reason to be introduced to. So in that respect, he was doing me a favor."

"Interesting." Ash stared off into space, brows furrowed as he pondered. "It's not the first time he's done that, either. I wonder what game he's playing?"

"I wish I knew." Woelfel still had his eyes closed. "I do know the man's wearing me out. I have to keep track of her whenever he's escorting her about, as I never know when she's going to need a rescue, but doing that naturally so that I don't seem obvious about it is beyond difficult. If the connections she's making weren't so useful, I would have found a way to put a stop to it. He's stretching my last nerve to the breaking point."

Hers as well. If Riana could just figure out his intentions, she'd feel more comfortable about the whole matter. "The odd thing is, I think part of the reason why he's doing it is because he genuinely likes me."

Both men looked at her in astonishment.

"No, truly," she defended. "After being in Court this long, I've gotten a sense for when someone is putting up a façade, and I don't sense that with Savir. Sometimes he's come and gotten me just to ward the ladies off. I've made him laugh several times, which his mother tells me is quite rare."

"I actually have seen that," Woelfel admitted. "How do you feel about him?"

"He's quite charming, when he puts his mind to it," she admitted freely. "If he wasn't an enemy prince, I'd say I quite liked him."

Ash gave her a pained look. "Dearling, please. Don't say that in front of me."

She leaned in and gave him a peck on the cheek in reassurance. "Not the same way I like you, of course. But I do wonder if that's why he gravitates toward me? Because he senses that I genuinely like him as a person. That and he has something up his sleeve."

"We all know he has something up his sleeve," Woelfel agreed promptly. "Savir doesn't move unless he has three reasons at least to do so. The question is, what?"

What, indeed.

CHAPTER TWENTY

Bexton was a skinny teenager that had a charming air about him and wits sharp enough to slice bread with. Riana felt sure that in six years he'd be a force to reckon with, as he'd grow into those slightly too-large ears and gain some muscle. As it stood now, he was cute in his own way and used that cuteness greatly to his advantage.

Riana had ostensibly hired him to show her about the palace grounds so that she would know where everything was and what areas she was not allowed in. Her excuse was that her cousin was busy with his own social schedule and didn't have the time to do it himself. In truth, she wanted Bexton for two reasons: one, she wanted a chance to fill the boy's ears with all sorts of rumors to spread about, and two, she wanted to do a pre-scout of the treasury. All she knew at the moment was that it was on the palace grounds, but that wasn't nearly enough information.

Strangely enough, Woelfel didn't have the slightest clue where it was, likely because he had never needed to know that information before and it would have looked very odd if he had tried to inquire about it. Since Riana was entirely new to Court she could ask silly questions like where things were without raising a single eyebrow.

As a tour guide, Bexton did well. He gave her the names of the place, a little information about what work was done there, and a funny story to go along with it. (The boy always knew an anecdote to share, some of them more illicit than funny.)

"Bexton."

"Yes, my lady?"

"I believe there is an age limit to being a page, is there not?"

"Indeed, my lady."

"When you do hit that limit," she said with a smile, "and if you can't figure out what else to do, or your plans don't work out, do consider being a tour guide for the palace. You're quite splendid in the role."

Bexton beamed back at her. "Why thank you, my lady. I admit I have entertained the notion from time to time."

"There's lords and ladies like myself that are newcomers to Court," she started ticking things off on her fingers, "new officials, other pages that are coming in, foreign officials—why, there's plenty of people coming in and out that would either need a tour guide or an escort about the place."

"Pages do some of that," he informed her. Still, he had that light of calculation in his eyes that indicated he was truly thinking about it. "But I do see your point, my lady. If I do apply for the position, will you be my reference?"

She couldn't possibly, of course, but agreed

anyway. "Of course, if I can, I'd be glad to."

"Excellent, my lady." There was a slight bounce in his stride as Bexton continued down the main hallway of the palace. "Now, if we take this door here, it leads out into the main courtyard and where the treasury, wine cellar, Royal Physician's office, musicians' quarters and the pages' offices are. Not precisely in that order."

Finally, the part she was truly interested in. They stepped through the door and into the colder air of winter. It was still mild in comparison to Cloud's Rest at this time of the year. Riana was grateful for it as she spent half her time out of doors these days.

"As you can see, the pages' offices are in this first building on your left." Bexton indicated a square building that stood two stories and looked remarkably similar to almost every other building in the square. They were all made of stone with columns out front and a truncated porch that barely sheltered the area around the front door. "It's basically there because it's more convenient to call for a page—" Bexton cut himself off and made a soft hiss that sounded like a curse. "My lady, quick, back inside."

Riana saw immediately why as Axley and Larcinese had stepped out of another side door and spotted them. Riana did not want to be caught out here with them, as there weren't many people and no one to come to her aid if they pinned her there. It was one of those dicey situations where there were just enough witnesses that she couldn't retaliate without breaking her cover but no one high ranking enough to dare stop the two lords.

She turned immediately and made for the door. Alas, moving quickly in eight layers of dress and petticoats was not really possible. The men lengthened their stride and caught up with her just as she had her hand on the handle.

"Come, Lady Saira, you'll make us feel unwanted," Lord Axley sing-songed. "Here, stay and let's chat a bit, shall we?"

These were not men that would pay attention to a mere page. Bexton was being utterly ignored and Riana used that to her advantage. She caught the boy's eye and motioned for him to go with a slight jerk of the chin.

He nodded back seriously and quietly left as if he had never been there. Hopefully he would bring back help, although who he could call was a question indeed. It would have to be someone of either equal or higher rank than Axley to get the man to leave her alone.

"I've seen you fluttering about the social scene like a butterfly." Axley had that smooth tone to his voice, a polished reflection that revealed nothing of what he really felt. "You go from person to person, striking up a conversation, able to speak to anyone. It's an amazing skill."

Uh-oh. He hadn't figured out what she was doing, had he? Riana gave him a baffled look. "A skill, my lord? I hardly consider it that. I just enjoy speaking with people."

"And you excel at gaining their attention," he crooned while taking a step in. It forced Riana back a step, caging her in that much more effectively against the wall. "I've watched you. Everyone smiles while speaking with you, genuinely, and continue to smile even after you walk away. Do you know how many people there are that can honestly be liked by the whole Court?"

It clicked in that moment. Riana realized that Axley wanted her to be an advocate for his cause. His reputation, and his minions, were not favorable in Court. He needed a voice that people liked and would pay attention to. Not—her eyes darted to Larcinese—avoid.

"I would be thrilled to have a woman with such excellent social skills campaigning for me." Axley took another step in, this time basically pressing her back against the wall. Even through her dress and cloak, the stone felt cold and she shivered. "Do you know much about my stance as a candidate for the throne? No? Do let me tell you the gist of it."

Riana pretended to pay attention as he started running off at the mouth but in truth didn't hear a word of it. Really, what did this creep think he was doing? Did anyone charm someone to their side by pinning them against a cold wall and forcing them to listen to some egotistic monologue?

He showed no signs of stopping anytime soon. Riana grew seriously tempted to break her cover enough to punch him in the throat. If she maimed him, just a little bit, he wouldn't be able to talk for the near future. Surely they'd give her a medal for that, as no one really liked the man anyway.

There was the sound of a door opening and Riana glanced in that direction, hopeful that it was Bexton back with a rescue.

Savir stepped through with Bexton at his side.

Her eyes widened. Bexton had fetched the prince?! Why him, of all people!

Something about her expression caught Axley's attention and he faltered mid-word, turning his head to look. When he caught sight of Savir a slight snarl curled his lip before he took a half-step back, making it less obvious that he had been looming over Riana.

"Lady Saira," Savir greeted, chiding her with a warm voice, "You are late."

Late? Oh. Riana gave him a slight curtsey—the best she could manage with her back still against the wall—and apologized, "I am sorry, Your Highness. Lord Axley had something he wanted to tell me."

"So I see." Savir approached and extended a hand toward her.

Woelfel and Ash would likely yell about this later, but Riana was profoundly thankful for the gesture and she took that arm without a second of hesitation. This might have been jumping from frying pan to fire, but at least the fire she knew would not be damaging her cover story or her reputation.

Axley audibly ground his teeth in vexation. Savir's enigmatic smile was somewhat mocking as he gave a nod to the men. "I'm afraid your conversation is at an end, Axley." Permanently was the unspoken word. "You've monopolized my companion long enough. She's mine now."

Larcinese and Bexton both choked. It took considerable effort on Riana's part to not do the same. What did he just say?!

Savir turned that innocent expression on

her, as if he hadn't just proclaimed something outrageous. "Shall we go, Lady Saira?"

"Of course, Your Highness." She kept the smile on her face although it felt like her face would crack under the effort of doing so. As they walked away, she could feel eyes burning into her back. Axley was not one to take such interference well. "Your Highness, I am grateful for the rescue."

"But you shouldn't have said 'She's mine now' to them," Savir added, fully knowing how she felt about that little remark. "I've always wanted to try that line. 'She's mine!' and then walk off confidently with the girl in question. It was quite dashing and romantic, don't you think?"

Riana gave him a weary look. "Your Highness, as a boy, how many times did you put a stick into a hornet's nest or down a snake hole?"

Savir blinked, expression nonchalant. "I didn't put any sticks in the holes. I merely found them. Maddox always did the investigating."

And that indeed was the perfect summary of the twin's relationship. Even now, Savir wasn't stirring up any hornets' nests, just finding them and neatly maneuvering his way around them. "You say that, but you came to my rescue, did you not?"

"Indeed I did. But then, you'll repay the favor in kind, will you not? The next time that I'm surrounded by a hornet's nest."

Ah-ha. So she was to be his next stick-holder while Maddox was gone? Riana had just known there was an ulterior motive lurking beneath that smile somewhere. She was of a mind to box Bexton's ears. Why the prince, of all people? "I suppose I should at least return the favor."

"That's the spirit!" he encouraged, smile becoming genuine. "For now, I understand that you were on a tour of the palace? To familiarize yourself with the place? Where did you leave off?"

Surely the man wasn't suggesting...no, he truly was, he intended to complete her tour with himself as the tour guide. "We had just entered this courtyard when Lord Axley caught me."

"Is that so? Well, it's dangerous to linger here, so let's go elsewhere and then return, shall we? I doubt the man will stay here for the rest of the afternoon after all."

Riana had no choice but to follow his lead. Mentally, she resigned herself to a lecture later from Ash and Woelfel. Bad enough to be rescued by Savir, but now to spend the rest of the day with him? And she wasn't going to be able to fulfill her objective of getting a good look at the treasury security, not with the prince literally at her elbow.

She'd better find a way to turn this to her advantage, otherwise she was doomed.

CHAPTER TWENTY-ONE

For the first time since their arrival, Ash left Woelfel's townhome. He was dressed in layers of grey and black, as was Riana, the better to blend in with the shadows. Woelfel was not with them on this mission for one vital reason—if they were caught, he needed the plausible deniability. Not that he wouldn't be on thin ice, but they had a few plans and stories in place to make it possible for him to cut ties with her if need be. They had to. It was vital that they not lose one of their best agents here in Court.

It neared four in the morning, the perfect time to sneak into the Royal Accounting Offices and the treasury vault that lay in the basement of the building. No one was about at that hour, and the guards that were positioned in the palace compound were more or less asleep on their feet. Hopefully they could sneak in and at least get a layout of the place. Riana didn't for a minute think they could somehow haul off the whole treasury (in spite of Edvard's wild fantasies to the contrary), but it didn't hurt to see how much damage they could do to the Iyshian economy.

They silently crossed through a side gate into the palace compound, one that only the servants knew and used. It was also one of the few still open at this hour of the morning, as the bakers usually started about now in getting the morning bread mixed up and rising. Guards patrolled by regularly, but no one was actually stationed there. Riana found this odd but Woelfel explained to her that every possible man that could fight was stationed elsewhere—either headed toward Estole or along the Overa-Iysh border to keep peace there. Overa was apparently a very restless neighbor.

Making it through the palace wall and into the courtyard was one thing. Actually getting to the right building was another. The various offices here all looked the same—big, blocky buildings made of the same hewn stone and tiled roofs. Only the signs differentiated them and they all hung out in front. Riana had no intention of waltzing along the main path. Her heart already thumped so hard it was likely to leap its way out of her chest soon. It didn't need any extra encouragement.

There was precious little sound except the wind in the eaves, trickling of the main water fountains, and the murmurs of the guards as they talked amongst themselves. At least this way Riana had a clear notion of where most of the guards were. Still, this low amount of noise bothered her. She was used to the ambient noises of a forest at night. Being smack in the middle of a city was not an experience she cared for. Even

Estole was not as cut off from nature as this.

Being the expert at sneaking, Riana led the way, moving lightly on her feet and with both ears strained to the max. She'd hear something long before she could see it. Her eyes were good, but it would take the eyes of a cat to see in this poor lighting. She peered around three corners, leading them along the back of the buildings, only mostly sure she knew where she was going. It looked more than a little different in the dark compared to her daytime tour.

"I think we're almost there," Ash breathed to her, his voice barely louder than a whisper.

Riana nodded agreement, then realized he likely couldn't see that movement, so paused long enough to put her mouth next to his ear. "If I'm right, it's three more buildings down, then two over."

Ash gave a grunt of acknowledgement. "Lead on, partner."

Smiling, she did so, praying this went right. She had a gut feeling it wouldn't. While they could fight their way out, Riana would really, truly prefer not to.

They eased down three more buildings, then stopped at the back edge to get a good look. From this angle, they had more moonlight pouring out over the area, and there were three lanterns lit along each side of their targeted building. Those lanterns shed plenty of light for Riana to see by.

For the dozen guards stationed all along the perimeter of the building as well.

Swearing softly, Ash propped his head to rest directly on top of hers, his chest pressed along her back in a familiar and comfortable manner. In a flash, Riana realized that this was what she missed, working with Woelfel: these casual little touches between her and Ash. It just wasn't the same working with the other man. She missed Ash too much in the process.

Pressing a kiss against her temple, Ash breathed into her hair, "Missed you too, dearheart, but focus."

"You started it," she breathed back, accusingly.

Ash snorted, but didn't deny it. Instead, he pulled out a pair of magical glasses from his shirt pocket and gave the situation a close study. "Me thinks...breaking in is not possible."

Riana could have told him that without the glasses. "The watch is much tighter here than anywhere else on the grounds."

"Likely the royal family's chambers are just as tightly guarded. But I grant you the point. Something about this tells me that they've had people try to break into here before."

Or they were worried someone would try it. Riana had seen signs that Zelman would drain his people dry for funds in order to meet his own ambitions. The elaborate parties he threw on a weekly basis despite being at war was a clear indication of where his priorities lay. If you drove someone hard enough into a corner, they'd eventually fight back, no matter the odds.

"We're not going to be able to do this with just the two of us." Ash eased back, encouraging her with a hand on her arm to follow him out. "Let's leave before we're caught."

Riana was all for that. In truth, she wasn't

really that disappointed. No one really thought that breaking into the treasury would work. They had done it more just to test the theory if it could be done or not. Well, that and to shut Edvard up.

They retraced their steps carefully back the way they had come. Riana was hyper aware of the time, and of the horizon, as she did not want dawn to break while they were still inside. They had spent at least a half hour getting to this point, the large clock on the main tower having chimed out the time as they moved. That left them a maximum of two hours before daybreak. As long as nothing went wrong, that was enough for them to make it all the way back to Woelfel's.

Of course, that very thought invited trouble.

Almost within sight of the side gate they had used to get in, Riana saw a shadow detach itself from the wall. Swearing, she grabbed Ash and flattened him to the wall, making their silhouettes as narrow as possible. It left them pressed tightly together, almost indecently so.

Ash, in a strangely jovial mood, whispered, "Now is hardly the time, dearheart."

Riana leveled a Look on him. "You have been hanging about Woelfel far too long."

"Can't argue that. What are you seeing that I don't?"

"A guard on the side gate."

Now it was his turn to swear. "Is he staying?"

"He doesn't look ready to leave anytime soon." Other than that, she didn't know.

In one accord, they turned and went the other direction, toward a different part of the back wall. Better to debate what to do next without a possible audience ready to chime in. Only when they were four buildings away, with the gate well out of sight, did Riana dare to even breathe. "Now what?"

"We find a low part of the wall to hop," Ash answered promptly. "Either that, or we find a place where we can get enough of a leg up to get over."

Riana eyed the fifteen foot wall looming above their heads. "That be quite the hurtle to jump. Even if we find a place inside, what's to break our fall on the outside?"

"I can manage it once we're over," Ash promised. "I just don't dare use magic in here. There's too many alarms that'll go off."

He had the eyes to detect things like that, not her. Riana trusted his judgment on this. "Then let's scout around and see if we can find something."

If they had been on the outside, trying to get in, Riana would have written finding something to climb on as a complete impossibility. The guards were completely paranoid about people hopping over the wall, and there was a hundred foot clearance on all sides to make it as difficult as possible. However, they didn't appear to take the same care with the inside. It stood to reason, right? Why try to prevent thieves from making their escape, when odds were they couldn't get in to begin with?

Riana blessed their shortsightedness. Or perhaps it was their laziness. She found a collection of crates tossed carelessly about behind one of the buildings. Judging from the smell, and the compartments inside the crate, this was the wine cellar for the palace. The building itself didn't stand very tall, suggesting it had a deeper basement, but the crates caught her full interest. Stacked up, they should give her plenty of height to get over, assuming that the weight and balance of them remained sturdy enough to climb.

The crates were roughly two feet by two feet, a perfect cube. In perfect unison, Riana and Ash started stacking them up like a staircase. One, then two stacked, then three, and so forth. They kept them flush against the wall to offer some stability and of course to give them easy access to the top. There was a slight hitch in that there wasn't enough of the crates to actually reach the top with this method. Ash went back down one, stealing from the bottom "steps" to help build up the top, but even still they were one short.

Ash lent her a knee and shoulder to boost her up and over to the top. Riana landed flat on her belly and stayed there, peering in all directions. It looked safe enough for him to come up.

However, Ash shook his head when she offered a hand. "Better knock some of the crates loose, make it less obvious what we did," he whispered to her.

Good point. No sense in advertising that someone had come and left again clandestinely. It would just heighten security and make their jobs harder later. So she stayed in a semi-crouch and kept a lookout as he went down and carefully scattered the crates about again. It made a little noise, but not much, as he set them down as gently as possible.

He was running out of room to maneuver in climbing back up, which made Riana nervous. She popped her head up a little farther, looking beyond the immediate area.

And that's when she saw them.

Two bored guards, not chatting, just strolling silently along on their patrol route. Riana's heart flipped into her throat and she waved at Ash frantically, trying to silently get his attention. They had fifteen, perhaps twenty seconds until those guards were on top of them.

Ash's back was to her, he didn't see her, and Riana couldn't call out a warning without giving the whole game away. In desperation, she tried the only thing she could: she screamed at him through their bond, an emotional sense of DANGER.

Perhaps he heard her. Perhaps he felt her panic. Either way, battle instincts had him off the crates in a flash, taking one of them from the top with him, so that he landed on the ground in a crouch. Without a second's hesitation, he flipped the crate over the top of his head, angled so that it looked like it was just leaning against the stack, but hiding him from sight.

Riana flattened herself to the top of the wall and didn't even breathe.

The guards went right up to the crates and stopped dead. "Again?" one of them asked his compatriot, tone more resigned than aggravated. "We've told them over and over, don't stack crates back here."

"Like they listen to us."

"But seriously, this is a huge security breach.

What if someone used these to get over the wall?"

"They'd have to get inside first."

"Alright, point, but what if they accidentally caught fire? It's a dry winter down here so far; one careless match or lantern, poof!"

"That I see happening before thieves use them to sneak out. In fact, we had a small fire outside the kitchens last week."

"I heard about that one. Should we try to move these things?"

Riana mentally started swearing. If they did that, Ash would be exposed in a second. She readied her throwing daggers and got a knee up under her. If they went for him, she'd jump down and take them out. It would likely alert any guard within hearing, but she couldn't just stand idly by and let Ash take them both on. He was not an expert at hand to hand combat like she was.

::Riana. Don't move.::

The thought came so clearly from Ash that she blinked, almost forgetting the situation they were in. Granted, they had been working on telepathic communication for weeks, but they had never actually gone through. Had...had their bond finally connected at a high enough level that they now truly were telepathic?

::Celebrate that later, dearheart,:: Ash scolded warmly.

::I'm a woman, I can multi-task,:: she shot back.

To this, he drawled, ::Do you really want to make me laugh with guards hovering above my head?::

Oh. Right. Good point. Riana clamped her

mouth and mind shut.

Fortunately for all, the first guard disagreed after a moment of thought, "Can't do it right this second, we'll miss our check-in at the next spot, and you-know-who is paranoid enough as it is. I'm not having him send people over to check on us. I'll skip that lecture, thanks."

"Well, alright, but let's at least make note of this and try to get back later?"

"Sure, I'd hate to have another fire to deal with. That last one was a pain."

Riana heard them move off, then pause.

"Wait, should we get a quick count of how many crates there are first? You know he's going to ask that."

"Oh. Hmm. That's probably a good idea. I don't want to answer 'lots,' he hates it when we do that. Let's both count, see if end up with the same number."

The guards went over the area twice, counting aloud and pointing at the crates. Riana didn't even dare peep over the edge of the wall, as motion attracted attention faster than anything else. Her bright red hair was only semi-covered in a hat right now as well, as it had been knocked askew when she had scrambled up.

Fortunately, they were satisfied with their count and left within minutes, heading along their patrol route, discussing what their boss would do when he learned about this. Riana continued to breathe shallowly until they were nearly out of hearing range and only then did she dare to lift her head. ::Safe to move?::

::Give them another minute. They're almost

completely out of sight. See anyone else?::

Panning the area, she took a good, hard look and strained her hearing. ::No.::

::Time for me to move, then.:: Ash shifted the crates back quickly, maximizing speed over silence, and made it to the top of the wall in record time. Even then, Riana felt sure that time was their enemy and every movement he made took far too long.

As soon as he gained the top, Ash threw a magical line over the outer edge of the wall, giving them a rope to climb down with. Riana scampered down and didn't breathe easily until they were on the opposite street of the palace road, well away from the watchmen. Only then did she feel like her nerves weren't going to snap from stress.

They paused on a side street, only shadows cloaking them, so they were hardly in the clear yet. Riana started to suggest hiring a night carriage when Ash blew out a breath and whirled, hugging her tight to him. He was overflowing with elation and relief, adrenaline still spiking. "I can't believe we just did that."

"Broke in and out of the palace grounds or transcended into telepathy?" she asked, hugging him back just as hard. "Both are the stuff of legends."

"Both. Either." Laughing, he pulled back a few inches and then kissed her soundly on the lips.

Riana blinked. Granted, the kiss was nice, but.... "Now you kiss me?"

"Blame it on the adrenaline." Leaning in, he kissed her again, more thoroughly this time, lips lingering.

Since her mouth was rather occupied, she had to scold him mentally. ::Your romantic timing is off, darling.::

::I can stop, if you wish?::

::Do and die.:: Now that he had finally made a move, Riana would skewer him if he tried to go back to being merely wizard-partners. She would have elaborated on this, but the kiss was a very nice one indeed and demanded her full attention. Winding her arms around his neck, Riana settled into a moment of pure enjoyment.

CHAPTER TWENTY-TWO

Edvard took the news of Maddox and his northern approach with a bellow, some cursing, and tossing several reports into the air. He looked ready to flip a few tables as well, but Tierone and Bria were seated there, and he did not dare cross either sibling. "A thousand soldiers! Maddox is up there with a thousand soldiers?! What are we going to do?"

The mini caller sitting on the table lit up with Ashlynn's voice. "There's only one thing to do. We have to put in a mobile barrier like we have for the southern border."

Broden saw sense as soon as she said it. There was no other way to protect both areas without running their wizards ragged. They were nearly exhausted as it was, trying to maintain a traditional barrier around Ganforth day and night. Granted, the academy had its own barrier locked onto the building, so they could evacuate into it if they needed to, but it would be a very tight squeeze. It would not be something they could do long term.

Bracing himself against the table top, Edvard asked, "Can you get it up quickly?"

"Actually, Master started building this in between the other three things he's juggling. He has part of it up already. If I can steal three people and do something makeshift, I think we can pull it off in a day. It's not as big of an area as the southern border—we don't need as much time to build it. Assuming that Lorcan and Kirsty can keep the wall up and functioning as they have been, of course."

Everyone let out a breath of relief.

"That's good," Tierone agreed, "but what about the channel? We can't close that off completely, that's where most of our food is coming from these days. Also, the barrier that you erect, will it rest on top of the water? Or does it penetrate below it?"

"Here's the bad part. It will recognize the water's surface as something 'solid' and will stop there. So someone could theoretically swim under the barrier. If they figure out that weakness."

Knowing their luck, someone eventually would. "But for now, lass, can we erect a wall that will cover the distance over the channel, something that can be popped up and taken down again at will?"

"Yes, I think so. It'll have to be sphere shaped, as angles will make it complicated, and it'll take more than a little redesigning and some finagling, but it can be done. That part will take more time, but still, not more than two days. Broden, did our pirate messenger give us a timeline?"

"The lad no' be much further ahead than the army, lass. He be on foot after all. He can move faster than a marching army, but no' by much."

"Curse Lugh's hands. So we'll have to maintain the barrier we have up right now and work to put the new one in place at the same time. That will be a severe magical drain."

"Work in shifts," Catriona urged. "Take breaks as you need them. We can't afford for anyone to collapse right now."

"Oh trust me, we all know it. And we're taking precautions. We're also letting the students do as much of the magical grunt work as possible to offset the burden. Still, this is going to be close in more than one sense. Edvard, Tierone, if you have any fighting men that can come over here and look menacing, I'd appreciate it."

"We'll send what we can, of course," Tierone promised her. "But there's not many to send at the moment."

"I know."

They all did, and there was no need for anyone to elaborate or explain further.

Thinking frantically, Broden tried to come up with something else they could do. Only one thought sprang to mind: "Can we no' try and sabotage the supplies?"

The whole room stopped and then looked at him appraisingly.

"That's true," Tierone approved, nodding his head slowly, a grin taking over his face. "They're out there with no support or backup of any sort. Their lifeline is those supply ships. Perhaps some guerilla warfare is in order. Let's see if we can sabotage those supplies. Who should go?"

"Not Broden," Ashlynn stated firmly.

In a stage whisper, Catriona told her brothers, "You really need to stop sending him out without Ashlynn. She absolutely hates it."

"You realize that every time I've tried, she just goes with him?" Edvard whispered back in exasperation. "I'm not sending Broden. No point in even trying."

Broden had to bite back a chuckle. "How about Amber? Lass has a good head on her shoulders, she should be able to round a few people up and do some fine skulkery."

The brother kings exchanged glances, found that the other had no objection, and turned in unison to Broden. "Send her," they said in one voice.

"Playing twins, boys?" Ashlynn drawled.

Tierone grinned, not that she could see it, and retorted: "I blame you and Ash. Bad influence. Who wants to tell her the mission?"

"Now as to that, it be best I go," Broden volunteered. "Being as I know the lay of the land a mite better than the pair of ye, as well as a few spots that be suited for chicanery."

"We'll leave it to you." Edvard puffed out his cheeks in a clear sign of stress and strain. "I do wish we had more of a plan than that, but we're too tightly stretched in our resources to do much more. I wish those rumored Overan mercenaries were real. I could certainly use them right now."

"Perhaps our anonymous benefactor will send them on the next shipment," Tierone joked with a grim smile. "But in the meantime, let's do what we can to stay alive. Do we all know what needs to be done? Yes? Then let's stop talking about it and go do it."

Amber Bragdon took the news of this assignment with a feral smile that sent a shiver up Broden's spine. "Sounds like a fine idea to me."

Eyeing her askance, he said slowly, "Ye seem a mite...enthused at the idea?"

"I absolutely hate being on the defensive," she responded with perfect loathing. "Some offensive tactics will make me much happier. Who do I get to take?"

Since she by and large had the most dangerous part of the plans, Broden did not see the sense in being stingy. "Ye take who ye'd like, lass. Try no' to yank someone away from a mission critical task, that be all I ask. And keep yer party small."

"No sense in bringing a lot of men with me," Amber agreed in perfect accord. "Just makes it harder to sneak around with. I'll take five, is that alright?"

"Bless ye, lass, that be fine. Have ye a notion on who to take?"

She stopped and stared absently at the army hovering outside their gates. Broden had caught her at the end of her shift, meaning she'd been on lookout at the top of the wall since daybreak that morning. She did not seem at all tired, however. Likely the thought of beating up a few enemies had pumped new energy into her. "Tant, Marissa,

Konrath, and Seth," she rattled off.

Broden blinked. That was exactly the people he had drawn on to do a rescue mission not so long ago. Seeing the mischievous glint in her eyes, he grinned at her. "Aye, lass, we know for a fact they be good people to take along on an adventure."

"Aye, that they be," she riposted, bouncing on her toes. "Can I have them?"

"As far as I am aware, they be free of any heavy responsibilities. Ye should be able to. When do ye want to leave?"

"I want to question our pirate messenger first, get some more details from him," Amber started ticking points off on her fingers, "and of course sit down with you and get an idea of where we can set up ambushes and traps. Gather up our own supplies, get a full night's rest—we'll need it later—and such. Tomorrow late morning?"

Even that seemed like not enough time, considering they were late in the afternoon now. But he trusted her to get the job done. "That be fine. Go contact yer people, I'll round up our messenger," and his payment, "and meet ye at Troi's office."

"Which one, city office or castle?"

"Manor house. Likely more quiet." Not to mention more spacious. The city office for the spymaster was chock full of people, so much so that squeezing a louse in there took considerable skill.

Nodding agreement and understanding, she bounced down the stairs and headed off, searching for her people. Broden watched her go with a shake of the head. It might be astronomical odds stacked against her, but it was not her he felt sorry for.

Those poor Iyshian soldiers would not know what hit them.

CHAPTER TWENTY-THREE

"I could not have heard that right," Ash declared, eyes threatening to bulge out of his head. "You want us to do what?"

"Try breaking into the treasury again," Woelfel repeated with an understanding smile on his face. "Hear me out, I have good reason."

Riana pinned him with a Look. "For this, you'd better have amazing and outstanding reasons."

Woelfel had hit them with this as they sat down to breakfast, and Mrs. Pennington gave him quite the glare for interrupting the meal, even as she sat a plate in front of him. Just like a child being scolded, Woelfel defended himself. "I know, Penny, but this is important! And we don't have a lot of time."

"You can spare five minutes to eat properly, Master Cyr." Still giving him that reproving look, she went back to the buffet and prepared plates for everyone else.

How many years had she been with Woelfel? The way these two acted, it was more like mother and son. Riana did wonder sometimes. Perhaps she'd find a moment to pry a little. "Thank you, Mrs. Pennington, that looks grand. Alright, Woelfel, tell me why you want us to risk life and limb breaking into a place that we couldn't actually enter the first time?"

"It turns out it was a bad night to attempt it," Woelfel explained, carefully swallowing before speaking and with a weather eye on Pennington as he did so. "I learned this morning that they were moving money in and out of the treasury when you two went in. They do this at night to prevent witnesses and for safety precautions. On a regular night, you wouldn't see near as many guards and even the palace patrol wouldn't be as hefty."

While all of that sounded reasonable, it did beg the question: "And why are we attempting this again?"

Grimly, Woelfel reported, "I received a pigeon last night from Troi after you two went to bed. Maddox has appeared north of Ganforth with a thousand troops."

Ash swore aloud and buried both hands into his hair, gripping it strong enough to rip strands out of the roots. "Tell me they stopped him."

"Yes, fortunately, they were able to manage somehow. Troi warns that all it did was buy them time. We must find a way to stop Maddox in his tracks. Unfortunately, there's only one of two ways to stop an army that is already deployed: you either defeat it or you bankrupt it."

"No funds, no supplies, and a soldier cannot fight," Ash agreed. "We can't defeat them. Our only option is to bankrupt them." A wash of exhaustion swept through him.

Riana felt the same, for they had been fighting uphill a long time without any real relief. Still, they couldn't falter now. To her, it felt like the twelfth hour. In fairytales, it was always at this point, when things were bleakest, that the situation would take an unexpected turn for the better. Surely the evil spell would be broken soon, they just had to persevere. ::Ash. Are you taking the world onto your shoulders again?::

He peeked at her, mouth quirked up on one side that might have been a sorry attempt at a smile. ::Trying not to, but...Riana. Truly, what are we supposed to do in this situation? 'Storm the treasury' isn't really a viable option.::

::Then we come up with one. But do not slump in on yourself so. We'll manage fine, as always.::

"Are the two of you seriously having a telepathic conversation in front of me?" Woelfel demanded incredulously. His eyes bounced back and forth between them, jaw dangling.

With a wink, Riana answered, "If you're desperate enough, you can do anything."

"Desperate enough?" Woelfel pounced on that with open glee. "Oh, do tell me the story. Does it have romance? Action? The best stories have a combination of those."

Sighing, Ash tried to redirect him. "Shouldn't we figure out what to do first?"

"No, absolutely not," Woelfel denied with a somber countenance that didn't fool a single person in the room. "This is vital information that I absolutely must have. Our whole mission might depend on it."

Ash gave up and went back to eating, letting Riana tell the story. She did so with flair, having had many years of story-telling practice, as it was the only past-time in Cloud's Rest during the winter. It didn't escape her notice that most of the staff found reasons to either be in the room or linger in the hallway as she told the tale. Then again, she wasn't surprised. Her joke to Ash about them becoming legendary with their partnership had a solid base of truth to it after all.

Woelfel stayed glued all the way through the end and he had a smile stretching from ear to ear. "Wonderful. Truly. She's right, though, you have no sense of romantic timing, Fallbright."

The wizard gave him an amused look, shrugged, and went back to eating.

"Now that you've broken through that barrier, you can speak casually to each other?" Woelfel pressed more seriously. "It's not straining or taxing in any way?"

"Not really," Riana responded, and realizing that she needed to eat before the food got cold completely, picked up her fork again. "It takes a mite of concentration, is all."

"It's more like we're mentally switching from one track to another," Ash sought to explain. "Say, if you were speaking in a foreign language, you would phrase the words in your head first, correct? Because it's not completely natural to you. It's similar to that."

"Ah. Yes, that makes complete sense. I assume that with enough practice, you'll not even need to concentrate."

"Perhaps," Riana agreed.

"Although we'll have to be careful," Ash warned casually. "The few records I've read from partners that were as close as us had a few warnings to pass onto the next generation. Most of them all said the same thing—that eventually, our thoughts would just bleed over to the other without any real intention. If we don't keep some kind of guide on it, it'll become very confusing."

Now there was a thought. Riana tried to imagine what that would be like and made a face. "I don't much care for that idea."

"Right? My head's confusing enough without your thoughts mixing in. Let's try and prevent that from happening."

"Agreed." Riana stabbed her last sausage and asked Woelfel, "Can we go back to the original subject? We need to bankrupt Iysh. How do we do so? Raiding the treasury will not be an easy task for two people."

"And we don't dare risk my position, so I can't go in with you," Woelfel agreed in perfect agreement. "You're right. I thought, the best we could do is perhaps buy Estole the help it needs. Can you break in and steal the funds needed to hire those mythical Overan mercenaries that everyone thinks we have?"

It really wasn't a bad thought. "It sounds viable to me but how much money does that take?"

"I think we should just take as much as we can," Ash disagreed. "That way we can hire as many as possible and if—heaven bless us—we have extra money left over, we can send supplies home."

She didn't even have to think over this suggestion. It was a good one. "Let's do it. Tonight?"

"We might as well," Ash concurred. "The truth is, we don't have a lot of time to play around with, and we've already done our reconnaissance on the place, so we know what we're getting into. Woelfel, we'll need to come up with some method of hauling large amounts of money out with us. I don't like the idea of us clinking about as we're trying to scale walls."

Woelfel chuckled at some inner vision. "Wouldn't that be a sight to behold. But point taken. Let's devise something today while we're waiting for night to fall. I take it that you'll want to leave in the bird hours of the morning again?"

"Not at four o'clock," Riana denied, mentally mapping out logistics and timelines. "Perhaps two o'clock instead. We need more than five minutes inside the treasury after all."

"Good point. Then let's plan for two o'clock." Woelfel rubbed his hands together briskly. "In the meantime, let's do some planning before you take a nap. You'll need the rest for tonight."

The break-in onto the palace grounds was worlds different this time. There were only half as many guards on patrol, to start with, and the silence of the main courtyards could have put a graveyard to shame. It actually spooked Riana. She felt like an ambush waited for them. She became hyper sensitive to every sensation around her, so much so that even a change in the wind had the fine hairs on the back of her arms standing up.

::I don't think there's an ambush here,:: Ash reassured her as he slipped further away from the side gate. ::Though I admit the silence is oppressive.::

::That be an understatement.:: Riana hated every second of this. And if it was just for Edvard's whim, she would have turned around on the spot and marched right back to Woelfel's house. Only the direness of the situation forced her to go on.

The path seemed shorter this time. Perception and memory was strange that way. They reached the corner that led toward the treasury far faster than they had last time, and Riana paused, peeking around carefully to canvas the area.

No one.

Frowning, she asked Ash, ::I know that Woelfel said the night we were here be a bad one, that there were more guards than usual, but is it not strange that there is not a single guard at all?::

::Strange is an understatement.:: Ash frowned, cuddling in close to her back like he had before. ::Let's pause and watch for a while.::

Riana felt better about waiting for a moment to see if a guard was just temporarily out of sight. She couldn't help but question, ::Why do ye keep cuddling up like this?::

::I'm cold.::

Snorting, Riana decided to let that one pass.

They waited more than a few minutes and still no trace of movement or sound from the treasury building. That sent Riana's already taut nerves singing. Something was very, very wrong with this picture. ::Let's edge in closer.::

::Riana, I don't like the look of this.::

::Ye be telling me? This smells.::

Ash stepped out and led the way, moving from shadow to shadow. He paused right behind the treasury building, not within its shadow, but close to it. Riana hovered right at his back, looking at every angle, hearing strained. Nothing. No, she didn't like the look of this at all.

::I hate to say this, but there aren't even any traces of magical protection up either. I can see where the spells used to be, but they're all disabled now.::

Riana gave the back of his head an incredulous look. ::Ye be jesting.::

::I wish I was.:: Ash turned his head just enough to meet her eyes, barely visible in the wan lighting of the moon overhead. ::Your call. Do we try the doors or not?::

As much as her instincts said to run for it, they couldn't afford to. If it really was an ambush, she and Ash would simply have to fight their way out. ::We have to try.::

::I was afraid you'd say that.:: Taking in a breath, he skirted around another elongated shadow and made it to the back of the treasury.

Security dictated that a fortified building like this only have one door to guard. So they had to walk around the front of the building, in plain view of the whole courtyard, in order to get in. Riana was sure her heart would fail before they actually reached the front, but somehow it managed to keep thumping. It threatened to leave her chest altogether because of the strain.

Ash took another breath, then sidled up to the door and grasped the handle. ::Ready? One, two, three!::

Riana was mentally ready for the door to just jangle, locks keeping it secure, but instead the door opened on noiseless hinges. What? Brows compressed, she slipped inside the building right behind Ash. Once inside, she paused, eyes adjusting to the total darkness.

::Wait,:: Ash directed. ::I can see with my glasses.::

Those fancy bespelled glasses of his were useful in more than one circumstance, fortunately. With them on, Ash had the eyes of a cat.

She heard him slip them on, then he cursed aloud in the foulest language she had ever heard from his mouth. ::ASH!::

"You can talk, Riana. There's nothing in here."

Almost afraid to ask, and truly not sure she wanted to hear the answer, she pressed, "What do you mean, nothing?"

"I mean nothing. No ambush, no people, and absolutely no money. The treasury is completely empty."

CHAPTER TWENTY-FOUR

"Empty?!" Woelfel parroted in complete bafflement. He kept shaking his head, as if he didn't believe his ears and was trying to clear them out a little. "I'm sorry, what do you mean by empty?"

"I mean exactly that, empty." Ash flopped into a chair next to the fireplace, taking a moment to get off his feet. Riana joined him, just as tired and cold. It neared dawn now, and she was feeling the effects of being up multiple nights keenly. Ash silently made way for her in the oversized wingback chair, an arm around her waist even as he tried to elaborate. His voice was heavy and laden with exhaustion, words slower than normal. "Empty shelves, empty chests, empty desks. The room is completely wiped of all funds. I believe the first night we were there, what we were seeing was not a transfer of money into the treasury, but from."

Woelfel dropped into the chair across from him, still stunned. "A government's bank is completely empty?"

"We really should have tried to get a better view of the front door that first night," Riana observed to no one in particular. "If we had, we'd have seen the transfer ourselves and not be blind-sided like this."

"Or we'd have been caught," Ash disagreed, not sounding bothered by the possibility. "It was difficult enough getting out as it was."

True. Riana was too tired to debate the point and let her head drop onto his shoulder. Cushioned between the fire and Ash, she was warming up nicely, comfortable enough that her eyes started to droop closed.

"We need to report this to Estole immediately." Regaining his energy, Woelfel popped up to his feet. "I don't know the cause, we'll definitely have to investigate this, but Edvard's wish has come true—Iysh is bankrupt."

"No, that's not quite what he was aiming for," Ash corrected, struggling to stay awake. "He wanted to bankrupt Iysh enough that they couldn't afford to send an army."

"They likely bankrupted themselves sending the army," Riana opined, eyes closed. Truly, it was marvelously comfortable right here.

"Riana, don't fall asleep there," Ash warned. "You'll wake up with a crick in your neck."

Drat it, the man made a good point. She forced her eyes back open. "So what does this mean? We can't steal any money to pay for mercenaries."

"Unfortunately correct," Woelfel growled, vexed. "That would have been handy. It also means, however, that Maddox is not going to be able to keep his army in the field for much longer. He's already been out, what? A month?"

Ash disagreed, "Depends on what you're considering the starting point to be. But we can't make any calculations on how long he can fight. We're not sure how much money he took with him to begin with."

"But we can guess, and even a rough estimation is good enough until we can put our hands on accurate numbers. If Iysh is truly wiped out, then Maddox can't stay up there any real time at all. This isn't a siege—it's a waiting game to see who will crumble first. The only real question is, can the army find a way around the barrier before their time runs out?"

Riana prayed that they couldn't. "We have to trust that they can't. But while we're looking for those numbers, we need to find the reason why Iysh is suddenly bankrupt as well. This is beyond strange to me. We've seen no sign that they're in dire financial straits."

"That is true," Woelfel agreed, sinking back into his seat. The way he popped up and down with false energy inclined Riana to think he was sleep-deprived like the rest of them and punch-drunk because of it. "It's a good question. Really, if they are so broke, then why is the Court functioning like it always is? Why haven't we seen any sign of depression here in the city? Why is no one talking about funds being tight, or doing cutbacks, or some sort of economical reforms?"

"Perhaps Iysh still has money, it's just been moved elsewhere?" Ash ventured uncertainly. "Although that begs the question why."

"Why indeed. We definitely need to investigate this. I'll start sending out queries to my colleagues immediately."

A stray thought popped out of her mouth before she could even think it through. "I wonder if this is why they only sent the wizard assassins that one time?"

Both men looked at each other for a moment before cottoning on. "Ah, you mean that time they attacked the barrier while it was being set up?" Ash asked. "Yes, that was odd, just a single occurrence. Everyone was sure it would happen again, but oddly enough they didn't try it."

"Perhaps they didn't have the money to try it," Woelfel agreed thoughtfully. "It does take serious coin to hire wizards, even the nefarious sorts. Perhaps you're on to something, Saira. Well. In the interim, what do we report home?"

Riana envisioned Troi's and Edvard's possible response to a message and winced. "If we say 'treasury empty but we don't know why' it will not go over well."

"Edvard will be delighted, at least at first. Troi will tear his hair out," Ash stated certainly. "But either way we need to tell them. Even if we don't know why, or aren't sure where the money's gone, they need to know that something is seriously amiss."

"I'm not saying we stay silent until we have all the answers," Woelfel assured him. "I'm just wondering how to phrase our report. We can't do a long, involved message by courier pigeon."

More's the pity. "Let's use rice paper to cut down the weight and write as much as we can."

"I vote Ash writes the note." Woelfel volunteered him with a sadistic smile.

"Why me?" Ash protested. "I've been sneaking in and out of palace compounds, I'm tired!"

Woelfel was quick with his rebuttal, tone matter of fact. "You have the smallest handwriting out of all of us and Troi needs a firsthand account."

Riana could feel Ash's vast reluctance to do anything that required brain power. All the man wanted was his bed, and she didn't blame him. Nearly whining, he demanded, "Do I have to?"

"The sooner it's done, the sooner you can go to bed," Riana encouraged, getting up so that she could pull him bodily out of the chair.

Groaning and mumbling inarticulately, Ash staggered his way to the desk and pulled out a thin sheet of rice paper and a pen. Riana stayed at his shoulder and read as he wrote. Right now, Ash's mind wasn't at its sharpest, and she wanted to make sure that he included all of the details that he should. Well, that and the fact that she wasn't sure anything he wrote right now would make sense.

Woelfel patiently waited, and when it was done, picked the sheet up and read through it himself. He nodded in satisfaction at the end. "Good enough. I'll send this off. Go to bed, both of you. I'll wake you if there's any news."

"You don't have to tell us twice," Ash grumbled, and stumbled out of the study.

Riana, feeling like she was eighty, followed right behind him. This spy business was fun, unquestionably, but it could certainly take it out of a person.

The blankets were warm, the mattress soft, the dream pleasant and lighthearted, and Riana lay in the perfect sleeping position so that not even one joint had the slightest discomfort. She was deeply asleep without any desire to wake up anytime soon.

Something roughly grabbed her by the shoulders and bounced her hard against the mattress, jerking her back into the waking world. "RIANA!"

That was Woelfel's voice and he never called her by her true name. Riana had awakened because of the brutal manner in which he'd used, but with that, her mind snapped to full alertness.

"What? Who died?" she demanded frantically, trying to get her balance together enough to stagger out of the bed.

"Not that," Woelfed denied with a frantic shake of the head. "Zelman is calling for you."

For several long seconds, that statement didn't make an ounce of sense. It was like Woelfel was speaking in a foreign language and she didn't know any of the words. "Zelman. As in, King Zelman? Of Iysh?"

"Yes, yes," Woelfel confirmed impatiently. "Are you actually awake?"

"I'm fairly certain I'm not," Riana denied, feeling like her head was spinning. "This has to be a dream. It's too strange."

"I wish it were a dream." Woelfel didn't waste another second trying to convince her, but instead went through the connecting door and into Ash's room. "FALLBRIGHT!"

Riana listened as the two men repeated nearly the same conversation she'd just had, and the sense of realness started to sink in. The King of Iysh wanted to see her? What for? She'd done so many suspicious things since her arrival that it made her paranoia scream. Worried, she sprinted into Ash's room. "Woelfel. How did the summons arrive?"

"By royal messenger. Trust me, if he knew what we were up to, it would have been guards waking you up instead of me."

A very good point. It let her breathe a little easier. "But there was no mention of why?"

"A king doesn't have to explain himself," Woelfel responded impatiently. "Now, get ready. He wants you at the palace in an hour and I know that it takes at least half an hour to get through all of the security and checkpoints to his study."

In that case, she had ten minutes to wash her face and dress. That didn't give her much time at all to look Court presentable. "Woelfel, send me someone to help with my hair, I won't have enough time otherwise."

"Penny is bringing up a pressed dress for you, she'll help."

Bless the man for the foresight. Or perhaps Mrs. Pennington had realized it herself. The woman was marvelously efficient. Either way, Riana couldn't waste another minute and rushed back into her room.

They might have set some sort of speed record in getting her ready. By the time Riana rushed down the stairs, she felt as if she had been in some sort of storm that involved pins and hair combs. Either way, she looked presentable enough to pass muster. Woelfel waited impatiently outside, ready to help her into the carriage, which she hopped into with alacrity. In a thrice they were off, moving at a fast trot through the daily traffic. Riana took a glance out of the window, only just realizing the time. "Is it noon?"

"Just past. You slept about six hours. I hope you got enough rest."

Riana snorted. "Even if I hadn't, there's enough adrenaline in me to keep me wide awake for the next three days."

Woelfel laughed, still tense but regaining his equilibrium. "I feel the same. Royal messengers are enough to scare me, but a summons directly from the king? It's nigh unheard of for a man of my position. I'm not ranked highly enough in Court to be important to him."

"I wish we had some inkling of what he wanted," Riana fretted.

"Just remember, don't make eye contact unless invited to do so by the king himself—twice. Always end speaking with 'Your Majesty.' Listen attentively and try not to disagree with anything he says."

That was a tall order to keep up for any length of time. Riana prayed, for her nerves' sake, that this meeting would be brief.

Entering the palace grounds during normal hours was—no pun intended—a day and night difference. There was activity, people, noise, work, and idleness mingled together from all the different classes as they went about their usual routines. Riana paid scant heed to any of it, instead trying to mentally rehearse at least the opening greeting to the king so she didn't make a farce of it.

The carriage stopped, a messenger met them at the door, and they were ushered straight through a side door that she'd had no idea existed. It did not lead to the elaborate rooms that she had been in previously but instead to a western wing that somehow seemed simpler and colder in comparison. There wasn't as much gold gilding in the molding, or statuary; that likely lent to her impression.

It was a very short walk down a broad hallway and into the first door on their right. The door actually stood open, so the messenger stepped right through, then took a side step to the right before bowing and announcing, "Lady Saira Vaulx and Lord Cyr Woelfel, Your Majesty."

Riana gulped in a breath, lifted her chin, and sailed through.

Damp air and smoke, that was her first impression. A roaring fire was in the fireplace off to her right, and it wasn't drawing quite right, so that smoke hovered around the ceiling of the room. No windows were open to help with this, leaving the air heavy and stuffy. There was a broad expanse of carpet, soft and thick, that led straight to a massive wooden desk that was strangely empty of anything but a single map.

Behind it paced Zelman.

This was Riana's first close up look at the king, as she had done her best to avoid him before this, and she had to admit she wasn't very impressed: a short, dumpy figure with thinning grey hair, a waxy complexion and an unnatural flush to his cheeks. The clothes he wore were expertly tailored to his frame—and she could not fault the tailors, but the man did not look like a king. More like a merchant, and one in dire straits, at that.

Remembering Woelfel's advice, she ducked into a deep curtsey and did not lift her head. "Your Majesty, it is a great pleasure to make your acquaintance."

"Saira Vaulx. Raise your head."

She almost did and then remembered, she had to be told that twice.

"I said raise your head, girl!"

What was with that angry tone? A sinking feeling in her stomach, she lifted her head. "Can I be of assistance, Your Majesty?"

"I hope so. I bloody well hope so! You're from Senn, yes? That's what I'm told."

"That's correct, Your Majesty." Riana shot Woelfel a look. Why would he ask that?

Zelman slammed a palm on top of the map. "Senn. Senn intends to secede from Iysh, doesn't it?!"

Well, they did, but how did he know that? Riana gave him a baffled expression, hands spread out in a warding gesture. "Your Majesty! What a thing to suggest."

"Don't play me, girl. My treacherous son, Hendrix, has been going around all over this country and speaking with people. Senn was the first place he went to. What did he say!"

For the first time in this man's presence, Riana was able to answer honestly, "I haven't the faintest idea, Your Majesty. I was not there when he visited and have heard nothing about it."

Not at all happy with this answer, he pressed, "I've heard reports that people are actually listening to him, although it's only the commoners, and they're not very useful. Still, it is maddening to think that he is trying to undermine me! Are you saying that no one in Senn paid him any attention? Do you dare say that to me?"

Riana hadn't actually heard much, as Troi's messages were naturally truncated in length. They had been able to infer most of what they knew based on his orders to them and the grand plan that they had made beforehand. "Your Majesty, I'm afraid that I cannot help in this circumstance. I have heard nothing from my family about Prince Hendrix's visit."

"PRINCE!" Zelman bellowed and swiped a tray of sliced fruit onto the floor, where it clattered and bounced in every direction. "Don't call that misbegotten whelp a prince! I do not acknowledge him! The day he was born, I should have strangled him and his mother! I knew the moment she announced her pregnancy that I would have nothing but trouble from him!"

Zelman picked up a glass from a water tray nearby and heaved it into the fireplace, making Riana jump. He started bellowing again, but this time he spoke with such fervor and speed that she couldn't make out more than one word out of three. She watched in growing amazement as a man in his late fifties behaved like a three-year-old.

No wonder the country was falling apart if this short-tempered man was running things.

After the first fifteen minutes, his behavior changed from entertaining to tedious. If she hadn't had a cover to protect, Riana would have either marched out or clobbered him first to shut him up. Instead, she was forced to stand there until he tired of his own voice. Her eyes glazed over, attention wandering, although she made sure to keep facing him and acting as if she were listening.

Two hours dragged by and he finally tired, sagging into a chair. Stabbing a finger at the door, he rasped, "Out. And the minute you hear from your family, tell me every single word they say about that lout."

"Of course, Your Majesty," Riana promised. She dipped into a quick curtsey and then made a swift escape.

Neither she nor Woelfel dared to breathe or speak a word until they were safely back in their own carriage and heading back to the townhouse. Only then did Riana heave out a breath and demand, "That idiot is a king?"

"Well, why do you think Edvard had such an easy time seceding?" Woelfel responded jovially. "And why so many were willing to follow him? Zelman's temper is legendary, second only to his stupidity. As tedious as that whole experience was, it conveys two very important things: one, he has no idea that you and Ash have been inside his treasury, which is very telling."

Yes, it was. Also heartening.

"Second, Hendrix is apparently making amazing headway in his conquest of Iysh. It's a bloodless one, yes, but an effective one. His persuasion to overturn Zelman must be extensive if the king is that agitated about it." Woelfel's expression fell into what Riana thought of as his 'Zigzag' face, the one where the spy's mind was obvious. "It's good news all around and we need to make sure to report it to Troi as soon as we're back."

While she agreed, Riana's paranoia planted a niggling doubt. "You don't think this is a trap of some sort, do you? That Zelman is manipulating us into sending word back to Estole to prove that we're spies?"

"I highly doubt it," Woelfel denied reassuringly. "He isn't the type to acquire proof when he suspects someone. He just arrests them and has the Courts sort the matter out. Besides, if someone does question us about it, we can say that we were sending a quick message home, asking about Prince Hendrix. We were hoping to give Zelman better information to go off of."

It was a plausible story, especially since the bird would be flying in that general direction anyway. "So no need to worry."

"Not about the bird at least." In a rare flash of black humor, Woelfel quipped, "The question stands as such: which will fail first? Zelman's sanity or Estole's walls?"

CHAPTER TWENTY-FIVE

The problem with high society was that their clocks were reversed. Riana had spent her entire life getting up with the sun and going to bed with the moon. The nobility in Iysh seemed to find getting up before eleven o'clock in the morning to be sacrilegious, and they were perfectly fine partying until three in the morning. Riana still struggled to adapt to this very different pacing and was not doing that well with it. Somewhere around midnight she started to feel tired, and by one, normally ready to call it quits. But of course, she couldn't, not if there were still people she could talk to and information she could wrangle.

This night was such a night. The party was still going strong even though it neared one, and it showed no signs of slowing down. Riana was beyond tired, however, and needed twenty minutes to just sit somewhere quiet. Even ten minutes would do. A quiet, cool place where she could put her feet up.

Fortunately, her tour with Bexton (and Savir)

had shown her some of the nooks and crannies that were not obvious at first glance. They were not in the main ballroom this time, but in an open atrium encased in glass, all so that they could see the winter sky. There were many hothouse plants in here, so that it felt more like early spring than winter. Riana went looking for a particular bed of white roses that hid a discreet door. There it was.

She slipped sideways past a crowd of tipsy ladies, opening the door just far enough to pass through and closed it quickly behind her. Ah, blessed silence. The room she had entered only had a fireplace with embers in the hearth, a small round table and three chairs situated about it. This place was meant for anyone that just needed a breather or perhaps a discreet meeting place. It suited her needs perfectly in that moment.

Sitting, she angled the other chair so she could prop her feet up and sighed relief. The blood pounded in the soles of her feet, indicating that they were likely swelling. Strange, she never had this problem in her worn-in boots, but these heeled shoes the ladies insisted on wearing fatigued her calves and feet every time she wore them more than a few hours. Why did women do this to themselves?

The door opened and a man slipped in. Riana just about jumped out of her chair when she realized that Savir had followed her in.

"Stay comfortable," he encouraged, juggling two glasses in his hands. "I saw you sneak in here and thought you needed a minute away from the crowd. So do I."

Riana wasn't sure if she really should leave

her feet propped up on a chair in the presence of a prince, but he said to stay comfortable... and he was handing her a hot tea that smelled wonderfully of citrus. Deciding to go with the flow, she took it and didn't move a muscle. "Ah, that's delightful."

"My favorite tea. The honey is good for a throat that has been overworked." He gave her a wink. "You're a popular woman, Lady Saira. Everyone wants to speak with you."

"I do feel blessed they feel so," Riana responded after another long sip of the delightful tea. Was there more than lemon in this? Ginger, perhaps? There was a slight zing on her tongue. "It just gets a little exhausting from time to time."

"I do understand."

She regarded him openly and for once tried to see it from his perspective. To be surrounded by people that wanted your attention, day in, day out, with no true respite your entire life... "Yes, I suppose you do."

"I'm glad I saw you duck in here. I wanted to ask, how are you? I understand that my father had a private audience with you the other day."

And he was extremely curious what that meeting was about. She could tell. "I'm somewhat confused on what the audience was for, to be honest. His Majesty did little more than confirm that I am from Senn before he went off on a tirade about Prince Hendrix. I confess I followed very little of what he said." She licked her lips and dared to press her luck. "How long has His Majesty...um...."

"Been a raving lunatic?" Savir finished the

question wearily. "I'm afraid for some time. He had bouts of depression and wild mood swings during my teenage years, but it wasn't until roughly six years or so ago, that he completely lost it. He does seem bent on blaming Hendrix for everything that goes wrong as well, although the heavens know why."

Perhaps it was the intimate setting they were in. Perhaps it was because he had brought her a cup of tea. Or perhaps it was because it was late at night and they both were tired of the crowds. Whatever the cause, Savir was far more open with her tonight than she had ever seen him. "I've heard that he exiled Prince Hendrix from the Court, but I never was given a reason for it."

"Me. I was the reason." Savir shook his head, expression becoming reminiscent. "Technically Hendrix is my half-brother, of course, as Queen Rosalind is not my biological mother. But we never felt that way, Maddox and I. She is our mother, and a good one to us. Hendrix has always been our little brother. We were incredibly close as children, more so I think because our father always seemed cold to Hendrix. We didn't understand the cause then and as an adult I confess myself still baffled by the attitude. The disobedient one was not Hendrix, but Maddox. He was forever stirring up trouble and getting into things that wreaked havoc."

Now that was an interesting piece of news. She also found it interesting that Savir's expression had softened in speaking of Hendrix. "Do you feel more distant with him as an adult?"

"Yes and no. I barely know him as an adult.

He was banished more or less from Court when he was eighteen. I haven't seen much of him in five years. And the stupid reason why he was banished? Because I told Father point blank I had no intention of inheriting the throne." Savir let out a soft sigh, weary and regretful. "Really, I thought it obvious. He preferred Maddox, everyone knew that, but for some reason he had it in his head that we three brothers should be competing with each other for the throne. What for? Why start that kind of internal conflict? There was no need for it. Neither Hendrix nor I wanted the throne."

"Was he perhaps frustrated at your lack of ambition?" It was the only reason that Riana could think of.

"Perhaps? But just because a man doesn't have a particular goal in mind doesn't mean he lacks ambition. I have plenty. It's just the throne I don't want." Savir shook the question aside. "At any rate, after that, Father raved for days. He was almost physically violent, he was so upset. Hendrix was the only one brave enough to step in and tell him that I had every right to choose some other path. That I wouldn't be a good ruler anyway. And he's quite right. A good ruler, the best king, loves people. Seeks them out, talks to them, wants to be in their company. I do well with them but there are also times—" he looked around in illustration "—that I need to escape from them and rest."

Riana thought of Edvard. There was not an hour that went by that he wasn't speaking to someone, unless one of his siblings had forced him to take a nap. The man thrived on being in people's company. She thought she understood what Savir meant. It took a certain personality type to thrive as the ruler of people and Savir didn't have it. He was wise to recognize that and seek a path more suited for him. "And for his support of your wishes, King Zelman threw him out."

"Sadly, yes. It caused a terrific rift in between my parents. Mother encouraged Hendrix to leave the Court, to travel about the country and do what good he could, partially to keep him safely away from Father."

So it had not been a true exile? Well, not initially. Riana had wondered about that, as Hendrix had been able to return to Court from time to time, he'd mentioned that. He just hadn't been able to stay.

"My mother doesn't speak to him unless something forces her to. Zelman now believes Hendrix talked me out of competing for the throne and blames my lack of ambition on him. Madness, all of it." Savir took a long pull from his cup and hummed approval. "I do love this tea. It's very calming."

"Yes, so it is." Riana was dying to figure out the recipe so she could make it again. "You don't strike me as the type to let the situation fester."

He toasted her with the cup. "You are perceptive, my lady. Indeed, I have no intention of doing so. I have plans in place, they'll just take a while longer to bear fruition."

Now that might be the most interesting thing she had learned this evening. "You won't tell me what they are, will you."

"I cannot." He smiled to take the sting out of it. "I can, however, provide a distraction so that we may linger here in comfort. How about a game of cards?"

She eyed the stack that he pulled out of his pocket. "You have no intention of rejoining the party, do you?"

"Not in the slightest."

She came home at nearly three in the morning, completely dead on her feet and more than ready to just fall face first into her pillow. Savir might have rescued her from talking to a hundred people but the man was intense in his own right. She made it all of three steps inside the townhouse before Ash waylaid her.

"You're just getting home? Do you know what time it is?"

Riana eyed him wearily. "Far too late. Or far too early. Take your pick."

Ash's frustration mounted. "These social events last far too late in the night. I bet you were flirting with the men again, you look exhausted, and I could tell earlier you were pushing yourself to be charming."

"Ah, that? That was because of Savir." She was tired enough that it took a second before she realized saying that likely didn't help her case. Not that she had a case to begin with, but still.

Brows slamming together, Ash growled, "He got you alone again, didn't he?"

Whole truth, half-truth, or full out evasion? "Ash, my darling, can we argue about this when my eyes aren't crossing with fatigue?"

"He did. I can tell." Ash growled like a wounded tiger. "Why does he always seek you out like this?"

"I don't know but he's helping me without realizing it. I've gotten very good information from him, and by association with the prince, everyone talks to me. It's a win-win. Assuming my nerves can hold out."

"I don't want you constantly in his company or flirting with him!" Ash burst out.

Riana strove to be patient but it was hard when she was tired. "I promise you can zap him after this is all over for having the audacity to flirt with me."

"I don't want to zap him later, I want to zap him now." There was an actual pout on the wizard's face.

She didn't say anything. Her look spoke volumes.

"And yes, I realize that I sound like a whinny five-year-old. You can ignore me. Go to bed, you're exhausted." Ash meant every word but his frustrations still pitched and rolled inside him like a ship being tossed in a stormy sea.

Putting both arms around his waist, she leaned against him, trying to channel soothing emotions his direction. "It'll be over soon, Ash. You just have to be patient until then."

"I know. I'm just feeling caged inside this house." He hugged her back, rocking a little from side to side. "It will be over soon. We just have to keep chipping away at Zelman until he crumbles."

From what Riana had seen, Zelman was tottering on the brink of destruction. It wouldn't take much more to push him over the edge.

Ash forced his feelings of frustration and claustrophobia aside and led her toward the stairs. "Come, dearheart, you're swaying on your feet. Go to bed. You still have a lot to do tomorrow. You didn't know when you signed up for this that most of your spywork would consist of flirting with noblemen and princes, did you?"

"And I can't even shoot at the ones that irritate me," she bemoaned, staggering up the stairs. "My feet hurt, too. I don't like the heeled shoes or the wide skirts."

"So the next time that Troi wants you to be a spy for him…?" Ash trailed off hopefully.

"I will tell him absolutely not unless I can shoot people," she stated adamantly.

"That's my girl."

CHAPTER TWENTY-SIX

Riana skirted the outside edges of the ballroom, heading for her next vict—er, potential allies. It had been a semi-productive evening so far, but she'd only been here two hours, and the night was still very young. Her goal was to get at least five people from the older generation to come away from General Quillin's camp and consider Hendrix as a good potential candidate instead. So far doing that had been akin to rolling mud up a hill in a snowstorm, but she at least saw some progress, which made her hopeful. Hendrix was due to come into town at some point, and she wanted him to have a good crowd to speak with when he arrived.

As she did a side-step, making way for a trio of ladies to pass her, she caught a glimpse of Axley and Larcinese coming her direction. Uh-oh. After what had happened last time, she did not want to be anywhere near them. That was not an experience she needed to repeat. Alright, where to run? Or hide? Her eyes darted about and she realized that she had actually passed a balcony door that would lead out to one of the outside terraces. Perfect.

Spinning, she made a beeline for it and darted through the door before swiftly closing it behind her. Phew, safe.

"My dear Lady Saira—"

Her head shot up. Savir?! Spinning, she followed his voice and found him leaning against the balustrade, a wine glass casually twirling in his hand and a sardonic look on his face.

"—we simply must stop meeting in such a clandestine manner," he continued, voice rich with amusement. "If we give the gossips such rich fodder to work with, it'll overexcite them and be bad for their hearts, you understand."

Drat it. Riana regarded him with equal mix of exasperation and amusement. Woelfel told her time and again to not mix with Savir more than she had to, but every time she turned around, there he was. "Your Highness, it's truly remarkable, how many times our paths cross in a single day."

"It truly is." He gave an elaborate look around. "And half the time it's in such dark, secluded corners such as this. My dear lady, if you are trying to seduce me, I must say that I'm perfectly amiable to such."

It was of course at this moment that Ash started paying attention to her emotions and felt something was off. ::Riana, what's wrong?::

She was not about to say "a prince is flirting with me, pay me no mind." ::I'm fine, I'll explain later,:: she sent back firmly. Frantically drawing on her experience with Woelfel and his sometimes irresponsible flirting, she tried to respond in kind, "Your Highness, you do make it so easy to rendezvous with you."

"I do, don't I?" he agreed charmingly. "It's one of those services I try to provide the young ladies."

She choked on a laugh. The rogue. He was an enemy prince, of course he was, but there were moments like these when she found she liked him a little. "I am very disappointed to hear that, Your Highness." She did her best to put on a disappointed face. "Does that mean any young lady would do?"

"Perish the thought," he dismissed. "Of course my dearest wish was to meet with you."

Riana had the hardest time not to roll her eyes. "How very flattering."

"You don't believe me," he mourned, lips twitching. "But I assure you—"

It was at that moment that Riana saw a movement out of the corner of her eye that sent her instincts screaming. There was a glint of metal in the lamplight in a place where metal shouldn't be, a movement and rustle of the bushes that spoke of sneaking, and a general feeling of wrongness that Riana knew well after years of being ambushed by bandits.

She had two seconds to make a decision on what to do. Moving meant blowing her cover, something that had been drilled into her, over and over, to not do under any circumstance. And yet...and yet...

Riana's heart revolted at the idea. Savir was not a bad man. He was not evil. He was, in many ways, remarkably like Hendrix. He had the same kindness, the same intelligence, the same charm if in a different fashion than his brother used. He was a man that was placed in a terrible position and was making the best of it. She could not hate him or think of him only as an enemy.

With that conclusion, it was obvious what she would do, and likely what the consequences would be. Riana threw herself forward, grabbing him by the back of the neck and throwing him down even as she pulled her fan shut with a snap of the wrist. When preparing for this role, she had armed herself similarly to how she had for Edvard's disastrous coronation. The fan was reinforced with steel, her hairpins were likewise weapons, and she had three throwing daggers either in a pocket or strapped to her thigh. If necessary, she'd used them all.

"Wha—" Savir managed, but had the sense to go down and not fight her hold on him.

Riana barely had her fan up in time to block the arrow that came whistling at the very spot where Savir had been standing not a second before. She knocked it aside, as well as the second one that came after it. With Savir obediently staying prostrate on the balcony, she grabbed one of her throwing daggers and threw it with precise aim at the man attacking. It hit with an audible, if truncated, scream of pain. Then the bushes he was hiding behind rustled harshly to the side as he pushed off and made a run for it.

Savir seemed to realize the worst was over as he stood and yelled out, "Night watch! Pursue an injured man running toward the east gate!"

There was a startled pause before a masculine and feminine voice called back, "Roger that!" and then the heavy sound of footsteps running.

"Hopefully they'll catch him before he disappears somewhere," Savir said calmly. "If he's gotten this far inside, he had help, so he might be able to hide somewhere and be smuggled out later."

A distinct possibility. Riana put the second throwing dagger she had palmed back into its holster and took in a calming breath. Well. That had certainly gotten her blood pumping. "Are there many assassins after your life, Your Highness?"

"Far too many. I've grown dangerously immune to them." He gave her a crooked smile. "Many people, you see, realize that I'm the strategist behind my brother. They think to take Maddox down by killing me first. They don't realize that Maddox isn't just a bull that only knows how to charge forward. He's capable in his own right. He's just not as patient as he needs to be sometimes, that's all."

Perhaps Savir saw him better than others, who didn't know Maddox as well. Or perhaps because he loved his brother, he saw him in a better light. Riana was in no place to judge, and saw no need to.

::Riana,:: Ash had a hard tone to his voice, ::why does it feel like you just got into a fight?::

Curse the man's ability to read her. There were definite downsides to their bond sometimes. ::I did. I'll explain later.::

::Now. You'll explain NOW.::

::Can't, I have a curious prince next to me, have to focus on him.::

There was a wordless growl.

"Well, Lady Saira, I admit myself impressed by your combat skills." Savir gave her a study from head to toe. "I must say, I didn't expect such skill from you."

Riana kept her smile at him steady, somehow, even as she frantically tried to come up with a plausible explanation. "You are aware, are you not, that the Land Northward is mostly lawless? Filled with bandits and pirates and the like."

"I am, of course."

"In truth, Senn is close enough to that land that we often saw bandits and pirates." Sticking to mostly the truth, Riana hoped for the best. "My father was very concerned about me being able to protect myself if ever I found myself alone on the road. He made sure I was taught from an early age the basics of combat."

"I must say, such training has served you very well," he applauded. "I will write him a letter personally thanking him for his foresight. For now, however, let us both go inside and report this matter. I want to catch our would-be assassin but also we must let everyone know of your gallantry, yes?"

Riana felt another moment of panic. "We do?"

"Of course, we do," he assured her, taking her by the arm and almost forcefully leading her back inside.

Resigned, she let him.

The night turned out to be exhausting, but not in the way that Riana had initially anticipated. Savir had dragged her straight to the palace Captain of the Guards, where she had dutifully relayed her own account of events. Then of course, the Queen Mother had heard and came over to get her own accounting and to make sure that her son was alright. Riana's hope that would be the end of it was immediately dashed when Greer Dunlap had come over and also demanded to know what happened.

After that, the situation became a badly kept secret, with the whole ballroom learning about it within the course of minutes. The ladies were amazed she knew anything about combat. The lords were impressed by her skills. Woelfel was ready to strangle her, she could tell, but couldn't do it because there were too many witnesses.

Riana was resigned to getting the lecture of all lectures until she found a way to turn it to their advantage. Several of the older generation came to speak with her and asked the whys and whos and whens of her training. Riana, in a flash of brilliance, stated that her father had taught her most of it but Prince Hendrix had taught her how to deflect arrows or throwing knives.

That, finally, gave her the foothold she needed. People were unaware that she had met Prince Hendrix in person or had actually been trained by him and his reputation rose a notch because of the association. After all, a man that would think to train a young girl—who eventually became a woman that protected his brother—was one that had amazing foresight and patience. Why, Zelman would never think to arm a woman in such a way, and look what it had done tonight! It had saved a prince from being assassinated.

Riana left the Court feeling triumphant right up until they climbed into the carriage.

Then, of course, there were no witnesses.

Woelfel pinned a look on her that would have felled a primeval tree. "Riana."

She winced and mentally brought Ash into the conversation, although he could only hear her, of course. "It was instinct." Mostly.

::What was?:: Ash demanded.

::I, ah, sort of saved Savir from an assassination attempt.::

::You did WHAT!::

Riana decided that telling Ash now was a stroke of genius. If she had delayed and waited until she was back, that would have surely destroyed one of her eardrums. As it was, it set her head to ringing.

"Ash is lambasting you right now, isn't he?" Woelfel said knowingly.

"Don't ask questions you already know the answer to," she retorted. "It was instinct. I saw metal gleam, a bush moving strangely, and I knew someone was going to attempt a shot from the shadows."

::Of course you did,:: Ash sighed. ::Bandit-honed instincts.::

::Precisely.:: "I had Savir down on the ground

in a second, deflected two arrows, and got my own dagger out before I even processed what I was doing. And as much as you two might complain, it's turned in our favor, hasn't it?"

Woelfel dearly wanted to chew her out for this, but it had, and he couldn't deny it. Sighing, he let it go with an open palm. "It would have been a disaster if not for your quick thinking. What made you think of bringing Hendrix into this?"

"I remembered Bria telling me that Hendrix actually taught her a little self-defense, and how he had visited Senn first after being more or less exiled from Court. I thought, the timing would be about right, for him to have an 'encounter' with Lady Saira at fifteen or so. Besides, I had no way of reaching the older generation, as they have little reason to like Hendrix. They want someone who knows combat and has a good head for leadership. Why not show that he does have that foresight and skill now, by passing myself off as one of his students?"

There was a contemplative feeling from Ash. ::How well did that work?::

"I feel that it worked well. I at least got people to talk to me tonight that wouldn't do more than a passing greeting before. What do you think, Woelfel?"

"It did seem to work in your favor tonight," Woelfel agreed, perhaps a tad grudgingly. "If we follow up correctly on this, keep the momentum of the thought going, we might be able to weaken the support behind Quillin. It certainly has worked better than everything else we've tried so far."

Riana smiled at him and tried very hard not to gloat.

::You failed. I can feel you gloating from here.::

::Oh, hush.::

"Be that as it may, Riana," Woelfel was back to glowering at her, "try not to make a habit of this, alright? And for the love of mercy, if you see an assassin anywhere near Zelman, don't hinder the man!"

She laughed. "I promise."

CHAPTER TWENTY-SEVEN

Riana did not like summons from Zelman. She in fact hated them. The man had only summoned her once and it turned out to be something of a disaster, so her opinion was entirely justified. This time, however, he had not summoned just her but also key members of the Court and some of the men and women that, while not holding any particular office, still carried a lot of political weight. Why she had been invited, Riana had no clue, but it didn't bode well in her mind.

She arrived at the main throne room with her heart in her throat and a dozen escape routes planned just in case. Ash was on high alert and standing by in an inn not far from the palace gate, ready to burst in if she called for him. Riana desperately prayed it wouldn't come to that.

As she entered the throne room, she found it occupied by perhaps thirty people or so. Every face was one that she recognized as she had spoken to all of them at some point or another. It made her a little insecure to be in this political hot bed without Woelfel at her side, but the liveried servant that had fetched her had made it clear no one else was allowed to come in with her.

Riana tried to stay near the back of the crowd, to be less noticeable. Alas, this failed, as Savir homed in on her location like a homing pigeon. He slid in to a vacant spot next to her and whispered, "Do you know why you're here?"

"I haven't the faintest notion, Your Highness," she answered honestly, pressing a palm to her thumping heart, trying to keep it from beating its way out of her chest. "Perhaps you know?"

"Ostensibly, it's to thank you for saving me the other day." Savir's tone indicated that was not truly the reason at all. "But my father is not the grateful kind and having summoned this crowd...I do not think we will like where this is going."

Riana nodded grim agreement. She didn't think so either.

"Savir!" Zelman summoned in a demanding voice. "Bring that girl up here."

Savir offered her his arm, and she let her hand rest inside his elbow, swallowing hard. Zelman's expression was filled with anger and hate. This man had no intention of thanking her for anything this evening. But she was trapped and couldn't flee as she wanted to. Keeping a neutral look fixed on her face, she walked arm in and arm to stand in front of Zelman.

The king looked down at her with cold eyes. "Girl. I heard from my son that you saved him from an assassin. Is that really true?"

Riana managed a curtsey. "Your Majesty. I did the best I could and am grateful it turned out well."

"Turned out well, she says." Zelman scoffed, throwing his head back and looking away from all of them. "Turned out well! If not for this girl's training, and sheer luck, we'd be short a prince right now. Why? BECAUSE OF HENDRIX!"

Riana blinked and slowly brought her head back up to stare at him incredulously. Come again?

There was a murmur in the crowd, a confused sound as people tried to follow Zelman's logic, but couldn't.

"That's right, my youngest son is to blame for all of this." Zelman threw out an arm in a sweeping motion. "ALL OF IT! If not for his disobedience, his greed for power, we wouldn't be facing such unrest right now! His mockery of my station, my right to rule, is what inspired Edvard Knolton to rebellion!"

As the king spoke, Savir gradually drew Riana away, stepping slowly backward until they were against the far right wall, out of the king's direct line of sight. Riana didn't breathe properly until her skirts brushed the wall, feeling like at least this way she wouldn't have to meet Zelman's eyes or control her expression so absolutely.

"Our bandits in the Land Northward, the pirates that plague our coasts, ALL OF THEM are due to Hendrix! We must stamp him out. His rebellion, his power, he's claiming the hearts of the greedy and preying on the stupidity of the commoners."

Riana stared at the man with growing distaste. She'd thought she hated the man before, but the feeling evolved the more she listened to his insanity. The stupidity of commoners? Edvard Knolton had depended upon "commoners" in order to establish a wise and just government. She was now very glad that it was he she'd met first, and seen what a king should be like. If she'd met Zelman first, then she would have lost all faith in humanity.

"It has to stop! Why, why can't you help me stop him!" Zelman jerked the crown off his head and brandished it like a weapon. "Is this a joke to you? Is my rule, my words, nothing more than the sound of a barking dog?!"

No, a barking dog at least made sense. They normally barked for a reason. Zelman's words had no reasoning at all that she could decipher. He was blaming his youngest son for things that were entirely outside of his control. The pirates? They'd existed for generations, past anyone's living memory. The same could be said of the bandits, until a certain foursome had walked in and wiped them out several months ago. Hendrix certainly couldn't be blamed for Edvard Knolton, as the Estolian king had made it quite clear—to Zelman's face no less—why he was revolting against Iysh.

Riana turned her eyes to the watching crowd of noblemen and women. There was not one person that was truly listening to their king. Instead, they looked disturbed by what they were witnessing. It was akin to a crowd watching a madman writhe and rave. Indeed, that's exactly what it was.

She looked to the man standing so quietly beside her and found Savir watching his father with loathing, perhaps a touch of pity. There was no love there of a son watching his father. That was the saddest thing of all.

"Lady Saira," Savir murmured to her, low enough that the words would reach her ears alone, "I intended to invite you here solely amongst my own family to give you heartfelt thanks for your bravery and quick-thinking the other day. I would be dead or injured if not for you."

She gave him a smile that was half grimace. "I do appreciate your words, Your Highness. I don't know how to tell you this, but...I have trained with your brother, Hendrix." Which was not actually a lie. She had. Hendrix was a good sparring partner.

"Have you." Savir regarded her thoughtfully. "So in fact, my brother's foresight in training a woman in turn saved my life."

"It would appear so." Her smile grew more genuine.

"Well. If I ever have the opportunity, I shall remember to thank him." Savir glanced up at Zelman, who was now almost frothing at the mouth, still ranting about Hendrix being the root of all evil. "I'm afraid he's on a roll now. He won't be stopping anytime soon and words won't reach him."

Zelman paced up and down the dais, screaming, ranting, even throwing his crown to the ground at one point. That made Riana jump. But she didn't watch him much—it was embarrassing for one thing. To see a grown man throwing a fit like a three-year-old was unbelievably embarrassing.

What she chose to focus on was his audience.

As she watched, she could visibly see each man and woman mentally turn away from Zelman or lose all faith in his abilities to rule. It was horribly fascinating to watch. Zelman had gathered these people up with some sort of ill formed idea to rally them against Hendrix and was instead doing just the opposite.

She had no idea how much time passed. There were no windows in this place or clocks, just the lanterns burning down. It was a good long while, she knew that, as her heeled shoes hurt her feet and she grew increasingly thirsty.

Zelman must have felt the same, as he abruptly stopped talking, a hand to his throat. He had literally ranted himself hoarse. With a hand, he waved an abrupt dismissal at them all before leaving through a back door, staggering a little from aching feet.

Relieved, Riana gave Savir a smile and quick curtsey but didn't try to linger. She wanted out of this place as quickly as possible. Lengthening her stride as much as the skirts would allow, she made her way out of the throne room, through the dividing courtyard, through the main hallway of the palace and toward a side door that would dump her on the street leading to Ash's hiding place. He had the carriage, which meant a neat and swift escape.

"Lady Saira!"

Swearing mentally, she stopped and turned, praying that whoever was hailing her would not be longwinded. "General Quillin. Is aught the matter?"

He caught up to her, extended an arm,

silently insisting on escorting her somewhere. The expression on his face suggested he had a serious matter to discuss. Intrigued, Riana took the arm and followed where he led.

In fact, he led her through the very door she had been intending to escape through. He did not, however, go into the main street but to a bench next to one of the open fountains. It seemed an odd place for a confidential conversation, if that was what he intended.

"I always speak to people out in the open," the general explained, no doubt reading the confusion on her face. "There are two reasons for this. One, no one suspects that I'm speaking of secrets. Two, this way I know for certain that no one can eavesdrop on me, as I'm able to see all around me at all times."

The man did have a point. "Are we speaking of secret things, then?"

"Indeed we are, young lady." He leaned in an inch. "I happen to know that Saira Vaulx is a sweet lass with midnight hair and a club foot. Met her once years ago, although the Vaulx family has likely forgotten that, as I was not a general then."

Riana's heart froze.

"I do not know entirely your identity nor will I ask," he continued, as if he hadn't just given her heart failure. "I have ascertained from your conduct and conversations that you are an ally of Hendrix's, here on his behalf, and I applaud your wits and courage. Not many people are capable of doing all of this. I shall not endanger you by asking anything about you."

Breathe. Riana had to remind herself firmly

to breathe. There was a panicked inquiry from Ash and she had to send back a reassurance even though she didn't feel at all calm. The very last thing she needed was him bursting through those gates. "General Quillin. If you intend to have me keel over from fright, you very near succeeded."

Laughing, the general shook his head in denial. "You've faced down a mad king and assassins. You have nerves of steel, young woman. I didn't think this would frighten you."

"You have more faith in my nerves than I do," she muttered. Straightening her back, she looked him dead in the eye. "You told me all of this for a reason. What is it?"

He gave her an approving nod. "Just so. I want you to pass along a message to Hendrix for me. I am on his side. Whatever I can do to support him, I shall. If he needs my help, send a message through you, and consider it done."

What this man just said was huge. Riana stared at him with jaw agape, quite sure her ears were pranking her. With a small shake of the head, she forced herself to focus. "Sir, are you sure? Your position—"

"Soon," Quillin interrupted, tone absolutely certain, "Zelman is going to lose all patience with Maddox and his lack of progress concerning Estole. I can see the signs of that well enough. Outbursts like today are not uncommon. When he finally does hit his limit, he'll call me out of retirement and hand the problem of Estole over to me. I cannot in good conscience wage war on Estole. Edvard Knolton has become the standard bearer of what a king should be. It would be a waste to kill him."

Riana felt this man's courage fill her heart and had the strongest urge to just reach out and hug him. "To borrow your own sentiment, my lord, just so."

He gave her a wink. "Prince Hendrix has a plan on how to deal with this mess, I assume?"

"He does."

"Then tell him to hurry up. Old men don't like to be kept waiting." Smacking his hands down on his knees, he pushed his way up to his feet. "Young lady, do you need an escort home?"

Riana shook her head. "I have someone waiting outside of the gates. Do you truly not have any questions for me?"

"The less I know, the better at this stage. You just pass along that message to Hendrix."

"I shall." Riana still felt that she owed him something. He had taken a considerable risk telling her anything. Standing as well, she offered, "General? When all of this is over—which will be soon—I'll be very pleased to introduce myself to you."

Quillin gave her a nod, expression pleased. "I'll look forward to that day with all my heart. Until then, young lady, I wish the both of us the best of fortune."

"Thank you, my lord." Macha knew they needed it. She watched him walk away and wondered, still mentally reeling, how in the world was she supposed to report any of this? People were likely to faint at the news.

Shaking her head, she headed for the gate, mentally rehearsing different ways to approach this. Hopefully she'd come up with something before she met with Ash. He was sure to demand what had startled her so, as she would in his shoes. If she didn't phrase it right, he might just keel over in shock.

CHAPTER TWENTY-EIGHT

Out of all the things that Riana had done, up to and including sneaking into the Royal Treasury, she considered tonight to be the most dangerous mission of them all.

They had been summoned to help Prince Hendrix.

The prince had been busy, going from one end of Iysh to the other, setting new land speed records while doing it. If not for the fact that he had spent the last five years traveling about the country, he likely wouldn't have had the stamina necessary to do it again in under two months.

Now he had clandestinely come to Kremser to secretly meet with several of the nobles. Riana and Woelfel had put together the meeting, as they needed Hendrix there to reinforce his alliance with the nobles willing to side with him. It was critical at this stage to do so, as Riana could only do so much. Hendrix needed to make personal connections with these people or all of their efforts would be for naught.

To that end, she of course had to be there, as she was the organizer of it all. Hendrix had sent a single message to them of when he would be in Kremser and where they could send him a response in return. The message he had sent was beyond cryptic as well—nothing more than a time, place and date.

Woelfel was again left behind as they didn't dare risk him, too. Ash took the precaution of a few glamour spells so they could move through the city while being in disguise, just in case. Between that and the cover of darkness, Riana hoped that they would arrive without anyone the wiser.

The meeting place was actually quite well established and popular among the nobility. It was known for its discretion—a necessity, considering what services it offered. When Riana had been told what the place was for she found the choice of venue both amusing and logical.

After all, who would think a political rally would happen in a well-known gambling den?

The building was not at all attention grabbing or imposing in any way. It was a three-story, red brick, with a wide front porch so that patrons could come and go with some cover from the weather. Two men stood on either side of the door in a nondescript livery that could have belonged to anyone and no one. Ash stopped and leaned forward slightly to give the man a discreet tip and a name: "Vanlandingham."

"Of course, my lord, my lady, please enter," the man replied, pocketing the money.

They strode through the double doors without a hitch. Riana couldn't help but wonder, ::Are we supposed to enter that easily?::

::I borrowed the face and name of a derelict noble that has a gambling addiction,:: Ash explained cheerfully. ::That's why he didn't bat an eye.::

::Oh.:: Riana thought that over for a moment. ::Wait, how did you know that he wouldn't be here tonight?::

::I also happen to know that he's currently in hiding from his creditors.::

::And how do you happen to know any of this?:: Riana asked in bewilderment. She was the spy, supposedly, and she had never heard of this man!

::Well, what do you think Mrs. Pennington and I do all day while you two are out spreading rumors?::

Mrs. Pennington. Of course. Riana felt like smacking herself in the forehead. That woman likely would put Troi to shame, she knew so much about the inner workings of Kremser's society.

The gambling den was not the smoky, dim interior that Riana expected. In fact, quite the opposite. It boasted vaulted ceilings, several massive chandeliers, thick red carpet and gaming tables set up in every possible location around the room. People were dressed brightly, chattering loudly and laughing even louder. They were clustered around the game of their choice, calling out numbers and bets, and either laughing or groaning when the outcome was clear.

Riana had to earn every coin she had with hard work and no small amount of danger, so she didn't understand gambling at all. Why risk anything on a game of chance that was more than likely rigged against you? It was more than nonsensical—it was insane.

Ash perhaps sensed her thoughts as he gave her a wry quirk of the brow. "You don't want to try?"

Giving him quite the look for that question, she drawled, "Does it look like I've taken leave of my senses?"

"You know, there's no safe way to answer that."

"There isn't," she agreed affably.

"Why don't I just assume we're here to meet my future brother-in-law and then leave immediately after?"

"Splendid thought," she congratulated.

Ash wisely left it alone and kept walking. "The note suggested a back room that had been booked for this. I wish I knew what he wanted."

"We'll see soon enough." It had better be dire. Anyone mixing with Hendrix in Kremser had a death threat hanging about their necks, ready to strangle them. Riana wasn't quite sure of the reason, but apparently Zelman was using his youngest son as the scapegoat for all problems. He hated Hendrix with a passion and Riana entertained no false hopes for anyone that dared to speak with the prince. They would be immediately executed.

Riana hadn't been sure on how they would find the back room Hendrix was squirreled away in, but as it turned out, it was easy to find. One of his retainers stood guard outside the door and upon seeing them, waved them inside.

The room was lush with reds and gold trim, like the rest of the place, but the sound more muted here. It could comfortably entertain perhaps fifteen or twenty people but fifty people must have been crammed in there. Riana took two steps inside and then came to a dead halt as she had no more room to maneuver. The air was hot and stifling with so many bodies pressed into such a small room.

"He couldn't find a bigger space than this?" Ash muttered, a little exasperated. Raising his voice, he called out, "Where's my future brother-in-law?"

From somewhere on the opposite side, Hendrix laughed. "Back here!"

"Can we meet in the middle?" Riana asked rhetorically, trying to shove her way through. If they tried to fight their way to Hendrix, and then back out again, it would take them most of the night.

Perhaps the prince realized this, as he called to them, "Stay put!"

Riana gratefully did just that even though she had to wait a small eternity for him to force his way through. People were trying to shift to give him a clear path, but the confines of the room made it very difficult to do so.

Hendrix popped in front of them with little warning, clothes somewhat askew and a bemused smile on his face. "Sorry, I wasn't expecting this many people."

"Clearly," Ash drawled, but even he wasn't put out about this. More people meant more support, after all. "I'm glad to see this. We're sure there's no spies in this lot?"

"As sure as we can be. We do take precautions about this sort of thing of course." Taking them in front head to toe, he asked in a lower tone, "Are you wearing a glamour? I can somehow see who you are but there's this shadowy over-layer that makes it difficult to read your expression."

"We are, security precaution." Ash shrugged as if this was to be expected. "To those that know who we are, they can identify us. Otherwise we look like someone else completely."

"Wise of you. Ah, then, let's go to another room so I don't ruin your efforts. What I need to speak with you about will be a dead giveaway to your identities."

Riana was grateful just to get out of the room. She had grown accustomed to Estole's crowded conditions, but being in here was claustrophobic and she didn't care for the sensation.

They went out and directly across the hall, into another room guarded by a retainer. As the door closed behind them, Hendrix explained, "I'm actually staying here, as it's the safest place to be in Kremser until night falls. The owner was kind enough to prepare a separate room that I could rest in. Now, Ash, Riana, I'm a little out of touch. How are things going?"

Ash gave him the short, succinct version, ending with, "We haven't been able to determine whether Iysh is actually bankrupt or if the money has been hidden elsewhere."

Hendrix kept shaking his head, back and forth, eyes incredulous. "There's no other safe place to put it, legally speaking. Unless my father has lost what is left of his mind and put the money into one of his lackey's bank vaults, the money should all be in there. Lugh's hands, did Edvard actually get his wish? Did we bankrupt Iysh?"

"Perhaps? I'm not sure as it's hard to prove anything. We got a partial copy of the Royal Accounting and according to it, Iysh should have plenty of funds available."

"It suggests to us that someone has been manipulating the books," Riana added, "but we haven't been able to figure out who."

"We have to figure it out," Hendrix stated, more to himself than anything. "If I take over the country only to have no funds to work with, then we're not making much headway."

"We'll continue to investigate it," Ash promised. "In the meantime, what did you want from me?"

"Ah, that. I've made my circuit, so to speak, and am almost ready to return to Estole. However, with an army hovering outside, I don't wish to try and enter the city. Too dangerous and it will make it difficult to leave again, if I need to do so. I was wondering, do you have one of those permanent callers that I can use?"

Ash shook his head. "I don't, but I can make something for you if you can give me about an hour and some sort of gold jewelry. Why, have you run out?"

"Unfortunately, yes. I'm amazed at how quickly I used them up." Hendrix made a face. "Even though I was trying to be careful with them. Does it have to be gold?"

"Not necessarily, but gold works best and

holds onto the magic longest. Silver and platinum don't do as well for some reason."

Hendrix pondered that for a moment. "I think I have a ring that's solid gold, will that work?"

"Certainly, it doesn't matter what type. You just have to hold it up to your face to use it."

Hendrix held up a staying hand. "Give me just a few minutes." He left the room and was back again before Riana could do more than find a chair and sit down. "Here."

Ash took the ring, gave it a quick look, and nodded in satisfaction. "This is fine. You shouldn't wait on me, though, as it really will take at least an hour."

"Just give it to one of my retainers before you leave," Hendrix requested. "I can't ignore my guests that long. Some of them are giving me some very interesting information."

"Information you'll pass along to us before you leave Kremser?" Riana prompted.

"Yes, of course, I'll make notes and send it to you via courier. Expect them in the morning." Hendrix paused with his hand on the door knob and gave them both a genuine smile. "I know it's been a long road, but we really are succeeding. I'm glad to see both of you well."

"We're relieved to see that you are too," Ash assured him. "We'll have a proper celebration when all of this is over."

"It's a promise." Hendrix gave them an analyst's salute and let himself out, closing the door behind him.

Ash gave her a quirked eyebrow, silently asking what she was going to do while waiting on him.

"I'm taking a nap," she informed him bluntly.

"Lucky," Ash moaned. With a sigh, he dutifully turned his magical attention to the ring.

Riana put both feet up on the couch, head resting on her arm, and took advantage of the quiet and security to just unwind a little.

Considering her anxiety in meeting up with Hendrix, it turned out to be almost anticlimactic. They left and returned without any sign that it had been noticed by the spies in Kremser. Riana was just as glad, truly, but she did have to wonder at how effective Zelman's spies actually were. If his own son could hold a meeting in the capital without tipping anyone off, what was happening in the world at large that the spies failed to report?

They entered through the back door, Riana doffing hat, gloves, and cloak as she moved inside. Mrs. Pennington rushed toward them, for once looking frazzled. That expression stopped Riana dead in her tracks, which made Ash stumble into her back. "What?" Riana demanded, not at all sure she wanted the answer to that question.

"The barrier around Ganforth has fallen!"

CHAPTER TWENTY-NINE

The inevitable happened three weeks after the Iyshian army started their siege.

The barrier protecting Ganforth failed.

It happened early in the morning after the first onslaught, and it cracked with an audible sound, like glass on the verge of shattering. The noise was such that it penetrated the air, everyone in Ganforth and on the docks of Estole hearing it. Broden had been heading toward a minor emergency on the docks when it happened, and when he realized what it meant, he did a sharp about-face and sprinted for the nearest caller. It was fortunately only one street behind him, so he reached in a flat minute, and frantically called through it, "Ashlynn! ASHLYNN!"

"If you're using my name, the world is on fire. How bad?" she demanded.

"The barrier around Ganforth just cracked."

There was no swearing, just a deadly silence that said more than words could ever convey. "Are you sure."

"Lass, it be visible even from here, and every creature known to man heard it."

"You say cracked, but has it fallen?"

"No' as yet, but belike any moment now."

"Report to Edvard then meet me in Ganforth." The connection abruptly ended.

Broden knew without her saying anything that she intended to call for help even as she ran toward the colony. He ran himself, huffing and puffing as he plowed through people. Such was his reputation that when people recognized him, they instantly made way, as they knew that he would not be running unless it was a true emergency. As he ran, he stopped any guardsman he saw and demanded the king's whereabouts. Most did not know, but a few had seen him, and pointed him in the right general direction.

It took far too long to find Edvard, who was doing his usual rounds among the guard stations, and Broden did not even try to wait before getting the man's attention. "EDVARD!"

The king's head snapped around, detecting the panic in Broden's voice. "How bad?" he demanded, not even sure what the emergency was, but knowing there had to be one.

"Ganforth's barrier is failing," Broden reported, his words nearly tripping over each other. "It cracked visibly no' twenty minutes ago."

So much had happened in such a short time, and Edvard had received so many warnings that the makeshift barrier around Ganforth would not be as strong, that the king just closed his eyes in a fatalistic manner. "How long before it fails completely?"

Broden shook his head and spread his hands helplessly. "I've no notion. Ashlynn knows and be heading that way. I will order the civilians either to come across or hole up in the academy. We can no' waste magic trying to protect the whole place."

"Bless you for your common sense," Edvard responded, weariness and frustrations battling across his face. "Do that. Do it quickly, before my people are caught in the crossfire. Draft anyone you need. No, tell me what you need, I'll send people to you. I want you as a first responder."

"All ye can spare," Broden responded, honestly not sure how much help it would take to evacuate Ganforth. "Call on Larek of Dahl, the man's got a good head on his shoulders and a work crew already organized for this sort of thing. He can take on the evacuated people."

"I'll seek him out. Go, Broden, go!"

Not knowing what else to say, and feeling time pressing hard against him, Broden whirled again and ran straight back the way he had come. As he ran, he caught the guardsmen he had seen before and passed on the message: Ganforth was being evacuated to Estole, get ready to receive people. By the time that Broden reached the docks, he was panting for breath. Sprinting around a city while talking at the same time was a bit of challenge for a man of his age.

Word must have somehow come ahead of him, or the people at the ferry were able to anticipate what needed to happen next. There was a boat ready for Broden and they launched as soon as he had both feet inside. He quickly had to sit before capsizing them.

"Master Mark," he panted, drawing in air like a leaking pair of billows, "did ye take Ashlynn across already?"

"I did, and barely came back in time to fetch you." Mark was an old sailor, past retirement age, that worked the ferry just to whittle his time away. Now he used every trick he knew to get more speed out of the dinghy to make the crossing as quick as possible. "Took her and two other wizards at the same time, Master Gerrard and Miss Kirsty."

Broden sent up a word of thanks. Three wizards were much better than Ashlynn trying to shoulder the workload alone. Of course, that meant Lorcan was now in charge of the southern barrier, him and whomever he could grab. "Did they speak of a plan?"

"They did, although it was all in magical terms, and I didn't understand more than one word in five."

Even if Broden had been in the boat he likely would not have fared much better. Being around Ashlynn almost a year had taught him more about magic than he had ever known, but that was not much of a measuring stick, either. He realized that whenever she spoke directly to another wizard, much of it went straight over Broden's head. He would have to ask those three when he caught up to them what plan they had concocted.

"King Edvard said to evacuate however many we could afore that barrier failed completely. How many can ye take, man?"

"Top load is fifteen," Mark told him bluntly. "Any more than that, it'll sink her. Am I taking any baggage?"

"No' a piece," Broden decided on the spot. "We've no' the room for it. Whatever they need, it will be supplied in Estole. Tell them to save their lives first, things can be replaced."

"It's sensible, what you're saying; I just know I'm going to get arguments from people."

"If they argue, take someone else first, or toss it back on shore. Do no' waste time arguing, move."

Mark gave him a solemn nod. "I will. I'll instruct the rest to do the same."

"Good man." Broden frantically tried to think if he needed to pass along anything else. The shore was in sight, he only had a few minutes. Ah, right. "Tell them to find Master Larek when they reach the docks, he'll know where to put people."

"Larek of Dahl? I thought so. Good man, that, got to know him when he was helping offload all of those merchant ships. I'll send everyone to him." Mark looked anxiously at the barrier, with the gaping crack running in a jagged line right through the middle. "How much longer do you think it will hold?"

Broden dearly wished he had an answer to that question. "Hopefully as long as it needs to." He did not have a better answer than that and he was out of time anyway. The dinghy bumped into the dock and Broden leapt off, scrambling to find his footing and sprinting as soon as he had it.

Here, at least, he did not have to frantically search for someone. He could feel Ashlynn clearly through their bond and knew exactly where to go. He found all three wizards not in front of the barrier, as he had expected, but instead at the inn, broadcasting instructions to everyone. Broden listened with surprise as he ran up. Gerrard was literally on top of the roof, booming out in a voice that could have surpassed thunder: "IF YOU CAN FIGHT OR TRACK, GO TO THE ACADEMY! SPREAD THE WORD AS YOU GO AND BE THERE IN HALF AN HOUR! EVERYONE ELSE, HEAD TOWARD THE DOCKS! YOU WILL ESCAPE INTO ESTOLE. TAKE NOTHING WITH YOU!"

He kept repeating that over and over as Broden skidded to a halt in front of Ashlynn.

Ashlynn, bless her, did not wait for him to ask questions. She gave him a breakdown of the situation voluntarily in between issuing orders. "This barrier was too makeshift, it had several fundamental weaknesses because we were literally throwing it together. You know how—yes, go there, and no we don't have room for any luggage, just go, Estole is preparing things for you, go, go!—what was I saying? Oh, right, you know how we had to build very strong pillars in order for the barrier to have a solid setting in front of Dahl and Estole? We didn't have time to build that here. There were just simple wooden posts instead. But the wood is breaking, it can't sustain that kind of magical energy for long without literally disintegrating."

"Which is why ye be no' even trying to fix it?"

"Exactly, no point." Ashlynn paused for a young man that looked barely out of his teens. "I'm sorry, what did you ask?"

"I want to make sure my grandmother gets across safely, but I also want to fight. Can I come back after seeing her across?" the man repeated anxiously.

"I can't guarantee you'll have the time. Either go or stay," Ashlynn directed.

For a moment he looked conflicted, not sure which was the better choice to make. Then he nodded, spun, and rushed off although not far before catching up with an old woman, presumably his grandmother. He took her arm and ushered her toward the docks, the grandmother struggling to hurry.

Broden was extremely sorry to hear that they could not somehow patch it and make do for a little longer. That had been his hope as he frantically made his way over here, although his realistic side had said the odds were not good on that option. "Ye cannot make another barrier?"

"Not one that functions the same," Ashlynn denied with a frustrated shake of the head. "Not before this one fails completely. Kirsty is over there now, patching as she has to, making it last as long as possible. We need at least three hours to get everyone out of here and I'm honestly not sure if the barrier will last that long. I have a bad feeling we'll have to erect a barrier over the center and hole up until we can get people shuttled to safer places. And escorting them is going to be an absolute nightmare with an army trying to get in."

A nightmare that gave Broden a headache just thinking about it. "Best avoid that. I will head back down to the docks, load up people as fast as I can and toss anyone in that sets to arguing with the ferrymen."

"Go," Ashlynn encouraged. "Someone needs

to, as people seemed oddly concerned with taking things with them."

It was odd, but people were strangely materialistic, even in circumstances like these. Broden ran back to the docks, throat nearly dry from thirst. He would have given his eye teeth to be able to quaff down a tankard of water, but they did not have the luxury for that.

No surprise to anyone, there were people insisting on taking some sort of heirloom with them on the boats. The ferrymen had their hands full trying to get people loaded, and arguing with the stubborn ones as they worked. Broden waded into the middle of it, sometimes just taking the bundle out of the idiot's hands and shoving them in, sometimes pitching the luggage into the water if they tried to argue the point further.

It was confusing, enough to make his head swim, as people swarmed on all sides. The boats were coming back and forth quickly, other boats joining in that were not part of the ferry, but fishermen local to the area that saw the problem and tried to help. Broden was not sure if Edvard had thought to send them or not but they were very welcome. The fishing boats could hold more than the ferry boats and so could evacuate people much more quickly.

Broden had no sense of how much time had passed until he forced himself to stop and actually look at the sun. Two hours? Had Kirsty managed to keep the barrier up that long? Looking about, he realized they only had another dozen people to load up. Was that really everyone? Worried, he jogged back through the streets, calling out to see if anyone was still lingering.

He did not receive any reply in return. Had everyone actually gone that quickly? Ganforth was not as heavily populated as Estole or Dahl, but they still had a fair number of people over here. Even with half of them going for the academy, Broden felt like they were a hundred people short at least. Maybe he had lost count in the confusion of loading people up, and some had gone on before he could even make it back to the docks after speaking with Ashlynn. Perhaps that was why his count was skewed.

Either way, it seemed his task was done. He headed back toward the docks and was greeted by a strange sight indeed. Four fishing boats were letting men off at the docks. As he watched, one of them finished unloading and quickly escaped back into the channel, returning to Estole. He was glad to see they had the sense to make sure there was no sea worthy vessel staying on the shoreline, but...what were all of these men and women doing here? He recognized more than a few faces, all of them either hunters or men he knew to have some fighting skills. Some of the women were ones that he and Riana had trained, fledgling guardsmen that hadn't quite completed the course enough to actually take up the uniform.

Legs beyond tired, he nevertheless pushed himself into a lope so that he could catch up to them more quickly. As his feet touched the wooden docks, a face he knew very well turned and gave him a grin. "Master Larek!" he greeted in surprise.

"Master Broden," the man responded,

extending a hand and clasping it. "We've all come to help you fight the blaggards off. King Edvard was asking for volunteers, anyone that felt they could join in on the fight. Are we welcome?"

Broden honestly felt like crying. His eyes were wet with unshed tears. "Always." Looking about, he saw that he had at least a hundred people. They were not the type he would put on a battlefield, but for what he had in mind, they were more than suited for the task. "Let's get into the academy. Fast and snell, now, afore the barrier collapses completely."

"Lead the way," Larek encouraged. "Most of us have never been over here before and aren't sure where the academy even is."

Broden immediately took off, encouraging people to keep up with him. He took the next street right and headed for the academy. Fortunately it was not far and when he rounded a corner and came within sight of the main doors, he spotted Ashlynn impatiently shifting from foot to foot, waiting on him. He dredged up adrenaline from somewhere to run the short distance to her. Ashlynn grabbed his arm as soon as he was within reach, jerking him all the way inside and shouted at the others, "Quickly, quickly, quickly!"

As soon as the last person passed her, she slammed the door shut. "They're in!" she yelled at someone out of sight.

The barrier around the academy snapped up and audibly hummed as it settled into place. Broden braced his hands on his knees, dragging in breath. He was seriously getting too old for this. "Everyone in?"

"Yes. Everyone out?" she demanded.

"I think so, aye. I ran through the streets calling to people but got no' a word in reply. Hopefully we caught them all." If not, they were on their own. "The outer barrier?"

"Will fail any second." Ashlynn let out a long breath, stressed and anxious, but trying not to be overwhelmed by the feelings. "You were literally the last person we were waiting on. Kirsty did her best but after a certain point she hit a limit. She said the Iyshian soldiers are just hovering out there, ready to pounce."

A terrifying thought, that. "Lass, I hate to ask, but what about Estole's docks?"

"Fortunately, we had to set up a separate system for them. Because there were a lot of brick and stone buildings—the warehouses—in place already, we just used them to set up the barrier on that side. That part is still intact. Mostly. I mean, someone clever can still swim under, but an army isn't going to be marching through."

Broden knew they kept saying that was a weakness, but it was not much of one to his mind. That was ice cold water, filled with winter runoff from the mountains, and would freeze a man if he was in it for too long. And once he was out, he'd have to instantly change clothes to avoid losing a limb or three. To Broden, the water was a very effective barrier all on its own.

Looking about, he realized that every square inch of the main courtyard was filled with people. Mostly volunteer fighters, huddling in with each other, speaking to each other in low, troubled tones. Broden knew that the barrier they sat in was more solid than steel. This one had ties to the very bedrock the academy sat upon. No one would be getting through this one. But they were also trapped in here, with limited water and food, and that was their weak point. Sieges were effective in that way—like as not you could starve your opponents into giving up.

Ashlynn's caller necklace lit up. "Ashlynn!"

Edvard? And he did not sound worried but a little relieved and excited. Broden cautiously hoped that something good had happened even as Ashlynn responded, "I'm here, Edvard. Tell me good news."

"To start with, everyone from Ganforth made it over safely."

Broden sent a prayer of thanks heavenwards.

"I had quite a few volunteers who wanted to go up and fight with you. Did they make it?"

"They did," Ashlynn assured them. "Everyone came in safely and the barrier around the academy is up."

"I'm relieved to hear it. I wasn't sure if they'd make it. Also, I just received word from Hendrix."

Ashlynn and Broden shared a speaking glance. Hendrix? How? "Isn't he running about the countryside?"

"He still is, but apparently he's won over most of the support he needs already. He heard from Ash and Riana what has happened here, and he's relayed word up to us that he will raise up an army to help."

There was absolutely no way that he could have heard him right. "Hang on, lad, Hendrix thinks he can raise an army?"

"No, he's absolutely positive he can. He's had more than one person tell him that they wish to fight. He's some distance out, not in danger of tangling with the Iyshian army, and he's going to visit every town nearby until he can pull a militia together. He thinks he can be here in five days."

Broden had a strangely still moment in his mind, all thought and emotion suspended. It felt like a cleft point, when things were about to change, and even though it was ridiculous, he somehow believed that Hendrix really could deliver on that promise.

"Can you last five days?" Edvard pressed. "Do you have enough food and water to sustain everyone for that amount of time?"

Ashlynn looked to Broden, eyes fierce. Broden was perfectly in tune with her in that moment. It would be a challenge, certainly, but one they were willing to accept. "We'll manage, Edvard. You focus on the southern border and don't worry about Ganforth. We'll take care of the rest."

CHAPTER THIRTY

Broden discovered something about Ashlynn during the siege against the academy. It was literally impossible for her to sit still. Granted, the situation was far from relaxing, and he did not expect her to laze about, but she acted worse than a cooped-up cat. Her impatience was such that while not actively clawing at the walls, she was ready to break something in order to sneak out.

After spending two days trying to settle her down, Broden gave up. He went to a man that knew the lass better than himself and demanded, "Gerrard. Can ye no' get the lass to settle?"

Gerrard looked up from the inventory list in front of him, pausing his count of food stuff in the pantry, a wry smile on his face. "I have better odds of halting the tide."

That was the answer he had expected. Grumbling, Broden slouched against the door jamb.

"Driving you crazy?" Gerrard asked in complete understanding.

"Granted, it be a short trip," Broden acknowledged in dark humor. "I did no' realize it afore now, but she has absolutely no patience, our lass."

"Absolutely none," Gerrard agreed and let the list dangle next to his leg for a while. "In situations like this, where she literally can't do anything but wait, she quickly loses even the semblance of patience. It's just as well that Edvard assigned her to be Sherriff of Estole. Even after all of this is over, having a demanding job will keep her from going stir crazy."

Now that was not a thought he had entertained before, but Gerrard was right. A brief mental picture flashed through Broden's mind of what Ashlynn would be like if she did not have a designated occupation. It was so terrifying he actually shuddered.

"Thankfully for all," and Gerrard was laughing at him now, "Edvard knows his siblings very well and understood that a busy Ashlynn is a happy Ashlynn, and as long as she's busy, she won't drive us to drinking."

"The man seems wiser by the minute." All of that was good, but it did not solve the immediate problem. "But what do I do with the lass now? Short of knocking her out."

"It might very well come to that." Gerrard frowned in consideration, staring off into space. "I think she's been wound up for so long that even when she has the chance to relax a little, she literally doesn't remember how to. Our choices are either make her sleep, or give her something to focus on."

Broden pondered that for a full minute. "Have any sleeping spells handy?"

"A full arsenal. It's the only way to survive as the sole adult with thirty children." Putting the list down, he cracked his neck from side to side, like a man gearing up for a fight. "Let's see if two old foxes can get the drop on her, shall we?"

For three days, Broden and Gerrard took turns tag-teaming Ashlynn long enough for someone to sneak up behind her and spell her back to sleep. It got progressively harder each time but Broden realized after that first day that Ashlynn actually needed the sleep. It was not until she had slept eighteen straight hours—after only being spelled to sleep eight—that it became apparent just how exhausted she was. Now that she was sleeping twenty hours a day, and eating regularly instead of bites in between emergencies, she actually gained a little color and flesh back in her cheeks. Even with them being on limited rations, she was faring better.

After seeing that, Broden swore he was going to sit on the lass and make her eat more regularly. She had been driving herself into the ground without him realizing it.

He was all set to do the same routine on the fifth day, but when he went to find Gerrard, he found the man in the middle of a call with Hendrix. As he stepped into Gerrard's study, the man caught sight of him and waved him through, Hendrix speaking loud enough for Broden to hear easily.

"—approaching the southern edge of Dahl, but we don't dare get much closer than this without risking engagement," Hendrix was saying. "I've got an army of three thousand, but they're oddly equipped and have no training actually fighting together. I don't want to put them in a head-on battle with Iysh. The outcome won't be pretty."

"Guerilla warfare would be the better choice," Gerrard agreed. "Broden just stepped in, let me catch him up. Broden, Hendrix is outside the barrier with a rebel army of three thousand volunteers."

That much Broden had caught coming in but it did his heart good to hear it, and a smile broke over his face. "Ye made good time, lad."

"That I did," Hendrix acknowledged with a gleeful laugh. "It's amazing how many came when I called. Even I was taken by surprise. But now that I have them, I'm not entirely sure what to do with them. What's the situation like over there?"

Lad likely felt as if he had entered the third act of a play with only a basic premise to go off of. "As to that, the Iyshian army be acting a bit strange, lad. They have no' made a serious attempt yet at the academy, just been raiding Ganforth for supplies. They ransacked the immediate area as much as they could, but even that did no' last long. At the moment, lad, ye got half-starved and very frustrated men on short pay camping outside the academy."

"Well now. That's a little puzzling. I can't imagine they're very happy freezing out there either. Did I mention that the wind chill is such that it cuts right through to the bone?"

Broden had no doubt of that. "Ye'd think they be more than ready to run at the barrier and find a way to end this quickly."

"I do indeed. This is very strange behavior. Why go through all the trouble of getting up there and then not do anything constructive?"

"Took the words right out of our mouths," Gerrard rumbled. "Your Highness, we've got men here that are rested up and ready to move. We want to figure out what their battle plan is, if it's not siege warfare they're interested in."

"I'm more than curious about that myself. How is the barrier holding up around Estole?"

"Fit as a fiddle," Gerrard answered confidently. "We had plenty of time to set that one up. Ganforth's was a makeshift affair, hence why it failed."

"Ah, is that right? I'd wondered what went wrong. Alright, if that's the case, I'm not going to approach the front door. I think you're correct, guerilla tactics will suit us better. It will be very difficult for me to take any men up to Ganforth. Can I depend on you to handle the north?"

"Of course," Gerrard assured him, brightening visibly. Then again, he was only mildly better at waiting than Ashlynn was.

"Then we'll divide this up and have some of us harry the troops north while the rest take the south."

Gerrard had a look on his face that reminded Broden of a wolf spotting interesting prey. "Hendrix, do you have a designated man that could lead the northern side?"

"Ah, that was my second problem. I've been

debating a few candidates. Why?" The prince was quick on the uptake. "Oh! I see what you're getting at. Broden, why don't you lead them?"

That would certainly be the better way to do this, to his mind. Broden would rather be out fighting anyway. "Gerrard, can ye let me out of this barrier?"

"I have a way of getting you out, yes. If you'll take the troops we have here for the longer forays, I can manage good distractions here to keep them from noticing you until it's far too late."

"Good. Then, lad, ye can expect both Ashlynn and I to take charge of the fighting up here."

"Is Ashlynn going too? Really?"

"Lad, I do no' think of meself as a suicidal man. If I left yon lass here by her lonesome and went out to have fun, do ye think I'd survive to see the next sunrise?"

Both men laughed and neither denied it. Candidly, Gerrard added, "At least this way we can stop hitting her with sleeping spells. I was starting to run out of tricks."

There was a pregnant pause as Hendrix mulled that over. Almost incredulously he demanded, "Wait, you've been bespelling her to sleep on a regular basis?"

"Lass be going stir crazy in here," Broden justified, a trifle defensively.

"Broden, I thought you said you weren't suicidal. How in the world did you get by with doing that and live to tell the tale?"

"She loves us too much to kill us." Gerrard ruined this confident statement by adding, "Although we just about hit the limit of her affections. Leaving her behind to fight would definitely mean the end for us."

"Then by all means, give Ashlynn an outlet for her pent-up frustrations." Hendrix paused and added in a softer tone, "I saw Ash and Riana when I was in Kremser. They're doing very well."

It was kind of Hendrix to give him such an update, as Broden did sorely miss and worry about his daughter. The only thing that helped him were the sporadic messages they sent to Troi. At least those told him they were alive, well, and succeeding. "Thank ye, lad," he responded huskily.

"Riana had a message for me to pass along to you as well. She said, and I quote, 'I finally got him, Da.' Do you know what she meant by that?"

Broden barked out a laugh. "It means she finally got Ash to the stage of lovers, lad."

"Truly?!" Hendrix sounded perfectly amazed by this but immediately counteracted his own outburst. "Actually, come to think of it, they did look rather intimate together when I last saw them. I'd wondered if something was going on, but they weren't overt about it."

Likely not; they were in the middle of serious business after all. "Well, I be looking forward to hearing the story properly later. In the meantime, lad, let's clear our doorstep, shall we?"

Gerrard's 'way out' was a small trap door and tunnel that led into a wine cellar and tapped into a cold spring that, with the right levers, could be shut off and used as a tunnel out. The sides of the waterway were stone, slippery and cold from water residue, but an easy enough climb out. Using it meant compromising the barrier, however, as he had to drop it temporarily to let them out. Even if it was no more than five minutes, it was five minutes of vulnerability that sent a cold chill up his spine. Fortunately, Broden and Ashlynn slipped outside with their hundred rebel soldiers without spotting a single enemy.

Before leaving the academy, Broden had taken an hour and split them up into different groups of ten, each responsible for a different area, and they were to go and come back as stealthily as possible.

He kept the last group of ten and looked about him. The moon overhead hung slim indeed, not giving them much in the way of light, and the darkness was like a welcome cloak about them. It would be easy to pull shenanigans tonight, but it was also easy to mix up friend with foe. Broden prayed that would not happen but was realistic enough to realize it would.

"Alright," he said in a low tone to his huddled group, "we be having the most interesting task of all. We be a-hunting for a prince."

One of them, a stout man with a raspy voice, spoke up. "Prince Hendrix said his brother was up here somewhere. You sure on that?"

"We are. Information came from an eye witness," Ashlynn confirmed. "He hasn't once been with the force around the academy, which means he's off elsewhere. We'd like to find his camp and, if at all possible, do our best to dish out some damage. If we're going to do anything to him, now is our best chance."

There were a few ginger nods as none of them were particularly keen on tackling a prince in the dead of night. Broden could hardly blame them. Maddox would only have the very best of bodyguards around him, and the prince himself was a good fighter. He was not easy prey. Still, no one protested, so Broden silently led off and was pleased when eleven people followed him.

It had been quite some time since he had skulked about the woods in the pitch black of night. Broden felt a familiar thrill go up his spine as adrenaline started churning. It felt somehow right to be out here, with the night song of insects and birds, the scent of ice and snow, all of it filling his head. His work in Estole was vitally important, and he respected the position he had there, but at times he truly missed just being out in the mountains.

They took a roundabout trail to go far north of where they knew the soldiers' camp to be, as Broden did not want to tangle with any night patrols or his own groups trying to work. It took them a little longer than he had planned, so that they were in the wee hours of the morning before they came all the way around. They had had a recent snowfall, little more than a light dusting, but it was enough to cushion all of the leaves and deadfall so that it made a noiseless carpet to walk on. Broden used that to his advantage as he stopped, crouched, and listened hard. Had they gone too far? He could not hear or smell anything that suggested men.

Ashlynn paused next to him, also kneeling, and pulled a pair of her magical glasses out of a shirt pocket. She put them on and panned the area first one way, then another, and back again. "I don't see anyone," she breathed to him.

This was becoming stranger by the minute. They had spent five days studying the enemy camp from the top of the academy; they knew that Maddox was there. They had assumed since he was not at the south barrier either, he had to be camped just a little farther out, far enough that even with magical enhancements, they could not see him.

An uneasy pit formed in his stomach. Broden motioned people to stay low and whispered, "Fan out in pairs. His camp is here somewhere. If ye find it, meet back here and wait. Everyone return in one hour."

There were grunts and silent assents before people split up and drifted off as silently as ghosts. Broden silently reminded himself to thank Edvard for sending him good men to work with. Otherwise he would never have given that order and would have ended up searching the woods himself.

Turning back to Ashlynn, he whispered, "No sign of a camp at all?"

"Not that I can see. Why did you think he was here, anyway? Why this exact spot?"

"Only clean water source available that his men had not already taken," Broden explained. "There be others, but they be farther north, past yon rise. Or much closer to the channel, which would make his camp visible to the shoreline."

"Which he wouldn't want to do," Ashlynn concurred thoughtfully. "I see. Let's move forward, see if we can find anything."

Broden had no intention of just sitting there and waiting for people to come back. It was bitterly cold outside, even with warming spells on him, and movement would keep him warmer. He got back to his feet and went along, carefully, as it was easy to miss things in the dark. Ashlynn had spelled his eyes so that he had night vision like a cat would, which helped. After her doing the spell on him so many times, he had adapted to it, mostly. Still, this was not the time to be careless and assume he could see everything.

They separated a little, no more than twenty feet, as both wanted to react if their partner suddenly fell into danger. Broden's internal clock ticked as he searched the ground. The snow from the other day had mostly melted and refrozen as ice, or stayed frozen in the thicker shade of the trees, which made for some interesting patterns.

"Broden."

Immediately, he turned and lifted his head up. "What, lass?"

"I think Maddox was here."

He crossed to her in long strides before kneeling and carefully studying what she pointed at. The remains of a cookfire lay nearby, nothing more than a ring of stones now, as well as disheveled dirt and a half-burned bone sticking out of the soot.

"Aye, lass, I agree it be a campsite no' used long ago. But why Maddox's?"

She pointed again, more empathetically, then lifted her hand away altogether. He had to tilt his torso and cock his head a little to finally see what she did, as he only caught an edge of it from his angle. There, in the snow and ice, was the half-imprint of Maddox's crest. It looked to have been left there by a sword lying in the snow.

"The only one that would have that crest on a weapon would be Maddox himself. It's treasonous for anyone else unless he's given them express permission."

That imprint was indefatigable proof alright. "I'm amazed ye saw that, lass."

"Why do you think I use the glasses and not the spell? They're able to pick out finer details."

He actually had wondered about that. Broden bent lower and put his nose a scant inch away to study it better. "Print's mayhap two days old."

"That's more or less my guess as well." Ashlynn rocked back to sit on her heels, looking at the abandoned camp site. "So the prince was here. Now where did he go?"

CHAPTER THIRTY-ONE

What followed was a grim game indeed. Now that they knew that Maddox was truly in their area, it affected the morale of Estole. After Broden and Ashlynn's reconnaissance of that night, several of the refugees joined Hendrix's rebel army. Hendrix's men performed guerilla fighting that made a hash of the Iyshian ranks. All of the northern troops were forced into a retreat as their forces were whittled down, until they joined the southern army at Estole's border. Hendrix's men did not let them rest but followed, sabotaging food supplies, setting fire to the tents, destroying any caches of arrows, and creating general mayhem.

It helped, but did not solve the problem.

Someone over in the enemy's camp understood magical barriers. Or at least, understood magical theory enough to figure out that what they fought against was not the standard barrier but instead a hybrid concoction of some sort. Broden had to assume that after that first week, when they did not make any headway, they must have sent for someone with magical expertise. It would naturally take time for him to arrive, especially while traveling on these winter roads, but arrive he did sometime after the northern barrier around Ganforth fell. It was at that point the southern border began to be battered in all the wrong ways.

Ashlynn stood next to him at the top of the wall, watching in grim anger as the enemy below her systematically hit the weakest points of the barrier in near unison. Broden understood enough about the barrier's construction to realize: "This be bad."

"Extremely so. Even the word 'bad' is an understatement." Ashlynn growled, the sound eerily like a cornered injured wolf. "I don't know who they got up here to help, but he's analyzed the barrier to perfection. With them strung out like that, hitting the point right in between the barrier's posts, they're literally hammering at the weakest point of the joints. Curse that man and the dogs that bred him!"

"I would offer to shoot him," Broden stated in equal frustration, "but it be worlds too late by now."

"I know it. They already know the weak points, it doesn't matter if we kill him now." Ashlynn slammed a fist on the top of the wall, angry and resigned all at once. "Broden, the barrier won't be able to hold out long under this pounding. This is one of its weaknesses and the reason why magicians normally don't use it. Under the right pressure, it'll break."

Broden had a feeling he already knew the answer, but had to ask anyway, "What can we do?"

"Not a thing. Not a thing that we aren't already doing. We're pouring more magic into it, shoring it up where we can, but we can't do that for much longer. It risks draining our wizards to the point that they'll suffer magic deprivation and collapse."

Having seen exactly what happened to Ash, Broden did not think that wise. They needed their wizards fighting fit more than anything. At the same time.... He turned and regarded Estole as a whole. There was no way to retreat anywhere. There was not a safe place to send anyone to. They had retreated as far as they could and even putting people inside of a building with physical walls would be nigh impossible with all of them.

Perhaps Ashlynn could read his mind or perhaps she simply had the same thoughts. Either way, she turned and said exactly what he was thinking: "When the barrier falls, there's no way to protect all of them."

"Lass, there has to be a way. If we can no' find one, we make one, but there has to be a way."

Ashlynn stared out sightlessly for several long minutes before she picked up the caller around her neck. "Edvard. Tierone. Hendrix."

She waited, then repeated the names again, louder, until all three men responded. "You can all hear me?"

"We can," Edvard answered, sounding subdued. "How bad is it?"

"I give it two days before the wall breaks entirely."

All three men growled out a curse. Tierone

demanded, "Nothing can be done on our end?"

"We're already doing what we can, but if we push ourselves recklessly then we'll be magically drained and you don't want that."

"No, indeed we don't," he immediately agreed, disturbed at the thought. "How much time do we have before the wizards have to stop?"

"Why do you think I said two days? As soon as we stop patching it with power, that thing will collapse like a house of cards."

Hendrix piped up: "I'm doing all I can to harry them from behind but they have a large enough force that they can protect the ranks battering at the wall. I literally cannot reach them from here. Edvard, Tierone, can your men attack from the wall? Even shooting people will help."

Ashlynn shook her head even though none of them could see it. "The way this barrier is constructed, we can't pass anything through it. It'll compromise the integrity of the wall if we try."

"Well, that's out, then." Edvard pondered this for a moment. "What can we do?"

"Broden," Hendrix spoke slowly, as if he were thinking aloud, "Didn't you say that Cloud's Rest has allied itself with us?"

"I did, aye."

"Let's do this. Let's gather up everyone that is mobile enough to move quickly and send them to either Cloud's Rest or Senn. If we can empty the city enough, we can put the rest inside of the buildings with permanent barriers erected, protect the citizens that way. Then we can fall to street fighting. It's dirty, but a wonderful delaying tactic."

"Wait," Edvard protested, "I agree we need a delay, but to what end? Are we just delaying the inevitable?"

"Heavens no, man, I wouldn't suggest this just to see an ugly end. I think I have the support I need. Let's take advantage of the barrier going down to get you out. We'll head straight to Kremser and wrest control of Iysh from Zelman. We can stop this army in its tracks that way."

"I feel bad about abandoning my people right as things go from bad to worse..." Edvard trailed off uncertainly.

"We need to move before it becomes a massacre," Hendrix argued. "I only came up here to help shore up your defenses. I didn't plan to stay for even this long. Edvard, if we stand still, we lose."

There was a pause as everyone held their breath, waiting for Edvard to make a decision. He blew out a noisy breath. "You're right. Of course, you're right. This is the only option. Alright, I'll go with you."

Broden personally felt that was the only viable option. Apparently Tierone and Ashlynn agreed, as they both voiced sounds of approval. Tierone added, "I think I should stay here. There needs to be at least one king on site to make decisions. But I agree, Edvard should go, one of us has to make a formal truce with you in order for this to be legally binding."

"Edvard, in the sense of expediency, Broden and I will be your bodyguards for the trip," Ashlynn volunteered. Or voluntold in that no-nonsense voice that Broden knew from experience all too well. "You can't afford to send a full entourage so you'll have to make do with the two of us."

Being a wise king, Edvard immediately agreed, "I wouldn't choose anything differently. Tierone, you're sure that you're alright staying here to deal with this madness?"

"We don't have any other choice, really. Besides, don't you want to see this through all the way to the end? You started this fight with Zelman in person. I think it should finish the same way."

Edvard let out a very evil chuckle. "I do admit I'm looking forward to a final showdown. Alright, Hendrix, we're in agreement. Hash out a plan for all of this and run it by us tonight. We need to move soon if we're to do this. Broden, I realize it's going to be a lot of travel back and forth for you, but I'd feel better if you and Ashlynn led the group towards Cloud's Rest. At least part of the way."

"If we really mean to do this in two days, we can no' go all the way," Broden warned. "But aye, I can at least get them set on the road and pushed in the right direction."

"Good enough. I just want to make sure they're retreating safely and not into an ambush of any sort. Hendrix, you have strong ties with Senn, you'll ask them for aid?"

"I will and arrange for transportation while I'm at it. How many boats do we need to ferry people up?"

"As many as they can spare. Let's move out all we can. It's going to get very harrying here in Estole for the next few weeks. The less burden we put on our supplies and wizards, the better."

Broden knew good and well that the only truly 'mobile' group was Larek's. He went directly there, catching the man's attention. "Master Larek!"

Larek had been hovering over a cookfire, but immediately got to his feet and crossed to him. "Master Broden. How bad is it?"

"Bad, man, but we have a plan. Those of ye that can move be either going to Senn or Cloud's Rest. We be emptying the city in order to make it a death trap in here for street fighting. Prince Hendrix plans to use that delay to go to Kremser and take the throne from his father."

Rocking back on his heels, Larek took this news with slack-jawed surprise. "Truly? He thinks he can win?"

"Knows he can," Broden corrected with a reassuring nod. "And feel free to spread that news about. But in the meantime, I need ye packed up and ready to move in two hours. Do no' try to move all at once, send people across to Ganforth as soon as ye can."

"Ganforth is safe, then?"

"Aye, the troops be long gone. It be a barren place now." He hated to ask this, as Larek had enough to juggle as it was, but Broden could not really think of who else had the leadership ability and connections to do it. "Man, I be honest—I can no' take ye to Cloud's Rest. I be set to guard the king and prince to Kremser."

Larek shrugged, not at all surprised. "I didn't think you could. There's a broad highway that leads directly to Cloud's Rest, correct?"

"Aye."

"Then I can't get lost leading everyone there." He gave Broden a cocky smile. "It'll be fine. They know we're coming?"

"We sent word ahead. They'll be expecting ye, but do no' expect them to be hospitable. Even with an alliance in place, they be no' a welcoming sort."

"Noted." Larek stared out in the general direction of Cloud's Rest, likely a thousand plans and logistics whirling in his mind. "How long do we have to get safely up there?"

"Two days." Broden grimaced as Larek gave him a patented, is this man mad look. "I did no' say ye had to arrive in Cloud's Rest, mind, just that ye need to be safely away from here in two days."

"For a moment, I thought you'd lost your mind."

"If that were to happen, it would have been long before now," Broden drawled. "Now, get people moving, and quick about it. I will try to meet ye on the other side. If no' me, then find a guardsman, they can start forming people up."

Larek gave him a vague salute of acknowledgement, turned, and started bellowing orders at people. Broden gave a glance skyward as he walked away. It was not even mid-morning yet. Assuming they could get the first wave of people over to Ganforth by noon, that still left six hours of daylight left to travel with. They needed to use it all to get people going. It would mean a cold, hard campsite for two days as they traveled, but they would make it.

For everyone else, it would belike be the work of two days to get them all sorted. But that was fortunately not Broden's headache.

Hitting the main street, Broden went searching for Ashlynn, as they needed to coordinate now that they had people in motion. Just how far of an escort could they do before they had to turn back? Broden was not keen on going very far out, because if anything went wrong, it would delay Edvard and Hendrix leaving for Kremser. That was the highest priority, to his mind.

Rounding a corner at a dead run, Seth plowed right into him, sending them both sprawling. Broden hit the cobblestone street hard, although fortunately he was able to tuck his chin enough to avoid bashing his head against the stone. Gasping for breath, he stared up at the cold blue sky overhead and sent a prayer that whatever had made Seth spring about like a madman was not another emergency. "Seth, lad?"

"Sorry, sir," Seth gasped, rolling to his feet. Being younger and more spry, he was recovering from the fall faster than Broden, and offered his boss a hand up.

Grasping it, Broden levered himself back up to his feet and winced as new bruises protested. "Lad, I be afraid to ask. What be wrong now?"

"No, sir," Seth denied with a brilliant smile, "it's finally right. Prince Hendrix just sent word that Overan mercenaries have shown up to aid Estole. They reported directly to him."

Broden blinked at him, the words refusing to penetrate or make sense. "Come again, lad?"

"Truly, it just happened twenty minutes ago. A mercenary force of two thousand appeared, reported to Prince Hendrix, and then engaged in the battle. Can't you hear them?"

Now that Broden was actively listening, he realized the sounds of battle had changed. It was indeed louder than before, more energetic instead of men battering at a magical wall. "Where did they come from?"

"They said they were hired to come to our aid by an anonymous benefactor." Seth paused and, having inside information, lowered his voice to ask, "The same benefactor that sent the ships?"

Likely so. But they had no way of knowing. "Lad, mayhap after this madness is settled, we will get to find out. Belike now is no' the time to be looking a gift horse in the mouth." More urgent questions rose to the surface. "Has our plan changed, then?"

"No, Prince Hendrix said that while the reinforcements are very welcome, they're still not enough to beat Iysh off with. He said keep the same time table and stick with the plan."

Broden did not think it was the wrong decision. They were only barely a matching force for Iysh in terms of numbers, but Broden did not think of the two armies as equals. One of them was far better trained and armed, after all. He did not want Estole's army to butt heads with Iysh if they could avoid it. "Then did ye come to tell me the news or help?"

"Yes," Seth answered, nearly bouncing on his

toes in excitement. "What do we do first?"

"Get these people out of danger, lad. That be our first priority." The mystery of the very welcome mercenaries he could sort out later.

CHAPTER THIRTY-TWO

"Colonel Rahimi, at your service." Rahimi gave them a professional smile, marred from being polished by the scar leading up from the left corner of his mouth. He looked exactly like his profession personified: a hardened mercenary with years of experience. Faint white scars lined his dark skin, one even trailing up through the temple and into his hair. Broden counted the injuries he saw on the man, eyed the way he carried sword and dagger on his hip, and fervently hoped to never meet the man on the wrong side of a battlefield.

Edvard stepped forward and offered a hand. "Well met, Colonel. Very well met, indeed. I'm Edvard Knolton."

The man was not an ounce surprised, which suggested he had very good intel before coming here. "King Edvard, it is my honor."

"I'd love to sit and chat with you a moment, but circumstances being what they are…" Edvard trailed off with a grimace and a circular motion of his fingers that indicated the entire situation.

Truly, they did not have the time or luxury for any sort of conversation. Broden and Ashlynn stood in the doorway to the command tent, guarding and listening simultaneously. Dawn hovered, they had just escaped from around the barrier, and it literally had hours before it would fall entirely. They had managed at midnight to squirrel people away safely behind barriers. The last of their refugees had been shipped to Senn yesterday morning. The city, for all intents and purposes, was open for combat without the civilians being in the way.

Now they were heading for Kremser with all possible speed, trusting on Hendrix's connections to gather up more of an army as they traveled, and hoping it would be enough to take Kremser. From Zigzag's intel about the lack of troops in the capital, it was possible, but only just.

"King Edvard, I'm fairly certain I can guess what it is you need to know. I wish I had answers. It was not I, but my superior, in contact with your benefactor. Only he knows the man's identity and he's sworn to secrecy until the war is won. He did tell me that when I learned who it is, I was likely to keel over in shock." Rahimi shrugged, expression rueful. "I'm afraid I wasn't able to weasel anything else out of him. He's notoriously fond of pranks and surprises, you see. He wasn't about to let an opportunity like this one slip by."

"Just that is helpful," Edvard assured him, although it was obvious that he wished he had had a more definite answer. "What else can you tell me?"

"We are on indefinite pay until this matter is resolved or we are ordered by you, King Tierone, or Prince Hendrix to retreat. I have orders to protect Estole, Dahl, and Ganforth at all costs. Prince Hendrix has given me a map with very precise markings to indicate where all of your citizens are holed up and I will make sure those locations are our priority."

Broden let out a silent breath of gratitude and astonishment. Hiring a mercenary force of this size took a sizeable chunk of money, and he had no idea how long their benefactor had hired them for. That was the one question he had been brooding over for the past two days—how long did they have this mercenary army for? After all, they had no loyalty or cause in Estole. When the money ran out, they would leave. Hearing that they were funded for an extended time gave him the peace of mind he needed to go to Kremser.

Edvard's eyes closed in a gesture of pure relief. "You bring me good news, sir. I thank you for it. Is there anything you need of me before I leave with Prince Hendrix?"

"Yes, Your Majesty, a few things. I need some way to stay in contact with King Tierone—I understand he's staying here? To command your forces on the other side? Good, good—so that we can work together. I don't want this situation to digress into an open brawl."

Turning, Edvard requested, "Ashlynn?"

"Of course," she assured him. "Colonel, if you'd give me something you wear? Something gold would be helpful. I have several callers on me, but they will only last a week at a time with constant use. Make sure to use them one at a time, to avoid draining all of them. Hopefully we're back before you run out."

The colonel thought for a moment before pulling off a signet ring on his right pinky finger. "Would this do?"

Taking it, she examined it for a long moment before nodding. "It will. Edvard, give me an hour."

"I need an hour with him anyway. We need to come up with plans, and alternative plans, to defend the place while we're away." Edvard shooed her over to a table to work before drawing both Rahimi and Hendrix to the table where a map was dominating the surface. "Tell me what plan you've concocted. Let's work out as much as we can before I go."

Broden stayed planted in the doorway, in part to guard, in part because there was a brazier right next to him that kept him warm in the cold morning air. Most of the camp (both theirs and the enemy's) was still asleep, although parts of it were moving. Broden had no idea until recently that armies actually fought from morning, after breakfast, until night like it was a regular work day. But of course they would have to, otherwise they did not have the stamina to fight day after day.

As he watched the camps come to life, he lent an ear to the three discussing strategy at the table. It was a different sort entirely than he had ken of. Mountain fighting and street fighting had very little in common. It was educational just listening to them.

Ashlynn came back to the table, laying out

359

five different callers, all linked to different types of jewelry or statuary. The men paused so that she could instruct Rahimi: "Each of these has a holding spell on the magic until it's picked up by you and used. So only use one at a time. Otherwise, even if you're not actively using it, the magic will slowly drain away."

"I understand, Wizard." Rahimi picked the ring up first and put it back on. "My thanks. King Tierone has one as well?"

"He has several and a wizard of his own so you don't need to worry about him."

"Good to know. King Edvard, Prince Hendrix, I think we could stay and plan for another three days, but in truth, battle is too fluid to have precise plans. I have an idea of what you want me to do, and I'll stick to it as I can, and adapt when I can't."

Hendrix clapped him on the shoulder. "Good man. That's all I can ask. In that case, there's no point in us standing here jawing. Edvard, let's go. We have an army to gather and a battle to fight."

In a flash of brilliance, Hendrix had sent out messages ahead of time via courier birds that he needed a militia force. It took three days for them to hit the first town on their southern route, and by that time a delegation lay in anticipation. Hendrix had barely lit upon the main street in town when the mayor bustled up to him. "Prince Hendrix!"

"Mayor Schwall," Hendrix returned the

greeting, sliding off his horse immediately and taking the man's hand. "Did you get my message?"

"I did, Your Highness, and was frankly relieved to hear that you are ready to make your move." Schwall was a small town politician, but still a politician, and offered a hand to the rest of the party. "I don't believe I've made your acquaintance?"

Hendrix stopped and politely introduced everyone. "King Edvard Knolton of Estole, Wizard Ashlynn Fallbright and her partner Broden Ravenscroft. Of course you know my retainers, Avis and Fitzpatrick."

"Indeed," Schwall responded, completely overwhelmed.

Edvard grasped his hand and gave him the smile Broden recognized as the one he used for charming people. "Harmony find you, Mayor Schwall."

"Thank you, Your Majesty," Schwall managed. "I feel quite honored to meet the man in person that started this whole revolution."

"Believe me, that was not my original intent." Edvard's smile went lopsided. "The only thing I wanted to do was protect my family."

Schwall relaxed into a returning smile. "By doing so, you protect all of our families. We thank you for all of your hard work. I received Prince Hendrix's message yesterday and immediately put out the call. I am pleased to tell you that I have three hundred men that answered. They are ready to leave when you are."

Broden was a little surprised by this. The town was not that big, barely more than Cloud's

Rest in population, and they could send out three hundred men? Remarkable. How fast did they have to work to prepare for the journey to Kremser?

"Mayor, we need to leave in the next hour, do you truly mean they are ready to leave when we are?" Hendrix pressed.

"I am. They have been on standby since this morning, as you indicated that you would be coming through on this day. I anticipated we would be, if not your first stop, one of your firsts. It seems I was correct." Schwall clapped his hands together with immense satisfaction. "Some of our townspeople also put together supplies for you as we weren't sure how well you would be able to prepare for this journey."

They would be a welcome sight. Broden knew that not much had been packed, partially because they had had little time to prepare what with seeing to everyone else, partially because everyone was loathe to take any food away with them when Estole was so low on it. Especially with a siege likely underway by now, ships would not be able to enter.

Hendrix clapped the man on the shoulder, eyes bright with feeling and perhaps a trace of unshed tears. "You are true friends, Mayor. I can't begin to express how glad I am for your support. We are very grateful for everything."

"We are glad to support you," Schwall assured him. "Be better to us than Zelman was, that's all we ask in return."

Hendrix snorted. "That's a very low bar to pass. How about instead I promise to be as good to you as Edvard is to his people? That's more of challenge and the leader that I would like to become."

"Hendy," Edvard drawled, "do stop, you're making me blush and squirm over here."

"We can all pat each other on the back later," Ashlynn prompted impatiently. "For now, we need all speed. Mayor, you say that everyone is on standby and are ready to go now?"

"Indeed, Wizard Fallbright."

"Then let's go, man, we're burning daylight."

Trust Ashlynn to keep the momentum up. Broden thought it but did not dare say it.

The mayor sprang into action and sent out a general call to assemble. Men came from every possible direction and formed, loosely, into ranks in the main square. The way they did this suggested to Broden that they had done some sort of drill to prepare for this moment. Seeing such soothed his heart a little, as it meant that they were not volunteering without any thought or preparation.

It took a little over an hour by the time they made it back on the road. They visited two more towns before they had to stop for the night at the fourth. In those towns, they managed to gather just shy of nine hundred men, an incredible force for a day's work and literally with two days of notice. The fourth town they stopped at for the night put them up in an inn, arranged for hospitality for everyone else in people's homes and even a few businesses, and were perfectly agreeable hosts.

Broden sank into a seat in the main taproom of the inn, grateful to be sitting still for a while and to have a hot plate of food in front of him. "Gods and goddesses above, but this be an extraordinary day."

Ashlynn had her head supported in one hand, looking beyond tired, although a smile wrinkled up her eyes. "It's astonishing what your word alone has brought about, Hendy. When you said you had the support of the people, you meant it."

"I did," Hendrix responded mildly, "but what's with the Hendy nickname?"

"You're family now," Edvard observed as if this were perfectly obvious and he could not begin to understand why Hendrix was even questioning this. "Of course we won't call you properly by name all of the time."

"Take it as a sign of affection, lad," Broden advised.

Hendrix tried to look unaffected by this but he was clearly pleased to be on a more friendly footing with everyone. "Does that mean I'm now accepted as Bria's fiancé?"

"Did I have a choice in the matter?" Edvard grumbled.

Ashlynn laughed outright. "No. It amuses me that you thought you did."

Edvard gestured to her with a "as she said" expression and did not dare say another word on the subject. "You told me that you had sent out several messages, but how many?"

"Every single town on our route south. I'm not sure how many troops we can anticipate," Hendrix added honestly. "I've been pleasantly surprised so far. I expected roughly half of what I got today. If this trend continues we'll have quite the force indeed by the time we reach Kremser."

"I certainly hope so." Broden sent several prayers up to the heavens to that effect. "I know you said that the journey will take six days from here, so does that mean—"

From Ashlynn's neck there came a muted sound. She immediately fished the caller necklace out and said, "Repeat that."

"Ashlynn," Troi's voice rang clear and very anxious, "I need to speak with either King Edvard or Prince Hendrix. Preferably both."

"We're here, Troi," Hendrix responded, brow furrowed. "You sound worried, what's gone wrong? Are the tactics not working?"

"No, Your Highness, they're working rather well. Our mercenaries are very good at their jobs and the Iyshian army is having an incredibly hard time going past the main street. That's going well." Troi took an audible breath before blurting out, "Miss Bria is missing."

Hendrix froze, staring at the caller as if doubting his own ears. Broden had a sinking pit yawning open at the bottom of his stomach and knew that everyone at the table felt the same. Bria missing? AGAIN?

"What do you mean my sister is missing?" Edvard asked in a dangerous tone of voice that promised racks and thumb screws if the answer was not to his liking.

"Sire," Troi, apparently realizing his king was Not Happy, had just the tiniest trace of raw panic in his voice, "we've searched all of Dahl, Estole, and Ganforth. Twice. Bria is nowhere to be seen. I've even had the wizards do a magical tracing

HONOR RACONTEUR

spell of some sort and they still couldn't locate her. They said that even if she were dead, it would have worked. We are convinced that she has been kidnapped and taken out of this area."

Edvard's eyes demanded an explanation from Ashlynn and she confirmed with a nod. "The searching spells have a certain radius to them. Get out of that radius, they're useless."

"We will of course do our best to track her down, but I have a suspicion that you'll see her before we do."

Perhaps Broden had spent far too much time around evil men, as he knew what Troi meant before anyone else did. "Ye mean ye think yon prince snapped her up when our backs were turned to use the lass as leverage."

Hendrix let his head thump to the table, shaking it back and forth in denial.

Edvard growled out several choice curses. "That is exactly something one of Zelman's whelps would do. After all, he's done it before."

"It did no' work out that well for him last time," Broden observed with a toothy grin.

"But it might work better this time," Ashlynn observed. "It'll take us time to figure out exactly where he's going and how he's getting there. We're assuming he's heading straight for Kremser, like we are, but we might be wrong. Maddox might have some other plan up his sleeve."

"Or it's not Maddox at all, but some other agent of Zelman's acting on his king's orders." Edvard rubbed at his eyes with the pads of his fingers. "I'm going to kill that man when I finally lay my hands on him."

If he could beat Broden to it. The archer had several arrows all with the king's name on them. Broden had a low tolerance for evil men to begin with and Zelman had exceeded the limits of his patience eons ago.

"Troi, try to verify what happened," Ashlynn ordered. "We'll do our best to keep a lookout for her as we travel. Maybe we'll get lucky. Have you notified Zigzag about all of this?"

"I'm preparing a message to him right now. If nothing else, maybe one of his contacts knows something."

"Right now, communicating with every person we can think of is our best course of action. We can never anticipate what someone else knows." Ashlynn put an arm around Edvard's shoulders, hugging him to her and offering some comfort. She, too, was worried about her sister, but Broden recognized that Hendrix was taking this the hardest. Edvard was not doing much better, either, as he regarded the safety of his family as his main priority and having Bria taken—again— left a bitter taste of failure in his mouth.

"That is very true, Miss Ashlynn. I'm spreading the word far and wide. Also, Sire, I'm offering an unspecified reward for any information regarding her whereabouts."

"Good thinking, Troi, reward whatever you think appropriate." Edvard regarded the caller in Ashlynn's hands with a sort of grim resignation. "I think we're reaching the limits of this booster of Ashlynn's."

"You're right," she informed him bluntly. "Troi, you know which route we're taking? Send carrier pigeons to your contacts along that route to keep us abreast of any progress."

"I will. Sire, our profound apologies, we have failed you."

"Find my sister. Figure out how she was taken. Apologize later."

"Yes, Sire." With that, the call ended.

Edvard threw his head back, taking in a deep breath. Broden was not sure if the man was fighting back tears or temper. Either way, he gave him a few minutes to gather himself back together. "Hendy. We'll get her back."

"And we'll murder the man that's taken her," Hendrix promised with a feral smile.

CHAPTER
THIRTY-THREE

"Wait, too many things are happening at once," Ash protested, expression pained. "Slow down, Mrs. Pennington. Start from the beginning."

"We have a spy in the innermost palace. He was the commander of the city guard until the new laws went into place. Since he is the second son of a second marriage, he lost his position and has played the part of a drunk ever since," she explained with forced patience.

Riana stopped reviewing the latest message that had come in via carrier pigeon and looked up sharply. A drunk lord? "Lord Halloway by any chance?"

Pennington gave her a sharp nod. "The same, Miss Saira."

"This means something to you?" Ash asked her.

"It does. I've met the man several times." Woelfel had said that he would explain about Halloway, but with one thing or another, had forgotten to do so. Riana knew nothing more than that the man was an ally of theirs, only not openly so. "What about him, Mrs. Pennington?"

"He heard of Prince Hendrix's army coming this direction and sent a frantic message to Master Cyr this morning saying that we were to not, under any circumstances, allow the army into the city."

Riana and Ash shared alarmed looks. That didn't sound good at all.

Ash pressed, "There was no explanation as to why?"

Shaking her head, Mrs. Pennington explained, "He has a very limited way of communicating with us. Only four people even know of his role aside from me—Master Troi, Master Cyr, and now you. He has a direct control over the city guard, and his position is too sensitive to jeopardize. We've only ever received three messages from him prior to this for that reason."

"This doesn't sound good at all." Ash rubbed his hands together in a round motion, thinking hard. "If that was all he could say then it must be very dangerous indeed. Woelfel knows this man better than we do, what does he think?"

"He is trying to enter the palace directly and find a better way of getting information from him without cracking his cover," Mrs. Pennington explained. "But he doesn't have very good odds of doing so. Prince Hendrix's advance toward the city is a badly kept secret at this point. Zelman will declare martial law at any moment and when he does so, the palace grounds will be locked down tightly. Only military personnel will be allowed in and out."

This just got better and better. Riana tried to sit on her frustration, as she needed to think coolly and logically. "Is there any way for us to communicate with Hendrix and Edvard that entering the city is dangerous?"

"We're not even sure which town he's in," Ash responded, equally frustrated. "And not every town has the carrier pigeons set up. The best we can do is inform Troi, have Troi send a message to him, and hope that message catches up with him."

That sounded very cumbersome and not at all likely to happen. Riana fidgeted in her chair. "Ashlynn is probably too far out to reach now?"

"Yes." Ash reached out, squeezing her hand, trying to settle them both down. Their emotions kept ricocheting and setting the other off. It was one of the downsides of such a close bond. "I'll have to wait until she's near the city. At the very least near the city gates. This will be equally hard to do. If it's too noisy, and it likely will be with them battering at the gates, she might not hear me calling to her. Our best bet is to try both."

Riana wasn't about to do one or the other. Good information became bad intelligence when delivered too late. That she had learned for herself in this business of spies and kings. "Is there nothing else we can—"

From the back of the house rang a distinct chime of bells, a signal that everyone knew well. It signaled a carrier pigeon returning.

In unison, all three of them popped up from their chairs and rushed toward the back coop.

Mrs. Pennington, old but spry, beat them there by a hair's breadth and scooped the pigeon out. He had a backpack on instead of a leg holster—a sign that the message he carried was lengthier than a sentence. She snapped the letter out of its pouch, setting the bird back inside, and unrolled the message.

Then her face gained a very grim cast.

"I'm not going to like this," Ash stated in a calm tone that belied the turmoil of emotions racing through him. "Say it."

"Miss Bria has been kidnapped."

Riana felt an odd distancing for a moment, as if she were in a surreal dream instead of standing in a potential war zone. Any second she would wake up and this whole nightmare would be over.

Ash put an arm around her shoulders, hugging her to him hard, snapping her out of that odd feeling and grounding her. She leaned into him as she desperately needed the grounding.

"How?" Ash asked in that too-calm voice. "When?"

"Three days ago and they're not quite sure how," Mrs. Pennington answered, her eyes scanning the note for a second time. "Troi is requesting we send out inquiries to everyone we know. He has no idea who has her or where she's been taken. All he's sure of is that she is not in Estole."

Riana took in a deep breath. This was no time to fall apart, as much as she would like to do so. She had friends in imminent danger that needed help. "Ash, draft a note to Troi explaining what we know. We need to get that off first. Then you and I will send out messages to everyone and try to find Bria. Mrs. Pennington, we're counting on your help in this."

"Of course," the matron assured them gently. "We'll all try to help. Perhaps—"

This time they were interrupted by the distinct sound of the side door slamming open and closed, accompanied by the quick trot of footsteps. "Where is everyone?" Woelfel called out.

"Back here, Master Cyr!" Pennington stepped just outside of the coop and into the hallway.

Woelfel spoke loudly before he was even into the room. "They'd already declared martial law before I could even make it to the palace. I couldn't get in to speak with him, and even basic messages were not allowed. We absolutely have to find out what he meant, otherwise our army is going to be slaughtered." Finally reaching the room, he stopped dead and eyed the message in her hands. "More news?"

"Miss Bria has been taken," Mrs. Pennington informed him with a grimace.

"WHAT?!" Woelfel demanded in dismay. "When, how?"

Riana still reeled with this latest news. Was everyone she knew and loved going to be in severe danger all at the same time? Was there no way to protect any of them? "Do we know when our army is going to arrive?"

Woelfel spread his hands in a helpless shrug. "It can take them anywhere between nine to fourteen days, depending on how many stops they make and how long it takes for people to actually respond to their call. We literally have to wait for someone to report a sighting or for the front gates to crash in before we know they're here."

"Never have I been so frustrated by our callers' limitations until now," Ash growled.

Mrs. Pennington clapped her hands, pulling them out of their complaints. "Focus on what you can do. We have very limited time to work in."

Riana took in a deep breath and made herself calm down. "You two focus on trying to find Bria. I'll do what I can to contact the army."

Due to all of the time she was spending around royals these days, Riana was able to secure an audience with Queen Rosalind without much effort. It took four hours to actually make the appointment and it was right before formal dinner that she could meet with her.

Queen Rosalind had her come into her morning room, a very feminine space obviously catered to the queen's tastes. It was light and airy, all of the furniture in whites, pale greens, and light oak. Even in the evening hours, it spoke somehow of daylight. It was a very relaxing space, which Riana appreciated, as her nerves felt stretched to the breaking point.

Somewhat to her surprise, Savir was there as well, relaxing in a window bench with a book. He rose when she entered, giving her a slight bow. "Lady Saira."

"Your Highness," she greeted in return.

Facing the queen, she gave a deeper curtsey. "Your Majesty. Thank you for letting me meet with you on such short notice."

"Of course, that's no trouble at all. Your note seemed quite urgent. Come," the queen invited, waving to a seat next to her on the couch. "Do sit down. Tell me whatever is the matter."

Riana promptly took the seat and tried to angle herself so that she could see both of them at once. "Your Majesty, I just received a very worrisome note from home. It was so urgently sent that I actually received it via carrier pigeon, which is a rare thing indeed. Your Majesty, Bria Knolton is missing."

Queen Rosalind's mouth formed an 'O' but it did not truly speak of surprise. For a moment, irritation flickered across Savir's face before he'd covered it with a frown. Mother and son glanced at each other, their eyes speaking volumes.

Riana knew she was right to call for this face-to-face meeting in that moment. She'd needed to see these reactions. These two definitely knew something.

Rosalind picked up Riana's hand and clasped it, offering comfort. "I understand your worry. Unfortunately I've heard nothing about the young lady's whereabouts."

"I see." Riana looked down, trying to make sure that her own expression gave nothing away.

"I will of course send out inquiries. Savir, you'll ask Greer Dunlap to do the same?"

"Of course, Mother."

"We'll do our best to find her," Queen Rosalind assured her gently. "I know she's a friend of yours, and of course she's very dear to Hendrix. I would hate for anything to happen to her."

Oh yes. These two knew something. And with the way they were dancing about the subject, they weren't about to disclose it. "Thank you, Your Majesty. I knew that meeting with you would be my best course of action."

Rosalind smiled at her, expression gentle. "I'm glad you did, child."

Yes, so was she.

CHAPTER THIRTY-FOUR

Hendrix called a meeting when they stopped for the night. People were setting up tents, gathering wood for cookfires and the like, generally making camp. Hendrix pulled aside the core people, letting everyone else do the camp chores, and sat them down on a fallen pair of logs just off the road.

"Before light fails us, I need to get a few things across. As I'm sure you've all realized, trying to take Kremser with a ragtag army is doomed to failure, no matter how big it is."

Broden had been wondering if anyone else realized that, or if they were riding on wishful thinking. "Aye, lad, we all ken that, I think. Ye've got a notion of what to do about it?"

"A few ideas. I want to run them all past you in order to see how much we can implement before we reach the city. I estimate we have another four days, which doesn't give us much time at all. I just hope it's enough." Hendrix angled himself so that he could speak to the whole group better. "Let me start off by saying this: the enemy likely knows we're coming and they likely have a very dirty tactic planned for when we do arrive."

"I think we all knew that," Edvard assured him. "You know what it is?"

"No, but I know what I would do if I was in their shoes. First, I'd give token resistance at the walls, to allow us through."

"Wait, what?" Ashlynn protested. "Shouldn't they be trying to keep us out?"

Hendrix shook his head. "They have a skeleton crew in the city right now. Zigzag confirmed that. It would be very difficult to keep us out of the city entirely for any real stretch of time. While it's well protected, they're not set up for a siege, either. Too many mouths to feed and the treasury, as we know, is depleted. Their best bet oddly enough is to let us in."

It almost made sense. Almost. "Let us in and then what, lad?"

"Bring us far enough into the city to trap us all inside." Hendrix leaned down and borrowed a few sticks and rocks to start laying it out on the ground. "Have a main force lying in wait on the road here, the one leading from the main gate to the palace. They know we'll want to make a beeline that direction. Then, have two elite forces here and here, on either side, a few streets over. Those forces will wait until we're engaged with the main one, then flank us on either side in a pinching movement. It'll decimate us entirely and will cost them very little resources or casualties."

The simple efficiency of it sent a chill up Broden's spine. "What be the odds they'll think to do this?"

Hendrix contemplated that for a moment before offering, "They're complete morons if they don't try this?"

Right. Extremely good odds.

"But you have a way around this," Ashlynn prompted hopefully.

"I have two. One, we realize that we're not going to just rush into the city willy-nilly and trust all will be fine. We go in systematically, clearing several streets in both directions, and then wait for reinforcements from our backup units to keep that area clear until we find those two reserve nests of enemy forces. We take them out first, then we proceed onward. Second, we divide these men up into squadrons and train them how to clear buildings."

Any training at all would help. Broden had been talking to everyone he could as they marched and discovered that very few had any sort of training or fighting experience to speak of. They were determined and fed up with a bad king, but not fighters. He'd grown increasingly worried about taking them into the city in this condition. Any training at all would give them higher odds of survival and all of them a better chance at actually winning the conflict.

"Ashlynn," Hendrix focused on her with intensity, "I've seen Ash create simple boards out of wood in seconds, dozens at a time. I've seen him log some pretty impressive trees as well. Is this something you know how to do?"

"Of course," she answered, almost affronted at the suggestion that her brother might know how to do something she didn't. "Why? What are you wanting me to make?"

"Shields."

Edvard let out a hiss. "Of course! I should have thought of that before. Shields would give them at least some protection. How big, do you think? A buckler size? Something larger?"

"Most shields are about the size of a man's chest," Hendrix answered with a weighing look at Ashlynn, gauging her reaction to this. "I'd like it to be about that size. What do you say, Ashlynn?"

"That entirely depends on how thick you want it, how many I'm making, and how many trees I have to work with," she responded candidly. "What's your order?"

"As many as you can," Hendrix responded promptly, proving he had anticipated this question, "three fingers thick and can you put a protective coating on the top to repel weapons?"

"Only if it's on the very top and the men understand that coming into direct contact with it will likely make them highly uncomfortable," Ashlynn warned. "Remember, my magic isn't a pleasant sensation to all."

"I do forget that sometimes," Broden admitted with a shrug, making them all shrug in return.

Ashlynn shot him a warm smile before continuing, "How many I make really depends on how many trees I can use. There's not many in this area of the country since it's mostly farmland out here. But I'll do the best I can to make sure that most of our troops have a shield, at least."

"Work it so that every squadron has at least a few shields in it," Hendrix requested. "That's the base of what we need. That way we have people who can cover the rest as they're fighting."

"That I can do," Ashlynn promised.

"Good. Now, Edvard, Broden, do you know how to clear a building safely?"

"Of course," they answered in unison.

Hendrix looked more than a little relieved, as well he should, as he had never seen Edvard in any kind of conflict. Neither had Broden, for that matter, but he knew the man trained with the guard on a regular basis. He might not have much in the way of experience but at the very least, he knew how to do it in theory. "Then while Ashlynn is logging trees, help me divide them up into squadrons and teach them."

"Of course," Edvard repeated, agreeing readily. He bounced up to his feet, already moving. "How should we divide them up? How large do you think a squadron should be?"

As they moved off, Broden lingered enough to ask, "Lass, ye be fine by yerself?"

She negated the worry with a flick of the hand. "There's trees right there, I'm surrounded by a little over a thousand people, I can't possibly be any safer. Go train people. Whoever gets done first gets to cook the other dinner."

"Fair enough."

They arrived in Kremser with a force of four thousand, eight hundred sixty odd souls. It was an extremely hodge podge force with little in the way of organization, but much in the way of determination. Hendrix spent most of the march organizing them as they moved, arranging them in ranks, assigning captains over groups, and so on. Broden watched him work and had to wonder—for a man that said he had only minimal experience in warfare, who exactly was he comparing himself to? He had plenty of experience from what Broden could see.

Kremser's spy network knew they were coming. It was impossible to hide their intentions and gather up a secret force of this size without it getting out somehow. Hendrix had not even tried. The walls and main gates had a strong force waiting for them.

They arrived late in the morning outside of Kremser's walls. Broden studied the situation from one side to another, not at all sure how Hendrix planned to get inside. Siege warfare was terrible in this regard, as the offensive force had to somehow get past those very sturdy walls. He had learned that intimately well at Estole.

Stopping dead in the middle of the street, Hendrix took one look at the situation and gave a grim smile. "And this is why I wanted Ashlynn to go with us."

Ashlynn perked up. "I get to break something?"

"All the things," Hendrix promised, expression a perfect match for hers. Straightening in his saddle, he waved her forward. "Wizard Fallbright, if I may request your assistance?" he asked mock formally.

"With pleasure, Prince Hendrix," she responded in kind, sweeping him a bow that would not have been out of place in a formal Court. Lifting a hand, she drew that intricate spell symbol in the air Broden knew well, spoke a word, and power burst forth like a lightning bolt straight at the gates.

They exploded in a shower of pebbles and splinters, leaving a smoking hole behind.

Chortling, Ashlynn blew another two holes just for the sheer fun of it, leaving it more than wide enough for four carriages abreast to pass through.

Voice laced with amusement, Edvard reminded her, "He has to fix those later, you know."

She wrinkled her nose at him but subsided. Broden noticed that Hendrix looked relieved. Been too afraid to request she stop, eh? Considering she had zapped him before, Broden did not exactly blame him.

Hendrix turned his horse around. "Captains, to me!"

The captains, already cued up, gathered and formed a rough semicircle around Hendrix, silent and anxious. Hendrix waited until he had all of them before speaking. "You know what to do. Block off the main streets, guard them so that we have direct access to the palace. Do not get sidetracked from that mission, no matter what happens, and please, please do not cut yourself off from an avenue of retreat. Be able to fall back at any point. I don't want to lose anyone in there. Do you understand me?"

There rang a chorus of assents.

"Then go. Squadrons one through six, you

breach the gates. We've got your backs."

Since Broden and Ashlynn were part of the first squadron, they immediately left. For anyone else, sending in a squadron of twenty-five men as the forerunners into a city would have been suicide. But not with Ashlynn as captain. She threw up a general shield to protect everyone as they bulled through what was left of the city gate. The gate was nearly as tall and wide as the street itself and she used it like a battering ram to force their way through. What soldiers were left did not stand a chance against her.

First Squadron consisted of men and woman who had training and fighting experience. They knew what to do without much input from Aslyhnn. As she moved through the streets, they peeled off and protected the sides, squashing whatever resistance they found. They always came back to the main street after that engagement, protecting Ashlynn and Broden's backs as they forged forward.

Perhaps it was because they were in battle, but Broden did not like the feeling in the city. There was a desperation, a bloodiness to it that had his heart thumping. Was this normal? It was not a sense of adrenaline but more like grim determination that pulled him forward, even though his heart was reluctant to damage the city like this. No one living here deserved to pay for Zelman's crimes.

Broden felt it just as well he was not a soldier by profession.

Ashlynn hit the fourth street corner and stopped, as planned, giving a chance for the other squadrons to catch up with her. Hendrix had pounded it into their heads to not advance too far too fast, as they risked being cut off completely from the main force. Even if they had Ashlynn with them, that would be foolish in the extreme.

Standing at her back, Broden kept a sharp lookout for trouble in every direction, trusting Ashlynn to do the same. "We no' be seeing many soldiers."

"It worries me," Ashlynn admitted. "I think they've set up a barricade of some sort ahead, letting these streets be a temporary loss. We're going to blunder right into an ambush at some point."

"Aye, that be me guess as well." Broden pondered that for a moment, watching absently as the rest of their squadron formed up ranks around them in a circle, covering all angles. "Well, lass, what do ye want to do about it?"

Ashlynn flashed him a hopeful look over her shoulder.

"Ye want to spring it," he interpreted, resigned. "Of course ye do. Why do I ask such silly questions?"

"I don't know, that's a good question, why do you?"

"Just on the off chance ye choose something sane for once?" he countered, not sure whether to laugh or cry.

"Now, Broden, have I ever taken the easier route? On anything?"

"There be always a first time, lass."

"Chances are it'll happen eventually," she agreed amiably.

"Chance be a fine thing," he groused. Sighing, he looked back toward the gate and saw that the other squadrons had nearly caught up with them. "No sense in pushing it off, I suppose."

"Let's go." Ashlynn turned long enough to shout back to the second squadron's captain, "We think there's an ambush ahead! We're going to spring it!"

He waved a hand in the air, shouting back, "We've got your backs, go!"

Four arrows in his hand, bow at the ready, Broden stayed just in Ashlynn's shadow as she cautiously went forward.

The streets were unnaturally quiet, so still that a graveyard would seem lively in comparison. Sound echoed off the brick buildings and the cobblestone streets in a loud ricochet that set Broden's already taut nerves screaming in protest.

It was in this abrupt stillness that Ash's voice rang loud and clear, "Ashlynn! ASH-LYNN!"

Swearing, his twin yanked the necklace out from under her shirt and hissed at it, "Keep your voice down, you idiot. I'm almost in the middle of the city."

"That's what I was afraid of. Turn around. Now."

"What?"

"You heard me. One of our spies reported that if the army entered the city, it would be slaughtered."

Hearing that, Broden grabbed her arm and started towing her in the other direction.

Ashlynn followed along behind him, demanding answers as they moved at a half-trot.

"Why?"

"We don't know. The spy is in the palace and martial law was declared before he could get a full message out. We've been trying to reach him properly for days now without any success."

Broden had to wonder, was Hendrix's idea the reason? Had they set up ambushes to flank both sides to crush an invading army completely? If that was the case, they had a counter-strategy, but he hated to forge ahead if there was more intel to be had.

"And why by the gods above wouldn't you call me before entering the city?" Ash berated her. "I've got information on this place, I'm here in the city, shouldn't you have called? I've been trying to reach you for days."

"I did call," she defended herself. "I didn't get a response."

"Did you re-attune the caller to 'direct' instead of 'linked' connections?" Ash asked in this tone that said he already knew the answer.

Ashlynn's face contorted into a comedic "whoops" caricature.

"Because I realized this morning you've been doing linked connections for so long you'd likely forgotten that was the setting. And so I changed my settings on this caller and was finally able to get through. Smart, sis."

"Oh shut up. I've had other things on my mind." Ashlynn snapped her fingers at her squadron as they passed them, jerking a hand to signal they were retreating. "Edvard and Hendrix also have a caller with them. Let's pull them into this."

"Good thought. Edvard, Hendrix, respond."

It took a bare two seconds before Edvard said, "I'm here. Ash, it's about time you called us."

"I've been trying to for several days. Ashlynn had the wrong settings on her caller, I couldn't get through."

"Oh, is that what happened?"

"Oh hush, the pair of you." Ashlynn stopped and silently asked Broden to do a headcount even as she continued talking through the caller. "Edvard, Ash says they have a spy in the palace that sent a warning. If we enter the city, we'll be slaughtered."

Hendrix abruptly came into the call. "How?"

"We don't know," Ash admitted in vexation. "He's locked in the palace under martial law and we haven't found a way to reach him. This is literally the extent of our knowledge."

"I don't like the sound of that," Edvard said, completely troubled.

"I don't think any of us do. Hendrix, Broden and I are currently on the corner of," Ashlynn turned and took in the pair of road signs nearby, "Market and Main Street. What do you want us to do?"

"Stay there," Hendrix ordered. "If they're going to do what I think they're going to do, then they won't move with only three squadrons in the city. Hold your position, keep a sharp lookout, and let me come up with another plan that will thwart whatever protocol they have in place. We can't afford a complete retreat at this point; we'll lose too much ground."

"Understood, that's what we'll do."

They hunkered down, crouching behind the shield bearers to gain the most protection. Broden had each man looking a different direction, ready to shout out at the least sign of movement.

Ashlynn stayed at his side, trusting him to look out for her safety as she continued the conversation with her brother. "Ash, what's the situation where you are?"

"Everyone has been ordered to stay locked up in their homes. If they have a basement, they're in it. We're actually geared and ready to come help you when Hendrix gives the word. I know where you are, roughly, so I should be able to carve a way to you if needed."

"Good. This spy in the palace, how does he know about the guard's plans?"

"Former commander of the guards before Zelman's inheritance laws yanked him out of the position. He's played a drunk lord ever since but his ties with the guard are still rather strong, as he served with them for several years. He's intimately aware of what they're planning. I wish he'd been able to get out before martial law was declared."

That made two of them. Broden absolutely hated this open position he was in. It felt like an arrow could come flying out from the shadows at any minute. It made his skin crawl.

The silence from their general was long and felt like several eternities strung together. When Hendrix finally did speak, Broden actually jumped.

"We've had a stroke of good luck! Our spy from inside the palace made it out."

"What?" several voices demanded all at once,

relieved and surprised. "How?"

Hendrix actually chuckled. "Long story short, my father has a magic talisman that transports him to the docks in case of an emergency. He stole that and used it to get outside."

Broden's mouth parted in delight. "Meaning the king has no escape route left?"

"Exactly. Two birds, one stone. I do love this man. Halloway says that the plan is this: there are three forces deployed toward the center of the city. There's one on Main Street, and two other elite forces waiting on either side, about six streets over. Their orders are to wait until the army has reached the main force and then they flank to either side, crushing us from every direction."

So, in other words, the plan that Hendrix feared they would have.

"The good news is, our spy has known about this plan long enough to help us with a counter. We're a little out of position for it, though. We need to hold the ground where we are and send our own force to the right, taking care of one of the flanking sides. Then we move up and around behind the main force—they're established on Baker Street—and take them. We have several citizens that have prepared temporary barricades they'll set down to help cut off any lines of retreat and make sure we can do this."

Broden shared a look with Ashlynn, almost doubting his ears.

It was Ash that said what he was thinking: "Wait, you mean our spy not only brought the plan to us, he also created a counter to it? Halloway, if you're listening, we're beyond grateful."

"No-not at all, sir," a new, unfamiliar male voice panted out. "General Quillin actually took charge of the barricades and set those up."

"Still, our thanks to you. We'll thank Quillin as well when we catch up with him."

"N-not at all," Halloway managed, still breathless.

"He's a little out of air at the moment," Edvard explained, tone amused. "The man did a mad sprint from the docks all the way around the wall to get to us. He barely had the breath to explain what we needed to do."

Made sense. If the talisman dropped him on the docks, then he would have had to run around a fourth of the city to reach Edvard and Hendrix, and that was not a small distance. In fact, Halloway's stamina must be impressive to pull it off.

"Ash, I need you and Riana at Baker Street, but don't engage just yet. Ashlynn, Broden, don't move. I need you to hold position and protect us while we deal with that right enemy group."

"Understood, we'll do that." Ashlynn kept the caller up in her hand, listening as Hendrix gave individual commands to his troops to support Ash and Riana as they dealt with the enemy. She didn't try to speak, however, as there was no need to. Hendrix had it all well in hand.

Four squadrons of troops, mostly formed out of the retired soldiers and guardsmen, jogged past them and went into a side street leading to Baker Street. Broden sent up several prayers as they went past but did not dare try to speak to Ash or his daughter. They did not need distractions at this point.

A mighty clash sounded several minutes later, screams and metal clanging against metal; the sounds of war. Broden saw magic flaring up into the sky like northern lights and knew that Ash was in the middle of battle, Riana undoubtedly with him.

It felt another small eternity before the sounds died out and Ash's voice came across, "They're down. Ashlynn, I'll meet you at the main force. We had very little casualties, I think we can be the rear attack."

"Do so," Hendrix ordered. "We'll reinforce Ashlynn's squadrons."

In a softer, kind voice, Ash added: "Riana is fine."

And this was why Broden liked Ash. "Thank ye, lad."

"Ash, Ashlynn, time your attack for the noon hour precisely if you can. Let's not give them any openings. Halloway, I'm counting on you to give the signal for when our people drop their barricades."

"They have orders to do it the very minute they hear me, Your Highness. If one of your wizards can give my voice a boost?"

"Of course," Ashlynn assured him. "Catch up with me."

"Then we all know what to do," Edvard said with immense satisfaction. "Go."

CHAPTER THIRTY-FIVE

Things did not go that smoothly, of course. In war, plans never do.

While they were able to deal well enough with the enemy on the main road, the same could not be said of the last group of enemy troops. They apparently had put together fairly quickly what was going on with the other two, and upon not receiving any orders, had rightly assumed that their commander had fallen in battle. So they did the very thing that Hendrix did not want them to do—they took over one of the monasteries nearby and holed up in it.

Ashlynn was all for blowing the place silly and charging through, but the monastery was so closely integrated into the city's infrastructure that doing so would cost thousands upon thousands of trillina to fix it again. Hendrix wasn't willing to do it and Broden did not blame him. There was no point in conquering a place if you were going to destroy it in the process.

Because of their caution, it took the rest of the

day of slow siege warfare and some trickery on Ashlynn's part to be able to get the gates of the monastery down. Once inside, it took even longer to finally get all of the enemy routed out. While they had dealt with the enemy, night had fallen, and no one wanted to try and take the palace in the middle of the night.

Well, no one except Ashlynn. The wait chaffed at her sorely but she bowed to everyone else's opinion (with vast reluctance) and they stayed the night in the monastery instead. There was a defensive position, almost enough beds, and even a goodly amount of food in the storehouses to feed people with. Really, it could not have been a better location to hole up in, which was likely why the guardsmen had chosen it to begin with.

Under the cover of darkness, two visitors arrived. One of them, with his fair hair and magic, was well known to every person and the sentries hailed him gladly, letting him through the gates. Broden caught the side gate opening and two people with hoods up coming in. This struck him as odd, as all of their people were already inside, so who were they letting in?

Worried, he snatched up the bow and quiver of arrows laying at his side and hurried down the stairs, waylaying them before they could get more than ten steps in.

The shorter of the two let out a laugh he knew well. "See, Ash? I told ye Da would catch us afore we got a dozen paces in."

Pulling his hood back, Ash grinned at Broden. "And I was so sure he'd be too busy to notice our entrance."

Broden lit up in relief and joy in seeing two of his favorite people in the world. Laughing, he threw both arms wide and caught them up in a bear hug. "Ah, it does an old man's heart good to see ye."

His daughter hugged him back hard, giving the same sigh, as if she had returned home after a hard journey. "Da."

"Aye, daughter." No other words needed to be spoken. For a time, he just held the pair of them and let his heart feel at ease.

"Is that Ash and Riana?" Ashlynn nearly flew down the stairs, taking them two at a time and hopping the last three, joining in on the hug with a bound. "How did the two of you get in?!"

"I think we said please," Ash answered, snaking an arm free to hug his twin to him. "Was that what we said, Riana?"

"Fairly sure the please did it," she agreed happily. "Ashlynn. Did Halloway make it to ye?"

"He did, and General Quillin, whoever that is, helped as well by putting up temporary barricades." Ashlynn drew back to look at the two of them. "Did you plan all that?"

They shook their heads in denial. "Had no part in it," Ash denied. "But we did get the report of what was happening. We were actually desperate to get Halloway out, as he had vital information, but he was locked tight in the palace. How did he manage it?"

"He stole the king's magical escape route," Ashlynn responded, sniggering.

Riana's eyes went wide. "Oh. Oh, to be a fly on the wall when Zelman finds that out."

"Right?" Ashlynn said in perfect agreement. "I'm soooo disappointed I'll miss it. But more importantly, I heard rumors that you're together now! Officially! Come, sit down and tell me every single detail."

"Well, we can," Ash turned to Riana with a mock-frown on his face, as if unsure of how to proceed, "but I would think she'd be more interested in us attaining the final level in our bond, wouldn't you?"

Riana gave a hum of consideration. "You're right, but let's not overwhelm her by telling it to her all at once."

Broden's eyes threatened to pop right out of his head. Ashlynn looked like a landed fish. "Ye did no'," he breathed, flabbergasted at this news. He had known that they were working on it, but still!

"Let's sit down, Da," his daughter suggested with a wicked gleam in her eye. "And I'll tell ye the whooole story."

They stayed up late talking, swapping stories and catching the other up to date. Still, at sunrise people were up, ready, and on the move. And while Riana and Ash were wonderful distractions, the twelve hour delay meant that Ashlynn was fit to be tied.

Everyone within range of her could tell. Even Ash could see it and he wasn't even on the same side of the palace wall as she was. They were stationed on the south side, around the corner from Broden and Ashlynn, while the others were on the east. But even from that distance, he could feel waves of palpable, taut energy, and the feedback resonated to Riana. It was likely a combination of stress, frustration, and worry over Bria, as they still had no idea where she was. Whatever the underlying cause, Riana knew this for certain: Ashlynn was going to be destroying things right, left, and center.

The doors and gates into the palace compound were guarded tightly. It would be near fatal to go through any of them. That was why Hendrix had vetoed the traditional method of siege warfare and chose to cheat outrageously with his two wizards. They lined up in three different areas of the wall, in between the gates, and waited with their troops poised and ready to enter.

"Now," Hendrix commanded calmly.

Ash lifted a hand and spoke a spell, the rock wall exploding into multiple pieces, showering dust and pebbles. Before the air had even cleared, people were piling through, shields up in defense. Ashlynn's side exploded at the same time as Ash's, and barely a minute passed before another concussion rocked the main courtyard as she blasted another section of the wall to smithereens.

Riana kept her eyes peeled and her bow at the ready as they went through the wall. Multiple enemy guardsmen ran their direction.

She knew full well that the men with her didn't have much in the way of fighting experience. Riana's first priority was always Ash, but she tried to look out for the others, too. Her hands blurred as she felled one guardsman after another, taking them down as quickly as she could.

Hendrix had said that the palace had a skeletal crew in place because Maddox had drawn upon it heavily in order to march against Estole. She saw now what he meant, as it seemed that she'd barely blinked before the guardsmen were down. In the midst of all that fighting they had made it all the way to the very interior courtyard without her realizing.

"How many did we lose?" Ash demanded, turning to take in a headcount.

"Two, sir," one of the men responded sadly. "Peter and Jim."

Riana swore aloud at the loss but was privately amazed that they had only lost the two.

Ashlynn and Hendrix's groups came up to the same point, all of them coming in slow to avoid running into each other. Ash turned and gestured. "Reynolds, you take command here."

Reynolds was one of the few who was a retired soldier and knew what to do. He gave Ash a salute, sharp with military precision. "Yes, Wizard Fallbright."

The same order was given to others, the command changing to another sub-captain, and only four squadrons detached from the group to go into the palace interior. Riana wasn't sure they actually needed four—not with two wizards in the group—but wasn't about to take chances. They basically had two kings to protect after all.

They had no way of knowing how many guards were still left inside the palace. Riana privately bet not many. After all, what would be the point of staying on guard inside the palace interior when the exterior courtyard had fallen? The palace was not fortified in any real sense of the word. It was huge and labyrinthine and even in the best of times, difficult to protect. Most of the guards would automatically be allotted for the exterior walls.

Forming up ranks, they carefully broached the side entrance that Riana knew so well. Since she was one of the few in the group that knew the palace—aside from Hendrix—she led the way, Ash right at her side. He had a barrier spell up like a battering ram in front of them, to attack or defend with as needed.

The halls remained eerily quiet and still. Riana had never seen the palace like this before. Every sound rang and echoed down the corridors, speaking of abandonment and loss. They came around each corner, one high, one down on a knee, the squadron slowly fanning out to cover branch hallways to prevent anyone sneaking up from behind. The precaution was necessary but after twenty minutes of walking about inside, Riana almost felt it foolish. Either this place was entirely abandoned or quite the ambush waited for them ahead. Either way, their precautions might be for naught.

"Where?" Edvard asked Hendrix and Riana, looking to them for an answer.

"Study?" Riana offered hesitantly. She was more familiar with the palace than Edvard, certainly, but only parts of it and did not pretend to know Zelman as much as his own family did.

"Study or throne room," Hendrix agreed,

expression closed off. "He always retreats to places of power when he feels threatened. I'm betting throne room, but let's check the study first. We'll pass it going to the throne room anyway."

No one saw any problem with this plan and followed Hendrix. They found the study empty of any living soul. Hendrix didn't seem surprised and headed toward the better bet. Riana privately wondered what they would do if Hendrix's guess was off. Did that mean they would have to search the whole palace? Sea monsters could get lost in this place.

The throne room of the palace was not actually connected to the main building. It was a separate room that shared the same roof, but not the same walls. There was an open grassy and flowered courtyard that separated the area, a garden spot that Riana knew people waited in while the king made judgments inside. Here, they finally encountered the palace guards.

Riana lifted a bow, ready to shoot immediately, but the guards didn't engage them. There were only eight to begin with, stationed along the wall, but upon seeing the Estolians advancing, their nerve broke. Tossing down weapons, they lifted their hands above their heads in a silent plea for surrender.

If they didn't want to fight, everyone was willing for them to surrender.

Hendrix signaled to the group. "Four to each corner. Two guard the hallways leading in. No one in or out but try to keep bloodshed to a minimum. Take these and put them on the bench over there and guard them until this is over. Ashlynn,

Broden, there are several wizards employed for my father's personal protection."

"We'll guard the outside," Ashlynn assured him, already taking a position to do so.

The way Hendrix phrased this made Riana think. "Odds are he has wizard guards inside with him, then?"

"Odds are."

Men moved out under his direction and Hendrix strode for the door. Riana expected a strategy session of how to handle Zelman, at least a conference between kings, but neither man tried to speak to each other. Did they talk about this on the way in? They must have.

Ashlynn, at some silent signal, moved ahead of the two men and threw open the doors before erecting a magical barrier around them, ready for attack just in case.

Riana and Ash, in mutual agreement, went through first. It was just as well that Ashlynn had prepared that shield, as they were immediately attacked. Ash swore and put up his own protective shield, shouting at his twin, "GUARD THEM!"

Snatching three arrows from her belt quiver, Riana nocked and let fly. The wizards here were smart enough to have a physical shield to protect against weapons, and they were quick to duck behind them. Her arrows splattered off them uselessly but it bought Ash precious seconds to react with, which was what she was truly aiming for.

Zelman sat on his throne, Queen Rosalind on one side, Savir on the other. A wizard kept a protective wall up in front of them, a portable version instead of fixed—Riana could recognize that spell in a glance. It was exactly like the one Ashlynn and Ash were both using. She caught Savir's eye and found him difficult to read, as usual. And yet...there was something about his eyes on her that seemed intense, like he was trying to tell her something. Why?

Riana's eyes went to Rosalind and found the queen openly pleading with her expression to not be reckless. Was it because they'd become friends? Or was there some other game afoot she didn't know about? With Savir, it was highly possible.

Standing, the king bellowed, "CEASE! I will not allow any fighting until I have answers!"

The wizards fell into a pre-battle readiness, not attacking, but not lowering their guard. Ashlynn shared a speaking glance with her brother and backed out of the room, releasing her protective shield as she did so, shifting that responsibility over to Ash, which he picked up smoothly.

Riana would be just as happy to get out of this without any more bloodshed. She didn't see a very high probability for it, granted, but was willing to play along and hope for the best. She put her arrows back in the quiver but left the bow in her hand. It would take only a moment to rearm and fire if needed. It was as much of a compromise as she could manage in this very taut situation.

Zelman stood, nearly shaking with rage, his face an apoplectic hue of purple. Stabbing a finger in Edvard's direction, he demanded, "Why aren't you dead yet?"

Edvard pretended to think about this for a moment. "Because my people are more capable than yours?"

The Iyshian King actually let out a wail, a demonic, screeching sound that hurt Riana's ears. "I WANT YOU DEAD!"

"Oh, do pipe down," Edvard drawled sarcastically, "you sound like a three-year-old. Hendrix, do something with him before I'm forced to stick a gag in his mouth."

Hendrix did not look at all pleased to take lead on this but gamely stepped forward. "Father. I have a petition here—"

"Petition," Zelman scoffed, throwing a hand into the air and looking away from his son as if he didn't even warrant the king's attention. "I exile you, disinherit you, and all you can think to do is get a petition from a bunch of peasants and rebels."

"I have a petition here," Hendrix continued with quiet authority, "from the dukes, marquees, counts, viscounts, and barons of Iysh. Most of them, anyway. They are tired of your rule and want you overthrown."

Zelman froze, his breath coming out in progressively harsher gasps. "...What did you just say?"

"I said the majority of the nobility in this country want you off the throne."

"You poisonous creature," Zelman breathed, his rage so great that he looked ready to explode with it. "I can't believe I bred something like you. You expect me to believe this? That my own will turn against me, after all I did for them? You forged those signatures! I won't believe such an obvious lie."

Riana hadn't actually expected Zelman to meekly step down just because of a petition. Men in power tended to stay in power.

Hendrix wasn't surprised either. He took two steps forward, facing off with the man that sired him. "I don't really care if you believe it or not. What matters is that no one really wants to suffer under your rule any longer. Haven't you wondered where your guards and staff are?"

Zelman, accustomed to being surrounded by people invisibly serving his needs, blinked and took note of their absence for the first time. He did sharp pivots, first right, then left, searching for people only to not find them.

"They're not here because you've lost their loyalty." Hendrix spread his hands in an open shrug. "You've lost, King Zelman. Step down gracefully. If you don't, you'll be facing more than political exile."

Zelman threw his head back and laughed but the sound was full of false bravado. "Like you have the power to do so! I know your weakness, boy. MADDOX!"

From a side door, the first prince of Iysh entered. Directly at his side was the one woman they had been searching desperately for—Bria.

Hendrix and Edvard let out a gasp of surprise and relief in unison, lengthening their stride to go for her, when Maddox caught Bria by the arm and drew her sharply toward him.

Riana felt that drawing her bow might be too much of a head's up for Maddox. He might be able to injure Bria before she could get to him. Instead she put a hand in a hidden pocket, ready to draw a dagger and aim for Maddox's eye. The grip he had on Bria was not life threatening but she didn't feel comfortable leaving the girl at his side. Besides, the way that Ash, Edvard, and Hendrix acted, if Bria was there for three more seconds, someone's temper was going to snap. Riana preferred to step in before one of those three came within Maddox's reach.

Just as she was pulling the dagger free, Bria caught her eye and gave a minute shake of the head, a clear warning in her eyes. Don't move? Why? Riana hesitated, but Bria's look in her direction didn't waver and she didn't look at all afraid. What was going on?

::Ash, Bria says do not move.::

Her wizard stopped dead in his tracks and gave her an incredulous look. ::Say what?::

::She's giving me a pointed look to not move. I don't know why either but don't jump into the fray. I think there be something else going on.:: In fact, the look on Bria and Savir's faces made her confident that there was another plan in play here.

Good brother that he was, Ash still was of a mind to jump in—she could feel the emotional struggle. But he also trusted her judgment, and so didn't lunge for Bria like he wanted to. Instead, he put a hand on Edvard's arm and gave him a pointed look that carried the message over to him.

Edvard didn't look happy about this—in fact, he looked like a mother storm on the verge of erupting—but he also kept his temper and impulse in check. He, in turn, grabbed Hendrix before the prince could do something, the same warning look being passed along.

"Ha!" Zelman crowed. "I thought that would stop you in your tracks. You're too weak, boy, you focus too much on the affairs of the heart. It's why you'll lose."

"Your callousness towards humanity in general has already caused two of your dukes to rebel, create their own countries, and now the rest of your people have revolted so thoroughly they basically let my army in through the front door," Hendrix shot back sarcastically, "and you dare criticize my leadership abilities?"

Riana lost focus of the argument as Zelman exploded—an easy thing to do, when he was enraged, she could barely make out one word in five—and chose to watch Maddox with an eagle eye. The twin princes were a study in opposites. Maddox was tall and broad, as muscular as Savir was slim, with hair more brown than black, skin tan from so many hours in the sun. If she had not known they were twins, Riana would not have even mistaken them as brothers. They were most definitely not identical twins. Maddox kept shifting from foot to foot, giving Savir impatient looks, although the reason why escaped her. He looked oddly as if he were waiting on some cue from his twin.

Savir was not in a hurry. In fact, his manner seemed almost lackadaisical, as if he were simply biding his time. Having interacted with him as much as she had, she knew good and well that he was always up to something. This lack of interest didn't fool her at all.

Just what was he planning?

Zelman's breathing was shaky and all over the place, indicating that apoplectic rage had taken over his common sense. He whirled to Maddox again. "Don't stand there like a statue! Do something!"

Maddox put a hand on the hilt of his sword but did not draw. "Such as? There's a wizard, two kings, and a very skilled archer in front of me. All of them armed. This is not a good defensive position, Father, even with your wizards."

"I DON'T CARE!" Zelman screamed, spraying spit as he did so.

Bria flinched and wiped a few flecks from her cheek, her expression one of absolute disgust.

"I want her dead—" Zelman stabbed a finger in Bria's direction "—and after you've taken care of that wench, kill Hendrix. With that traitor gone, their so-called rebellion will be done with, as they have no other candidate to replace him with. Don't be so difficult, Maddox, and move!"

"I have never once threatened any member of my family," Hendrix protested, voice rising in octave as he spoke, "and you'd have my fiancée killed? And then me? By my own brother's hand? Are you mad?!"

"You're the one that brought this upon yourself!" Zelman snarled at him, nearly shaking with rage.

"You exiled me over nothing!" Hendrix riposted, his own temper dangerously at a breaking point. "The only thing I did was support Savir when he declared he had no intention of taking the throne! You punish me for no reason and now that I'm here, you want my own brother to kill me?!"

Zelman's face turned ice cold, for all the world as if he were speaking to an insect instead of his own son. "If he is to be king, he must deal with contenders."

Silence fell so thick and heavy that Hendrix's breathing sounded like war drums. Riana was floored by this declaration. Even to their faces, Zelman had no remorse in dealing with a "contender." Was this man's heart made of stone?

The queen had been silent all this time, but she finally spoke, breaking the silence with a simple question, spoken calmly and evenly: "Hendrix. What was your plan, if you were able to remove your father? What did you intend to do with me, Savir and Maddox?"

Hendrix croaked, "I would never harm a strand of hair on your heads if given the choice. If you backed me, I'd leave you where you are. If you weren't willing to do so, I was going to offer you a choice in exile."

"I see." The queen's face softened a little. "I'm glad."

"Mother, please," Hendrix pleaded openly. "Don't force my hand on this. Don't make me your enemy. I am not yours."

Maddox shot another impatient look at his twin, the fidgets nearly uncontrollable. Riana's hand twitched for the quiver. She had no idea what the twins were up to, but there was definitely some other plan in play.

Her attention on Savir and Maddox was so absolute that she nearly missed the back door of the throne room opening a crack. Her eyes darted that direction and saw a brief burst of light as a spell flew out with unerring accuracy. Ashlynn had snuck in through the back. Almost before Riana realized what had happened, Ash spun on his heels and flicked out his own spell, hitting the other enemy wizard who wasn't guarding himself well.

Both enemy wizards fell bonelessly to the ground, felled by the twin wizards.

There was abrupt silence, everyone a little stunned by the speed and efficiency of the attacks.

Sometimes Riana forgot that Ash's fighting skills were battle-honed, and even in situations like this, he knew how to get the drop on his opponents. She gave him a quick smile. ::Nice shot!::

::Why thank you, dearest.:: He gave her a swift smile before refocusing.

Zelman stared at the downed wizards for only a brief moment before he snapped his fingers at Savir. "Grab one of the shields, be useful for once. I won't stand for this treason in my own palace, in my own throne room; it's unconscionable. Maddox, I demand that you do something."

Shooting another look at his twin, Maddox drew his sword. Savir gave him a minute shake of the head in response. To Riana it was clear: Maddox wanted to move, Savir was saying to wait. But wait on what?

Zelman grinned nastily at them. "Finally, you'll get what's coming to you."

"Father?" Maddox asked, taking a step in front of the king.

"What?" Zelman snarled.

"I abdicate my right to the throne."

For a moment, Zelman looked like a landed fish. "Wha—What did you just s—?!"

Without even batting an eyelid, Maddox rammed the sword into his father's chest, cutting the king off mid-word.

The room froze all over again, staring in disbelief as Zelman slowly crumpled and fell backwards. He wasn't even able to do more than gurgle before his eyes glassed over.

What...just happened? Even though Riana had seen it with her own eyes, she couldn't process it, couldn't take it in. Had Maddox just killed his own father?

"Got tired of his ramblings and playing along with him," Maddox stated to the room in general. He retrieved his sword, cleaning it against his father's robes with a casual swipe before sliding the sword back home again.

Growling in frustration, Savir gave his twin an aggravated look. "Mad-dox."

Shrugging, Maddox looked deliberately elsewhere.

Hendrix croaked out a sound, cleared his throat, and tried again, "I don't understand."

Maddox gave him a shrug and a slight, enigmatic smile.

Barking out a short laugh, Edvard slapped a hand against his thigh. "You were never on Zelman's side."

With a nod of confirmation, Maddox elaborated, "Had to play along, though. After what happened with Hendrix, we knew he'd throw us to the wolves as well if we didn't."

Bria, strangely, wasn't as surprised as the rest by Maddox's actions. Instead, she stared down at Zelman with an oddly clinical study. "You're going to get in trouble. You messed with Savir's plan."

"Didn't feel like waiting for the rest of the audience to show up. Besides, he's used to me doing that." Maddox grinned at his twin.

Hendrix dared to cross the room and wrap his arms around Bria, an embrace she readily returned. "I'm alright," Bria said softly, her words meant for Hendrix alone and so barely audible to everyone else. "I, too, was just playing along. Maddox needed me to be a trophy to Zelman, prove to him he was trying, to buy more time."

Riana stared at the dead king, the realization slowly sinking in that with his death, they had won.

They had won.

She let out a breath and felt like the world itself was lifted from her shoulders. "We've won."

Ash spun and caught her up in a hug that lifted her feet off the floor, his feelings of relief and victory a perfect mirror for hers.

Edvard slung an arm around them, one held out to accept Ashlynn too and she joined in on the impromptu hug. Broden was right behind her; Riana and Ash shifted arms to incorporate them into it, their joy so intense that they bounced a little with it.

"I'm so glad that you found a way to sneak through the back," Edvard congratulated Ashlynn. "Those wizards were a bit of a problem. For that matter, I'm glad you and Ash are so in sync that you could tell which wizard he would aim for."

"She always goes for the left one," Ash explained absently, still basking in their victory.

"I do not," Ashlynn objected, still smiling. "I go for the right opponent first."

"My right, your left," Ash objected without truly paying attention to the argument.

"You mean my right your left," his sister corrected.

Edvard hastily interrupted, "Not a twin argument now. Please. Let's bask in the victory for a while. Hendrix! I think I'll go outside and announce our victory, we have a great many people anxious to hear from us."

"Let us all go," Hendrix countered. He took two steps toward the door before he stopped and offered his free arm to his mother. "Mother?"

The queen was staring down at her dead husband with sad eyes. "Not one will mourn his death. Not one will grieve him."

Hendrix crossed to her, putting an arm around her shoulders. In the gentlest tone that Riana had ever heard a man use, he asked her softly, "Are you sorry that he's dead?"

Looking into her son's eyes, those eyes that were so like her own, she gave him a small shake of the head. "I do not. And that is the saddest thing of all. He was a terrible king, a worse father, and an equally terrible husband. The best I can say for him in this moment is that he was never abusive to me. I hope, my dearest son, that you never follow in his footsteps."

"Guide me," Hendrix requested, a heartfelt plea, "so that I do not fall into the same pitfalls."

"I will," she agreed readily, a tenuous smile

blooming on her face, "but I don't think I need to worry about you much. You are good at taking counsel and that was the one thing your father could never learn how to do. You have good people that stand with you." She looked at all of them, smile firming. "People that will walk through fire with you. As long as you have them, I know you will be fine."

Riana felt the same. A man that could take counsel, that could be teachable, would never end up like Zelman.

Her eyes falling on the king's corpse once more, the queen said with quiet authority, "I have heard Savir and Maddox's declarations to abdicate the throne. They are so noted. The king is dead." Lifting her eyes to Hendrix, she declared, "Long live the king."

EPILOGUE

Quite the crowd gathered at the palace steps. People from all walks of life were there, speaking to each other in low tones, antsy and excited. Riana stood on the steps leading up to the dais, in a more formal getup than she thought appropriate for the situation. Hendrix insisted that everyone be in formal attire, as this was a coronation ceremony, but did that mean she really couldn't have her bow? It was low odds at this juncture, granted, but there could still be loyalists hanging about, wanting to take a shot at the kings. The situation made her nervous enough that she had once again strapped every stiletto dagger and weapon she could in hidden pockets and as hair ornaments. This time, she was not the only woman to do so.

The entire royal family, from both countries, stood arrayed on the dais. If there were less than a thousand people in the palace's main courtyard, Riana would be very surprised. They were crammed into the space like sardines and she knew that many more people were outside the palace walls, trying to listen in. Several sound spells boosted peoples' speech so that as many people as possible could hear the proceedings. A few wayward boys had even figured out how to climb up on the roof of a nearby building so they could get a better view of the proceedings.

They had spent two weeks reforming matters, re-instating lords, ladies, and government officials that had been dismissed due to Zelman's stupidity. Axley and all of his cronies were rotting in a dungeon cell, as Savir had more than enough information on them to prove them guilty of numerous crimes. Considering their characters, Riana hadn't been the least surprised to learn about it. General Quillin had happily written a statement saying he had no intention of taking the throne and then offered to take the palace guards in hand until they were able to sort things out. Under his capable leadership, they had enough guards loyal to Hendrix standing in the palace now to offer some measure of safety. If that wasn't enough, they had four wizards nearby to ensure it. Still, Riana felt very nervous about this whole situation. Undoubtedly because the first coronation ceremony she'd ever attended had been an unmitigated disaster.

Savir took a side step closer to her and whispered, "What has you so on edge?"

"The last time we had a ceremony like this one, it was an assassination attempt," she groused.

"Ah. Well, this one isn't. Relax."

Easier said than done. Seeing that people were still milling about a little—although what the holdup was, she couldn't imagine—Riana dared to ask a question that had been plaguing her for the past two weeks. "The empty treasury. You're behind that, aren't you?"

Blinking innocently, Savir pointed a finger toward himself as if to say, Sweet little innocent me?

"I thought so." Riana had gotten to know him a little better now that his mask was off and was happy to see he felt easy enough around her to tease. "Hendrix said the country isn't actually bankrupt, but he didn't get a chance to explain more than that."

"He's been a little busy," Savir explained cheerfully. "I could go into a long-winded explanation, but here's the gist of it: I cooked the books."

Riana choked on a laugh. "What!"

"I have been for about two years now, ever since Edvard Knolton declared Estole's independence. I had an idea of where all of this was heading and I saw a chance to get both Maddox and I safely out of the line of succession. Really, we both knew we weren't suitable for the job and felt like Hendrix was the better choice, but Father wasn't easy to maneuver around. After Edvard won the first battle, I knew this day would come eventually. So I started sneaking small amounts out of the treasury with every transaction. A little here, a little there, but the country spends a lot of money on a regular basis. It added up to a considerable sum after a while. I stored it all in my personal vault and Maddox's, as no one would dare to look there. After this ceremony is complete, we'll give it all back, minus some interest." Seeing her flabbergasted look, he defended himself mildly,

"I'm not generous enough to help my brother completely for free, you know."

Apparently not. "You really managed to empty out the treasury just doing that?"

"Well, no, Hendrix moved a mite faster than I anticipated. So I bought a few supplies and shipped them to Estole, as I knew you needed some, and I still had money left in the treasury, so I hired some Overan mercenaries. Riana kept going about telling everyone she'd met them, after all; why not turn the lie into a truth? That, finally, did the trick."

Her father was standing in front of them and when he heard this, his head whipped around. "Lad, ye be behind all that?!"

Savir smiled at him, an outrageous twinkle in his eye.

"Well." Broden seemed a little caught for words. "The mercenary commander did say that when we finally learned who our benefactor was, we'd lose our teeth over it. Ye be the one that sent that message to Troi, too, I bet. The one with the list of spies."

"That I was." Savir pretended to think on that for a moment. "Is he still mad about that?"

"Mad do no' begin to cover it."

A loud bang peeled out as the end of a staff was knocked into the granite steps. Everyone automatically looked toward the front. Maddox stood with the royal scepter in his hand, a long shaft that had the seal and a miniature crown on the very top of it. In a voice loud enough to carry over the crowd—thanks to Kirsty's spell—he called out: "Lords, ladies, people of Iysh, Dahl, and Estole! I am Maddox, First Prince of Iysh. I hereby formally abdicate my right to the throne. I present to you the Third Prince of Iysh, Hendrix, as the rightful heir to the throne."

Maddox stepped back, Hendrix stepped up, swirling his formal cape in a dramatic touch as he knelt before the High Priest of Macha, God of Battles and Sovereignty. Two other priests were in attendance as well. Riana noted that all of the trappings and decorations were in place this time.

The high priest held a simple crown of braided gold over Hendrix's head, hovering but not touching. In a sonorous voice, he proclaimed, "We recognize Hendrix, Third Prince of Iysh, as the new King of Iysh. We bless him with wisdom, with patience, with justice, with mercy, that his rule might be long and his people prosperous. The king is dead. Long live the king!"

"LONG LIVE THE KING!" the crowd shouted back at him.

The coronation ceremony from generation to generation didn't change much, Riana had learned that while preparing for this one. That meant that Zelman had been given the same blessing, if by a different priest, with the same gentle admonitions to be a good king. Had the man not been paying attention to that while being crowned? Or had he forgotten it over the course of time? Riana had to wonder. If he had just heeded those words during the course of his reign then maybe he wouldn't have ended up being stabbed by his own son.

Hendrix stood up, a crown solidly on his head, and beamed. The mood must have been infectious as his people cheered him, relieved and happy to have a better man on the throne. Taking a half step back, Hendrix gestured toward Edvard and Tierone. "I present Edvard of Estole and Tierone of Dahl. I recognize them as the rulers of their countries."

Edvard and Tierone came around to kneel in the same area Hendrix had, the high priest holding a crown between their heads and repeating the same words. Their crowns had been hastily crafted the past two weeks—which had been part of the reason for the delay—and were somewhat representative of the men themselves. Tierone's was iron instead of a precious metal, rimmed in the barest hint of gold on top and bottom, practical and without fanfare. Edvard's was silver, a thin circlet that rested on his head with only the Estolian crest as a single ornamentation on the front. He had designed it to be light and easily worn for an entirely practical reason—the mantel he wore was heavy enough, no reason for the crown to make the job heavier.

The crowns were placed upon the heads of both men and they stood again. The high priest gave them the same blessing and admonishments before he announced once more, "LONG LIVE THE KING!"

The watching crowd was perhaps a touch more enthusiastic as they shouted back, "LONG LIVE THE KING!"

Riana shouted it with them and grinned. Seeing the people of Iysh so readily support two foreign kings was a good omen for the future.

Hendrix stepped forward again. "My people, I wish to make a few announcements as your king. First, some appointments: my mother will remain as the Dowager Queen of Iysh. Maddox shall remain the First General of the Royal Army. Savir shall from this day forward be the Head Minister of Finance."

Riana choked. Was that a good idea? The look Hendrix shot his brother was in equal parts amused and warning. Savir beamed back, innocently. No, definitely a bad idea. Riana was just as glad this wasn't her country or her call to make.

"I also declare," Hendrix continued, "an official end to our war with Estole and Dahl. I offer a formal peace treaty with trade agreements to King Edvard and King Tierone. Will you sign a treaty with me?"

This was very much a formality as the kings had been in close discussions about this very topic for days now. They had all the details already hammered out. A writing table was hastily brought out with a stool, and each man sat and signed in triplicate so that each king had his own copy of the agreement. Then they stood, shook hands, and gave a wave to the cheering people.

Riana could hear the difference in their voices. It wasn't enthusiasm this time but abject relief. Every person there was heartily sick of war. They were tired of it robbing their finances, their peace, their very lives. Having spent her entire life fighting, for one reason or another, Riana didn't know what to think of this new age of peace.

Perhaps Ash felt her turmoil over it as he leaned in, an arm around her waist. ::What, dearest?::

::If I'm not fighting, what am I supposed to do?::

Ash pondered that for a moment. ::Whatever you want to do.::

Whatever she wanted to do? Well, now, there was a concept.

More practically, Ash added, ::Or more like, whatever Estole and Edvard need us to do. You do remember that you're a Provost for Ganforth, don't you?::

Actually, there were days she did forget. War did that to a memory. ::I suppose it's a silly question. I'll be busy running about as usual, won't I?::

::I can guarantee it. Even before the war started that was the case. Estole is a pretty country but a demanding one. Not to mention all of the rebuilding that we'll need to do.::

That she knew. But she wouldn't trade it for anything.

Edvard bounced over like a puppy; she could practically see a tail wagging. "That went splendidly. No assassins this time."

"Edvard, is that your definition of 'splendid?'" Ashlynn asked, laughing. "Truly?"

"Do you know how rare it's been for the past year that no one's been trying to kill me?" he riposted, not at all bothered by his sister's needling.

"The man do have a point," Broden observed. "Well, now, lad, what be next?"

"Next," Savir answered, not looking at them but at the crowd, "we make some war reparations toward Estole and Dahl. Sending a little money home with you to help with the rebuilding will help, yes?"

"Abundantly," Tierone agreed as he came up and joined them. "Considering Iyshian soldiers ran roughshod over a third of my farmland. We have a lot of rebuilding to do once we're home again."

Riana felt that statement was the best candidate for "understatement of the year." "Tierone, as you were the last one to leave home to travel here, you would know how to answer this question best: How bad is it?"

Tierone gave a shudder. "Don't ask. Really. It's better you have hopes and dreams before you see it yourself. You won't see much of Ash for the rest of the summer, that much I can promise you."

That was not in the least bit comforting.

"First, however, we need to have a royal wedding." When all he got was surprised faces, Edvard made a face at them. "Do you really think I'm going to leave Bria here without her being properly married to Hendrix first? They've been engaged for a while, they're not about to separate now, and I'm not even going to try dragging her off again. Hendrix will tear the treaty in half if I even try."

"Wise of you," Savir murmured, biting back a laugh.

"So, wedding first," Edvard finished firmly. "She's got a week before we really need to leave for home."

"A week?!" Ashlynn and Riana protested in unison.

"A week," Edvard maintained.

"Edvard, a week is not enough time—" Riana started.

"The dress alone—" Ashlynn spluttered at the same time.

"She's got two female wizards at her beck and call, and a queen. I'm sure between the four of you, you can do something about the dress." Edvard was not budging an inch on this. "A week. We have two countries to rebuild, I can't give her more time than that."

"Why don't you go talk this over with Hendrix and Bria?" Savir suggested. "If all you're giving them is a week, then every moment counts for them."

Edvard considered that for a moment, realized it was a valid point, and turned smartly on his heel to follow the royal couple indoors.

Watching him, Savir opined, "I think he's about to realize that negotiating terms is easier with a king than a bride."

Rubbing her hands together and chortling like a demented gnome, Ashlynn strode after him. "This ought to be fun to watch."

Broden, shaking his head, followed, with Savir right behind.

Ash turned to Riana. "Go with?"

She shook her head. "I've had enough conflict to last a lifetime."

He resonated perfect agreement. "Then, my lady, how about we have a proper date? The whole city is a giant festival today, surely we have earned the right to a bit of pleasure."

"Why, Ash, it's like you read my mind."

::My dear lady, perhaps I did.::

HONOR RACONTEUR

ABOUT THE AUTHOR

Honor Raconteur grew up all over the United States and to this day is confused about where she's actually from. She wrote her first book at five years old and hasn't looked back since. Her interests vary from rescuing dogs, to studying languages, to arguing with her characters. On good days, she wins the argument.

Since her debut in September 2011, Honor has released over two dozen books, mostly of the fantasy genre. She writes full time from the comfort of her home office, in her pajamas, while munching on chocolate. She has no intention of stopping anytime soon and will probably continue until something comes along to stop her.

Her website can be found here: http://www.honorraconteur.com, or if you wish to speak directly with the author, visit her on Facebook.